MAX ABADDON AND THE GATE TO EVERWHERE

A Max Abaddon Novel

By Justin S. Leslie

Paperback ISBN: 978-1-7353035-3-6
E-book ISBN: 978-1-7353035-2-9

Contact Information Email: Abaddonbooks@hotmail.com
Facebook: @Maxabaddonbooks
Website: www.JustinLeslie.com

"A person lives three lives. The first one ends with the loss of naivety; the second, with the loss of innocence; and the third, with the loss of life itself.It's inevitable that we go through all three stages."

—Adam – Dark

PROLOGUE

A History of Demons

"**M**om, please!" I exclaimed. Being six years old and having trouble sleeping because there was a monster in the closet was always the setting for a bedtime story.

"Lie down, and I'll read you an extraordinary story," Mom said, walking in and placing a cup of ice water by my bed.

She flipped the wall switch off and turned on the bedside lamp, which let off a calming orange glow that projected various objects' shadows on the walls.

"What's it about?" I asked curiously.

"You'll see," she said, opening the green-and-gold embossed book on her lap.

There once was a world of Gods called Terrum. It was a place of magic, and large enough that even the heavens above had a place to reside in. Kings of Armies, Queens of Fairy, Gods of the Pantheons, and what were called the Others all lived in harmony.

One day, the Kings, Queens, and Gods of Terrum came to the Old Gods wanting more. Knowing that they couldn't make everyone happy, the Old Gods came up with a plan. They would give a Plane of existence to every one of the groups while the Old Gods remained in control of Terrum. The groups rejoiced at the news, but would soon find that all that glittered was not gold.

The Old Gods were smart and knew one day the masters of the Planes would want more. When the fighting started, the celestial war was more than even the Old Gods had imagined. So much so that several of the Planes were destroyed.

To control what was left, the Old Gods created the Over and the Under. Planes to control the others, again leaving the Old Gods out of the vicious cycle of the power-thirsty realms. These were given to the strongest of the remaining Gods and Fallen Angels.

With that, Heaven and Hell were created. Heaven would control the lands through the use of justice and goodwill. In contrast, Hell would control an army of the Undesirables and violent Demons made from celestial beings that had been accused of treason or other crimes against the Old Gods. Unlike what stories often told, the Fallen Angels had gone against their will, becoming the Lords of the Underworld. They had never truly fallen, leaving many of them spiteful and angry. This army would become undefeatable, filled with lost souls: the currency of the Old Gods and a never-ending pool of soldiers who would serve them if it was ever needed.

As quickly as they were put in place, they took control of the other Planes, giving the Old Gods power once again, even if the other Planes didn't realize it. But that would not last.

The Hellion Legions grew restless. The Angels that had been forced to work in the Under were not happy; many wanted to go back to what was called the Light. Before long, the Old Gods realized they had created an army even they could not defeat.

As with any rebellion, it caused a great divide. The battle raged for millennia, until one day, the final Plane shifted from Terrum, forever breaking their connection. Out of that battle, Earth was born, a piece of Terrum flung to the other end of the cosmos on another Plane. Knowing they couldn't survive independently, the leaders of the remaining Planes bound their realms to Earth.

In doing so, the Over and the Under were forever separated.

Unable to come back together, a balance was again struck. The Fallen now in charge of the Under knew they couldn't defeat the Hellion Legions, though they could control them. Most of the Fallen just wanted to go back to their everyday celestial lives.

In a final play by the Old Gods, they sent their undesirables, lost souls, and criminals to what became Earth. The Demons . . . The Hellion Legions had one more battle to win. Instead of fighting, the Legions laid down their arms, realizing that the battle was not winnable. A truce was made, and the Demon Accords were chartered.

With no one left to fight, the Hellion Legions and Demons looked for their new home, wanting Earth for their new Plane. No one expected the Lords of the Underworld—consisting of the Fallen Angels—to have been working with the Celestials to make a deal. Earth was the prize, and it would not be good if the Legions destroyed it. The Lords of the Underworld buried the Legions, violent raging monsters of unbelievable strength, locking them away till this very day.

Over time, the other occupants of the underworld became more twisted and crazed in their pursuit for souls. The currency of the Everwhere. The place of balance between all the worlds. A place inhabited by spirits. The Lords couldn't fully control the Demons without the help of the Legions, but they could keep them on the Plane in the Under unless called upon. That is the history of Demons.

The end.

"Are the demons bad?" I asked, yawning as the story took its toll on my body.

"Most of them. They long to be on Earth. To walk in the sun, to smell the ocean, and to take whatever souls they want," was the last thing I remember her saying before fading into dreams of angels and demons fighting side by side against a dark, ancient enemy.

CHAPTER 1

Abaddon and Associates AA . . .

I t was only 8:00 p.m., and I had already set five buildings, an RV dealership, and several cars on fire, all while being completely sober. "Hey, boss, he's running into that big warehouse," Petro chirped over the radio.

The man was moving at unnatural speeds, leaping over tall buildings in a literal single bound.

"I see him," I replied, letting out a huff of air from having sprinted the last quarter mile down the Jacksonville loading docks. Running through the open spaces between stacks of cargo containers, my feet splashed through the large puddles on the ground, creating ripples that reflected the moon's reddish harvest hue.

One week ago, I'd had an actual customer come in for consulting advice at Abaddon & Associates, AA for short. It had taken some time to figure out that I had named my consulting firm—which consisted of just Petro, Phil when he wasn't performing his NCTS duties, and myself—after a recovering alcoholics program.

The attractive middle-aged businesswoman needed me to find her husband, who just happened to have a slight addiction problem and an infatuation with the magical world of which he was not a part of. It was obvious the two were well off, so I wasn't prepared for, well . . . for the day and current late-night jog I was on.

"There's a hole in the roof. The assface is going into that big building," Petro said as I stopped in front of the metal monstrosity.

"I'm going in," I replied, grabbing the handle and melting it into glowing goo with hellfire.

Petro zipped down behind me, avoiding the molten metal.

"Something's not right with that guy. I'm right behind you," Petro hurriedly said in an unsure voice.

The air in the building was stale due to the oppressive humidity. Light shone in from the opening in the ceiling, filling the auditorium-sized room with gray shadows. The hole in the roof was big enough for a container to be dropped and arranged.

The smell of night and salt water from the ocean permeated the area. I had chased Mr. Bellman throughout the northeast side of Jacksonville, starting around the football stadium. While he had been leaping through the air, I had been using a new trick. Being quarter demon, quarter Mage, quarter witch, and quarter human, a few perks had become available, one of which was properly using the tracking spell on my staff if I could hit my target with it.

Mr. Bellman had started slowing down a few miles away from the port authority. I had taken the Black Beast, my trusty old black Dodge Ram, through the area at less than acceptable speeds. I was sure Kim would have something to say about it if she ever showed up.

I had called Phil and Kim as soon as the first red lightning bolt had come from Mr. Bellman's hands.

Taking my first step in, I avoided the natural light filling the space. The area was filled with containers providing suspicious, dark hiding spaces in every corner.

"Hey, I know you're in here," I said, seeing his outline in the far corner on top of three connexes. When fully charged with the tracking charm in my staff, my sight allowed me to see the person if I was within a few hundred feet. This complemented the tracking spell that pointed in their general direction.

The man shrieked in an unnatural tone, sounding like a feral wolf. I put the staff back in my newly modified blazer and pulled out the Judge. The Judge was a gun that was just that: judge, jury, and executioner; it was enchanted. If it deemed you guilty and that you needed to be relieved of whatever existence you had, it would do so. The gun also had a nasty habit of not firing at all, having some type of "higher" judgment on the person it was aimed at. This often led to the right decision being made and awkward situations when you pointed at someone, and it didn't fire.

He stood up, a red glow coming from his hands and eyes. It was my first real look at the man today that didn't involve him trying to kill me with the flaming lightning he was shooting in my general direction. He looked as if he was either about to break out in a song and dance, or throw everything he had at me in one last stand.

As he let out another howl, I leveled the Judge at him, pulling the trigger. A loud boom echoed in the night air, muffled slightly by the shower-like humidity.

The bullet fizzled out in a shower of sparks as it slammed into Mr. Bellman, stunning him long enough to buy me a few seconds to go to trusty old plan B. What is plan B, you ask?

Slamming the Judge back in its holster, I pulled my will, creating a baseball-sized sphere of hellfire in my right hand and slinging it at the man as he pulled up another wall of the sparkling, crackling lightning. I would need to figure out why plan A hadn't worked later.

The two collided in a spray of hellfire creating a bright

wall of splattering light. The immediate smell of smoke filled the air as hellfire flew into several directions, catching whatever flammable material was around.

Mr. Bellman let out a howl, shooting another arch before I could pull up a shield or spell. One of the spreading tendrils smacked me in the arm, spinning me around and slamming me into a container as I dropped to my knees.

"That hurt," I said under my breath, noticing the man was moving slower than before. I looked up as the smell of burning fabric filled my nostrils like something that had been burnt on the stove.

The enchanted corduroy blazer I had received on my 30th rebirthday had recently been improved. It didn't resemble the snappy sports coat it used to anymore. It was now longer and looked lighter from the outside. The inside, however, was what counted. It had more room and additional armor coverage.

I reached in and grabbed Durundle, the flaming sword once owned by Charlemagne. It was enchanted, and much like the Judge, had a slight mind of its own. The sword, however, wasn't as discriminating. It just figured out how aggressively it was going to dispatch whatever was at the other end. At times, it manifested as a flame-dripping sword; other times, it appeared as if it had just come out of a smelt, glowing red with hellfire, with my favorite being when it decided to do its best lightsaber impersonation. It had only done that once. Tonight, it went with glowing red hellfire.

"*Ignis!*" I yelled, bringing the blade to life as the man took two lumbering steps toward me. Getting to my feet, it was clear something was wrong. I wasn't going to take any chances. The man was now twenty feet away, the red-orange glow flowing from his hands growing to create a haze around him.

Cu-chunk, cu-chunk, rang through the air as the man exploded. The sounds were coming from a shotgun—not just any shotgun: Phil's.

I stood there, watching in slow motion as his flaming head flew through the air, forcing me to catch it for a second in my left arm like a football before I threw it. Phil ran around the corner just in time to catch the burning skull, accidentally lighting his beard on fire.

After a minute of dancing and smacking his face, Phil finally stopped moving.

"You see that, bruther?" Phil exclaimed, taking in the scene and the pile of gore. Phil looked at his shotgun then at me. "Normal ammo. That bloke did the exploding on his own," he concluded, popping a smoke in his mouth and lighting it off a small fire starting on a pile of pallets.

Phil's beard was burnt to the point of no return. It would have to be shaved off. The smell of burning hair permeated the area around the body, mixing with Phil's cigarette smoke.

Smoke was starting the fill the air as other parts of the building finally caught fire under the aggressive direction of the hellfire that had been thrown around. A red glow started emanating from the shadows.

"Hey, boss, Kim's here. I'm not sure if you noticed, but the building's on fire," Petro said over the radio as the sound of police sirens started howling in the background.

Like a bad cliché, Phil and Kim had shown up just in the nick of time. Phil and I looked at each other as a wall on the far end crashed to the ground.

"Time to go," I told Phil as he put on a glove, reached down, and scooped up the head. He made the same face a child would if his parent were about to make him eat boiled brussels sprouts.

"I'm trying to get ahead," Phil said in his thick Irish accent with a mix of chuckling, coughing, and gagging.

Taking one last look around, I put up Durundle, as visions of the burning scene etched themselves into my memory.

The sirens and lights danced off the buildings and stacks of containers. Standing with her hands on her hips was Kim Kinder, the one and only Senior Field Marshal for the regional OTN office. In other words, she handled the cases that weren't your everyday, run-of-the-mill crime and which were more likely to be explained by magic.

"I have to hear this," Kim said, a slight smile reaching the corners of her mouth.

Over the past year, I had done everything in my power to get her to go out on a date. It had finally worked three weeks ago, ending with a call to check out a grisly murder scene. It had really killed the mood.

She was five and a half feet tall, fit, blonde, and had only recently started opening up to me on a personal level. Kim was pretty in a strong way that lent itself to endless hours of training. The scent of vanilla and honey radiated from her body, both deliberate and subtle at the same time. Tonight, she was dressed in dark jeans with a blue T-shirt and a light jacket to cover her service pistol.

Since the Balance, regular law enforcement departments had mixed feelings about the work she did. Some were curious, others standoffish, blaming anything they couldn't figure out or solve on Mages or Ethereals. To be honest, there wasn't much truly magically driven crime that happened out in the open. Centuries of working under a veil of secrecy had made it the norm not to be caught or exposed.

That's right, the Balance had taken place. Just like that, the regular world knew of the existence of the magical community. At least the part of it the Supreme Council wanted to divulge. There were still plenty of things that had gone unmentioned, and for a good reason.

The world as a whole had taken it rather well, mainly due to the underwhelming size of the community they had been exposed to. A few places, as predicted, hadn't taken it as glowingly. Certain rural areas and already sensitive inner cities had seen days of looting, riots, and general chaos. Some smaller, less developed countries had fallen into dictatorship-like rule out of fear.

The plan had been to ensure this was corrected using the might of the new combined worlds. At the end of the day, the plan had worked. Many of the smaller countries, while still unstable, had found peace, and the general chaos had settled back into everyday life.

A cheeseburger, after all, was still a cheeseburger, and a beer . . . I needed a beer.

One thing that hadn't been predicted was the massive surge within religious communities. Faith was not just an abstract anymore. While not everything had been laid out to the general public, it had been enough. This would cause issues later, but for now, there was general calm.

For the most part all the Mages I knew still kept to themselves Mages I knew still kept to themselves. Like myself, they felt like more of an anomaly or attraction than anything. That is, minus the Vs. Vampires loved all the attention. They had even opened a chain of themed, exclusive restaurants in three major cities.

Jacksonville, Florida, as predicted, boomed. Its status as a major hub for everything magic in the US turned it into a new type of "Magic Capital," as it was nicknamed.

When I'd started advertising my services in St. Augustine, the office had become an immediate magnet for tin foil hat–wearing nuts and overly curious people. After a few months of people figuring out that I was always at the bar next door drinking and not selling T-shirts stating, "Hey, I'm a wizard," the traffic had died down.

I had been awarded a place on the Junior Council due to my actions over the past two years. Ed, after his injuries, had been promoted to the Senior Council, and he had authorized me to do official Council business when I deemed it necessary. While I wasn't working at the Atheneum anymore, I was still part of the team in a roundabout way.

Finding Mr. Bellman was one of my first official consulting cases involving regulars. I had done a few odd jobs, but they had been mundane tasks; catch a Fiend Hound or see if my house is haunted. My business card and window sign were simple:

Abaddon & Associates (AA)
Consulting commercial and private. Questions answered.
Rebirthday testing. Council-certified castor dealer.
See a consultant for rates.

Phil walked up, dropping the head in front of Kim and garnering a gasp and a slight step back. The smell of burning flesh and Phil's now deceased beard lingered in the humid air. Petro buzzed down, directly taking back off after smelling the charred remains. He had a weak stomach.

"I don't think Mr. Bellman will be causing any more issues tonight. I've been chasing him through town for the past hour," I said, waiting on a response. Kim took a minute to let the situation in front of her sink in.

Phil lit up another cigarette as loud voices came from the other side of the cars, the dock's fire team finally arriving to put out the blaze I may or may not have started.

Kim pulled up her phone, showing me the screen. "Was this you?" she asked, pointing to a line of reported fires on a map leading from the football stadium to the docks.

"Me? No, him," I said, pointing at the head.

Kim clicked on a video of Mr. Bellman shooting his fire lightning at me and setting a small, empty medical office building on fire.

"See? I was trying to get the guy to stop. That's why I called you," I said, wishing I hadn't as she pulled up another video.

This one was of the RV dealership we had gone through. It clearly showed me launching a small ball of concentrated hellfire at the man, only for it to be deflected and land in an RV, immediately lighting it on fire.

"You got me on that one," I admitted, looking over at the man raising his voice at Frank. It was odd that Frank was there.

Kim cleared her throat. Again, she pushed fast-forward on the video, showing the entire dealership engulfed in flames.

"You have good insurance, I presume?" Kim asked, smirking at me. She was being playful, yet making sure I knew that setting large parts of the city on fire was not acceptable.

"I think," I said, looking over at Phil.

"Bruther, this doesn't look like any normal consulting gig. The guy was in full-on crazy mode in there, slinging Lord knows what type of magic around. I would think this would be considered Council business, and with that, fall under their umbrella," Phil said in quite possibly one of the most intellectual statements I had ever heard him say.

I stood there looking at the two.

"Sounds like something the marshal's office will need to be involved in as well," Kim hinted as they both stood there looking back at me. Petro came to hover behind them, holding his nose with one hand as he mimed for me to pull out my Council badge.

"Right," I said, pulling out the small shield intricately inlaid with the Council's seal. "I'll need you two to pull up what you can on Mr. Bellman. I'm going to need to make a call."

"Call to whom?" Kim asked.

"Mrs. Bellman. Kim, do you have something we can wrap

that thing up in? We can get what's left to Jenny and let her check it out. Something wasn't right. According to his wife, he was a regular guy, an addict. Not to mention, infatuated with magic. I would like to see his blood work. I'll gate Phil back through the Postern; he can get that mess off his face. I'm kinda looking forward to seeing the new and improved Phil," I said, again overhearing the loud man who was obviously an employee of the docks.

Phil and Kim picked up on my mood, shook their heads, and followed as I walked up behind Frank.

"Hello, Max," Frank said in his smooth, calming yet commanding voice without turning around. Vampires had a way of doing that.

"Hey, Frank, had dinner yet tonight?" I asked, looking at the bald, short, strong-looking older man.

"No . . ." Frank drawled out.

Vampires were oddly fascinated with humanity, not like the movies would have you believe. Some liked human blood, but they were the exception, and a rather nasty one. Vs or Vamps, as they were called at times, were cursed—for lack of a better term—Fae from long ago. Some Ethereals considered them diseased Fae. This curse happened when the Plane shifted and the first Ethereals set foot on Earth—war had torn their Plane of existence mostly apart. It had been a final message to the Fae, but the plan had only been partly successful.

They didn't even drink blood. At least not the normal ones. They depended on highly developed synthetic blood that allowed them out into the sunlight, to eat regular food, and avoid ripping people throats out. This ability to let them live partially normal lives had made them forever thankful for the two regular scientists who helped formulate the product.

Frank had gone through a type of rehab after having acquired a taste for human blood. That, however, was a story for another day. The issue here was that people still were not convinced, and if not infatuated with them, they were mostly scared shitless.

"What?" the man asked in a gruff voice, seeing the three of us come from behind Frank. "You're that Max guy that was in the news."

I sighed, knowing he was talking about the footage from a few months back showing me doing what I do best: setting a car on fire. Hey, that guy had it coming.

"Yup, and this is my favorite Vampire friend, Frank," I said smiling, letting him see the whites of my teeth. Frank just shook his head.

The man took a step back, showing his unease.

"I was just asking Bill here a few questions, nothing major," Frank purred, now playing the part, not liking the man's reaction.

"Do you know this man?" I asked Bill, holding up my phone and showing him the picture Mrs. Bellman had given me.

Bill paused just a second too long. If you're going to lie when someone shows you something, do one of two things. Look at it like you are sincerely trying to remember (people appreciate the effort) or immediately say no.

Bill had glanced at it, recognized the man, looked up, then paused before saying no. He didn't shake or move his head at all. Frank also picked up on it; however, he was probably going by the man's heart rate.

"Tell you what," Frank said, turning around and making a funny face at the rest of us. "Kim, can your team take a statement from Bill and call me afterward?"

Frank was, as of a month ago, the Senior Lead Investigator for the CSA in the Southern US. This meant that he worked directly with Kim, but had slightly more pull in the grand scheme of things.

That was perfectly fine with Kim. She had been offered more positions than she could digest and had turned them all down to stay in the field. I respected her for that. I also hoped it was because of me.

Since the fire was close to being put out and the damage was minimal, I helped Phil gate back to the office, from where he would gate to the Atheneum with Mr. Bellman's head. Petro had done a great job of telling us how disgusting it was and how bad it smelled meanwhile.

Jumping into the Black Beast, I took out my phone. I had a phone call to make to Mrs. Bellman.

CHAPTER 2

Ordinary World

P etro buzzed the door open as Mrs. Bellman walked in. She looked at Petro with hungry curiosity. Mr. Bellman hadn't been the only person with an interest in the magical community in the family.

"Thanks for stopping by," I said, standing up from my desk. We had changed the old Transitions Office into the headquarters for Double As, AA for short. The rest of us just called it the shop.

Thanks to Devin's housewarming gift, and with Tom's approval, most of his and my old office at the Atheneum had been moved to the new space. The walls were covered in bookshelves adorned with an assortment of things I had collected over the past two years. In the back of the office was the desk that had once supposedly belonged to King Arthur. It wasn't round, so I was skeptical at best.

The icing on the cake was the bar from the old office—the same bar, including the sliding mirror that went down into the lab that, as before, didn't quite fit the space it occupied. In St. Augustine, in the downtown area, anything a few feet underground was more than likely in the water table.

The door to the Postern was another story. According to Tom, that room really wasn't in the Atheneum. It was nowhere and everywhere. I had also set up a gate in the office's back room with a stone from the Evergate. I would take it with me in the event anything happened. The Evergate had ten stones total. One had been taken by Petro's brothers, but had been returned during a spring break. Another I always kept on me, and a third here in the offices of AA. If there was a reason there were ten, neither Tom nor I had figured it out. We had set two others to help Ed navigate the Atheneum until we could come up with a way to get him out of his wheelchair

That's right, Gramps was back. He, of course, had left soon after to God knows where to do who knows what.

"I'm assuming this isn't good," Mrs. Bellman said as she took off her overcoat, handing it to me.

She smelled like she had just put on Chanel before walking in. Mrs. Bellman was dressed in a pair of casual slacks and a blouse that indicated she had gotten dressed up to come into the office. She was slender and tall, having hands that spent more time concerned about moisturizer than hard work.

"I'm going to need you to come with me to the Atheneum to look at something," I replied, seeing the shift in her face.

"You need me to identify his body," she said with a sigh. "The Atheneum? Isn't that the place that everyone talks about? Some big scary old castle?"

Her voice was smooth and reassuring. She knew what she was here for, yet Carol Bellman had still gotten herself together. I was starting to think she was doing it out of respect and not any other reasons. You know, such as trying to seduce the mysterious Mage.

"I'll drive us over."

"Don't you all gate or whatever it is you call it?" Carol said as Petro flew back into the room, landing on the desk.

Before I could respond, she stared at Petro and asked, "Is he a Pixie?"

"I'm standing right here, lady. Believe it or not, I can talk and do things like read," Petro said, used to the stigma Pixies carried.

I looked over at Petro. "It's going to be a long night. Can you run ahead and see what's going on?"

"Sure thing, boss," he replied before zipping into the air over and through the Evergate.

"Sure we can't take that?" Carol asked.

"Have you had dinner tonight?" I replied, knowing the usual effects gating had.

"Yes."

"Have you ever gated?"

"No, I don't think I know anyone that has. Well, the Chesters down the street say they have, but they are full of shit," Carol replied playfully. The tone was odd, not fitting the situation.

"Then we ride."

Handing Mrs. Bellman her overcoat back, we walked out jumping into the Black Beast. I had driven back to the office, a straight shot down A1A, and was in desperate need of a drink and some rest. Kim and Carol were going to get along just fine.

That was a lie.

I have a feeling Kim is going to make me feel stupid about dealing with her, I thought in my snooty inner voice.

The ride to the Atheneum was typical. I didn't even do the radio test due to the situation. Pulling off Highway 16 into the inconspicuous entrance path, I could tell she was more excited than upset. Mrs. Bellman must have known the vibe she was giving off, as she settled back down.

Phil was standing outside with James smoking a cigarette. "Bruther, Jenny's waiting," Phil said, letting me know to go directly down to her lab. Phil had completely shaven his beard off, only leaving a layer of hair on his face. He looked ten years younger, as men often did after they shaved their beards off.

"James, how's it going? We didn't get a chance to talk earlier," I greeted, shaking his hand.

"All good. You still owe me a drink from last year," he replied, making sure I knew that I owed him some time. He was a good man and an even better regular agent. James came from a traditional Black southern family and had a way of making you feel comfortable around him.

"Mrs. Bellman, please follow us," I said, forgetting how many people were now working in the Atheneum.

The entrance had been turned into an official-looking facility. While it still held its traditional gothic look and feel, the inclusion of two security desks and a small wall barrier made it feel too official.

Carol's eyes reflected the glowing yellow light of the massive iron chandeliers, but what made her mouth gape open was the large stone globe water feature in the middle of the entrance. The globe was the size of a small house. I had done as Phil had instructed and avoided drinking the water out of it. He saw me remembering and grinned. It was the first time in several months I had been in the facility.

"Is Kim here?" I asked Phil, grinning back. He just shook his head, knowing I wanted to say something about his now missing beard. I would miss watching him drop things in it while eating as we made fun of him.

"Oy, she is. I don't think she's pleased about the fires, mate. You may owe her more than a drink."

I sighed, knowing I had probably ruined a night of her reading to her cats, or as I figured she actually did, nightly jiu-jitsu classes. I just preferred the visions of her with cats instead of her learning how to kick my ass. Plus, I really wanted an actual evening out with her.

"Jenny, Kim, I'd like you to meet Mrs. Bellman," I introduced once we arrived, looking around the room. Petro buzzed over and landed on my shoulder. The room was always immaculate and smelled like a combination between a sterilized hospital room and a garden.

"Hey, boss, you're going to love this," Petro whispered into my ear, waving at Kim when she looked over at us, raising an eyebrow.

She wasn't upset. Instead, Kim was engaged. Something was going on.

"Nice to meet you, Mrs. Bellman. I'm not going to hold this any longer from you. Mr. Bellman has passed away. We just need you to identify his remains," Jenny started in her educated yet reassuring tone. She was probably one of the smartest people I had ever met, and on top of that, the new de facto boss of the Atheneum. Let's not mention she pretty much had also been the boss when Ed was in charge anyway. Also, those two had officially come out as in a relationship. To be clear, they had been in the most obvious secret relationship of all times. They loved each other, and everyone knew it.

"Remains?" Mrs. Bellman whispered.

I stepped forward before Kim could. Knowing her, she would show Mrs. Bellman the remains with little to no bedside manner. "Carol, I don't want you to think about how this happened. We can talk about it later. I just want you to know we are going to get to the bottom of it."

Kim, as I figured she would, walked directly over to the basketball-sized lump on the table and pulled off the cover, exposing Mr. Bellman's head. Called it.

Carol was wearing sunglasses with a light brown hue; she turned, covering her mouth. "Jesus, that's him."

Mrs. Bellman broke down crying, walking to the corner to avoid her husband's head on the table. I looked at Kim to see a smile, not on her mouth but in her eyes.

Jenny and I walked Mrs. Bellman out into the hall. "What

would do that? I mean, he was just out doing drugs, right? Or having an affair? I wasn't expecting this."

"We will find out. I'm going to get you home tonight, and we can talk tomorrow or the next day," I said, putting an arm around her. She pulled in closer than Jenny or I expected, garnering a look between us.

"Mrs. Bellman, we will need to see some of your husband's things. Someone will be reaching out, as Max mentioned," Jenny concluded, bringing the situation to a close.

"Max, can you take me home?"

I looked over at Jenny as she gave a slight shake of her head. She needed to tell me something.

"I'm sorry, I need to work on this. It's become an official investigation, and I'm better served here. James is by the stairs and will take you home. Get some rest, and I'll call you tomorrow," I said.

James walked over and escorted Mrs. Bellman away. You could feel the ice coming off Carol as she left, shuffling like a robot in need of an oil change, unlike her normal, practiced posture.

"So, what's up?" I asked as Jenny let out a breath she had been holding the entire time, allowing the tension out of her body.

"Well, I don't think she had anything to do with this mess. Remember when I talked to you about Ethereal drugs?" Jenny asked in her motherly tone.

"Yeah, sure, but nothing that would make you explode and make your head go flying off, right?" I said, hoping I hadn't missed anything.

"From what I understand, Phil didn't help the situation with his little play toy," Jenny replied as she walked back through the door.

Kim walked up, smiling. "Looks like we have an honest-to-God case that doesn't involve the end of the world, fake Vampires, or overgrown cats, and I'm not going to lie, watching that CCTV footage of you was impressive," Kim said excitedly. Something was going on that was getting her blood flowing. "Oh, and I need to tell you. Do that shit again, and I'll arrest you personally."

Thoughts of her handcuffing me crossed my mind. Kim shook her head when she saw my expression. Petro opted to land on the shelf and avoid proximity with what was left of Mr. Bellman.

"Alright already. Stop looking at me like I'm a unicorn. Spill it," I urged.

"We know three things. One, Mr. Bellman was a regular and in no way had any level of natural Etherium in his body before this. Second, he has ungodly amounts of a Fae drug called Kracken in his system. Well, what's left of it. The last thing is about the drug itself," Jenny informed me as she walked around the table and put on a pair of gloves.

"Hey, Kim, you used to work narcotics, right?" I asked, figuring out why she was so engaged.

"Five years. It's where I got my start," Kim answered, walking over to me and getting a better view of what Jenny was about to do.

Jenny took the cover off the head, turning the face directly toward us. "Look at the eyes," she said as she pulled one eyelid open, pinning it back with some shiny clamp that was probably worth more than my life.

"The drug is exceedingly high end and rare to find here. It's more common on the Plane; however, even there, it's very costly. An elite drug, if you will. To a Fae, it is like getting a shot of steroids and cocaine all in one, all while turbocharging the subject's Etherium. It has an even more drastic effect on the human body, though it's very dependent on the concentration. You can literally give a dose to a regular person and grant them the short-term ability to do magic by giving them some level of Etherium. It all depends on the type the person takes to figure out the experience they are going to have and/or abilities —" Jenny was cut off by Kim; she didn't seem to mind as she popped open the other eyelid as well.

"If you take enough, you will definitely have a bad day. There are only a handful of reported overdose cases. Up until now, since your world was off the books, so was the drug. It wasn't considered illegal. Now, it's a big, fat, Do Not Pass Go, Go Straight to Jail offense. If you're caught peddling this stuff, it's game over. As a matter of fact, it is considered, as of two months ago, one of the most dangerous drugs out there, and in turn, one of the most sought after. The local marshal's office busted someone selling fake Kracken. You have to have serious money and connections to get the real stuff."

"Max," Jenny cut back in. "Remember last year when you took that potion that turbocharged you before Tom poured it out?"

"Yeah, I was like a beast after I took it. I wanted more, but as you noted, Gramps poured it out and told me to stay away from the stuff," I said, getting a clearer picture of what had happened. "So this stuff makes you explode if you overdose? I think there was a movie made in the '80s about people smoking crack and exploding."

"*Frankenhooker* is not a viable source of field research," Jenny replied, getting a chuckle out of the group staring at the head.

"Look at his eyes," Jenny continued.

They were blood red with no indication of white. Burn marks scorched the skin around the openings. The burns were not from the fire, but rather from the glowing haze I had witnessed seeping out of them like fog rolling off a pond in early spring.

"One indication of Kracken use is bloodshot eyes. It's a

quick way to figure out how much of the product the person has taken. Also, per the burns. The flames would not have burned the skin of a real Mage or Ethereal, which tells us the person is not a Fire Mage. I think the report should be back," Jenny said, nodding over to Kim.

Kim walked over as I watched her move, clicking the mouse on the computer and centrifuge on the desk. "It's over a thousand parts and says 'Unknown.' Jenny, look," Kim requested, needing some help with the medical interpretation.

"God, it's like his blood is pure Kracken, and . . . something else. I'm not sure, some type of accelerant. It's like he took the purest dose he could, mixed with something else to make it even more powerful. I don't understand. This may take some time," Jenny muttered, putting on her glasses and banging the keyboard at a furious pace.

"Enchanted Vampire blood," Petro said as he flew over to the table.

"What?" Jenny asked, turning.

"Vampire blood. I can smell it from here. You just had to ask," Petro said, grinning as he played with his majestic mustache as he often did when gloating.

Phil let out a simple, "Yuck."

"Explain," Jenny commanded, her curiosity eclipsing the fact that she had a disembodied head on the table with its eyes propped open.

"Well, if you get caught doing that on the Plane, it's instant death. Vampire blood is infectious to the Fae. It can turn them into Vs, or even worse. In humans, it's like an accelerant. Remember all those movies where young girls or guys drink Vampire blood and get all super sexy time?" Petro said, gyrating his hips. "Same thing. It takes whatever it's attached to and does whatever it does. There are shifters back home that drink the stuff all the time to stay in human form. Kind of a trendy thing," Petro finished as I motioned for him to stop gyrating.

I looked over at the head. "We need to figure out where he got the stuff, and if there's any more out there," I said, pulling the cover back over the head.

"Precisely," Jenny agreed as she walked over to her phone. "I already texted Ed that we will need to talk later. I'm going to see what else I can find on the drug. There're a few books in the stacks dedicated to Kracken; it used to be considered a miracle potion. I'm sure the Council will want you involved."

"I'm already involved. Just not officially until your report goes up, and they ask. I need to get back to the office and get some things situated," I said as I saw Phil nod, signaling it was time for a drink at some point in the near future. "Kim, you have a minute?"

"Sure," she replied as we walked out into the hall, the murmur of conversation picking back up behind us.

"Sorry about the mess. Do you need me to fill anything out?"

"Paperwork?"

"Yeah, something like that. That whole side of the docks was a mess, and the RVs?"

"Don't sweat it, but consider yourself on retainer as of this morning, and don't think about sending me a bill. Look, I can help, but when big things get damaged, it gets touchy, especially after the Balance. Some people are just looking for an excuse to make Mages and the like look bad. You're one of the good guys; we'll clean up what we can. I've already made a few calls. Oh, and before I forget, here," Kim said, handing me a note, her hand lingering a second longer than needed.

"It's a name and number. Cecil?" I asked, looking up.

"While you were heading back, I made some calls. I got this as you were pulling up. He's a V that got in some trouble in the past and was caught with Kracken. It wasn't illegal then, but what I can tell you is that he works out of Jacksonville and has had a steady stream of shipping containers coming in at the docks. I've already made a few inquiries," Kim said, smiling.

"Perfect. Let me check this out. Call me if you hear anything; I'll do the same. Hey," I paused. "It's like old times."

"About time," she said as she looked me square in the eyes.

Over the past year, I had been busy—as had Kim—with the Balance. Everything was happening so fast, and time had just passed. My weekly attempts to get Kim out on a date had turned into monthly, which had turned into an actual date, as mentioned before, that hadn't ended well.

"Let's get together tomorrow and talk things over," I said lightly.

Kim smiled, nodding her head approvingly and walking back into Jenny's lab as Phil stepped out.

I looked down at my watch; it was almost 1:00 a.m. "Petro, go time, partner. Phil, I'm going to have to take a rain check."

Phil frowned slightly; he wanted to have a few drinks.

"Bruther, drinks tomorrow, FA's. Promise," he demanded.

"Promise," I answered as Petro flew over and landed on my shoulder.

"Pinky swear." Phil reached out his tattooed pinky. I had also not been meeting my quota of drinking nights with Phil. Studying the Postern, endless nights of practice (including Council meetings), and setting up AA had taken a toll on my social life.

I exchanged the time-honored tradition, sealing our fates for tomorrow evening.

We gated back to the office, leaving the Black Beast to be picked up later.

I sat behind the desk as Petro landed by the keyboard. The office still smelled like Tom's old office. Leather, whiskey, and burnt hickory. Taking a deep, cleansing breath, I opened the drawer and pulled out a small bottle of bourbon along with a cup and a cap for Petro.

"Casey good you're up this late?" I asked him. He had gotten married to Casey, and the two now lived in a section of the house behind the walls that apparently used to house a Pixie family. It made sense, as FA's next door had a setup for them as well under the bar. Recently that had changed, as they were now allowed on the bar top.

"Boss, she's fine. What's the plan?"

I pulled out my phone, punching in the number on the note Kim had given me. Petro gave me a confused look.

The phone picked up after two rings. "Cecil," the V on the other end of the phone said in an assured voice. Sounds of upset conversations were going on in the background, as well as sirens. He was at the docks.

"Hey, it's Max Abaddon. I hope it's not too late. How's it going?" I asked, figuring the only reason he would pick up the phone is if he knew who I was.

"I know. I'm a little busy right now."

"My business card must be getting around. Hope everything's alright, and things cool down some for you. Are you free tomorrow to have a conversation?" I asked, getting a jab in on what was probably some of his burning containers.

"No. You can call my office and set up an appointment."

Figuring I would flex to see how far I could push the Vampire, I pulled my trump card that wasn't really official yet.

"I'm going to have to call this one. By order of the Junior Council—"

Cecil cut me off before I could finish. "The docks. Noon tomorrow," was the last thing he said before hanging up.

Once Jenny talked with Ed, I would be officially on Council business. My status on the Junior Council did give me some privileges. One of the main perks was sitting on the Council Intelligence Committee. I was an intel guy in the army, and enjoyed the continuity—plus the access to information others didn't have. My status as caretaker of the Atheneum and Postern was, for the most part, no longer. I had quit. The Council hadn't known how to react to that, so it was just treated as if it had never happened.

AA was more of a side business to support my weekly beer habit. While Mrs. Bellman was my first true consulting case, I had figured a way to navigate the murky waters left after the Balance and still have the best of both worlds. The fact that I had recently been introduced to the magical community a year or so prior to the Balance put my feet firmly in both worlds. Not to mention I had decided to be an independent Mage. The whole episode with Carvel and Darkwater trying to have me executed or expelled from the magical community had left a bad taste in my mouth. Carvel's mother, on the other hand, had left the taste of pie. She had cooked me one after I had saved her son's life. It's a long story.

I set the phone down as we took the final pulls from our drinks. After filling Petro in on the conversation and information Kim had given me, we called it a night, agreeing to meet in the morning for Petro's favorite: Golden Grahams.

CHAPTER 3

Three's a Crowd

My morning ritual had improved over the past year. I was even able to afford one of those fancy, one-cup coffee machines everyone was so crazy about. As if deemed by the gods, it started its daily awaking ritual, filling the air with the smell of rich Colombian coffee.

As my feet touched the thick Persian rug beside my bed, I realized that I still needed to catch up on a lead for one of the gates in the Postern. Last year, I had learned that the Postern was, in fact, a weapon. Tom, whenever he was around, spent all his time going over it with me. We had figured out how to use three of the ten gates. Gramps had been impressed that I had figured two of them out. He had even told me a few stories about getting a couple of the others to work, only to have "issues," whatever that meant.

The new digital clock I had purchased read 6:30 a.m. A rather rude combination of beeps and dings came from the angry box as I clicked the snooze button. My new room was on the second floor of the office building. The same floor that Trish, the ever-trusty owner of FA's and my new landlady, had at one time stated was off-limits due to an incident.

Since Petro was now officially married, I wasn't as worried about him spending his mornings sneaking into my room.

Plus, I had started sleeping naked, which had also helped deter his interest. I missed it. I reached over, putting on my castor as a light wave of relief poured over my chest. I was still a reasonably new Mage by all accounts, which meant my body hadn't fully regulated to the Etherium flowing through my veins.

I now had a slightly smaller black-tiled bathroom that was filling with steam as I walked out after turning the water on, letting it build up.

Most Mages wore a castor all the time, as it stored a little extra energy. There were all types. Nice dive watches like mine, or watches like Phil's, which looked like a leather bracelet with an old timepiece on it.

For years before we met, Jenny had been designing castors, and I, as of last month, had a handful in stock to start selling. She said it was part of her retirement plan.

The need for a castor only came if a person had some type of lineage from the Plane, and also only after thirty years of gestation. The best part was that you basically started aging at the speed of slow. For every ten years that passed, a male Mage would on average progress about half a year. While this wasn't the case for all Mages, it was prevalent in males for some reason. The term for the celebration of turning thirty was one's rebirthday.

During the Balance, a documentary on castors had been made, only to be buried in one of the twenty or so on-demand channels. Jenny had been part of it, and the group had even thrown her a party to celebrate.

I reflected for a few more minutes as I looked at the now modified blazer I had received on my rebirthday. It had a dark burn mark on the front resembling a dried-up, massive ketchup stain that I would have to address. Or as it often did, it would just address itself, as it was enchanted.

After several minutes of standing in the steam-filled room after taking a shower, I looked down, pulling all the moisture from the air and creating a pocket of fresh dry air in front of my face. It was a trick I was learning in case I ever got stuck underwater for longer than anticipated.

I walked out and found Petro waiting for me in the hall.

"Hey, boss, hope you had a good night because I had a doozy," Petro said as he flew up in the air, heading toward the kitchen.

"I slept well. Woke up feeling a little nostalgic. Remember my rebirthday? I keep thinking about how much things have changed," I told him as I followed him toward the kitchen.

The kitchen was on the second floor and relatively up-to-date, considering the rest of the building's age. It smelled like old wood that had been exposed to water and overly heated oil at one point. In other words, it smelled like a well-used kitchen you would find in a typical home full of people.

I reached into the cabinet by the refrigerator and pulled out a box of Golden Grahams, shaking it lightly as I set a bowl down for myself and a small cap for Petro.

One thing I had learned was that if you ever wanted to make a Pixie happy, all you had to do was give them some Golden Grahams. Petro and I had shared hundreds of bowls over the past two years, sitting at the Atheneum kitchen table and talking over the day's plans.

The routine was simple; I would take a few flakes, put them in a plastic bag, crunch them up, then pour the crumbs in a small cap followed by the correct amount of milk. That part was important; eating cereal the way it was engineered always produced satisfying results. In many cases, Petro just ate the flakes whole.

Since his marriage to Casey, things had changed slightly, and we only got to do this about once every other week.

"So what's the plan, boss?" Petro asked, reaching down and scooping up a mouthful of cereal. A slight frosting of milk permeated his mustache as he reached down and grabbed a small napkin, wiping his face.

"We're going to the docks to have a little chat with Cecil. As I mentioned last night, he's one of the few people in the area that's ever been connected to the stuff. I don't think we're walking into any trouble today, but the fact that he was down there last night is not a coincidence," I said, taking a mouthful of cereal as well.

"What about the Council? If you go off doing this without their permission, it might become an issue. Anyway, are we still on the clock and getting paid by Mrs. Bellman?" Petro replied, bringing up a good point.

I clicked open my phone, sharing the screen with Petro. There was a text message from Ed giving us the go-ahead to speak with Cecil, making this official Council business.

Petro squinted his eyes, reading the message out loud in his best impersonation of Ed, "*Max, I've talked to the Supreme Council, and they are good with you working this until we get all the details together. We have everything else with the fires you started handled, as long as you don't do that again. Just do me a favor and don't do anything until we can get more details or a few more people freed up to help. If something changes, I'll let you know.*" He looked up from the screen with a skeptical look on his face. "He seems to be giving you a pretty long leash."

"*Us*, Petro, he seems to be giving *us* a pretty long leash," I said, making sure that he was fully aware that others were involved. We both sat there for another few minutes, eating our cereal and reflecting on the message.

My phone dinged with a message from Phil. It consisted of nothing more than several question marks and beer emojis. I took a deep breath, looking over at Petro.

"What is it, boss?" Petro asked, picking up his now empty cap and putting it in my bowl.

"It's Phil. I don't want to leave him out of this; I also don't know if it's the best idea to have him go down there with us today. One thing I do know is that if I don't go have a drink with him tonight, he's more than likely either going to chase after me with a shotgun or start calling me names again."

A few months ago, after not being able to meet up with him for afternoon drinks, he had started calling me names. These included Squishy Nuts, Barfy Face, Assback, and his classic go-to, Nerd Legs.

Petro and I looked at each other, obviously more concerned about the name-calling than anything else.

"I'll give him a call in a little bit. I want to meet up with him after we leave the docks; maybe we can grab a drink afterward and see if he's heard anything. Lastly, I want to give Kim a quick call before we leave and let her know what we're doing," I said, figuring it would probably be a good idea to stay in Kim's good graces.

"Let me go talk to Casey; I'll be back in a little bit. When are we leaving?"

"In about an hour. I just remembered the Black Beast is at the Atheneum. We're taking a road trip. I'll talk to Phil when I go over to grab her; just head over when you're done. Tell the old lady I said hello," I told him as Petro fist-bumped the air. He enjoyed going on truck rides; it was part of the whole "they enjoy human activities" thing about Pixies. Plus, we always turned the stereo up to eleven and rocked out to the latest Planes Drifter song.

Whenever I went to the Atheneum, it was usually later in the day. Now with a full staff of what seemed to be roughly forty people, the facility was rather lively at 7:30 a.m. The sweet smell of doughnuts and bitter coffee filled the air; it was shift change.

Security guards were stationed at the front entrance, and the gate that I came through today was the one to the right. It was a special gate and, besides the Postern, one of the more powerful ones I had used. Most gates were only attached to one location. One way there and one way back. This gate would let you come and go from several other places. I had even spent time talking to Tom about it, to see if it was like the Evergate in the Postern. It wasn't. In fact, it was far from it. Being at the Atheneum is what stabilized the gate. Long story short, it took more than a few spells, sanctioned by the Council, to keep it up and running, and Ying.

"I'm here to pick up the Black Beast and talk to Phil. The Council gave me the go-ahead to investigate the situation that occurred last night," I said grinning.

"I heard a little bit about it from Mrs. Bellman on the way home. She was pretty shaken up, but something was weird about her. She was very interested in the Atheneum and asked me a ton of questions about magic," James replied quickly, as the other guards looked impressed.

"If you can think of anything that stood out when she was talking, let me know," I said, putting my keys and phone in the tray before walking through the scanner that had recently been installed. It was the latest in Mags-Tech technology; it scanned for unauthorized spells, enchantments, glamours, and in general, anything that wasn't supposed to be in the building.

Phil wasn't hard to find; you could hear his voice coming from the back of the hallway as he walked out of the dining room.

"Morning, sunshine," I said, walking up to him as we both raised an eyebrow and looked at each other, smirking. Very rarely were either one of us up this early in the morning, and even more uncommon was both of us being ready for work.

"Bruther, what's got you in here this early in the morning, besides the free bagels?" Phil asked in his thick Irish slash Texan accent, popping an unlit cigarette in his mouth and letting it roll around.

"Coming to see you, sunshine, and pick up the Beast," I said chuckling.

"Figured. I got a note from Ed as well. He told me to work with you until we get more information—I have a feeling we're the ones getting that information. Jenny wants me to take what's left of Mr. Bellman to the Council labs."

"Great. Hey, I'm heading to the docks with Petro later. Keep your communicator handy; I'll let you know if anything pops up. Maybe this time you could be a little less shotgunny, though," I said, smirking.

Phil put his hand over his chest. "Mwwaa? Shotgunny? I'm thoroughly offended."

We both laughed as he walked me to the truck. Petro joined us, having gated in after talking with Casey.

As previously described, Phil was a blue jean, dress shirt with the sleeves rolled up, vest-wearing, long-haired with an undercut, tattooed, half-Irish, half-Texan, hipster-looking guy. If you were ever to call him that, though, he would, in turn, beat you into the ground just to prove he was not a hipster. Sadly, he had just had his long beard burned off less than twelve hours ago; he was still getting adjusted to that.

He was an Earth Mage, able to achieve staggering feats of strength. Phil, however, preferred to use regular weapons often loaded with "special" ammunition. His father had been Fae and his mother a tried-and-true Texas woman. He always liked to say he was raised in Ireland but grew up in Texas.

The Black Beast sprang to life as Petro took his seat in the cup holder while I turned up the radio, riding the whole way to the docks with blaring music.

We pulled up to the docks only to find the parking lot completely full. Not only had the night prior generated a significant amount of additional work, but it had also garnered the interest of the local news channels.

Smoke still filled the air from the storage building, and

the smell of burning plastic started coming through the air vents of the Black Beast.

"Game time," I said, looking over at Petro as he grinned.

Things had changed over the last few years, and as I wasn't under the strict thumb of fourteen bosses anymore—well, maybe just one or two when on official business—trips like this had become substantially more enjoyable. The Council actually liked my anonymity to a point. It gave the bureaucrats an excuse to blame me if something ever went wrong.

Even though the Balance already had roughly twelve months in the books, Petro still garnered attention everywhere he went. Pixies weren't exactly something you saw every day, unless you were me and had to watch him eat snacks in his underwear when he had had too much rum to drink, or if Casey had kicked him out of the bedroom.

A plainclothes police officer walked up, looking over us suspiciously and at the same time with wary recognition.

"Can I help you?" the middle-aged, extremely fit, overly passive-aggressive officer said.

"Max Abaddon Sand," I replied, pulling out my Council shield, garnering an even more wary stare.

The man picked up his radio, talking into it like we weren't there. I could feel Petro positioning himself behind my shoulder. He wanted to dust the guy, ensuring he had to go home and change his clothes, and more than likely, burn them.

Depending on the intent, Pixie dust could have a relatively good or bad reaction if a person was exposed to it on purpose. Stress the *on purpose*.

"Yeah, that Max guy is here. Okay, yes, hold on," the officer said, putting his hand over the phone. "Mind if I look at that badge?"

"Sure. My favorite color is blue—well, actually, that's a lie. It's red now. I'm an Aquarius, and I'm fairly sure I didn't start that fire last night," I said while handing my Council badge over to the man.

The man read off the numbers on it. His voice was clipped, yet still professional. I was betting on at least one divorce, a drinking habit that may even best mine, maybe even Phil's, on the weekends, a 350 credit score, and to top it off, probably a few citations for behavior issues. Come to think of it, I kind of liked the guy. That is, if all those things were true. Well, maybe half of them at least.

They were already checking if I was on the clock. I paused at that thought. The civilian police force was getting smart, and for the most part, ignored most of what I usually dealt with. They still handed OTN (other than natural) cases over to Kim's team.

I had texted Kim to let her know what would be going down at the docks this morning, fully expecting her to pay a visit.

The man handed me the badge back. "You're clear. Hey, you know what happened here? Rumor is you had something to do with it," the officer said, running his hands through his hair.

"I'll help you out with that one if you tell me your name," I replied as Petro came from over my shoulder, hovering between the two of us.

"Neil. Name's Detective Neil. I've heard a lot about you; I am surprised we haven't met before," Detective Neil said, letting out a breath.

The shuffle of reporters and regular police officers started to fill the air as the dockmaster walked out of the main administration building.

"You ever been married before, Neil?" I asked as Petro zipped off toward the commotion.

"Not anymore; divorced. All I got out of it was the old beat-up RV that I live in and a taste for cheap booze," he answered, motioning me to follow him.

Note to self, get to know this guy better. I had been looking for more contacts on the regular force. The issue was, most seemed to be either enamored by anything magic or scared. Neil, he didn't give a shit.

As we got closer, and as I suspected would happen, eyes and a few cameras turned in our direction, just like any time we showed up and the local media got wind of a Pixie and possible Mage in the area of a likely crime scene.

The dockmaster walked up to the podium with the local fire chief and a police officer on either side of him, getting back the attention of the cameras.

"Good morning, thank you for coming out. We would like to report that the fire is now under control and that the scene is under investigation for possible arson. I'd like to hand the podium over to Fire Marshall Bill."

It took me a second to pick up on the man's name, snorting out loud and garnering a look from Detective Neil. It was immediately clear we were both on the same wavelength as he cracked a smile.

"Good afternoon, ladies and gentlemen," the fire marshal said in a New York accent, which seemed out of place for Jacksonville. "We have a few leads at this time; however, we don't have anything for public release. There was a report of a fatality during the fire. As soon as the area's deemed safe, we will let you know. I will not be taking any questions."

Typical, I thought to myself. As soon as something happened on some type of state or federally regulated property, there was always a press conference with a police officer, fire department member, and government official.

A few reporters barked out questions to Detective Neil and I as we stood there. Petro was hovering over my left shoulder.

"What a bunch of dumbasses, boss," Petro whispered in my ear as I nodded in agreement.

"Tell you what, let's go behind the tape over there and talk," the detective said, ushering reporters to get out of the way.

To be fair, I think Petro liked the attention. I'm not saying I did, but I didn't mind the random pretty woman passing by giving me a second glance.

We walked out of earshot of the reporters. Detective Neil turned and looked at me, lighting up a cigarette. "You know about all this?" he asked in a genuinely curious tone. His voice was almost gravelly, probably due to years of smoking, only exercise keeping his lungs in working order.

"Everything, considering I was here last night. The guy was strung out on some kind of magical drug, shooting fire lightning out of his hands. One of my buddies showed up as the guy was getting ready to zap me again, and he exploded." I watched the detective burp, blowing smoke from his cigarette out of his nose without opening his mouth.

I figured it wouldn't hurt to tell the guy the truth. The way I saw it, the department probably took most of what he said with a grain of salt, hoping he was sober.

"Hmph," was all the detective said.

My phone chirped with a text from Kim. *Be there in an hour. Don't fuck anything up.* She was serious, and had even dropped the f-bomb on me.

"Here's my card. Call me if you need anything," I told him, checking the time and remembering I had a meeting with Cecil at the other end of the dock.

"What's that guy's deal?" Petro asked as he hovered over my shoulder, the two of us walking away from the crowd.

"I don't know," I said, figuring that the guy pretty much just thought I was crazy. "I don't think the guy really cares. Smell anything funny?"

"Yeah, I can smell the Vampire from here. He's not alone,

boss. There's something else familiar, too," Petro answered as I looked over my shoulder at him. He was squinting his eyes, taking in the scent.

Pixies had an unbelievably great sense of smell. They could tell pretty much immediately who or what somebody was. It was also good enough to tell how many different people were in a building before they even walked in if it wasn't too large or sealed off for some reason.

"That looks like our ma . . ." I trailed off as I stared at Marlow Goolsby talking to the black Vampire.

Petro picked up on the scene simultaneously, buzzing slightly further in front of me to get a better look. What the hell was he doing there? As if the two well-dressed men talking could sense Petro and I walking up behind them, they both stopped and turned around.

"Greeeeat," I said loud enough for them to hear, drawing the word out.

Marlow looked over at Cecil with a questioning glance. He spoke first as he often did, attempting to take charge. "I should've known as soon as I heard that something of particular value was on fire that you'd be involved," Marlow stated in his clipped professional tone.

As always, Mr. Goolsby was dressed to the point of exhaustion in a spick-and-span black suit with an optimistically white shirt. His blond hair was parted precisely, and his brown eyes continued to look out of place, a scar splitting his left eyebrow. Mr. Goolsby's face was angular and strong. The smell of fresh basil mixed with an eccentric sweet tang of orange wafted from him as he turned away from Cecil. As on every other occasion I had met him, I wanted to punch him in the face.

Cecil, on the other hand, was different. Looking at Marlow Goolsby, you knew exactly who he was and what he was about. You might not know what he was doing, but the rest was not left up to the imagination, and he made it perfectly clear. Cecil wore a tailored Burberry pattern suit, including a matching vest.

His skin was dark, almost to the point of being completely black, and his face radiated intelligence, drawing you to him. He was, after all, a Vampire. Cecil wore a castor much like mine, which Vampires often didn't bother with. He also sported identical gold rings on his pinky and index fingers of both hands, topping it off with a gold chain hanging over his vest. He wasn't as cut and dry as Marlow, but it was apparent he was the type of man—or well, Vampire—who would just have somebody else do his dirty work.

Cecil also had a group of Vs with him, clearly looking like a gaggle of cartoonish thugs.

"Morning, gentlemen, did I miss the party? I heard they were serving all-you-can-drink mimosas right down the road," I responded in my best Southern drawl as Petro snickered.

Cecil began to speak as Marlow held up his finger, the look of disdain on his face clearly evident. The two men did not like each other, but they appeared to have some kind of joint interest in the situation.

"You know very well what happened here, Max," Marlow said in a clipped tone that I hadn't heard since I'd almost burned his building down. "I think the three of us need to talk, privately."

Just to prove the point that Marlow wasn't entirely in charge, I repositioned my Council badge, making sure that the two had a clear view of it.

Marlow chuffed. "Don't insult me. I'm one of the few human representatives on the Council; you would be better served to put that away and talk to us privately," he said, making it clear that he absolutely wanted to have a conversation off the books.

Cecil slowly walked over. I could feel his eyes taking in

every molecule of my being and Petro's. He was, as I assumed, intelligent, and unlike many others, didn't make the mistake of ignoring Petro. After all, the Warrior of the Freeze was about the bravest person—or, well, Pixie—I had ever met.

"I've heard about you, Max and Petro," Cecil started in a raspy yet smooth snakelike voice that made me want to yell out "Cobra" at the top of my lungs. "If all the stories are true, you can cast hellfire."

Just to make sure that the two gentlemen were perfectly aware of where I stood in the situation, I pointed a finger over to the smoldering building. While I hadn't been wholly responsible for it burning down, there had absolutely been some hellfire involved.

Marlow let out a huff of dissatisfaction. He was waiting for me to say something. The three of us stood there. We were again playing a game from a book that everybody in the sales world had read at one point of their lives.

Marlow walked over to a large black SUV, opening the door. The last couple of times I'd run into Marlow, he hadn't had a driver; either he really liked to shuffle himself around or he honestly didn't trust other people.

Cecil got in, and I followed. Marlow held up a hand as Petro began to enter, forcing the Pixie to stop and making dust fall lightly from his wings.

"Hey, boss, you going to let this asshat treat me like this?" Petro demanded, his face turning red. I knew that look. If Marlow was smart, he would put on some sunglasses before he needed an eye patch. Petro was extremely good at giving people permanent pirate costumes for Halloween.

"Do me a favor; go find Detective Neil. Find out when Kim's going to get here and try to link those two up. I'll take care of the asshattery," I said, winking at him. I had a feeling he wasn't going to let this go.

The door shut, changing the pressure inside the vehicle.

It was obviously bulletproof and more than likely able to withstand a chemical attack. All three of us started talking at the same time. I sat back and watched the Vampire and Marlow Goolsby jockey for position.

"Is it just me or is there some tension in the air? Maybe you guys need to go out on a date," I joked, accomplishing my goal and garnering angry stares from both men.

Marlow paused to let Cecil speak first, again winning the "see who's in charge" game. At least between those two.

"I lost a lot of money last night in this fire. My understanding is that you were here and had something to do with it. What I'm more curious about, however, is why all my containers were moved to Marlow Goolsby's storage building that same day," Cecil stated, looking over at Marlow and wearing an aggressive expression on his face.

The two men hated each other; it was apparent they were both in business for themselves.

"I would think all of this would be covered under insurance," I started, looking at the two men as they sat back in their seats. "So, I take it illegal Ethereal drugs aren't covered under any new insurance policies since the Balance."

The two men looked over, burning a hole through me with their eyes. I figured I had pretty much just hit a grand slam out of the park.

"Choose your words wisely, Max," Marlow cautioned sternly. "Cecil, maybe if you weren't shipping illegal narcotics, we wouldn't be having this conversation."

I decided to chime in. "You guys do know I'm here representing the Council, right? Like everything you do, say, think, breathe, whatever, may be used against you at some point in a manner that may not be in your best interest."

"Is that a threat from one Council representative to another while on official business?" Marlow asked. I glanced over, seeing Cecil shuffling. Vs did that kind of thing when they were nervous or about to lose it.

I knew what Marlow was doing; he was forcing me to decide. I would either stay in that vehicle during the conversation unofficially or asked to leave officially. Much like everything Marlow did, it was for his benefit. On a couple of occasions, he had even manipulated the team and me to do work for him—or clean up, as I liked to call it. I wasn't in the mood to get in the middle of their little spat.

"I tell you what. Whatever it is between you two gentlemen, that's none of my business. I'm here to talk to Cecil officially, and I prefer to keep the bullshit to a bare minimum." I reached over to the handle as Cecil barked loudly.

"Goolsby, is this one of your puppets? Max, I know who you are, and you have a rather nasty reputation of helping him out. I would recommend not doing so in this case," Cecil said, not only warning me but mainly directing his threat at Marlow Goolsby.

The sound of Goolsby taking a deep breath filled the empty void after the outburst. "So be it," was all he said. It was clear the conversation was over. I opened the door, stepping out of the vehicle as Cecil stepped around the other side. Marlow sat inside the vehicle, lingering for a few seconds as he calculated his next move.

Stepping out and looking at me, it was clear he had made his decision. Like the rest of us, he knew the Vs had excellent hearing. He delivered his message to both of us as Cecil walked toward the office building. "These are my docks, and this is my town. New business of this sort, operating without my knowledge, will not be tolerated. I'll be in touch," Marlow finished as he walked around the front driver's seat of the SUV.

The thing about Pixies is that they're highly creative and great with electronics. And Petro wasn't just creative; he was the king of being creative. He was also the king of not taking other people's shit. The SUV's engine purred to life as the stereo blared through the bulletproof siding and glass with "Hit Me Baby (One More Time)" by Britney Spears. The tint on the windows prevented me from seeing Goolsby's face, who I was sure was highly irritated. A few muffled pops and clanks put an end to the pop onslaught. He had shot his radio dead.

The vehicle finally pulled out, the sounds of crunching asphalt under the tires and clicking rocks overtaking the once Britney Spears–filled scene.

"Man, I still like that song," I admitted. As if on cue, Petro appeared over my left shoulder, landing lightly. His face was blood red, with streaks of tears coming from his eyes.

"I'm not even angry; I'm impressed. Hope he doesn't try to kill us," I said, joining Petro and letting out a full-on belly laugh that shook every inch of my body.

Cecil turned around, staring at the both of us and wearing an incredulous look on his face.

"We'll be right there," I said, winding down.

"Tell me to buzz off one more time," Petro added, also calming down.

"Any word from Kim?" I asked as we both restored ourselves to normalcy.

"She'll be here in about an hour. Apparently, they found another body in a similar condition. I talked to that Detective Neil guy. He smells like a combination of you and Phil after he's been smoking and you've been drinking all night. That guy is in rough shape. I think even before the Balance, he wouldn't have given a damn if I was floating around in front of his face," Petro said, running the sentence together rapidly like a fast typist beating a keyboard to death.

We walked over to the office, noticing the cameras were all turned toward us as we strutted into the building. While they were still far away and separated by tape and a line of uniformed officers, those cameras could probably see a split hair on the back of my head. I had learned to be smart around video, especially since the Balance. There was now a whole new fad on social media: catching Ethereals and Mages doing things and posting the videos. One of my favorite ones was of a highly intoxicated Water Mage peeing out in public, manipulating it, and causing a stir. I'll leave the rest up to the imagination.

The office was old and had extraordinarily little attention paid to it. The furniture was mid-80s, as were the cheap printed pictures on the wall. At some point, someone had tried to update the space by adding cheesy old black motivational posters behind the main desk. The No Smoking sign on the door was obviously ignored, as the smell of stale smoke from cheap cigarettes and overly cold air-conditioning permeated the room.

Cecil's demeanor had changed as he sat behind the desk. Vs oftentimes had the ability to switch off and on their emotions.

"You didn't have anything to do with that little sideshow. I can smell your nerves," Cecil said, steepling his fingers. His voice rolled around the small enclosed office.

Petro flew down to one of the cracked leatherette chairs as Cecil's eyes followed him.

"You have a problem with Pixies?" I asked, putting a little rumble and bass in my statement.

"I think we all just need to calm down, Max. I've never seen a Pixie so brave. I believe your name is Petro," Cecil purposefully addressed Petro in a show of respect that very few Ethereals showed his kind. He let out a nice chuckle to cut the tension in the room. I understood from spending plenty of time with Frank that Vs did have a sense of humor. In fact, it was often more disturbing than my own.

"This isn't a social visit. I'm sure you know why I'm here. We talked to Mr. Bellman's wife and the federal authorities. He had been spending a significant amount of time here. I don't think it's a coincidence that he was heading back here last night in, let's just say, a little bit of a rush," I said, not willing to sit on the dirty chairs, making Cecil have to look up at me.

"Have you ever heard the story of the rock and the stone, Mr. Abaddon?" the V asked out of the blue, using my name too politely.

"No, but I'm pretty sure that, just like every other V, you're going to tell it to me in some dramatic fashion no matter what," I said flatly.

Cecil let out an unnecessary breath of air, thoughtfully flattening his lips. Petro rolled his eyes, something I knew he was doing when his left wing twitched.

"There once was a rock on the side of a road. A young boy picked it up and threw it through a window, smashing the glass. Two weeks later, the boy went inside the abandoned building, and while not paying attention, slipped and fell on the broken glass, cutting himself badly when he landed, hitting his head against the same rock. The boy was scared badly and took this as an omen." Cecil paused, ensuring we were both completely captivated by the story. I looked down, checking my watch just to make a point.

"Years later, a young man was walking down the street. A car swerved in the middle of the road, avoiding an animal but driving into a pond. The driver hit their head, knocking themselves unconscious as the car started to sink into the pond. The young man looked around, panicking as no one else helped. He looked down and saw a stone at his feet. He picked it up and rushed to the sinking car, throwing it at the back windshield and smashing it. He jumped in through the window and pulled the young woman to safety.

"The young man stayed with the young woman for some time as the paramedics and a tow truck showed up and pulled her vehicle out of the water. A young police officer walked over and handed the young man that stone, saying that his actions had saved the young woman's life. The two were later married and kept the stone on the mantel of their home. Time passed, and one night, a thief came into their house, thinking they weren't home. He was surprised to find them there and panicked as they woke up. He grabbed the rock as the wife came downstairs, smashing it over the woman's head and killing her instantly while her husband was checking the rooms of their children." Cecil stopped and looked at us. We both looked back, waiting for the punch line.

"So, what's the point of the story, besides wasting our time?"

"And depressing us," Petro added.

Cecil stood up, throwing a rock at me. After a little shuffling, I caught it, looking down at my hand. The stone was heavy and angled, and a slight tingle of power came off it.

"Ahh, you feel it," Cecil said. He stood up and walked over to me, taking the rock back.

"The young boy was the young man. It was the same rock that ruined and made his life. It also ended his wife's," I said, getting an uncomfortable vibe from the stone the longer I held it.

"Yes."

Petro chimed in, wanting to know the ending. The man had a way of pulling you in. *Vampire . . . I know*, I thought, keeping focused. "The man? What happened?"

Cecil grinned, knowing he had accomplished his goal. He took off the hat he was wearing, exposing a long scar. He also unbuttoned the top of his shirt, showing us what looked like the start of several large scars. "I ate him. The thief, that is."

We sat there for a minute, taking that in. A part of me felt sorry for him, while the other knew exactly what Cecil was capable of doing.

"I get it. That happened to you. It's a great story, but what does it have to do with any of this?"

"You live by the sword, you die by the sword, Mr. Abaddon. Or for that matter, the stone. The story is what you make of it. Are you a stone or are you a rock, Mr. Abaddon? I think I know the answer, but I recommend staying on the shelf as you were meant to," Cecil finished, walking back behind the desk and pulling out his phone.

"I'm not here to play your psychosomatic games. Mr. Bellman had an enormous amount of Kracken in his system. As a matter of fact, I watched him explode, though the shotgun blast probably didn't help. My understanding is that you happen to know about that product. I—we figured if somebody was in the area with it, you might know something about it," I said, watching Cecil go through a range of emotions before landing on understanding.

"Ah, I see. You're here because of a coincidence. Straight and to the point, as foretold. For that, I can tell you that I'm not aware of anything out of the ordinary."

He was playing the "don't lie but don't tell anything else" game. For the most part, Cecil seemed genuine; he was a crook for sure, but maybe not a murderer.

"Can you tell me anything about the stuff?" I asked, seeing if he had any further interest in talking.

"I could, but I'm sure your friends can supply you with that information. It's time for me to go," Cecil finished with finality.

"Stick around town. It's not official, but as soon as the marshals show up, it will be," I said, seeing if that statement would give me some room for further conversation. Cecil nodded at both of us as he left.

We walked out, getting hit in the face by the humid air after being inside with the cheap air-conditioning.

"What do you think, boss?" Petro asked as Cecil, and his crew pulled out of the parking lot.

"I thought he was supposed to stay here. I don't think

Goolsby's visit was planned. Those two have it out for each other. I think we may need to figure that out. So, you think he's in on it?" I asked, seeing Kim's silver sedan pull up.

A car alarm, followed by Christina Aguilera, could be heard in the distance as Petro snickered.

"Let me guess, he turned on his blinker and set off his stereo and car alarm," I said, shaking my head. "He dealing in the stuff?" I asked again after the distraction.

"Him, oh yeah. I could smell the stuff on him. It smelled different, though. I can also smell that crap all over this place. I'm going to talk to Kim. I'll send a note to Jenny to get some folks down here as well . . ." Petro said, drawing out the word and following with, "Incoming."

The stereo from Cecil's car landed directly at our feet with a plasticky cracking echo. The smell of burnt plastic reached my nose. Claw marks were embedded around the edges of the once vibrant flat-screen radio. He had ripped it out and thrown it, ensuring it landed precisely in front of us from a block away.

CHAPTER 4

Getting Ahead

I stood there looking as Petro buzzed over to Kim. I checked my breath discreetly, realizing that there were a few cameras pointed in my direction. I reached into my pocket, pulling out my phone and dialing Phil.

"Bruther, done already?" he asked before I could speak.

"Not yet. Marlow was here, and Kim just pulled up. Do me a favor. If you see anything come over social media or the radio, let me know. There're cameras everywhere here. If there's a bunch of pictures floating around of Cecil, Marlow, and myself talking, it may become a headache later."

While Marlow Goolsby was an official member of the Council, he was only a member of the Junior Council. Since the Balance, the Supreme Council would only allow a regular to hold a post at the junior level. While beneath most positions Goolsby had held in his life, it was still higher than 99.9 percent of the rest of the general population.

We figured he was working on a way to move into other levels and ranks of the Council to further his position, but no one had truly nailed down exactly what his goals and intentions were. Tom did nothing more than refer to him as a criminal, and that was good enough for me.

I watched as Kim opened the door of her car, wearing

a smile. The sun was shining off her smooth dark hair as she held two cups of coffee. I turned to walk in her direction, seeing Neil moving a little faster than usual toward the silver sedan as Kim stepped out.

Petro had zipped over and was floating in front of her. He had a habit of doing that and unloading a whole thirty minutes of conversation in two.

Neil and I both converged on Kim at the same time. How the stoic detective arrived so quickly was a mystery.

"Morn—" Neil and I said at the same time, interrupting a duel of cheesy banter.

Neil looked down at the coffees.

Something was off in his posture toward Kim. Petro sensed it too and positioned himself over my shoulder, a slight breeze coming from his rapidly fluttering wings.

"Good morning," Kim said objectively to both of us. She handed me the extra cup of coffee as a scowl crossed Neil's placid face.

"Just the way you like it," Kim said, putting her focus back on Neil.

"Kim, it's been a while," Neil greeted, rubbing the back of his neck.

What in the one-legged Fiend Hound was I watching? I could feel Petro thinking the same thing by the change in the rhythm of his wings. He knew I liked her. He knew I liked her a lot.

"So," I interjected, only to be politely cut off by Kim.

"Max, can you give us a minute?" Kim said in a honey-covered voice that soured in my ears.

"OK," I said, slowly backing up and walking toward Cecil's now dead radio.

One thing being a quarter demon had done, and I was finally starting to realize it, was to sharpen some of my senses.

Over time since my rebirthday, the one sense that had sharpened like a spear was my hearing. Unfortunately for me, there was so much background noise that by the time Petro and I got back to the dead car radio, their conversation was garbled.

"What do you think they are talking about? Police stuff?" I asked, looking at Petro as he landed on my outstretched hand.

"No, I don't think so . . ." Petro trailed off as we both came to the same conclusion.

"Gods and graves, that guy—"

"Neil," Petro corrected.

"Neil is Kim's ex-husband." The words rolling off my tongue turned bitter.

My memory finally kicked into gear, and I remembered her talking about Detective Neil last year.

"You sure about her, boss? She screwed that guy all up. He's a walking shit show. Maybe a badass as well, but nonetheless," Petro said, making me do my obligatory fake motion of shooing a fly off. The little guy hated that.

"There's a God, Petro. That much I'm sure of. Unfortunately, that God does not want me to ever date," I joked, taking a sip of the coffee. It was perfect, just the way I liked it. Psychotically black, making me reset. "The guy's messed up but seems to be alright. It probably explains why he didn't blink an eye when we walked up. I bet he knew we work around Kim," I continued, sipping more of the coffee and making sure the two knew we were watching them talk.

"I bet that's why he's hanging around," Petro said, making an even better point.

"Man, being married has made you smarter buddy." Petro scrunched up his tiny forehead, trying to figure out if that was a compliment or a joke.

"Max," Kim called after a few more minutes of heated

conversation. Introductions were again made as she clarified things were over between the two.

"Ben will reach out with any updates we get," Kim said, smiling at me. She was making a point to both of us.

Before I could open my mouth to embarrass myself, my phone rang with Phil's ringtone. Garth Brooks's "Friends in Low Places" blared.

Petro whispered, "Awkward," barely loud enough to hear.

"It's alive!" Phil bellowed.

"What?" I responded, putting the phone on speaker.

"Damn thing's . . . !" The sound of screeching tires sharply rang from the small speaker. "Head!" Phil yelled as the sound of crunching metal made all of us grimace. The phone went silent as I looked at Kim.

"You can track his location on your computer, right?" I asked. She was already in motion.

We had trackers on our phones that we knew about this time around. I pulled out a gate stone from the Evergate. "If you can figure out where he is, I'll be able to get to him."

Last year I had—with some help, of course—figured out how to use another gate. The Seekergate. Simply put, if one knew the location they wanted to go to, and it wasn't warded, they could get there through the Seekergate. I could get to the Seekergate by way of the Evergate, both in the Postern. See where this is going?

I'd learned that the Postern was built not only as a weapon, but also as a deterrent. Tom had been entrusted with it, as I was now. He had managed to figure out a handful of the gates. I had worked out another two. Better yet, it had taken him over two hundred years; me, about one. During World War II, Tom had lost the ability to use one of the gates, unfortunately losing the key to the Mirrorgate, which would take one to the in-between, a place where souls stuck in purgatory or doing whatever stayed. That left another few gates to figure out.

"What's going on?" Neil asked, confused.

"Found him," Kim said as I looked at the map, forming a clear image in my mind of the location.

"You guys need some help?" Neil again interjected. Petro was buzzing over my shoulder, having pulled his sword out. He winked at me with a slight grin.

"Sure," I replied as I pushed my will into the Evergate stone. A shimmering dark gate formed in front of us as I grabbed Neil by the arm, pulling him through. Don't worry ... over the past year, I had become very proficient in gating and not tearing people in half taking them through.

Walking into the Postern, Neil dropped to the floor, lurching up what appeared and smelled like stale doughnuts and coffee. The guy was a mess.

"Never gated before, huh? Could have fooled me," I said, walking over to the bound safe on the table in the middle of the room. I was the only person able to open it. No questions asked. We had even decided to take Tom off the imprint of the binding.

"The hell, man?" Neil complained, working to stand up on his feet as I pulled out the Seekergate key and jammed it into the door.

"Sorry about that," I said, walking over and picking him up again before pulling him over to the other gate. His legs hadn't found purchase yet, so it was easy to bring him along once again for the ride.

Concentrating, I formed a vision of the location in my mind and stepped through, dragging my new best friend. Well, the person I just met who happened to be Kim's ex-husband. Petro was already tucked under my blazer as was the routine. Going through the Seekergate, we had to be touching or connected. If not, one could find themselves under the ocean.

The pull from the Seekergate was a little stronger, again bringing our new companion to his knees. The whole trip had taken less than a minute.

Looking around, a few things were immediately clear. First, Phil was glowing white while holding his knockoff Thor hammer, standing beside a burning unmarked sedan. Next, and probably the oddest thing I had witnessed or been part of since taking acid in college and getting into an argument with a taco for five hours, was what looked like a see-through ghost pirate wearing Mr. Bellman's head.

The head was in the same state as it was last time I'd seen it attached to a body. The eyes glowed with reddish-orange vapors; the body was different however. It was moving erratically, as if it didn't know where it was, or more precisely, why it was holding up a severed head.

The creature flailed around as a blast of flaming lightning cut through the air, branching off and hitting the car, creating a small explosion.

Being fully charged, Phil took it in stride, while Neil, Petro, and I went flying back several feet.

I quickly looked over at Neil, hoping I hadn't made a mistake bringing him into this fight. Luckily, the detective who had clearly enjoyed his fair share of liquor this morning was shaking his head, reaching for his pistol.

Petro flew out from his position, ending up twenty feet in the air. I reached under my blazer and pulled out the Judge.

I drew up the weapon and aimed dead center of the head, pausing for a few seconds to take in as much of the creature's details.

Beating us both to the punch, Phil leaped forward, slamming the hammer into Mr. Bellman's head and creating a large spark of flames that knocked him back several feet. The same stuff that had him before was driving the ship—well, what was left of him.

A small section of Mr. Bellman's skull also vacated the premises, generating even more confusion from the ghostlike body.

Several pops rang out as bullets went whizzing by to my right, not landing on their target, merely going through the blank space that was occupied by the apparition.

"What the hell is that?" Neil asked, still on his ass with his pistol held up.

"A reason for you to get your shit together," I replied, squeezing the trigger and letting the Judge do what it was made to do. For a moment, I was hoping that it wouldn't just fizzle out, but like before, either Mr. Bellman wasn't guilty of the crimes he was committing, or it was negated by whatever magic was controlling his body.

If Mr. Bellman was indeed innocent, then maybe the apparition wasn't. Phil was starting to get back up, realizing what I was doing.

As if luck had decided to actually show up today, the round slammed into the body, going from incandescent green to flaming red, slowly starting to burn at the edges. The creature fell to its knees, or whatever was holding it up.

It looked as if somebody was burning a cigar by taking a long drag from it. The ends of its fingers and legs started burning, creeping inward toward its center. Within another second, the light in Mr. Bellman's head winked out as it dropped to the ground in a crunching thud.

Petro dropped down to eye level, and we all four stood there and watched. After taking our attention off the now lifeless head, I quickly realized that it had revealed the apparition's actual head. Again, the word pirate flashed in my mind.

Who he was, or had been had left him dressed as if he were starring in an old Errol Flynn movie. He had a patch over one eye and what looked like a rag covering his hair. With the long earring hanging from his right ear and the open white button shirt, it was abundantly clear he wasn't from around here. The leather clasp holding his apparitional sword at the bottom started to evaporate. Small trails of light looking like embers floated up into the sky. He had been judged.

Neil again vomited after his nerves settled and the initial shock of gating twice started to kick in.

"He's not going to be doing much for a while," Petro commented as we both snickered.

"Who's this bloke?" Phil asked walking up, the glow of his body starting to dull as he pulled the energy back into his body.

"That there is Kim's ex," I said out loud.

Phil looked down at the man then shifted his gaze up to me, a smile reaching the corners of his eyes without showing on his face.

"I don't think he's going to be gating for a while, bruther," Phil concluded as the sound of sirens started to fill the air.

Phil had been driving on J. Turner Butler Boulevard, heading toward the FBI building, when the vehicle had shot off the road on the south side of the interstate, landing in an open field next to a retention pond. Flames were still bellowing from the smoking vehicle, and people were slowing down to watch the scene unfold. Cameras and flashes could be seen in the vehicles passing by.

"Great. Paperwork and the news," Petro said, saying what the both of us felt. While normal to us, regulars were still trying to comprehend the depths of the new world they had been introduced to.

"Maybe not. All those folks are seeing is a burning car and the four of us. I doubt they can even see you," I said to Petro as he landed on my shoulder.

Kim's sedan, as well as an ambulance and two other police cars, pulled into the grass. A fire truck was coming from the other direction, slowed by traffic.

As the good marshal jumped out of her sedan, her attention went immediately to Neil. He was still on his hands and knees, retching up what was left of the stale doughnuts and sour coffee in his stomach. A smile came across Kim's face as quickly as it disappeared, only noticed if, like me, you were staring at her intently.

Kim walked up close, whispering in my ear, "I think it's about time we finish that date." She walked over to Phil, ignoring the man on the ground as the uniformed police officers rushed to pick him up.

"Lass, you should have seen it. It was all ghost, severed head, and fire. The damn thing cut the roof of the car in half before I could get out. I'm never transporting a dead body part again," Phil complained as Kim just looked at him, grinning at his obvious enjoyment of justified violence.

"I'll make a note of that, sunshine," Kim replied and walked over to the head as Petro, Phil, and I shouted at the same time for her to stop.

Petro buzzed down to it first, a concentrated look on his face. He was smelling the odd spectacle; Pixies had a nose for things. After a few seconds, Petro buzzed over. "All clear. I don't think it's coming back this time. I can't even smell any of that drug on it."

Kim hissed, "Dammit, we needed a sample."

"Tell you what; we're close to the building, so get one of those guys to take it. I'm sure there's something useful left in it . . . on it?" I said, trying to justify my statement, still excited about the possibility of a date later. I looked over at Petro making a discouraging face.

"You're probably right," Kim said, pulling out her phone and dialing Ben.

"What now, bruther?" Phil asked, noticing he had burn marks all over his shirt and jeans.

"I say a drink is in order. Not much else is going to happen here, plus that car isn't going anywhere," I replied as a rumbling explosion came from the engine, causing the surrounding spectators to flinch.

Kim talked to Ben for a few minutes, hanging up and confirming he was on the way. Ben was Kim's cousin and fellow marshal. We didn't see much of Ben, but he always seemed to show up and clean whatever mess we had created.

"You boys going for a drink?" Kim asked, standing beside me and watching Neil slowly get to his feet.

"On my honor," Phil bellowed as Petro joined in.

"It would be my honor, my lady, to escort you to our favorite water hole and protect you from these two mongrels," Petro joked as I held out my phone, shaking it to remind him he better call Casey.

After Petro's call to his wife, we were in the clear for drinks. He had promised her the one thing she wanted more than anything: practice bringing children into the world, or actually, the act of doing so. On several occasions, I had informed Petro that wasn't the best leverage he could produce in an attempt to go out drinking with his buddies.

After gating back to the old Transition's Office, now dubbed Abaddon & Associates, we took a few minutes to get cleaned up. Kim had volunteered her car to take the head to the FBI building.

Walking into the front office after getting ready, I saw a letter sitting on the desk, as well as a message on the answering machine. "Work? I guess word gets out fast of how awesome we are," I said. Petro zoomed in, excited to see what had been dropped off.

"How did that get in here, boss?" Petro asked as Phil

walked out of the bathroom drying his hair with a towel. While he didn't live in the office, he made himself at home doing things like cooking in my kitchen and using my towels to shower. To be fair, I had been working on getting him to move in and help split the rent which, oddly, hadn't been due since I moved in. I did, of course, have the best landlady ever.

Trish was the owner and bartender of the Fallen Angel and landlady of my attached office slash apartment. She was smart, sexy, and more than likely, the most intelligent person in the room at any given time. Trish was ageless. I don't think anyone knew how old she truly was. Tom had told me not to even try to figure that one out.

The bar catered to the magical communities, Ethereals and Mages alike. At times, regulars wandered in only to be thrown off by the wards. Before the Balance, Trish had done an excellent job of making sure they gated to the right location, having them think it was just an eclectic bar.

I opened the envelope while pushing play on the answering machine. Having a business once again had forced me to get some type of landline.

A professional male voice, obviously calling on someone else's behalf, filled the room. "Mr. Abaddon," the voice started, using the last name reserved for the magical community. "On your desk is a deposit for a new castor. My client understands that you sell custom pieces and would like to keep the purchase discreet. Please spare no expense, as you will see by the enclosed cash. Preferences are listed; it will be a lady's watch. Please contact me at the number listed on the envelope."

We all looked at each other. "Bruther, that's two for one this week. Your first big case and sale. Jenny's going to be ecstatic," Phil told us, walking back upstairs to finish getting ready. I could hear Kim swearing at him about closing the door.

"What do you think, Petro? A mysterious envelope full of money, a crazy drug case. It seems like things are picking up,"

I said in a manner reflecting my thoughts that things were, in fact, picking up. I just wasn't sure yet if it was in a good way.

"Boss, I think you need to figure out who's buying that thing. The smart lady—"

"Jenny," I corrected.

"Jenny will be excited. She told the girls that we could help if we ever sold one. This one looks like a big score right off the bat." Petro hovered over to the cash and started counting it in his little hands.

"That's the thing. Most people aren't discreet about purchasing a castor. Do me a favor and let her know before we head out. I'll get this money over to her tomorrow. That is, after my cut," I said, reaching over as Petro sorted out a few bills and nodded his head approvingly as I pulled them out of the massive stack and put them in my pocket.

"That's about five hundred bucks. I'll let her know," Petro replied, closing the envelope back up.

"Thanks. We need to figure out some type of finders fee. With that stack of cash, I doubt my cut is going to make a dent in it."

Petro sent a text to Jenny only to have her call to go over the details. She was, as predicted, excited. After five minutes of getting her to calm down and the group staring at me, we headed out for the long ten-foot walk to the entrance of FA's.

"Look what the gate dragged in," Trish greeted, the smile on her face lighting up the room. "I haven't seen you two together in quite some time. To what do I owe the pleasure?"

The smell of buttered, almost burnt steak and old copper filled the air, welcoming us to sit down. Petro had the story condensed down to thirty seconds in an unbelievably quick puking of words.

"Then it was like *boom,* and I was like swooping down—" Petro was going on before Kim cut him off.

"How about a round of drinks. I'm paying tonight, gents," Kim announced as Trish shook her head.

"Not a chance, guys. They're on me tonight. That is, unless Max decides to play chess with some random stranger again at the bar," Trish said, taking a jab at my little incident a few months prior.

We all settled into the first pulls of our drinks, letting out a collective, "Ahhh . . ."

"So what now?" Phil asked, being the only one to finish his entire beer in one pull.

"That is the question. I don't know about you guys, but that looked like an apparition," I said, taking another pull of my Vamp Amber.

"What?" Kim asked.

"Ghost, lass, a ghost," Phil clarified, having another beer set before him without even asking.

"About that, I think Tom's coming back to town this week. We need to run this by him; I don't know any other necromancers in the phone book," I said, noticing Kim had scooted slightly closer to me. I could feel her breath as she talked.

"An apparition—" Kim said, being cut off by Phil as he chugged his other beer.

"Ghost, lass."

"—ghost sprung out of Mr. Bellman's head and tried to take over? Oh, and the ghost was a pirate?" Kim said finishing her thought.

"Yup, that sounds about right," I said, finishing my first beer and getting another. After that, we all took another pull of our drinks in a coordinated effort. Trish stood there looking intrigued before finally chiming in.

"Did the spirit act confused, as if he didn't know why he was there?" Trish asked as we all looked up at her.

"Sounds right," I answered.

"Dammit, have they found any other bodies?" Trish questioned, pulling a glass of Magnus out from underneath the bar top and taking a drink.

Kim spoke up first. "They did this morning; not the same but close. This time they only found an arm and a leg, plus, well, they just found bits," Kim said, shaking her head. "While we were on our way over, I got the message that there were no traces of Etherium or Kracken in the body."

"You know, that might mean whatever was trying to take over the body got what it needed. Did the head, after all this happened, show any signs of the drugs or anything else?" Trish inquired, asking more questions than I had heard her make in the past.

"Not sure yet," Kim replied.

"What are you getting at?" I asked respectfully, knowing there was more to Trish than met the eye.

"Sounds to me like someone loaded up some drugs that amp a regular body enough to use magic and, with that, attempted to bring over a few souls from the Everwhere. You know that friendly place you paid a visit to over the summer?" Trish said as the wheels in my head started spinning. Being that Phil had a few hundred years on me, I was behind the curve.

"Someone's trying to raise the dead," Petro said, followed by a burp. It didn't take much to get him feeling good. After making that statement, he zipped up, heading over to the jukebox and playing "Riders in the Sky" by Planes Drifter, a cover of an old tune by Sons of the Pioneers.

"How the hell does he know these songs?" I asked as Kim leaned into me with her shoulder, laughing.

I sat there, trying to figure out any possible connections and drawing a blank. Necromancy was the least practiced—not to mention fairly illegal—type of magic. It was highly controlled and sanctioned not only due to its somewhat question-able practices, but because there was also a lack of Mages and Ethereals who could even do it.

Being a necromancer was much like existing as an Earth, Fire, Wind, or Water Mage. It was the one thing that Gramps, whom I now called Tom since finding out he was alive, was.

According to Ed and Jenny, there were less than five known necromancers on Earth, and of those five, four of them worked for the Council, one of them being Tom.

"Possessed drugs?" I threw out to the group.

"No, more like someone is practicing necromancy," Trish said, confirming my thoughts.

I could almost feel Kim's breath as she leaned over to talk to the others; the light smell of honeysuckle coming off her kept drawing my attention to her. "We actually had a few OTN cases like this in Chicago a few years back. I'm getting them sent over on the box later."

The box was the all-seeing, all-knowing computer that tied the civilian's and Council's systems together and sat at the Atheneum in what was called the crucible room. It sounded fancy, but it was nothing more than a command center with monitors and computers, the latest and greatest technology Mags-Tech had to offer.

"Let me know when you send them over; I'm getting with Tom as soon as he's back. I'm sure he's heard what's going on," I said, taking the final pulls of my beer.

Drinking wasn't one of my figure-people-out tests, like the cereal or radio assessment, but I had found that watching a person drink could tell you a fair amount about them. What someone's drinking, how they drink it, not to mention where they are drinking, told you a lot. For me, by the time you got to the last pull of a beer, it was usually too warm to be enjoyable. Just like with cereal, when you got to the bottom, it was not how it was meant to be consumed anymore. Besides, if somebody finished every last drop, they weren't leaving an offering to the beer gods.

I unknowingly took the last pull, finishing my bottle.

Phil and Petro erupted. "He did it!" Phil bellowed as the group caught on, having heard me rant about the last pull of beer on multiple occasions. This was followed by money being exchanged from bets placed on prior occasions. Being a former intelligence analyst in the army always had me analyzing things this way. It was a habit I was sure everyone who knew me wished I'd drop.

"Ha, ha, joke's on me. Look, I think this is just ramping up, and if Cecil and Goolsby get into a turf war, things are going to get even worse," I said as Trish cocked her head sideways.

"Cecil? As in the V?" Trish asked, the poison coming out as the name crossed her lips.

"You know him?" Petro asked back, starting to slur his words.

"Yes, he isn't allowed in here. Ever. As in permanently banned," Trish said, walking over and picking up her cell-phone. She punched the keys feverishly, looking back up.

"What did the guy do?" I asked, already figuring the answer.

"He used to come in here and push that crap to my guests. If he is involved, no good will come of it," Trish said as she noticeably didn't distribute another round of drinks.

After a few more minutes of talking about things, the group decided it was time to leave. Walking to the exit, Kim stopped me as Petro and Phil went through the door.

"Hey, I meant it about us going out. Let's try for this Friday if nothing goes crazy," Kim said, looking me in the eyes. That gave me two days to get some work done.

"Friday it is. Tell you what. I have an idea. I'll pick you up around seven?" I offered as we looked at each other. The pause was longer than usual, and started to feel like we were pulling closer to each other.

"Hey," Phil bellowed, stepping back in and stopping the moment from being whatever it was about to be. "Let's go."

"I'll call you tomorrow and let you know what I find out. Can you gate me to the Atheneum?" Kim asked as we joined the others.

Phil interjected, "I'm heading there; you can come with me."

I looked back to wave at Trish, who had obviously been watching Kim and me. A smile spread across her face, once again lighting the room up. It almost looked as if she were lightly blushing.

CHAPTER 5

Anyone Home?

T he next morning, I awoke to multiple text messages and voice mails. A text from Kim, two emails from Ed, a voice mail from Tom, and four more messages from Jenny wanting the envelope of money plus the instructions for the castor we had been commissioned to make. Did I also mention it was 11:00 a.m.?

I could hear Petro's light knock on the door. "Hey, boss, get up. Kim's here."

"Hold on. Just give me a minute. Tell her to get a cup of coffee; I'll be right down," I said, letting out a stale breath. The previous day had drained every ounce of energy I had, leaving me passed out till well after wake-up time.

My phone, as if knowing I was awake and needing to prove a point, started buzzing. Ignoring it, I got cleaned up and dressed, throwing on some jeans and a T-shirt. I had grown my hair out to below my ears, which forced me to do some type of grooming. After a quick look in the mirror, a light spray of cologne, and a breath check, I walked downstairs to see Phil and Kim standing there.

"I see you got my message," Kim said, referring to my clothes. "I want this to be unofficial. The more off the clock you look, the better."

"Sure, that's what I was thinking," I said, doing my best to cover up my oversleeping. Phil squinted his left eye, seeing right through my attempted coverup.

Petro flew out from the back room with Casey. She was dressed in a yellow top and leather pants with two small swords hanging off either hip.

"Casey, good morning," I greeted, seeing Petro's nervous glare.

"Morning, hope you enjoyed your late slumber. I'm going with Petro today. He made me a promise, and I need to make sure he comes back with all his parts intact," Casey said in a cool voice.

Pixies were by far the most interesting species to come from the Plane. Most had been here since the Great War, with Petro being not only a little bit of a celebrity but an exception.

Many had come to Earth in whatever way they could due to their status on the Plane, where they were treated as servants, mistreated, and from all accounts, ignored as nothing more than pests, which was a grossly inaccurate way to describe Pixies. They were smart, brave, and for the most part, the same as everyone else, minus the whole thing where you had to convince them to keep their clothes on around each other.

Their most intriguing distinction, however, was their uncanny ability to work and detect magic. Female Pixies also had an extraordinary IQ level, which was why so many of them worked with Mages in their labs. The males, on the other hand . . . I trailed off, looking over at Petro brushing his mustache and adjusting his crotch. Let's just say they were brave, not scared of any fight—unless that fight was with a female Pixie.

"That might not be a bad idea," Kim said, smiling at her. "We could use some brains today."

Phil, Petro, and I looked at each other, rolling our eyes

simultaneously.

"Sounds like you haven't checked my messages," Kim continued, picking up a cup of coffee with Fae honey and handing it to me.

I let out a sigh, taking a seat behind the desk.

"What's the score?" I asked, taking a light sip from the perfectly brewed treat. While upscale coffee shops did sell the stuff now, it was still too expensive to buy on a day-to-day basis, even to the point of robberies. This one undoubtedly came from Trish. Kim must have stopped by to see her about something.

"Ben has another body secured as we speak. Frank is with him. Nobody knows about this, and it's off the books as of right now," Kim said quickly, getting the point across that we needed to get moving.

"You think that's a good idea?" Phil asked, making a good point.

"That will be perfectly clear soon," Kim replied, taking a seat in one of the armchairs in the lobby. "Get yourself together, and at least check my message."

"Yes, ma'am." I saluted her and finished the coffee, shaking off any sleep left in my system. Being discreet, I grabbed my blazer, sword, and short staff. The sheath for the sword was enchanted. The sword went in, and the blade disappeared. The sword came out, the blade reappeared. It gave me the ability to carry the thing pretty much anywhere. I had yet to figure out where the metal went, and had decided on not even trying. Magic . . .

To stay off the radar, we all piled into the Black Beast. Even though it was in the ownership of a new Mage, it was still a black Dodge pickup truck, fitting right in.

"Where are we going?" I asked, pulling out onto the main drag heading toward A1A.

"Sawgrass clubhouse," Kim replied, sending out a text at

a furious pace.

"We have a tee time?" I joked, getting a slight smirk from her.

As if ordained by some cosmic comedy show, my phone rang, Aslynn's name flashing across the LCD screen on my dash. As luck would have it, I hadn't talked to her since last year when Kim had made it clear she didn't like her.

I let out a breath, sending the call to voice mail. The silence lasted a good two minutes before Phil decided it was time to fart. In all fairness, I appreciated the comic relief and believed he did it on my behalf. Turning the radio up, Planes Drifter belted over the stereo, keeping the rest of the ride's conversation to a minimum.

The parking lot for Sawgrass was empty. I turned the radio off, as the tires crunched on gravel.

"You weren't kidding; this must be off the books, at least for now," I said, getting an eerie feeling. Places like this were usually somewhat busy. Today, it was utterly devoid of anyone. I started to wonder why Frank was there and not another CSA agent or marshal.

"We don't want anyone that may be on the take seeing this," Kim said, opening the door and jumping out of the truck. Her feet landed with the muffled thump of combat boots.

"I better be getting paid. I'm guessing I'm on the clock?" I asked, half being a smartass, half genuinely wondering.

"You're on the clock. That means you must clock out to talk to Aslynn," Kim drawled playfully. At least I hoped so.

Phil had brought his smaller wannabe Thor hammer and a 357 Magnum. It looked new. The shotgun, as Kim had pointed out, would draw too much attention. I had to remind her to look around at the group. She'd agreed, however, thought the fully automatic 12-gauge street sweeper Phil usually carried needed to stay put, especially considering how expensive things were at the golf course.

"Dammit, I almost forgot," I said, clicking the message button on my phone. I had forgotten to listen to Tom's message.

"Max, I'm at the old house; head this way when you can. A lot to catch up on. Ed filled me in on yesterday's events. I think he'll be here this afternoon as well. And for the love of the gods, call your mother!"

Gramps was back at the Atheneum, giving me a little extra motivation. I had started calling him Tom to avoid confusion in public. Any chance I had to spend time with him was a top priority. Training and working on the other gates in the Postern was what had prevented me from spending time with Kim. I had learned more about magic from Gramps in two months than in two years of combined training and getting into sticky situations.

"What is it, boss?" Petro asked as Casey flew overhead.

"Tom's back," I said, looking at the others. "We all may need to take some time later to go over everything with him. If I were a betting man, I'd put a hundred on necromancy."

Kim motioned for us to follow her up the path, leading us to a couple of waiting golf carts. Angel was there leaning against one.

Angel was a V. She was alluring, and the most amazing woman not only I, but pretty sure anyone else had ever laid eyes on. Angel had a slight limp as of last year, and I had my suspicions she was, in fact, agent Two. I didn't have the nerve to ask her, though.

"Hello," she said in her clear, concise, yet sultry voice.

"Hey, lass, you driving?" Phil was the first to respond. The two liked each other and had worked together before I came into the picture.

She grinned. "I wouldn't let you drive me if I needed to get water and was stuck in the middle of the desert," she replied as Phil jumped into the passenger seat.

Kim and I jumped into the other cart as Petro and Casey stretched their wings beside them.

"Yes," Kim said without me saying anything.

"Yes what?" I asked as we lurched over a speed bump.

"Yes to our date. Remember, you owe me dinner and a drink tonight," Kim replied smiling.

"Hopefully we can get this wrapped up before seven. Guess where I'm thinking?" I said, overlooking that Kim was good at getting things out of people. I was hoping the old "figure out where she wants to go" trick would work.

"Since I know your plans include FA's, I was thinking . . ." Kim again drawled out, tapping her finger on her bottom lip. "Seafood at OC White's, plus live music? It will keep us close just in case, not like that really matters to you. It's normal night, if memory serves."

She was right. We all used to do normal nights before the Balance, where we would go out to a regular place. The intent was simple: to hang out for the afternoon, grounding us in the real world. I smiled, nodding my head, not wanting to overthink it. She was in a good mood and was obviously pushing to spend some time with me.

The first head on a spike showed itself as we pulled up to the clubhouse, rounding the entrance walkway. The scene was medieval. Whoever had done this was making a statement.

"Yup," was all Kim said, knowing what I was thinking. On the spike was the head of one of the Vs that had been with Cecil yesterday. Petro zipped down, shaking his head while holding his nose. Casey clearly had a stronger stomach as she stopped by the head, sniffing the air.

"How many are there?" I asked as Kim pursed her lips.

"Ten in total. That includes the head in the middle of the entrance hall. It looks very much like Mr. Bellman's, but with a hole in the middle of it," Kim said in a low voice.

The carts came to a stop as Angel stared at the severed V head, not giving away any emotions. Vampires were touchy about their kind after all the strife they had endured over the years. Even if they didn't like each other. It was an odd family, all sharing a unique struggle. At least, it appeared as a struggle to some.

"I take it he didn't pay his membership dues," Phil said, immediately jamming a cigarette in his mouth and striking a match off his leather castor.

"He was one of the lucky ones," Angel spoke, avoiding eye contact with the grisly scene.

"Petro, why don't you keep an eye on things out here while the rest of us go inside," I suggested, knowing his pride would be hurt if the gore inside was any worse than what we had just witnessed. As brave as he was, Petro couldn't stomach blood, not even if he had spilled it himself, which he was extraordinarily good at doing when needed.

"Sure thing, boss. I smell something familiar out here anyway," Petro said with a puzzled yet familiar look on his face, pulling out his sword.

"Casey, you could go in?" I asked as she came down, motioning for me to lay out my palm for her to land.

"Sure thing," Casey agreed in her high yet distinguished voice. "As long as my husband's outside, we'll be safe on the inside."

Petro's face lit up with pride. I had a feeling I was somehow contributing to their mushy lovefest in the middle of a massacre.

Frank greeted us at the door, his expression as neutral as Angel's. It was clear that most of the bodies inside would be that of Vampires.

"Frank," I greeted, nodding my head. "Is the area secured?"

"It is for now. As soon as word of this gets out, things are going to get rather messy. I called in a few favors to keep this place shut down and have reached out to Davros for guidance," Frank said, nodding his head to Phil.

Phil threw him a smoke even though Vs didn't really breathe. It was more of a habit; at least that's what they liked to tell people.

"We are good with whatever Davros wants to do here, but it needs to happen soon. Cecil will find out about this sooner rather than later, and when he does, I have a feeling he will be paying Mr. Gools—" I cut Kim off.

"Goolsby, just Goolsby. He's no mister anything," I interrupted, frustrated.

"Goolsby will be getting paid a visit soon. I would rather them not rip the city apart," Kim continued, putting her hand out in an ushering motion for us to go fully through the opening.

It's hard to explain the way a dead Vampire smells. It's not like a normal body. There's a sweet tang that lingers, not overly putrid but also not completely unpleasant, almost like a musky aftershave that you have to think twice about wearing.

The clubhouse itself was grand and opulent, showing its acceptance of the elite population of Northeast Florida. Besides the blood and gore now in place, it was the kind of building most ordinary people would never get the chance to visit.

"Gods and graves," I said, taking in the gruesome scene. The entrance was covered in dark purple—almost black—Vampire blood, as well as various organs that I had no clue what they truly were. Two more severed heads lay on either side of the walkway, both looking inward, their eyes gone from their skulls. What appeared to be entrails were strewn on the stairwell going around to the upper level.

Hanging from the chandelier directly above the center staircase swung four headless bodies. The corpses lightly swayed in the air as black, mucus-like blood dripped from their shoeless feet. Whoever had done this was no stranger to violence. I looked over to see Phil wide-eyed, not caring that he was smoking inside the clubhouse. He had even pulled out his flask, taking a pull of it to steady his nerves before blindly handing it to me.

Phil, like the rest of the team, knew what the repercussions of this would be. There would be violence between the two factions. Goolsby had played his card. In fact, he had played his card a little too well, more than likely drawing the attention of other Vampires outside of Cecil's control.

Vampire blood also had another unappealing trait besides its smell: it attracted bugs at an alarming rate. Anything within the building that crept or crawled was already flocking to the bodies.

Angel walked back outside as Frank spoke up, "Kim, you think we can get this cleaned up at least?"

"I can't get anyone here for another two hours," she replied, handing out face masks she had strategically placed in her back pocket and forgotten to give out first.

"That's going to be too late, if it's not already. I have a feeling that someone left breadcrumbs leading here. Frank, can you and Angel keep this place empty for at least thirty minutes?" I asked, knowing of only one person—well, demon —that could clean this up quickly enough.

Belm, your friendly neighborhood demon, was a friend of my prior mentor's son and happened to be a relative. I had come to find out that also meant that I could reach out if needed via a simple spell. A simple, illegal spell.

I walked over to the others. "I'm going to need a minute," I said, the others getting the message and leaving out the front door. What can I say? A lot had happened over the past year.

Pulling out a small knife, I walked over to the counter, pricking my finger before letting six drops of blood hit the cool marble. Placing my hand over the blood and pushing my will out, the drops started to levitate.

I murmured under my breath the incantation Tom and Belm had shown me. Unlike eerie, spooky apparitional voices one sees in movies or reads in books, this spell was very much like placing a phone call through blood magic. Something that we had even tried to use to locate Lilith to no avail. While I could talk to Belm in my headspace, getting him to show up was a little bit trickier.

While I had to use gates and the Postern, a true demon didn't. Belm, in reality, was different than your standard run-of-the-mill demon. He was more than that, something I and the others had yet to figure out. He didn't show up on any of the radars set up to track demons.

Within seconds, the smell of ozone filled the air as Belm stepped out from behind the counter. I opened my eyes to see him standing there in his regular biker/greaser black leather pants and jacket, sporting a blazing white T-shirt under it. His hair was, as always, slicked back to perfection with what looked like a gallon of oil.

The smell of freshly cracked pepper overtook the scent of ozone.

"You rang," Belm rasped out, doing his coughing laugh. He paused, looking around the room. "Been busy? Looks like the apple didn't fall far from the tree," he quipped, using the one thing as bad as Vogon poetry: demon humor.

"Not me this time. Can you help get this mess cleaned up?" I asked, giving Belm a straight-faced glance letting him know this was important.

He pursed his lips, sniffing the air and holding his hands out while he scanned the room. "Oh, you have a mess on your hands." Taking a deep, raspy breath, Belm continued after a reflective pause, "We have a mess on our hands."

"These are Cecil's men. Goolsby and Cecil got into it yesterday. Not sure what's what, but we don't need this splashed on the news or leaking out just yet," I said, filling him in on the current state of affairs.

"Cecil, the dope man? If he's in town, there will be trouble. I may have to give Jamison a call. This is the kind of shit he loves to be in the middle of. I'll get this cleaned up; you have any bags?" Belm said in a moderately clear manor. He knew this was serious.

I looked over at Belm, realizing I hadn't figured out how he was going to clean it up for us. My gut had just told me to reach out to him.

"I'll be right back," I said, walking outside.

"So?" Phil asked as Angel walked up, handing me the head of the V in a bag. She followed by giving me a stack of body bags. I had a feeling she knew what I was up to.

"Getting a little help," I replied, not giving away my visitor, who I was sure everyone except Kim and Phil knew was inside. As I figured they would, the two stared at me.

"OK. Belm's going to help clean up, then we can take a better look around," I said, walking back inside, the smell of Phil lighting a smoke wafting behind me.

Much to my and everyone's amazement, all the blood was now gone. The bodies once hanging off the chandelier were now on the floor lined up neatly beside each other, their respective heads laid neatly in a pile. The only untouched item was the severed head. It was obviously missing a body with a gnarly hole in the middle. I had only been outside for a handful of seconds. "What about the one in the middle?" I blurted out, referring to the out-of-place head.

Belm, shaking his head, just smiled, waving at everyone before disappearing in a cheesy puff of smoke he did on purpose.

"I'll call Ben," Kim said in a confused tone.

"Frank, any chance you have people keeping an eye on things at Goolsby's?" I asked, taking a deep breath.

"Nothing to report. Cecil, on the other hand, already has people out looking for these guys. Vs just kind of know when things like this happen," Frank said with a blank expression on his face.

"Great. Casey," I called out, wanting an expert's opinion. My voice echoed in the empty room. "That head with the hole in it. Any chance it may come back to life?"

Casey buzzed down, spending several seconds studying the mangled head. "I don't think so. It doesn't smell like the other one. There's nothing here at all. No magic, no Kracken, nothing. It's like something drained it of everything. I can usually smell things even on regulars. Nothing here," she said with confidence.

"Let's get what we can while we're here from the e-meter. Even if it doesn't give us a reading, it will let us communicate that to Jenny. Phil!" I called as he turned around, shaking his head.

"Bruther, I'm not messing with that thing after last time," he said, blowing out a lungful of air.

"There's a bottle of Ambrosia in it for you, little fella," I said, smacking the plastic bag in my hand and walking over to the head. After my time in the army and the past few years, gore didn't have the same effect on me as it once did. Not to mention that the head didn't have a face to relate to.

Phil walked over after a few more huffs, putting on the gloves Kim gave him and helping me get the head in the bag.

"I'm going to call ahead so Jenny is ready. I don't want any more surprises. Casey, let Petro know it's time to go. He's done a great job protecting us in here," I said as she poked out her chest, proud of the compliment for her husband.

Petro buzzed in, now able to handle being inside with the absence of the gore that Belm had taken care of.

"Hey, boss, this place stinks!" Petro chirped as Casey hovered behind him.

"We know. Anything to report outside?" I asked, handing the Evergate stone to Phil so he could open a gate.

"Nothing besides the severed head on a pike," Petro said, smirking. "I heard sirens heading this way."

"How far out?" Kim asked, looking at her watch.

"Angel was walking out to slow them down at the entrance. Maybe ten minutes or so," Petro informed us, flying over to Phil standing by the gate. Phil had left the bag for me to pick up. I shook my head.

"I'll call when we get some news. Everyone's at the Atheneum," I said, looking at the group walking over to the gate.

Kim and Frank looked at each other, knowing things were about to get busy.

"How long was it till the head of Mr. Bellman re-awakened?" Tom asked as he pushed a silver rod into the stump of the neck of our latest victim. Petro had left to go look up some information on the box as Phil, Tom, Ed, Jenny, and I stood around the examination table in Jenny's lab under the Atheneum.

Jenny had opted for red hair this year. I looked at her as she rolled her eyes. Life Mages had a bad habit of taking on the characteristics of the people they worked on. For Jenny, it was her hair. If she used her magic on someone with red hair, she could then take on that trait. It was her way of getting a cheap color job.

"Ahh, a day at most. The damn thing just started humming, and next thing I know, I have a floating head in the car growing arms and legs. It was making all kinds of sounds. Mad as hell and wanting out of the back seat," Phil said, looking at the disembodied head with disdain.

Ed was in a wheelchair most of the time, and we had worked out a system to gate him into the labs underground to avoid the stairs. I had taken two of the gate stones from the Evergate, setting them up for his use. While it had him always going to and from the Postern, he was able to maneuver around the facility with relative ease. Last year, after the fight at Castle Rock, Ed had been injured to the point of forcing him into a wheelchair. All the king's horses and all the king's magic couldn't put Ed back together again, so to speak.

Jenny was set to have him leave for Japan in a month to have reconstructive surgery on his spine. From what the doctors had told her, Ed would be able to walk again, just not at a sprint. That was the thing about magic. Being that severely injured by magic as many times as he had been last year prevented him from being cured by magic. Sure, magic could be used to speed up the healing process, but unless you were a Life Mage or had some other way to do it, these types of wounds required physical, old-school medical intervention.

"Right, so by definition, this head would be close to that timeline?" Ed asked, leaning back in his chair.

"No, as Jenny stated, Mr. Bellman still had some level of the drug and/or reading of Etherium. This head is what I would call deadweight," Tom said, pulling out the rod.

"So the other head was still alive?" I asked as Tom patted me on the shoulder, smiling.

"Kracken does have that effect. Not the alive you may think, though. More like keeping a small part of the person's essence in place." Tom let out a breath.

"Soul, bruther. He means soul," Phil interjected.

"If that's what you want to call it," Tom replied, not appreciating Phil's simplistic opinion. Necromancy was, after all, Tom's specialty. "The problem is, Phil," Tom started back, wanting to get a lesson out at the same time, "the body you and Max dealt with had channeled something from the Everwhere. The in-between—"

"That's the place I went to a few months back, with the ghosts and stuff, right?" I asked, already knowing the answer.

"Yes. Whatever or whoever that was, took control of Mr. Bellman's body in an attempt to literally come back from the dead," Tom said as Jenny handed him a small copper bowl.

"It's the same," Jenny said, putting her hand on Ed's shoulder.

"What's that?" I asked, leaning over to see the contents.

"Jenny here took samples of the blood from both victims and did an old-school spell to figure out, not what's in their systems but what's not," Tom said, setting the bowl on the table.

"They are identical. The Kracken in their system stripped the blood of pretty much everything. I can state with 99 percent accuracy that our other victim also experienced the same fate," Jenny responded, dumbing it down for the rest of the group.

Same as last year, finding out what exactly was missing had proven to be more helpful than looking for information.

"Right, so do we think this other victim's parasite got what it wanted?" Ed finally spoke up.

"Without the body, I'm not sure. In the other case, we found the rest of it splattered all over the docks. Here, as Casey stated, the head was the only thing at the clubhouse from the host," Tom explained, pausing as he spoke. He was thinking as he talked to the group, a distant look growing in his eyes.

I sat there thinking about my trip to Everwhere. Something was nagging me but not taking hold of my thoughts, as if something was blocking a memory.

"Someone is spiking drugs with souls to do . . . what?" I

drawled out.

"Bring them back to life. Something that would require a lot of effort to do," Tom chimed in before the others.

"Effort?" Jenny asked.

"Someone went to the Everwhere and captured those souls. Something, I'm sure Max can verify, that is not an easy task," Tom replied, looking over at me.

"I'm not exactly an expert on the Everwhere. I just lost a bet. Look, when I was there, they were almost like real people. That thing we fought was raging; something that didn't seem to want to be here," I said, contemplating if I had messed something up once again.

"Didn't you run into some crazy fella?" Phil chimed in, my memory again foggy on it.

"Yeah, I did, but can't seem to remember it clearly," I slowly responded.

"I'll get a memory potion whipped up. Macey, Lacey!" Jenny exclaimed, giving the two Pixies instructions on what she needed.

"Right. Tom, do you think Max's trip to the Everwhere has anything to do with this?" Ed asked, rocking in his wheelchair, his hands pushing and pulling the wheels lightly. He was thinking.

"No, not at this point. I don't think it would matter either way. I need to talk with someone. For now, we need to keep the Council in the loop on this. What about Goolsby and Cecil?" Tom asked as he walked toward the door, stopping to put the silver rod in a red container marked with a hazard symbol.

After the Balance, even OSHA had shown up at the Atheneum. Various new protocols and safety requirements had been put in place. To keep things from getting out of control, Jenny had made sure to wipe most of the inspector's memory of his inspection. While frowned upon, it was something that was necessary in some cases.

Any location that had regular employees or people had to work with the local authorities fell under these rules now. This was still a gray area, and made for hours of interesting commentary by local regular officials.

"I'm going to have Max and Phil check in on them both. I've already talked with Kim; she has her ear to the ground," Ed said, looking down at his phone as it vibrated. A frown took hold of his face. "Party's over. They've found another body. The Council is requesting we come in and report. Max, in case you are still wondering, you are on that Council by proxy."

"No field trip?" Phil put an unlit smoke in his mouth.

"That will have to wait. Hopefully we can get in and out this evening, and you can hit the road," Ed said, looking around the room.

"I am getting paid for this, right? On contract?" I asked, still trying to figure out why I was taking orders from Ed.

"I believe this is official Council business, and as noted, it's your duty to help in such matters. Plus, I'm sure you enjoy being on the inside looking out versus—well, you remember," Ed said grinning, knowing I was going to help anyway. "I'm sure you can turn in an expense report."

CHAPTER 6

The Not So Secret Secret

"**B**y that, you mean lie?" I stated out loud to the closed chamber meeting, my voice echoing off the gray stone walls. The team had gated to the Council halls, only to be shuffled into a small chamber to discuss Jacksonville's current situation. Phil had stayed behind to keep an eye on things while Jenny, Ed, and I had to go sell our souls.

Carvel, Ana, and believe it or not, Dick Holder (Inspector Richard Holder for those not worthy) sat across from our team. The other body had turned up in London at a shipping dock. The Dunn now had a box as well that cross-referenced the cases, immediately linking them.

The Senior Council Intelligence Committee, now lead by Carvel, had intercepted the notification and deemed it classified, taking it off the system until released. This happened whenever an OTN issue came up that the Council wanted to keep in-house.

"No," Carvel replied, looking at Ana and not our team, clearly looking for her to jump in. "We need to keep this contained until we know what's fully going on."

"To be clear, we are saying this is Council business and does not concern the marshal's office," Ana said in a smooth yet authoritative tone.

I could feel Ed pushing a thought in my mind as I let go of the grip that I had learned to build around my thoughts. *They don't know,* was all that came through. What they knew or didn't know was unknown to me. That being said, the message was clear: don't mention Kim and their current involvement in the situation.

As soon as the thought crossed my mind, Ana looked directly at me. Her stare cut through my soul like a knife, followed by a grin. It's times like these that either Ed was talking to everybody in the room subconsciously, or I had no clue what was going on.

"So what are we supposed to tell the local authorities?" I asked, figuring in my mind that I was talking about the police and not the marshals. In a moment of brief reflection, a flash of Kim's ex-husband even went through my mind. "What a douche," I murmured under my breath.

"A what?" Carvel asked, finally joining the conversation.

"Nothing. It's just this dude I met the other day. So Dick, tell me, what's up in England?" I said as Jenny rolled her eyes while Carvel sat back, letting out a breath. The good thing about Dick was that he could take it all in stride. He had been born and raised in the East End and was as stubborn, egotistical, and old-fashioned as he was fat. He opened the Twinkie cellophane wrapper in front of him, furthering my point, making a distracting noise before answering.

As if ordained by the gods themselves, Inspector Holder decided to answer my question with a mouthful of half-eaten Twinkie. "Omph, amphhh . . . Bloody nutters ran-in a local business chap in Southampton. All that was left was his body; head was gone. Those weirdos . . . I mean Mages at the Dunn did some tests. They threw some data in that box they always tap on, and all kinds of alarms started going off. Next thing you know, I'm getting a call from Ms. Ana Vlad here," Dick said, looking over at her and winking. "She says something about a few deaths possibly being connected in Jacksonville, Florida, and . . . well here I am."

The rest of the group took a minute to revolt with Inspector Holder's disgusting manipulation of the Twinkie he had just eaten. What was even worse was the slurp of coffee that he took directly afterward. It was long and drawn out, the type of slurp that was almost always followed by a belch. In this case, it absolutely was. To make matters worse, Inspector Richard Holder started the unwrapping of another Twinkie.

"Have the local authorities gotten ahold of the story yet?" Jenny asked, putting the meeting back on track. She had a way of doing that.

"No," Ana answered for the eating Inspector. "We are more concerned with the incident in Florida. I have it on good authority that the Vampire Masters will not sit idle if Mr. Gool —"

"Goolsby, just Goolsby," I barked before retreating, quickly realizing who I was talking to. The guy was sleazy, and I didn't like others holding his name in high regard.

Ana smiled. "He will be held accountable if he had anything to do with the many deaths of our kind. The issue is, as you know, Goolsby is one of the only regulars on the Council, and this may end up getting chaotic. We would prefer that not to happen. Ed, I am asking you to call him upon your return; he respects you. It needs to be official and by the books. Goolsby will need to take a position on this. I'm hoping that he isn't involved, for everyone's sake, and this is nothing more than some drug-running incident as we are currently painting it to be. Am I clear on that?"

We all agreed without speaking, the expression on everyone's faces clear.

"Does the Council have any information on the drug or who may be hunting in Everwhere?" I asked, wanting to get to the point. I understood they wanted to police their own, but

I wanted answers. Seeing a man blow up in front of you after shooting laser fire lightning out of their eyes will do that to a guy.

"Not as of today," Carvel interjected. Ever since I'd saved his life and his thousand-year-old mother had baked me a pie, he at least tolerated me. I think he even liked me enough to work together. "I understand you visited Everwhere some time ago, but as it always is when you are involved, things are probably not as they seem."

I saw Ed lightly nod toward Carvel in a sign of respect. "Agreed. We think that someone or something is doing this. What we are not sure about is why. Plus, the targets seemed to be selected. We need to be figuring out why or how Goolsby," Ed looked at me, "and Cecil are involved. They most certainly are." Ed's voice was classic, timeless in many ways, making people listen.

"Max?" Carvel asked, looking over. This was something I hadn't expected. He wanted my opinion.

"I'm more concerned about the bloodbath about to take place in the streets of Jacksonville. I would hate to be around when that episode of *Cops* is filmed," I joked, the humor lost on the group.

"Ed, do you think you'll need any help? The Supreme Council wants the Atheneum team on this case, as it's in their backyard. As is everything else lately," Ana added, setting her firm jaw.

Did I ever mention I was in love with her and, well, her beer? I happened to get drunk one night and send her a text devoting my lifelong loyalty if she would let me tour her brewery, since she was the owner of Vamp Amber. Ana's response had been to send me a keg of the stuff and a box full of hats and bumper stickers for the beer. Even Vs had to have a marketing team.

"Soon enough. It all depends on what Max is saying; if

things get crazy in town, then yes. If we can keep things calm, it will just be a matter of time trying to figure this out. Might I recommend at least pulling Kim and the OTN marshals in? They will be needed. I agree with your point about the local authorities, but . . ." Ed said in a final attempt to keep Kim and the team on the case.

"Has Bert been around lately?" Dick asked. Bert had been Kim's peer since before the Balance. He was a straight-up regular guy and a good cop. I'd met him on a handful of occasions. He was glued to the West Coast most of the time.

"No, not for some time. They have him in some vault in Hollywood, by the sounds of it. After the Balance, from what I heard, when they figured out a bunch of actors and actresses where Mages or Ethereals things got—and are still—dicey," I said, regurgitating what Kim had told me.

"Very accurate assessment," Ana replied. "Excuse me while I make a call."

Ana walked out of the room while the rest of us sat there staring at Dick eating his third Twinkie.

"Dick, how's gating treating you?" I asked to cut the silence.

After another few seconds of chewing, Inspector Holder spoke up, "Well. Some Asian lady gave me this belt. I can go from the Dunn to your spot and here. No more of those bloody airplane rides."

In reality, Chloe used to spell him and gate Dick to wherever he needed to go.

After another minute, Ana walked back in. "You can pull in Kim and the rest of the marshals working out of the Atheneum. That's it," she said with finality.

After saying our goodbyes and talking to Dick about dropping by, we gated back to the Atheneum. The rest of the team went their separate ways. Tom and I, as we always did when together, discussed the Postern.

"Any luck on the new key?" Tom asked, referring to the key I'd found after breaking the clock my mother had given me on my rebirthday.

"Not yet. I tried a few things. It seems to be tied to the Mirrorgate; I just can't figure it out. Here," I said, grabbing the journal off Tom's new (yet still old) desk. He had gifted me his previous one, which had apparently belonged to King Arthur and which was also rectangular. We had stopped by the Postern on our way to the office and grabbed the journal from my place. Opening the pages, I found the picture of the key.

"And?" Tom asked, wanting to see what my take was. It was clear he knew this journal inside and out.

"The picture is an opposite of this key, like a mirror. All the others I can set on their picture, and they line up. What I don't get is the gate itself. It only has four reflective panels and a sliver of mirror around the edges. I'm guessing it has something to do with time."

"Maybe," Tom replied, pointing down at the picture below the hand-drawn gate. "I do know that's not glass; it's highly polished silver. It's so pure and manicured that it looks like mirrored glass. Old mirrors were nothing more than flat, polished silver. The whole reason Vs couldn't see their reflection back in the day," he explained. "I never knew that key was in the clock. It was a gift given to me by an old friend, and used to sit by your mother's bed. She always said she would give it to you if things sorted themselves out. Did you ever figure out the trick of the clock?"

I looked over, puzzled. "Trick?"

"Do tell me you at least set it and used it once."

"I did. I can't think of anything that happened, though. I just went to sleep."

"Precisely. If you set that clock, it would make you go to sleep. It was enchanted to do just that," Tom said, shaking his head.

"I don't think that has anything to do with the gate. Hold on . . . what if the whole point of the gate is not to use it in a normal way. Like in a dream, or opposite somehow," I said, seeing a grin finally appear on Tom's face.

"Now you're cooking with gas. Did you see the drawing? I added it. The originator of this journal just drew the gate. I never had this key, but figured the mirrors symbolized something, like with the Evergate. The gate stones symbolize a foundation, much like the gate. The Seekergate uses an actual key, symbolizing the path to where it is you are going. The Mirrorgate has been debated to mean two things: literal time and what I think is the ability to be in a mirrored reality, possibly like a ghost. Plus, don't forget the gates themselves could possibly need more than the keys to use them. That is why you will see normal keys and intricate gates or intricate keys and normal-looking gates. It took some time for me to figure that out."

"How long?" I asked, having had this conversation before. Tom just chuckled as we spent the next thirty minutes coming up with ways to try activating the gate.

"Gods and graves, it's getting late," I said, realizing I needed to text Kim and take a rain check on the night out. "You sticking around here for a few days?" I asked as Tom walked me to the Postern gate.

It reminded me of FA's being in multiple places and not at the same time. The issue was, it would only open for Tom and myself since moving. The main door at the Atheneum had an extraordinary dragon inlaid into the door. The one in my new place was due to the Evergate, and a little voodoo from Devin.

I gated back to the apartment around 9:00 p.m. to find Phil and Petro watching cartoons in the office. This time it was old episodes of *M.A.S.K.* The one where the Camaro had wing doors and lasers, of course being able to fly.

"Hey, boss, any news?" Petro asked, not taking his eyes off the screen.

"They want to keep this one in-house. Plus, it looks like we may be taking a field trip to England." That got the two's attention.

"What? That old fat bat trying to get us to come over and do his dirty laundry?" Phil exclaimed in a jesting flourish followed by a few choice minor curse words. The kind of cussing I could actually understand.

"They found another body. The team wants us to check into it as soon as we figure out if things will stay calm here. The Vs think Goolsby has something to do with this. Him being one of the few regulars on the Council is going to get messy fast; Ed should be talking to him at this very moment," I told them. "Ana wants to know where he stands, plus I'm curious to see how much he knows. The thing is, I'm just not buying anything yet. Then again, who knows, I've never trusted Goolsby. He may have played his hand in the open for once," I said, grabbing a beer out of the downstairs mini fridge that was—thanks to Phil—half empty.

Phil, sensing my anguish, flipped me off. He didn't even look over his shoulder, knowing what I would see by the sound of the refrigerator opening.

"Thanks, guys. Maybe it's time you just move in and help around here a little," I said, directing the statement at Phil.

"Bruther, tell you what. We get this behind us, and I'm game. I've been dragging my arse to get some money saved up," Phil said, pointing over to the brown bag by the floor with a twelve-pack of Vamp Ambers in it. I walked over, smacking him on the back of the head. Petro dusted lightly, snickering at the interaction.

"How much money?" I asked, knowing he was much older than he looked.

"Ahh, you know, enough," he replied as Petro again

snickered.

"He's got enough to buy whatever he wants. The clunk just wants to stay close to the old place," Petro said as Phil's face became thoughtful.

Petro was right. Phil used to work with his wife at the Atheneum. After her death, he seemed to be bound to the place. Its walls reminded him of her. Apparently, the room he stayed in was the very room they had stayed in together.

"Hey, man. It's all good. It would just be nice to have you around more," I told him as Petro agreed. The three amigos together at last.

"Well, until you and Kim finally figure out you like each other," Phil interjected, letting out a bellowing laugh afterward, shifting the subject.

"Anyway, we need to get some rest. I have a feeling things are going to get rocky fast," I added, walking over to check the stack of letters and my email before calling it a night.

In the stack of mail was a check from the person representing whoever was getting the castor commissioned. I let out a breath. I had forgotten to talk to Jenny about it earlier. Inside the envelope were further instructions and preferences, as if the person knew I needed the information. Also sitting in the crisp, white paper was a check for ten thousand dollars. With this and the deposit things were looking up.

Taking a lungful of air, I wheezed, "Holy shit . . ."

"What is it this time? Your nudie magazines came in?" Phil joked.

"Man, you need to get with the times," I said, holding up my phone. "People don't get nudie magazines in the mail anymore."

Phil just stared. He was obviously one of the few people left on Earth that had a physical subscription to *Big Buns Bonanza* magazine.

"Whoever this is means business. Remind me to get this to Jenny," I said, walking upstairs as Phil got up and collected his things.

CHAPTER 7

Vampires and Voyeurs

"**W**hat?!" I exclaimed as the knock on the bedroom door grew louder. My new bedroom was significantly larger than the one I had at the Atheneum. Instead of filling it with useless things, I had just brought my furniture from Tom's house over and nothing more. The mix of open space and lack of furniture generated a piercing echo whenever someone knocked on my bedroom door, which, at 3:00 a.m., shouldn't be happening.

With that thought, I sprang from bed, shaking the fog out of my head. I could hear Phil at the door; I could even make out Petro hovering directly outside as well.

"This better be good," I muttered, seeing the two of them in their gear.

"Hey, boss, maybe you should stop turning your phone off at night. It's going down," Petro said, spitting out the sentence faster than he usually did, indicating trouble.

"Bruther, the Vs moved on Goolsby. Riverplace Tower is a damn war zone." My brain started to catch up to my feet, putting me into motion. Phil tossed me a small tube of blueish liquid. "Bottoms up, sunshine!"

I blindly drank the contents, feeling a sudden surge of energy. The taste was familiar, and my brain eventually connected that it was Jenny's turbo coffee potion, one of the first potions I had ever learned to make. I wasn't a big potions fan, but this stuff was useful.

Ten minutes later, the three of us were standing together, listening to Kim on speakerphone. "Come in at Friendship Fountain; we will meet you there. It looks like they came from the river," Kim said as she hung up.

Friendship Fountain was about a block away from S. Main Street leading up to the Acosta Bridge.

"Phil, have you had a chance to talk to anyone else?" I asked, checking my gear over one last time, the hilt of Durundle peeking out from underneath my arm. The uniform I was wearing was the same one I'd had over the past two years: black tactical gear, including a vest, and enough loops to hang about anything I wanted on it. After taking Mouth's advice, I'd stopped making it a habit of carrying every single enchanted piece of equipment I had. On my right hip was my service pistol, and in a neat holder on my side was the short staff I had made a year back.

"No, bruther, just Ed and Jenny when they woke me up; the girls got a hold of Petro. I was talking to him about that very thing. I've got a feeling one of the other Vs on the Council tipped them off to avoid an all-out war," Phil said in a serious tone.

The three amigos, back together again, all walked into the Postern as I pulled out the Seekergate key. Envisioning Friendship Fountain in my mind, I placed the key in the keyhole, turning it as the gate shimmered to life. The fountain itself was large, round, and shallow. Water shot into the air from set angles. It was the type of fountain you would often find someone trying to run through in the middle of a hot day; it happened to also overlook the river.

Walking through the gate, the feeling of magic being used close by washed over my body. It was clear that Petro also felt the same thing. Someone was using some serious fire-power.

Ben walked up with a curt look on his face. "Ready to go?"

I spoke up first, looking over to see Kim on a radio, buried in a deep conversation. "What's the score? Do you know how many Vs are trying to get into the building?"

"Trying . . . ?" Ben asked with a slight tone of exasperation in his voice. "They're already inside."

"Something smells weird, boss," Petro said, dropping back down to eye level after getting the lay of the land.

"Yeah, I can smell it too," I replied as Phil looked over, lighting up a cigarette and shaking his head. Over the past year, Phil and the others I was close to had figured out my dirty little secret. To be honest, I had actually sat them all down and told them over drinks one night, only to be told that they already knew. They also recognized I had some additional skills that often were hard to explain. Quite frankly, I was still trying to figure them out.

Petro and I were picking up traces of something from the Plane. It could be anything from a creature or some type of item being used in the attack.

I looked down at my phone, noticing I had another missed call from Aslynn. She had been trying to get a hold of me for the last three days. I clicked the off button on my phone, seeing Kim do the same as she walked back toward the group. A team of ten more marshals walked from around the corner behind us, also looking as if they were ready to clock in and do violence. Or hopefully, in this case, prevent it.

"They want us to go in. Max, as a member of the Council, you are the senior official on-site. I also just talked to Ed, and he highly recommends we make sure this keeps contained. We know there was some fighting in the parking deck, but whatever's going on is happening inside the building," Kim relayed in a militaristic fashion.

"We can't gate into the building; it's warded. I've tried it before." That got me a sour look from Kim.

"I say we just knock on the front door," Phil said, spitting the still-lit cigarette on the ground.

Ben, Kim, Phil, Petro, and I all looked at each other, nodding our heads in agreement.

"We do need to let them know we are not going to take this kind of thing lightly. Plus, we can also play this off as coming to the aid of a fellow Council member. Either way, I agree with Phil. Let's go knock on the front door," I said. The team of marshals circled Ben for instructions. The three of us were obviously not invited to that conversation.

It was immediately clear there would be repercussions later. Three mangled bodies in various stages of dismemberment were strewn around the white marble lobby. Blood painted the walls, and bloody footprints were not only on the floor, trailing in the direction of the stairwell, but on the walls and ceiling. A Vs trademark.

"How many?" I asked Petro.

"Ten, maybe eleven. They have someone else with them. I'm thinking the extra person is who we smelled earlier."

Without saying a word, the team of marshals split up into two groups of five, one being led by Ben and the other by Kim.

"Where are you guys going?" I asked as Kim walked up to the three of us standing in front of the elevators.

"The teams are going to take the stairwell. As you can tell, it looks like that's the way Goolsby's visitors went. We are going to take the elevator," Kim said matter-of-factly, winking at me. She was sexy when she talked like that.

"The stones on this one," Phil said, shaking his head as we walked into the elevator. I pushed the button to the thirteenth floor—better known as the Blue Room. This was the place I had basically caught on fire, as Belm, Chloe, and I met face-to-face with the Eater, a rather nasty Mind Mage.

Goolsby had threatened me on several occasions to never show my face again in his place of business. Oddly enough, I had been there on two occasions and had yet to be slapped on the hand by Goolsby. Or set anything else on fire.

As the elevator rocketed toward the heart of the building, a jolt followed by a loud crash garnered everyone's attention. While we had pressed the button for the thirteenth floor, it was evident by the over two-minute ride at high speeds that we were going significantly higher. At times, I even wondered if the building was tall enough to justify the fast yet longer than needed ride.

During the trip, I thought that either Goolsby wanted us there or was too preoccupied to give a shit. The man had a way of pulling me and the others in to do his dirty work.

As soon as the bell rang and the elevator doors smoothly slid open, it was clear he was preoccupied. Flashes of blue light shot down the hallway in front of the open elevator doors as another rumbling jolt reverberated throughout the building. Automatic gunfire spattered and ricocheted off the far walls where we had once sat at the bar talking to the overly tall bartender. The hostess stand was shattered into pieces, several chunks lodged into the sheetrock. Shouts of orders rang out from the right side, obviously coming from Goolsby's offices.

A light gray glow started to cover Phil as he pulled up his shotgun, simultaneously squeezing the handle of the hammer that he carried. Petro was already at the roof of the elevator, ready to fly out and up. He knew to be careful when Vs were present.

The shitty thing about big nasty fights was that things

never happened to go as planned. Ever since I had realized I was a mix of about every type of being out there, my body at times moved a little faster than the rest.

I lurched forward, pulling out Durundle. "Ignis!" I yelled as the elevator doors slammed shut behind me before my counterparts could exit. Green balls of plasma, followed by actual normal bullets, whizzed by. It wasn't that shots weren't scary; it's just that whoever was firing them was either old fashioned or on their last leg. If you didn't have any power left, even Mages deferred to bullets.

"Shit!" I yelled, diving through to the other side of the hall, again finding myself ducking under Goolsby's bar with a flaming sword. I took a second to home in on the sounds around me. Gunfire, check; spells, check; yelling, check. *Sword fighting?* I thought, hearing the distinct sound of a blade taking a chunk out of its victim. It sounded as if three parties were dancing on the dance floor.

Taking a deep breath, I chose to head away from the offices, figuring that would only put me face-to-face with the Vs or whomever Cecil had sent. It was also the direction of what sounded like a secondary struggle.

"Coming through!" I yelled, running next to the wall and immediately jumping into the dining room as a flurry of gunfire erupted overhead.

I looked up to see a V brandishing a short rod much like mine. The V jumped out from behind a far table with a look of confusion on his face.

It was either my flaming sword or the blade from a blurring third party that neatly sliced his head off. The look on the V's face morphed from confusion, to realization, to cold eternity as his head slid forward, dropping the V's body right behind.

The blur shifted after seeing me. It looked as if a cloud of smoke was wielding what looked like an old cutlass blade.

"Pirates . . . I hate pirates," I said in my best Indiana Jones impersonation of his hatred for snakes.

Lurching forward, the blur leaped through the air, connecting with my flaming blade in a hissing metallic clank. The edge was iron and must have also been enchanted, holding up to Durundle's blows.

We exchanged rapid swings, neither finding an opening. The blur was hard to focus on as I kept trying to lock onto something solid. I pushed my will into my hand, lashing out a short arch of hellfire and pulling it back into my body, a neat trick I had recently learned.

The heat worked as planned as the blur started to take shape. I could finally make out arms and legs. Again, their blade swung down from the guard, forcing me to maneuver at lightning-fast speeds to stop the sword's downward momentum from cutting me in half.

Taking the opening left by what I now deemed in my mind as the floating blender, I again pushed my will out, this time catching the anomaly with a flash of hellfire. The effect was immediate. A hiss of anger and pain came from the shifting form.

Just as I was about to finish the fight, two more Vs came in from the far side. The distraction was enough to allow the floating blender to reset. Seeing their team member's fate, they immediately zeroed in on me standing there holding my sword. Pissed didn't properly describe the look on their faces.

The two new additions looked at me with focused hate as the sword-wielding blur flew past, the scrape of our blades echoing in my ear.

"Hey, fellas. That wasn't me, promise," I belted out as they let loose several spells. Tables shattered as the wall behind me exploded, more gunfire and spells being introduced to the party.

I dove behind the knee wall that separated this space

from the bar, the cover giving me a minute to regroup. As the two Vs leaped toward me, arrows whistled through the air, meeting their marks and dropping the two instantly. They must have been enchanted.

Several more arrows whistled down the hallway as the almost seven-foot-tall, half-Asian, half-Black bartender, Rex, popped up from behind the bar. If he was this good with an arrow, I was starting to wonder why he hadn't helped last time we had gotten into a fight.

"Clear," Rex said in a flat, almost bored tone. The sounds of gunfire came to a halt, as did the sounds of spells being cast by the Vs.

I quickly realized I was kneeling with Durundle burning brightly in my hand. The elevator doors opened, and the sound of pounding footsteps from the stairwell filled the shuffling silence.

The whole thing had happened without me hurting or killing anyone. Bonus for not setting anything on fire either. I quickly extinguished the blade, standing up as the rest of the team arrived. Goolsby's goons came out from behind the hallway past the elevators.

"Rex, old buddy, been a while. Any chance I can get a drink?" I asked as the tall man shook his head, reaching down and grabbing a beer bottle, throwing it at me. He put his fingers to his lips in a hushing motion. It would be our little secret.

I ducked down, taking several quick pulls from the cheap light beer. OK, maybe not friends, but we would work on that.

Kim rounded the corner just as I stood up. Smoke from the gunfire, as well as the smell of sulfur, lingered in the room. It was clear the Vs had not achieved their goal.

"Where's Goolsby?" Kim asked as Phil walked over to the two Vs on the ground with arrows sticking from their chests.

"Not sure. Rex, where's the boss?" I asked as he nodded toward the back office area. Before we could move, Goolsby walked out, holding an assault rifle. He was in the fight, and clearly—by the looks of his attire—ready for it.

Kim looked over, eyeing me up and down to make sure I was in one piece. In all fairness, I wasn't sure if I was. The burn mark on the back of my coat verified that I had been hit by a spell.

As anyone in the sales business would tell you, the first person to talk was the loser. Goolsby was taking that approach once again as he stood there looking at us.

Phil yelled in the background, "Bunch of Vs with no heads over here. They never got ahead in the fight."

The joke went flat as Goolsby spoke. "Max, you

are . . . ?" he said, letting me finish the statement.

"Here to rescue you, princess," I replied, holding back a belch from chugging the beer. George Lucas would be proud of me.

"We are here because of what was discussed with you earlier. We received reports of movement on your location," Kim interjected, knowing I was just going to agitate the man further.

"I see. Again, Max?" Goolsby asked. This time he had a stressed look on his face, as if he wanted to know my opinion.

I finally snapped out of it. "Oh, yeah. So, I don't think your folks killed those headless Vs. Minus the ones with arrows in them."

"The ones Rex shot will be fine; we will, of course, turn them over to the marshals. Are you sure you didn't have a hand in that?" Goolsby asked, implying I had done the head whacking with my sword.

I stepped forward as he squared up, staring a hole through me. "I didn't do a damn thing but come here and, unfortunately, help save your ass once again. Oh, and there was a blurry-looking blender thingy floating around with a sword cutting off their heads, but you wouldn't know anything about that, being that you were wherever it was you were."

Goolsby sighed. It was the first time I'd seen him do that. He relaxed, letting the tension out of the grip on his weapon. "Not one of mine. I'll check the CCTV footage." Goolsby paused, looking at me. "Max, are you growing taller?"

Funny thing, I was. Over the past year, I had added three inches to my mediocre stature, making me start to stand out in a crowd. After talking with Tom, we had landed on it being the demon part of me adding to my build. It was also one of the reasons I'd had my blazer modified. He was the first person besides Petro to comment on it.

"Growing pains," I said as Kim let out a breath, setting the conversation back on track.

"We will be reviewing that with you," Kim stated, squinting her eyes, sizing me up.

"I don't think so. I'm on the Council, and that makes this accorded territory," Goolsby responded calmly.

As if on cue, Phil walked over. "Accorded mess. This place is a crime scene, and as a Council member, you are bound to cooperate with both regular and magical authorities. It's in the Balance proclamation accords. This is both of those types of scene thingies at this point."

Phil had laid down the law out of nowhere. He didn't do that often, but when he did, people listened. He had a certain reputation.

Kim nodded, looking back at Goolsby. I guessed that he was somehow deleting the footage as we stood there. Petro flew over to the group with a pissed off look on his face. Apparently, he had gotten sucked into the elevator shaft and gotten stuck, not being able to open the hoistway doors.

"OK, I'll get a copy to your team," Goolsby murmured, letting his face go slack.

"CCTV? Count me in," Petro said, buzzing off toward the

back offices. He enjoyed TV, and even more so, reality TV. This fit both the bills.

Unfazed, Goolsby tracked back to my prior statement. "Like an apparition with a sword?"

I was still trying to compute what exactly it was I had just gotten into a sword fight with. "No, it was solid, but wasn't. I can tell you the iron blade it had was a significant item," I replied, taking the edge off my tone.

Goolsby stood there shaking his head, pursing his lips. "Is anyone on the way to see Cecil?"

Kim looked up from her phone; she was sending out a message. "They are, and I would not assume they are—"

Kim was cut off by one of her agents. "This is one of Cecil's guys. We picked him up for drugs a few months ago."

The look Kim gave the young agent said everything it needed to say. A good year's worth of night shift duty in Alaska was heading their way.

Goolsby lifted his chin slightly. "I'll be in my office. I expect the Council will be looking into this. In the meantime, I will be making sure none of my other assets are being attacked."

The statement was final as he turned and walked off, leaving Phil, Kim, and me standing there. Petro was already on the hunt for the video.

"What an arse. He's up to some dodgy stuff," Phil said, lighting up a cigarette much to the dismay of the other agents. Again no one questioned him. No one ever did, except maybe Jenny and Kim on occasion.

"Yeah, he is. He's also on the Council, and if I was a betting man, I'd say we are here by design. That was only a handful of Cecil's goons. The guy's not a heavy hitter like Goolsby; at least, I don't think he is. Whatever that thing was that cut off those heads didn't like the fact that a third party showed up," I said as Kim licked her lips, ending with a popping smack.

"You know something? I have the feeling that if we—well, you—hadn't shown up, whatever those things were very well may have taken both sides out. Goolsby was being honest when he said it wasn't one of his," Kim said, making a damn good point as Phil and I nodded in agreement.

Petro buzzed over. "Good news and bad news. The CCTV system is fried."

"The good news?" I asked, having figured out that would be the case.

"I found this," Petro said, handing Kim a small plastic bag the size of a marble.

"What is it?" Kim asked as he dropped it in her hand. The material inside was blood red and powdery. It almost looked like crack with coloring in it.

"Kracken, but not the normal stuff. It's the turbo stuff," Petro replied as we all looked at each other.

"Where did you find it?" I asked him as Kim passed it around.

"In the elevator shaft, which is scary as hell, by the way. I don't think that elevator goes up and down. Anyway, when the elevator finally appeared, this was on top of it. Like someone had dropped it. Even better, something stunk in there as well like . . . like that one guy before he went *boom* at the docks."

Goolsby's assistant and Rex walked out in an obvious attempt to supervise our presence. I looked over at Kim, ignoring the two as I pocketed the baggy.

"Any idea how many bodies are up here?" I inquired, seeing the last of the marshals walk through the stairwell.

"That was the text message I was looking at. Ben thinks around fifteen. Some of the bodies are pretty messed up." Kim grimaced. There would be consequences.

"Goolsby's people?" I already knew the answer.

"None, just a few people that need medical aid," Kim said

as we walked toward the elevator.

"Hey, I need to check a few things out. Something's been bothering me. All this is really pinging my radar. You mentioned they found a business card linked to both locations?" I said after making sure we were out of earshot.

"We did; I'll text you a copy. Weird shit, some company called B&B LLC. Has a skeleton on the back. I was going to check it out in the morning," Kim said as she mean mugged one of the younger marshals, forcing him to wander off in another direction.

"Let me guess, the address is by the docks." That got me an approving grin from Kim.

"Goofy looking and smart," Kim said teasingly. "I still haven't wrapped things up from this morning."

"Ha, ha. Dinner tonight? I'm going to get some rest, then go check this place out. You good?" I asked, figuring I would at least be polite.

"Mr. Independent Council Mage, I don't think I have much say so in what you do. Plus, I would rather you go. I have enough weird shit going on right now; it's going to be a long morning. You owe me a cup of Trish's good stuff, and yes on dinner," Kim said as she hit the send button on her phone. My phone dinged loudly, receiving the message.

As an independent Council Mage, I was afforded certain flexibilities. Not only was I considered a consultant, but I also had just enough weight after the past two years to get myself out of most types of trouble. My call to leave the Atheneum had ended up being one of the best choices I had made over the past decade.

Well, besides that one time directly after the Balance that I went out and decided to show off. I set a bar on fire that night. Luckily, no one was hurt, and the shock of it all kept me out of trouble. Come to think about it, that might actually have been one of my worse choices of late.

"Kim," I said before everyone else was around. "You know they don't want your team or the civilian authorities digging too far into this. You find something, talk to Ed or someone you trust. It might be nothing, but again . . ."

Kim nodded in understanding.

"You ready to go?" I asked Petro, also nodding at Phil as they arrived.

"Sure thing, boss. The old lady is waiting up for me," Petro said, doing his normal waist gyrations.

"It's past 5:00 a.m. in the damned morning, bruther," Phil said, the signs of exhaustion starting to show. To be fair, I was in the same condition. *Sleep, I need some sleep*, I thought as we boarded the elevator. The building was still warded enough to prevent me from using the Evergate. That little skip home would have to wait till we were outside.

After a few minutes of clearing things with Ben outside, we gated back to the apartment. Within twenty minutes, we had all passed out. Half-drunk beers, which we thought were a great idea, sat on the end tables.

CHAPTER 8

The Jolly Roger

T here's a certain feeling of accomplishment when sleeping in past noon. You far exceeded the extra hours' quota met by so-called "lazy people," and you absolutely sent the bold statement of I'm going to be up late tonight. I rolled over, realizing my phone was vibrating. It was more than likely what had woken me up before dinner and cocktails.

I pressed my palms against my eyes hard, forming purple spots in my vision as I slung my legs over the side of the bed and made contact with the cool floor.

After a chug of the room-temperature water sitting on the nightstand, I grabbed my phone, yawning. "Damn," I said into thin air, reading the texts.

Tom had messaged me about needing to discuss last night, followed by Kim telling me she would be resting till later in the day. I paused, grinning at her thoughtfulness. Jenny had left me a lengthy message about the castor she was starting for our customer, whom I had yet to meet. It was really her customer, but who was I to argue. She was meeting with their contact later today.

Rich people, I thought, *always paying others to do their work*. Not that I had anything against people with money; hell,

Tom was probably unforthcomingly rich.

I also had a note from Petro. Casey had apparently put him on what he called *mating* duties for the day.

Phil was set to cover at the Atheneum for the evening. It was much like fire watch in the army or being on call as a doctor, CSA agents such as Phil also had their weekly rotations on the graveyard shift.

I let out a breath, realizing I was going on a field trip by myself. After getting cleaned up, I walked into the kitchen, looking at the picture of the card Kim had sent. After a few cups of coffee, I decided to head downstairs to print out a copy using some of my card stock.

Advances in printer technology had convinced me that magic was somehow involved. A little person with a small enchanted stick made whatever I needed come out of it. I used the paper stock I had purchased to make my business cards and printed both sides. The cards turned out nice. I wasn't sure what was pushing me to do that, but I had a hunch it would get me further than pulling out my phone and showing a picture.

I hated people that crammed their phones in your face. "Look at how pretty my child is" or "check out this amazing steak I ate last night," the list goes on and on. Although, I did at one point have a photo of Phil passed out with anatomical cartoon characters drawn on his face courtesy of Petro and me. I guess I did show that one off a little too much before Phil politely took my phone, charged his hands, and threw it into the stratosphere.

I looked down at my phone and realized I also needed to call Aslynn back. She had a knack for always calling at inopportune times, especially when Kim was around. I stretched, scratching my undercarriage and hitting redial.

"Max, it's you," Aslynn said in a rushed, desperate voice.

"Glad to hear from you, Asly—"

"Are you at your new place?"

"Yeah. Hey, what's up?" I asked as there was a knock at the front glass door. I kept the blinds drawn to keep out the light, and more often than not, nosey people—or things, for that matter.

Aslynn had been, at one point, a mild love interest of mine who also happened to be the daughter of Nuadha Danann, better known as Ned, a Senior Council member and full-blooded Fae. He also happened to be my sponsor when I had first started out at the Atheneum.

I walked over and opened the door. Aslynn rushed in, literally falling into my arms.

"Gods and graves, you okay?" I asked. She looked around, alert, and glad to be off the street. She reached up, hugging me closely and forcing me to pull in a lungful of air.

"It's Dad. He's gone missing, and I can't find him anywhere," she blurted out, light tears coming out of her emerald-green eyes glittering down her face. She was Fae, and as stunning as they came.

I walked her over to the desk, grabbing her a cup of coffee from the small break room downstairs.

"Things have been crazy lately; maybe he's out on assignment," I said, gauging the *oh shit* level.

"No, he never does anything without letting me know something. Ever. I mean *ever*," she said, emphasizing that "ever" was a very long time.

With women, I usually wasn't as blunt. I had a thing called manners, but now was not the time. "Why do you think he is missing specifically?" I asked. She shifted moods, seeing I was paying attention.

"He was called to go to some private meeting about four days ago and never came back. Dad never does that to me. Even worse, I got a hold of Jamison, and he doesn't have a clue either, which made him worried. He told me to contact you, as it will be a week or two before he gets back," Aslynn said, sniffling slightly.

I leaned back, taking this in. "We need to let Ed and Tom know. They care about Ned, and if they know something, which they should, they will let us know."

Aslynn smiled slightly, taking a sip of her coffee. "Okay, can you let me know what they say?"

"I'll do you one better. I'm going to the Atheneum to drop off an envelope for Jenny; you can ask them yourself."

Aslynn looked apprehensive yet happy that someone was doing something. I paused, standing up.

"Let me grab a few things. I'm leaving as soon as I drop you off. Why did you wait to tell me?"

"My brother was very specific. He told me to get hold of you first," Aslynn said, standing up and giving me a hug that lasted a little too long. I reflected on that statement, knowing Jamison had some minor divination abilities.

As if the gods themselves knew where I was at that very second, Kim called.

I let out a breath, knowing I had to take the call. I put a finger up, walking to the back. "Hey, what's up? I thought you would still be sleeping."

"I was, till the reports came in on the red substance. It's the same stuff, and even better, the blood work Jenny was working on also matches, meaning both our victims had the same junk in their systems at some point. The material we found is that substance," Kim sluggishly said as Aslynn walked around the corner.

"Can I use your . . ." She paused, seeing I was on the phone, grimacing and mouthing sorry.

It was too late. "Is that Aslynn's voice in the background?"

"Uh, yeah, kinda. I mean, she stopped by. I'll fill you in later," I said as Kim took a deep breath and hung up.

"Shit, shit, shit," I said under my breath.

"Was it your cop girlfriend?" Aslynn asked as I silently pointed toward the bathroom.

After several minutes of brooding and getting my stuff together, we gated to the Atheneum and filled Ed and Tom in on Ned. This was apparently a bigger deal than I'd thought, as they immediately went off to the crucible room. After dropping the envelope about the castor off to Jenny, it was time for my little field trip.

The address to B&B LLC was by the docks and easy to locate through the Seekergate. Time had proven several ways of focusing to get exactly where I wanted to be, but it wasn't an exact science. There had been times when the Seekergate had simply told me to kiss its ass and not worked. I chalked this up to bad location info in my mind.

After concentrating on the location, I pushed my will through my body and into the key. The gate shimmered to life as the smell of the ocean permeated into the Postern.

Stepping through, I found myself staring at a bustling parking lot. The building on the other end was sleek and modern, with a ten-foot-tall fence surrounding its perimeter.

Walking closer to the facility, it became evident money was made here. The view of the intracoastal and manicured feel of the place made it clear. You ever notice how the closer you get to a nice office building, the more expensive the cars are? This building was no exception. Large, black, decked-out diesel trucks and even meaner-looking sports cars deliberately turned their noses up at the back rows of BMWs and lesser models. This place clearly had a chain of command.

The guard shack at the front entrance looked to be one of the only main points of entry. Most office buildings had what was lovingly known as "rent-a-cops." This place had an honest-to-God Amazonian-looking woman standing outside the gate door. She was at least six foot five and coming in at a strong, not fat, 230 pounds. Her uniform was pristine and manicured, and the weapon on her hip sat like an afterthought. My instincts decided it would be best not to pick a fight with her.

Whoever she worked for was not cheap. She might even be an employee of the facilities. The railroads, like CSX, headquartered in Jacksonville had their own police force after all. Cameras followed my movement as the front of the building came into focus.

Gray smoked glass wrapped the structure like cascading water. Other than the front door, no other points of entrance— or for that matter, windows—made themselves known. A flagpole with a black flag sporting the same skeleton as the card flew slightly below the roofline.

I let out a huff as the tall, dark-skinned woman walked forward, obviously not thinking I was a threat. I had decided to throw on some dark jeans and my latest Planes Drifter T-shirt Abby Normal, the lead singer, had sent me over the summer. The recently modified enchanted corduroy blazer came to my knees, making the outfit even more eye-catching.

"Can I help you?" the woman asked in a deep, throaty voice. A radio silently buzzed in her ear. It was the type that you tucked under your shirt with a coiled cable leading up to your ear. I could pick up on things like the light radio chatter I was not supposed to hear with my newfound heightened senses.

"I'm here to see Bruce Teach," I said, holding out the business card I had printed this morning.

She paused, getting instructions from whoever was watching on the cameras. She was good at what she did, and shifted just enough for me to notice. "Bruce is not here at the moment," Linda, as I now made out on her name tag, said, getting another message over her radio. "Please follow me. He is at the dock."

"Dock?" I asked, not questioning the response. We walked in through the gate alongside the privacy fence, not walking toward the building.

"Mr. Teach is on his yacht. You do know what that is, correct?" Linda said, not missing a beat. Her tone was flat, meaning that was not a joke.

We walked through another gate to see a 400-foot-long mega yacht, the kind you saw in West Palm Beach or Miami. There were a few in Jacksonville, but not nearly as many. I hadn't noticed it due to the other boats in the area when I gated in.

The boat was also wrapped in the same smoked glass, not giving anything on the inside away. We continued walking toward the dock, arriving at another security gate manned—well, womaned—by what looked like Linda's twin sister.

"Wait here," Linda said, walking over and talking to her partner.

I had tried to will a gate while in the courtyard of the building with no luck. The place was warded. While the gates in the Postern were more powerful than most, they still had limitations. Betting the yacht was also warded, I focused my attention on the two shipping vessels sitting in the dock a few hundred feet down from the back of the facility. They were obviously part of the operation.

Old rusted pylons shot up from the saltwater leading up to large open decks full of cargo containers. A crane reached out, surgically picking off containers. That would be my target.

"Mr. Abaddon, please follow me," Linda said as the other woman stared. She used my middle name. In the magical community, that was the real deal. It was given at birth without the parents' input. Yes, hospitals had been aware of the other world way before the rest of the world.

The Council had a group of old clerics that assigned one's middle name through some type of divination, or otherworldly sight if any trace of Etherium was present. I had no clue that every child ever born in a hospital was tested, but they were. All thanks to Mags-Tech labs.

"Hey, how do you know my name?" I asked. I hadn't introduced myself. Linda didn't say a word as we walked on the gangway onto the main deck. Another round of security guards greeted us.

The boat read *The Jolly Roger* on the side. I needed to freshen up on my pirate history.

"You will need to leave all your weapons here," Linda said, looking sternly at the two men standing there. They looked as if they were her brothers. Tall, dark, and having the same facial features.

Last year, I learned not to take everything with me when going out on official business; it usually ended up drawing more attention than not. Today I had brought my service pistol and short staff. In my mind, the staff wasn't a weapon but more of a tool. I had used that to pass it off on more than one occasion.

I slowly pulled out my pistol, dropping the magazine and clearing it on the table. The two men just stared as Linda lurched forward without warning, grabbing the staff from its holder under my arm.

"Hey, at least buy a guy dinner first," I said, garnering at least one momentary smirk from the guards. *Hah*, I thought, *at least they are not robots.*

"He's clear," Linda said as the two men walked up to me, one positioning himself in front and one behind. Linda went away as we walked into the interior of the luxurious vessel. Plush carpet, light wooden panels, and the smell of fresh flowers greeted us.

After a few more turns and twists, we walked past a door slightly cracked open. For a moment, I thought I saw Councilman Darkwater sitting there.

"Excuse me," I said, stopping and turning around only to slam face-first into the guard's chest. "Omph . . . I think I have a frien—"

I was cut off by the guards politely moving me down the hall. They weren't being physical; it was more like the look and behavior a mother and father would give their eleven-year-old child when they found him drinking a beer and reading a nudie magazine. I may have done that once.

The two men walked up to a closed door that was significantly more fortified than the others. Delicate silver artwork was etched into it, giving off a radioactive level of energy.

The doors opened as a large, burly black-bearded man stood up from behind a gilded desk. I hesitated, thinking it was the man I'd run into in Everwhere. I quickly realized it wasn't, as he clearly had both his legs and was several years younger. My thoughts landed on him absolutely being a relative.

The room was old-school opulent. Gold and silver covered most of everything in the space. The smell of cinnamon lightly filled the air.

"Max," the large man said in a booming voice. He reached out a hand the size of a bear claw. Gold rings with inlaid gems adorned each finger.

"I'm at a disadvantage, I'm afraid," I replied, betting this was the Bruce from the card. I reached out my hand, pushing a little will from my demon side into the grip. The large man paused for a second as his eyes momentarily went into laser focus.

"Bruce Teach, as I'm sure you read on my card. I believe I know who you are," Bruce said, attempting to take over the conversation.

I wasn't going to let that happen. It was time to shit on his day. "I got a coin off a man that looked just like you. Had a peg leg and all that," I said, seeing if I was right.

Bruce froze, a sneer forming on his face as his muscles

rippled throughout his body. "You what?" he clippingly said. See, I told you. I won that round. "You know my father?" Bruce asked. His posture indicated that he was either figuring out a way to beat me to death or genuinely wanted to know.

Figuring I would see how far I could push him, I let it rip. After spending more than one minute with the man, I was sure he was trouble. Not the Goolsby type of world-shaping trouble, but the same type as Cecil. Goolsby at least had some sort of code and intention to act like he was on the right side of things. This guy . . . nope. Plus, I was pretty sure I had seen Darkwater in the room we'd walked past earlier. That guy was not on my Christmas card list.

"Well, wasn't too long ago. He gave me the coin after he was shot by a flaming arrow in Everwhere. I kind of left him in the graveyard after that," I said, seeing the rage building in the man.

As soon as it came, it left. Bruce took back control of the wheel and taking a step back behind his desk. The thing I liked about going out on my own was that I could do things my way. Well, Phil probably would have pulled a gun on the guy, but that's beside the point. I wasn't doing work for my consulting business; this was official Council business, and the man standing before me knew it without me saying a word.

"Sit," was all the man said. Figuring I had pushed him enough, I obliged. "I'm sure you're not here to talk about my father, and frankly, I'm not sure how you know about this. But I do know about you, and was interested in meeting you. What is it you want?"

The man was on the program. Straight to the point, like me. "I'm here on Council business looking into several shipments of contaminated Kracken. You know anything about that?" I asked, throwing the full plate in the trash can: food, silverware, and all.

The slight shift in his eyes told me all I needed to know.

However, I didn't believe he knew I was sharp enough to pick up on that small of a detail.

Pausing just a second too long, at least by my standards, the man's voice boomed again. "I know who you are, and I'm sure by now, you know I've been around for more than a few years. Whatever it is you're looking for is not here. I thought you wanted to talk business about that coin, but I was mistaken. I need you to leave my property."

"After this meeting?" I asked, figuring he was done with the pleasantries.

"Now," Bruce bellowed as the guards rushed into the room. "My business is just that, my business. Tell the Council they shouldn't throw stones in glass houses, and next time they send a lackey, tell them to send a real man."

A neat little trick I'd learned last year: I pushed my will into my hands as hellfire erupted from my palms. It wasn't enough to catch anything on fire but enough to shimmer off all the gold and silver. To top this trick off, I relaxed my sight as blood-red flames danced on my now glowing lava pupils.

Everyone froze, not only the two goons but Bruce as well. "We have a problem?" I asked as the rest of my little trick took hold. The temperature in the room went up well past 150 degrees. I told you it was a neat trick. On the back end, it also didn't take a lot of effort to do since, besides the heat, I wasn't really letting anything go.

"Raaaghh, ha, haaa, arrrghhhhhh!" Bruce exclaimed, the laugh coming from his gut. It wasn't the type of laughter to change the mood of the room but the type that said: "game on." Great, I had only been alone for a few hours, and I was already making new friends.

I turned, walking out of the office, not letting the flames in my hands or eyes go out. The two goons reluctantly shuffled out of the way as Bruce continued to laugh maniacally. "Dead men tell no tales," was the last thing I heard him say as I walked out of sight.

My walk back to the security gate at the dock was quick as the two women met me. They had obviously been told to escort me off the property. I politely went.

That man was a Mage, and he had something to do with all this. I was betting on him at least transporting the drugs. Either way, things had clearly escalated.

I walked to the end of the parking lot, activating the Evergate stone and walking into the Postern. After a minute of checking my messages, I turned to the Seekergate and walked through onto the container boat I had picked out.

According to the slip I found hanging off one of the containers' doors, the boat had recently been loaded and was soon going to leave port. I'd ended up gating into a concealed area on the back side of the ship surrounded by containers, with a stairwell leading down into the guts of the boat.

"The Port of Southampton, England," I read to myself in my best Inspector Dick Holder impersonation. He was from the East End of London, and his voice made that clear, or in his case, not so clear at times. I remember the inspector mentioning a businessman in England that had met a similar fate to the ones here. Southampton, to be precise.

"What a coincidence," I murmured, scanning the other containers. I started to focus, as something was pinging my radar. In other words, something was making the hairs on my arms stand at attention. There was magic on this ship. Strong magic.

The container on the opposite side had what looked like the same shipping tag, but it was placed on the container door like a sticker, not a tag. Something was telling me this was important, and I needed to take one of these back to the team to do more digging.

Reaching down, I pulled off the sticker to find a rather familiar symbol. A small scarlet-colored letter *T* with a smaller

H in the background presented itself, the ends of the letters flaring out. This was the symbol of the Thule Society.

Looking around, the other containers all had tags hanging off and not stuck to the door like the one in front of me. The shipping information was all the same. I reached my hand down, lightly touching the symbol with my finger, wiping it off instantly. This was a symbol to mark this container as special. I bet the others all went on their merry ways as decoys or real business while this one got on the short bus. I made sure none of the other containers in the immediate area had markings. As I suspected, they didn't.

Voices came echoing up from the stairwell. "Are you sure you saw someone up there?" a man murmured. Without my newfound heightened senses, I never would have heard that.

Shifting behind the far container, I pulled out an Evergate stone and my short staff. "I don't have to see anyone," the calculating, cold voice of Pearl sliced through the silence. The other man shut up for good measure.

Pounding footsteps came from the now lit stairwell as a streak of lightning billowed out, filling the humid air with the smell of ozone. Pearl wasn't taking any chances. I was also betting he didn't truly know who was there, just that someone with some magic in their tank was in a place they were not supposed to be. Plus, I gave off a strange vibe, being who I was.

I smacked my staff on the container as thick, billowing smoke poured out its end. The effect was immediate and jarring to anyone that was on the other side of it. The smoke was the thick kind that you could feel sticking to your body, not enough to choke a person but enough to make anyone second-guess their next step. I could fill an area the size of a small house with smoke in less than five seconds. Being that I was using my staff—a blended item—it was, unfortunately, a one-trick pony until I could recharge it.

Lightning again crackled through the air, now muffled

and dampened by the smoke. As I had learned before, Pearl's little trick would significantly decrease the amount of time I had. Today wasn't the day. I needed to get back.

I willed power into the Evergate stone, slipping through quickly into the Postern.

After another second, the gate closed, and the Postern was as if nothing had ever happened. I took a deep breath, reaching down and grabbing my phone. They would know I had taken the label off that particular container. I just wished I had been able to get inside.

CHAPTER 9

A Certain Moral Flexibility on Date Night . . .

The dining room was packed, with only the trusted individuals allowed in the secured area. It was clear the
group was in there to keep out of earshot of the others
working in the now full offices. Even Aslynn was present, sitting beside Jenny who was looking at the castor she had been
working on for her rich client. Frank and Angel stood at the
head of the table, rapidly talking to Ed and Tom while Petro
hovered over, wrinkling his nose at me.

Instead of heading back to the apartment, I had decided
to walk out of the Postern into the Atheneum, figuring what I
had just witnessed was a huge break. I still had access to the
recently installed security door in the dining room. The security lock had been added before the ball last year.

"Guess I missed the party invite," I chuckled lightly as
the room stopped and stared at me.

"Right. Close the door, Max," Ed said, all business, as
Frank continued to talk while reading off a tablet.

"Reports indicate that a Mage was videotaped on scene
prior to the fire starting on the container vessel," Frank said,
looking directly up at me, holding up the tablet with a crystal
clear picture of my face on it walking through B&B LLC's parking lot. I decided I would just call it Black Beard; by this point, it

was beyond evident that it was a modern-day—or not so modern-day—pirating organization fronting as a real company.

"Who, me...? I just went to talk about the business card we found. I literally just got back from there. I need to call Kim. She may want us to wake her up for this," I said, walking over to the table as Petro landed on my shoulder.

"You stink, boss. I can't nail it down, but whatever it is, you smell," he said, changing his mind and taking back off.

"Kim is the one that sent this," Angel said in her sultry, professional tone, interrupting Frank before he could talk. "I want to be clear with everyone in this room. After last night, the Vampire Houses are restless. Davros is even asking what we are doing, and has personally requested a meeting with Mr —" The room cut her off before I could, tired of my correction.

"GOOLSBY!" came in unison, a slight groan in their tone.

"Max, I think it's time you fill us in on your little field trip," Tom said, walking over.

"First things first. Does anyone want to guess who just tried to kill me? Bueller... Bueller... anyone?" I said sarcastically, trying to lighten the mood. Phil at least contributed with a slight chuckle. Without any guesses, I threw the business card on the table as Jenny scooped it up, quickly beating the keyboard of her laptop as if it owed her money.

I spent the next thirty minutes going over my visit, still astonished that the container ship was on fire and burning in the water. They had installed a monitor on the far wall of the room, and we all glanced at it to see updates throughout my story.

Much to my surprise, the only person lacking in questions after I was done was Tom. He was stoic, as if deep in thought. Ed walked over, sitting beside him, and I watched the two having a private conversation. I couldn't get my ears to focus on what they were saying, and figured they had a way to do that. After all, both men were hundreds of years old.

"So you think this kid is Blackbeard's son? The guy you think you ran into while in the Everwhere earlier this year?" Frank summed up in the most Captain Obvious way he could. Vs always wanted the last word.

"I'm pretty sure he was the guy, and yes. All this is connected, and now that we have this shipping information, we need to get it over to Dick and let the team at the Dunn do some homework," I said as my phone chimed with a message from Kim.

Kim was almost here. She had driven down instead of taking the gate we had set up for her to use. Regulars could use gates, however, it took a good amount of energy from them, and it wasn't cheap. Plus, it had an adverse effect on their stomachs and its contents on most occasions.

Gating was done by the use of blended items, and these were heavily monitored. Basically, you either had to be rich, or work for some organization that reported to the Council somehow. Only a select few regulars were licensed to use gates.

"I agree," Tom spoke up, finally done talking with Ed. "They knew we would be looking at that ship by the end of the day. They're sending a message. A ship that big tells me they don't really care. If the only issue had been that you didn't like this . . . Bruce, I think you called him, it wouldn't automatically mean he is in bed with the Thule Society. With Pearl showing up, though, that's another story." He paused. "Max, can I speak with you for a few minutes?" He nodded toward the door. It was clear he wanted to talk out of earshot of the others. I texted Kim, letting her know that I would be down in the offices in a few minutes.

After the short walk to my old office, which was actually Tom's, he walked over to the bar, pouring us two glasses of Magnus.

"Pearl used to work for Blackbeard," Tom said, starting the conversation after we both took a pull of our drinks. "Ever heard of the Black Pearl?"

"Like from the movies? I'm not too smart on it, but sure, I guess. Why does this feel like a flaming bag of shit is about to be dropped on my doorstep?" I asked, taking another pull.

"Because it is," Tom responded, making it clear that the connecting dots were not in our favor. "Look, if Blackbeard's back, it means that the Thule Society is getting closer to its goals. Most people don't know the true history of pirates, who they were, and what they really did. You ran into Blackbeard in Everwhere. I didn't say anything to you, but that is what I have been checking into recently. He was supposed to be, well, let's just say he was supposed to be under lock and key. Not in Everwhere figuring out a way back to Earth."

I took a minute to let the parts that I understood sink in, finally forming a question. "Devin oversees keeping those types under lock and key. I understand that. Why Blackbeard, and why now?"

"That is the question only a few of us are asking.Plus, a few others are involved in keeping those types secured. The real purpose of pirates was to smuggle souls and whatever else others wanted from the Planes. You've seen it yourself; this is the second time Lilith and that lot has tried to figure out a way to bring things over to Earth, which by now I'm sure you understand is not one of the Planes," Tom said, finishing the rest of his drink in one swallow.

"It's like an episode of Scooby-Doo. You always know it's Old Man Jenkins or some shit. I get what they are trying to do and why, to a point. The thing I don't get is why pull Goolsby and Cecil into this," I said, finally getting to the point Tom wanted to talk about. His posture shifted as he walked over to the far corner, turning on an old record player. "Praise the Lord and Pass the Ammunition" by Kay Kyser and his orchestra came on, a classic written back in 1942 in response to Japan's attack on Pearl Harbor.

I may be a youngster, but I know my music.

"That's what I can't figure out. As you said, it's clear to a point why, but not entirely. The drugs and those two goons fighting seems odd," Tom said, lightly tapping his foot.

"What if this Bruce guy wants to be the new heavy hitter in town?" I thought out loud as my phone chirped with a text from Kim simply stating *here*.

"No, that's not it." Tom sighed, letting out a breath. "I'm starting to think that Pearl and whoever are trying to bring the old gang back."

"Old gang?" I asked, often forgetting how old Tom was.

"If the souls of Blackbeard's gang are in Everwhere, they can—in theory—bring them back to life. He was a necromancer," Tom said, picking up another record and blowing dust off it as he put it on. Fats Waller came out of the old record player. "Ain't Misbehavin'," an old Harlem anthem from the 1920s, came out the coned speaker. The lack of bass created a unique, nostalgic sound.

"You're saying there truly is a way to bring people back from the dead?" I asked, finishing off my drink and standing up.

"Yes," was all Tom responded as he turned, walking over and patting my shoulder. He was remembering days gone by, and how this all was coming together. "Look, we dealt a blow to the Thule Society last year. If they are going to these lengths to get whatever they want done, it may be worse than we think. It's just that there's something we are missing here."

He dismissed me after a few minutes of contemplation. I nodded my goodbye as he turned to look at his stack of records. I walked into the dining room to find Kim talking with Petro and Phil.

"Look what the cat dragged in," Kim said as Petro flew over.

"Bruther, what was that all about?" Phil asked. He turned the radio down on the table, obviously there for his shift later.

"Looks like everyone's alive and well this evening," I replied as Petro whispered in my ear low enough for only me to hear.

"She's wearing perfume, boss. All over the place."

Petro was telling me she may have gotten a little dressed up to come over, which was obvious by her attire. I let out a breath, finally realizing I had asked her out for dinner tonight. With everything going on, it had completely slipped my mind.

Petro, sensing my idiocy, played defense. "Hey, boss, I know you wanted me to cover for you while you got ready. I'm here now."

A look of confusion that turned into realization crossed Phil's face at the same time. "Oy, yeah, bruther. We have it covered."

"Here I thought you had forgotten about me, fire boy. These two just filled me in on most of everything. At least we'll have something to talk about over drinks," Kim said, looking smug.

"Let's head to my place. I need to get freshened up, then dinner it is," I said as the other two let out a collective breath. I had, in fact, forgotten about tonight. Before we left, Ed set a meeting for the morning while they got everything over to the Dunn in England.

We gated back to the apartment, and after ten minutes, were ready to go.

"Where are you taking me tonight?" Kim asked, her mood light. I could still tell she was tired and had gone out of her way to make time tonight. She looked amazing. She was wearing a pair of tight-fitting blue jeans with slightly heeled shoes, the straps wrapped over her toes. Her red blouse was loose and hung lightly off her shoulders, showing off her sculpted physic, her days working out in a cult-like gym making themselves known. Her hair was straight, a change from its usual ponytail, and as many women in Florida would tell you, it took not only time but patience to get ready for a night out.

Kim didn't always wear the same perfume, and tonight, she smelled like Chanel; or at least that's what I thought it was, comparing it to the smelly advertisements in magazines. Of course, she had a clutch purse that I was sure had at least one gun and some other weapon in it.

"I was thinking about that seafood joint with the outside patio. OC White's," I said, seeing if she was interested.

She grinned. "I love that place. It's been forever. Hopefully they have live music outside," Kim replied as we walked out the door.

Luckily for me, the place was within walking distance and not too crowded for a Thursday. Kim reached out, taking my arm as we walked.

"Thanks for asking me out. It's been crazy lately," Kim said, starting the conversation. "How about today? I mean, really. I know the Council wants to keep us out of this."

"It's bad, from what I can tell. Bringing people back from the dead and all that kind of stuff. Plus, as you heard, I ran into Pearl today. I don't think he knew it was me though."

"I need to tell you something. It's important," Kim said as we stopped in front of the Bridge of Lions, turning left.

"Alright," I replied, taking a breath when looking over at Ordius, the once Keeper and now concrete lion, standing resolute.

"You know how the Council was watching you last year?"

"Yes ..."

"Well, I found out today that the regular government is watching you. Especially after that situation at the docks," Kim said, shuffling her feet lightly.

"That's nothing new. You mean like the local police?" I asked, seeing how big this was.

"No, the FBI and . . ." Kim paused. "The marshal's office. They want to learn everything there is to know about you. Ever since the Balance, there are more people involved in that group than I can count."

"Okay, look," I said, smiling at her. "This isn't anything new; I'm used to it. What's so important this time around?"

Kim took a visible gulp. It was time to deliver the bad news. "Councilman Darkwater was just assigned by the Council the oversight of the marshal's office division associated with OTN cases." I stood there looking at her as my jaw slightly dropped open. "Max, that means that while he is not in charge of the marshals directly, he can dictate what we do in regard to Mages and Ethereals."

I stood there with a blank look on my face, already knowing the man hated me and was more than likely the Thule Society's plant on the Council.

Taking my look as me not understanding, Kim laid it out. "The first thing he did was pull all the files related to you. I wrote some of those files. Then he presented a surveillance plan for approval this morning. I got a call from Ben, as he is in charge of that kind of stuff. He shelved it till we had some time to talk."

"Asshat couldn't get me through the Council as I'm on it, so he is taking another route. Sneaky little shit," I said, apologizing afterward for cursing in front of a nicely dressed lady. We started walking again, seeing our targeted dining location.

"Look, there's not much to worry about. It seems kind of desperate. That, or he absolutely has no clue how closely you work with our office. That's one of the reasons I wanted to make sure we got some time this evening. We probably need to keep an eye out moving forward," Kim continued as we walked up to the hostess, immediately being seated outside.

"The only reason you wanted to get some time together?" I asked, letting her know that while I appreciated the heads-up, I had become accustomed to the scrutiny. "Hey, that guy is a clown. Plus, I'm pretty sure I saw him today. I figure he's the reason my face came over your feed earlier, especially after telling me this. Guess it makes more sense now," I said, and with that, we shut down the serious talk.

We ordered drinks and listened to music while waiting for our food. Talks of planned vacations that would never happen and making fun of Phil were easy filler while waiting for our dinner. As we talked, Kim put her hand on mine, both of us enjoying the normalcy of the evening.

"Why are you so calm about this?" she asked as our plates arrived. We had both ordered the same shrimp plates.

"There's just not much I can do about other people trying to get into my business. You don't think the Council doesn't have someone keeping an eye on you?" I asked winking. "Besides me, that is."

We both chuckled lightly. "I guess you're right. I shouldn't be blind to it. All the political bullshit these days just makes this whole thing not nearly as fun as it used to be," Kim admitted, taking a mouthful of food.

"You call all the crap that happened over the past two years fun? I better step my game up on this date."

"Date? Okay, this is officially a date," Kim said, grinning as I instinctively knocked on the wooden table.

"Remember last time we went on a date?" I asked, finishing my Vamp Amber. Restaurants had started stocking certain kinds of Ethereal spirits. Not the hard stuff, but Vamp Amber was for sure the most popular.

We both sat there, shaking our heads. The night had ended up in a high-speed chase and what I was sure was a drunk troll.

"The only date," Kim reminded me.

After finishing our meals, we headed toward the Bridge of Lions to walk off the food and drinks.

Ever notice how right when things are going well on a date, you're glad you brought a sword? The screaming started as soon as we walked in front of the turn off for the bridge. Howls of pain and joy all mixed into a chorus of hate. Something was on the loose and not playing nice.

We both looked at each other before shaking our heads.

"Of course we had to talk about a normal evening," I said, pulling Durundle out from under my arm without igniting the blade yet.

Kim had already pulled out her service pistol, changing magazines to the glowing blue loaded rounds used to take care of the not so normal things. I was having trouble figuring out how she had fit everything in her mysterious purse.

I hit the SOS button on my phone and whispered into my charm, calling for Petro. After testing the enchanted charm, it had never taken more than five minutes for him to arrive; those five minutes being while he was in Jacksonville and I was in Canada. Long story . . .

We picked up the pace, running past the bridge and seeing a jet of flame erupt from the old fort followed by a guttural bellow.

"Flamey sword time," Kim said as I stopped at the entrance gates.

"Yup, flamey sword time. *IGNIS!*" I yelled as the sword decided to turn into the glowing, straight-out-of-the-forge, dripping-flame style for tonight.

Petro buzzed out of the dark like a dart. "Boss, I can't leave you alone for five minutes. I was just try—"

He was cut off by another shooting pillar of flames coming from the fort. A charred body landed roughly thirty feet away from us, bouncing off the ground. The pile of flesh sat there smoldering, the smell reaching our noses.

Kim reached back down to her purse, sending out a message on her phone. The sounds of a crash filled the air as we both looked at each other again.

"Petro, see what's going on up there. Be careful," I said as we both put in our earpieces. Kim and I shuffled out of cover, running up to the entrance. The doors had been bashed in, splinters of wood covering the ground.

"Boss, it's not good," Petro said in a calculating tone. "I think it's something from the Under."

"A demon?" I asked, not sensing one close. Yup, I could tell when one was around.

"No, something else. It's nasty," Petro said as another pillar of flame ripped through the air. He dove out of the sky, stopping in front of our faces with his chest heaving. The fire had taken him by surprise. "There are people in there. Some are hurt bad, boss."

I looked at Kim as she nodded her head, knowing what was about to happen. I returned the nod as Petro took back off into the night on instinct, more cautious this time. The sound of sirens echoed in the background.

Spinning around the entrance corner, I charged forward, slamming against the wall and finally seeing what was causing the problems.

The creature was roughly seven feet tall. Its legs were short, only lending a few feet to its overall height. A bulbous gut hung over a heavy-looking pair of armored leather pants. Two chains crossed its chest, covering an uncountable number of scars. It looked like one of those big, scary-ass monsters from *The Dark Crystal*. Its face looked like that of a boar, and two horns jutted out from the corner of its mouth. What got my attention more than the sheer hellishness of the creature, though, was its pitted cleaver. Blood was visibly dripping off its edge. The whole scene was chaotic and chilling.

Someone darted out from behind one of the doors as the creature turned, swinging its cleaver as it let out another screeching bellow. The beast thumped toward its newest victim as I noticed several other bodies lying on the ground.

I was going to end this now.

I lurched forward with Durundle in my right hand as I collected a ball of hellfire in my left. It hadn't noticed me. As the hulking mass lifted its arm to swing its weapon, I let the ball of hellfire loose at the same time as Durundle, creating an accompanying blast.

The plan immediately changed as the hellfire just absorbed into its body, the blast from Durundle only getting its attention. The attack I had launched would have melted through a car. It was the most powerful offensive hellfire spell I knew how to use. I paused, seeing the person on the other side finally reach the far wall. He was out of any immediate danger.

The beast lowered its head, opening its lower jaw and letting loose a pillar of flame directly at me. I dodged quicker than it expected, ducking into the gift shop and finishing off what was left of the door.

I took a second to refocus, realizing that neither hellfire nor getting close enough to use Durundle was going to work. "Water," I murmured to myself under my breath. "I'm by the damn ocean." While I wasn't as good at using water magic as I was at hellfire, it all landed on how much access you had to said element. I could create hellfire out of thin air. Water, on the other hand, I had to get from somewhere.

The sounds of gunfire echoed as Kim let loose a flurry of rounds, the blue ammunition whistling through the humid October night air. I motioned for her to get back. After all, I was about to pull a metric shit ton of water through the entranceway.

The rounds landed on their target. Kim was an ace shot.

The creature staggered back, not hurt but stunned. The attack and whatever was in the rounds had taken the creature off guard. I took a deep breath, focusing my will on the water and pulling it toward my body. I was guessing that since hellfire didn't do it, maybe water would. Elemental magic had a way of affecting people like that. Something would get through.

Dizziness took hold as I felt the pull of water rushing toward me. The feeling of my stomach dropping told me I had pulled too much from my reserves. Mages and Ethereals had a limited amount of Etherium, and it took time to recharge the gas tank. On a good day, I could throw hellfire around for an annoyingly long time—at least for those on the receiving end of it. Water, on the other hand, took everything I had.

Water came flooding in through the entrance as the beast lowered its jaw, directing another pillar of flame toward the dark void I was hiding in. The wall of flowing water slammed into the creature's face like a wall of bricks. It fell back with the force of the attack.

Petro came over the radio, knowing I would be spent. "You okay, boss? That was one hell of a water show."

"Yeah, I'm going to need a minute," I said as my phone started buzzing. It was a simple text from Tom: *INCOMING!* "Go to ground, buddy."

Petro took my advice, flying through the entrance now void of channeled, violent jets of water. Kim jumped in the room, her pistol at the ready, as the creature swirled around as if on cue, letting out another guttural howl as it dug its hooves into the ground, charging.

"We need to go out more often," I said hoarsely, shaking off the dull void from my little water show.

Kim's face went flat as she pulled up her pistol. For some odd reason, the expression on her face went from neutral to disbelieving in the next second. I turned around to see the charging beast shift to the left as an orange-and-black striped animal the size of a rhino drilled into it. The violence of the impact shook the gift shop.

The new addition to the circus sideshow was best described as a tigerlike battle cat. The sounds it made reminded me of the ones from Castle Rock last year, ripping into the Thule Society goons.

The beast let out a howl as it tried to get up. Its short legs made the large cat's attacks focused. The beast, not to be outdone, swung its cleaver with laser-like precision; it wasn't the first time it had fought on its back. As the battle cat raised its head—opening its insanely large mouth and showing fangs the length of a human leg—it was apparent it would be its last.

Kim, Petro, and I all looked at each other in confusion. The massive cat flung its mouth down on the beast, taking its head in its mouth with little resistance. While catlike, its legs were stacked with muscle and looked to have some type of armor covering them. The pattern on its fur looked like that of a tiger, just black and orange, no white. Its tail was capped with a silver spear.

The massive cat went flying with the beast as it crushed its head in its mouth. The spear-shaped tail slammed through its body, shooting out the other side with a spray of gore as the beast's body went limp. The battle cat backed off the disgusting mass, its reverberating purring shaking the ground. Its eyes were glowing blue as it leaped into the air and out of sight.

"What the hell was that?" I asked out loud, standing up.

"A big cat," Kim replied as she handed me a piece of gum.

"Bad breath?" She nodded. "Dessert later?"

"No, I need a drink," Kim said as Petro landed on my shoulder.

"That was a shifter; a big one. I think that other thing was a hellion," Petro informed us, taking in the scene as well.

The beast started to dissolve into a pile of e-core as the enchanted silver took over. Marshals and Mages started pouring into the fort. Angel and Frank landed on the far side as Tom walked up with Phil in tow.

"Hello, all," Tom greeted as Phil walked over, rolling his eyes and offering us a smoke after seeing our condition.

"No, thanks," Kim told Phil as I stared at Tom.

"I see you all met Oscar in all of his glory. He gets a little fired up when things from the Under show up," Tom said, walking toward the pile of goo.

"That was Oscar?" Kim started. "The same Oscar I found in that abandoned house full of cats by your parent's house?" she asked me.

"Guess so. I thought it was Ordius for a second. I don't think I'm going to let Oscar on my lap anymore," I replied as Petro started telling Phil what had happened.

"I'm going to check on the team. There are dead regulars here. This isn't going to be easy to cover up," Kim said, taking a deep breath. "Drinks later," she reminded me before walking off.

Petro and Phil caught me watching the sway of her hips, the two letting off various whoops and caws at me.

"You guys?" I asked, looking at the two and flipping them off politely.

"I've still got duty . . ." Phil drawled out.

"Petro?"

"I'm still on baby-making duty. We were right in the middle of su—" I cut him off.

"Alright, tomorrow then. Hell, we all probably need some rest anyway. Any word on Cecil?" I asked, moving out of the way for a group of local police.

"He's been called to the Vampire Courts," Frank said, making the three of us talking jump.

"Cecil will be back in a day or two. With the deaths of his men at the clubhouse and at Goolsby's, the meeting will be more of an accountability discussion," Angel continued, generating another jump from the group.

"Let me ask you two something. Is Goolsby going to get some blowback from all this?" I asked, spitting out the quickly hardening cheap gum.

"Nasty habit," Angel said, looking at me.

"Chewing gum?"

"No, spitting," she replied before she realized what she had just implied. Even Frank started to laugh as Angel turned what I assumed was red before storming off. Her limp was still slightly visible. I was pretty sure I knew how she got that.

Phil wiped tears from his eyes before lighting up another smoke. "Bruthers, you know she can kick all our asses. Well, except maybe mine."

A small rock flew out of the dark corner of the courtyard, hitting Phil in the back of the head, the thrown object smacking hard enough to knock the cigarette out of his mouth.

"I don't know yet," Frank finally answered. "Something's not lining up. I think if no more Vamps die, things should be manageable. Any more deaths and things could go south quickly."

Tom walked up with a small jar full of e-core. "Got what I needed. I'm heading back. Max, mind if I hitch a ride?"

"Sure," I said, pulling out an Evergate stone. "I have a few questions about Oscar. You know, the cat that used to sleep in my bed at night when I was a kid."

CHAPTER 10

Home Sweet Home

T he faces of the prior leaders of the Atheneum and Postern stared at me as we walked up the stairs in the old house, the sounds of water splashing from the small water feature in the foyer. Tom's home was an odd addition to the Atheneum.

It was roughly 10:00 p.m. by the time we finally got settled in the old office with a drink in hand. We had seen James on the way over from the Postern, and I'd promised as always to have him over for drinks.

"So . . ." I said as I leaned back in the red leather chair, letting the tension out of my body now that we were back at Tom's office.

"Oscar!" Tom yelled as banging noises came from what once was my little room. I loved that space.

I turned to see a roughly five-foot, overly tan middle-aged man walk out of the room wearing sweatpants and a baggy T-shirt. The T-shirt didn't hide the fact that he was layered in muscle, resembling Arnold Schwarzenegger in his Conan prime.

"Max," Oscar's purring yet cheesy voice came out. "Glad you didn't need any help tonight."

I stared as Oscar walked over, sitting down. A smug grin lingered on his face, and I noticed a light layer of fur barely visible covering his body. Oscar licked his forearm, smoothing it over his face.

"Why is this the first time I'm seeing any of this?" I asked, taking a pull of my Vamp Amber, letting out a burp.

Tom spoke up as Oscar continued grooming himself. The whole thing was as awkward as I'd heard shifters could be. I had yet to meet a shifter in human form other than Al to the best of my knowledge. His eyes were hypnotic, deep blue to the point of glowing. You could almost see the magic coming off his body.

"Well, before you turned thirty, that was a no-brainer. Over the past two years, it's been by choice. Oscar has been working for some time to get off the radar of several people," Tom said, filling in the gaps.

Oscar stopped, looking up. "I only shift when a demon or a hellion is around—kind of a nervous tick. I've not had to worry about that for at least twenty years. That seems to be changing lately. I can smell it in your blood, by the way."

"About that," I said as Oscar grinned a fanged smile. "Is this as human as you get?"

"I'm relaxing. If needed, I can push a little harder. I prefer to stay a normal old house cat. I don't age that way, and people are more prone to pet me," Oscar purred as Tom handed him a drink.

"Oscar is at least nine hundred years old. At least I think. I found him as a cute little kitten," Tom said, reaching over and scratching behind his ear.

The whole scene was weird, but my night had degenerated into another episode of *The Twilight Zone* by this point.

"Max, I've noticed something," Oscar said, thankfully smacking Tom's hand off. "You seem to always be asking the wrong people the right questions, and the right people the wrong questions."

I sat there with a puzzled look on my face. "Coming from a man—well, cat—sitting here licking himself?"

"He means you need to figure out what the hell is going on, and fast. Not to mention that we need to remember who is pulling the strings here," Tom replied, looking down at his watch.

"Lilith. You're saying we need to get to her," I said, noticing Leshya walking in with a tray of snacks. "Thanks, I've missed your cooking." Leshya just smiled before walking off. She looked different. I couldn't put my finger on it.

"Maybe it's her, maybe it's this Darkwater guy, which I doubt. I'm not sure, but Oscar has a point. This game of cat and mouse has been going on for a couple of years now. As soon as I heard Blackbeard might be involved, I knew it was time. Oh, not to mention that a hellion legionnaire showing up is probably worse than a demon, but we can talk about that later. The Council is meeting in the morning. You need to be there," Tom said, standing up.

"No way I'm missing that one. I was thinking it was about damn time they brought out the big guns, especially since Ned's gone missing," I said grudgingly.

"About that, it's not widely known yet. It may freak people out; you know how everyone has been after the Balance. Jamison should be in town soon to take care of Aslynn. She likes you, in some odd, big brother kind of way. Anyway, the last thing we need is the Council thinking regulars are kidnapping full-blooded Fae. We wanted to see if we could locate him first, but we are reporting it officially in the morning," Tom replied, mirroring my sentiment.

The two of us took deep breaths while Oscar excused himself.

"Hey, I heard Sarah is going to be working at FA's?" I asked, changing the subject. Tom walked over to his replacement desk, setting down his drink. It was curved and looked like it had been made by the same person who had made King Arthur's not-so-round desk.

Sarah was a sore subject for Tom. She was one of the first people I'd met at FA's other than Trish. In reality, she had drugged me so Tom could make sure I would not freak out when I found out about the world on the other side of things, as I used to call it. They had wiped my memory, only to give it back to me when they deemed the time was right. The entire episode had come to light after we'd destroyed the Fountain of Youth.

I had only seen her once since last year, and it was only in passing. According to Tom, she lived on the Plane, and was only here to help him with something. I was curious about Sarah, as Tom clearly cared for her. Tom, as always, was full of secrets.

"She is. I'm not saying it's the best idea, but it's time she leaves the Plane for good. I think you have company," Tom said, looking reflectively at me. He had a way of doing that.

My phone dinged with a message from Kim. *I'm at your apartment. Where the hell are you?*

I quickly grabbed a cucumber cream cheese sandwich, standing up. Leshya knew they were one of my favorite snacks, and had made them knowing I would be here. The creamy, soft flavor mixed with the spices sprinkled on top. The crunchy, perfectly sliced cucumber was as fulfilling as a cold beer at 5:00 p.m. on a Friday. They were small and cut in perfect squares on fluffy—what I assumed—Wonder Bread. Knowing she was probably watching somehow, I took a bite, letting her know it was a fantastic treat. Oscar obviously also liked the sandwiches; he was already halfway through the tray as I walked out of the office, gating back to the apartment.

"We need to grab a drink," Kim said as soon as I walked out the gate. She had changed into a clean pair of jeans and a Rolling Stones T-shirt. I liked the look on her.

"Woman after my own heart," I replied, dropping my coat on the desk. "I'm going upstairs to get cleaned up. I'll be down in five."

After five minutes of banging and rushing around the bathroom, including putting on way too much cologne, I walked downstairs, ready for what I had figured was the last relaxing moment we would have for a long time.

FA's didn't have much of a crowd for the first time in months. I assumed the hellion probably had something to do with it. People knew that St. Augustine was the main FA's and word gets around.

"Slow night?" I barked as Trish looked over, a worried look on her face. "Bad Mouth" by Fugazi blared through the jukebox. Trish snapped her fingers as the radio turned down. Something was up. Kim looked over, surprising me by grabbing my hand. She knew it as well.

We walked up to the bar as Trish planted two Vamp Ambers on the bar top. "Thanks?" I said quizzically. Kim and I had a lot to talk about, but it could wait a few minutes. "What's up?" I asked, taking a pull of my beer. Trish was, from what I could tell, some type of Egyptian demigod. Or at least that's what everyone liked to think. I was more along the lines of believing it.

Trish took a deep breath, pulling out a glass of Elf Juice from under the bar. I grimaced, not being a fan of the stuff. It was an acquired taste. It also had an effect on regulars that could only be described as that of a Pan Galactic Gargle Blaster. If you don't know what that is, then chances are you'll probably never try an Elf Juice.

"I need to show you something," she said pensively, walking around the bar. Kim and I stood up, going to the far end of the bar top as Trish raised it.

"Kim, I need you to understand something. I know Max's dirty little secrets," Trish said as I smirked at her, the both of us walking behind the bar for the first time. The view of the place was clear and eclectic. "We all have them. I trust you, but I'm not sure this is the best thing for you to see right now. This is my dirty little—well, big secret. And you betray my trust only once."

"I give you my word. Hell, that's about all some of us have these days," Kim said as Trish, reading something in the statement, nodded in approval.

Kim and I looked at each other as we stood in front of the kitchen door labeled "Employee Only." Note "employee" was not plural. We were about to meet Amon, FA's world-famous cook. No man, woman, child, Mage, Fae, or V had ever stepped foot in the kitchen, let alone met the cook. A sinking sensation dropped in my stomach. I was actually more nervous than I'd been earlier.

Trish took a steadying breath and opened the door. Oddly enough, there was a solid silver and iron door behind that one with several intricate-looking locks etched into it. She raised her hand, murmuring an invocation as the mechanisms smoothly slid open one by one.

As the door opened, warm yet clear light spilled from the kitchen. It wasn't LED-bright, but it wasn't dull either, creating a calming effect. Rich smells from supremely prepared food filled the air. A light bang came from around the far end, from the direction of what appeared to be the freezer.

There were big grooves in the floor from what looked like a large blade being lodged in it. Memories of last year when Ying Yue—the leader of the Gate Mages Guild—had decided to stop by and size me up came to the surface. Trish had yelled for Amon, and the distinct sound of a blade slamming into the floor flooded back into my memory. He hadn't come out but had been about to.

"Amon, we have guests," Trish said, picking up a dirty towel and setting it in a sanitizer bucket. The kitchen was organized and clean. Amon took pride in his work. A steak sandwich sat in the window, ready to go out and smelling amazing. The odor of grilled onions and peppers caught up to my watering mouth.

A rumbling yet articulate voice came from the freezer as the door swung open. "Max and the brave one," Amon said as he stepped out, mist surrounding the large figure as he stood fully upright.

Kim and I both tensed up, but didn't dive for cover. The spitting image of the hellion we'd battled earlier today stood in front of us with an immaculately white cooking apron on, holding a large cleaver in one hand and half a cow in the other.

The similarities were striking. Tusks protruded from a larger than normal maw, rings and various jewels dangling off them. A large, overly round belly protruded over stumpy legs, Amon's torso making up most of his mass and height. While splotchy and off-colored, his skin was better taken care of than the other hellion. Amon's eyes looked human, with red pupils slightly shadowed by an overhanging forehead.

This was the creature that had made some of the best food I had ever tasted. I immediately looked at his hands, one outstretched in placation as he lumbered forward. A grin crossed my face.

"It's a pleasure," I said, taking his interestingly articulated large hand in mine. Kim stood there, still registering the sight. It wasn't lost on me that regulars were still adjusting. While Kim was more acclimated than most, the sight of a hellion was enough to take anyone off guard.

After a pause, Kim took a step forward. "Sir, it's nice to meet you."

Amon bellowed loudly, "Gaffawaaa!" The porcelain dish

stacked by the window waiting to be served shook. Trish followed with a slight snicker.

"Sirrrrr, ha, I work for a living," Amon drawled out, getting my attention. It was a reply someone who had served in the military would give.

Kim grinned, the mood shifting. I was betting it was Trish doing that little trick she did.

"Well, now you know. Even more, I think you all need to talk," Trish said, walking over and picking a chip out of a bowl only to have Amon snap the towel out of his pocket at her with lightning speed.

"Ouch!" Trish howled playfully.

"That's for the guests, love," Amon said as Trish stuck out her tongue. The two were fast friends, the type you could tell had been through enough together to never question each other. The banter reminded me of Ed and Tom.

"Military? Enlisted?" I asked, second-guessing my own interest in tasting a chip.

"Let's go in the back," Amon suggested as he lumbered around the corner. The room on the other side was like something out of *World of Warcraft*. Deep, rich-colored rugs made from silk hung from the walls and covered the floors as large, overly ornate chairs sat in various locations around a curved desk, looking again like Arthur's and Tom's desk. I was starting to think Rooms To Go had had a sale in the 1500s.

Dull light came from actual open flames in two large open-pit fireplaces. On top of one sat a slat for, I was guessing, heat exhaust. The scene only got weirder from there when I realized he was actually pulling out a pizza from the opening.

"Hungry?" Amon asked, slapping the pizza on the stone table in the center of the room. The smells that filled the air caused a bliss similar to that of one's first kiss. Rich meats and the scent of herbs and spices immediately generated drool. I was watching how agile he was with his large hands, almost surgical.

We all sat down around the table as Amon moved the large chairs. Trish was smiling, obviously knowing what was coming. Amon pulled out the giant pitted butcher knife, slamming it onto the poor pizza with hammering force, making the room shake. He put his hand out, shrugging in placation. Trish pulled four beers from behind her back, setting them on the table as she always did.

Kim looked over, grinning. "Best date night ever," she said as I blushed. I agreed. It had been several hours since the run-in at the fort, and all that exertion had, in fact, brought back my appetite.

After a few minutes of silent eating—yes, his food was that good—Amon spoke up, answering my questions. "I thought you would like that one, Max. I was in the military: the hellion legions."

Trish interrupted. "Amon was a hellion general," she said, taking a pull of her Vamp Amber.

I whistled. "What do you know about what happened tonight?" I asked, getting to the point. I wanted to know about Amon, but the fact that Trish and Amon knew what had happened already set off all kinds of bells and whistles.

Trish responded as Amon nodded at her. "You are going to find out soon that the people in the fort were, in fact, regular politicians. They were holding some kind of fundraising event tonight, from what they said. A group of them came in here earlier. There were a few Mages with them, as well as a V whom I didn't know. I could tell the senator was not part of the magical community. As you know, I have severely restricted regulars' access into the Fallen Angel. Present company excluded, of course."

"Okay, so he's a politician and came in for a drink. Why does that matter?" I asked as Kim ate her second piece of the thin-crusted masterpiece. Amon's grin widened upon our every bite.

"He came in not having any trace of magic in him. I handed him the old menu; you remember, the ones that only work for magic types?" Trish said. Memories from the first time Ed had come into FA's with me flooded back like the nostalgic taste of cereal you hadn't tasted in twenty years.

"I have a feeling that might have changed?" I said, starting to think about the number of people I had run into over the past week taking Kracken, the ever-popular drug that would give regulars a taste of magic, if even for only a few minutes.

"Well, he was talking with this V, and they went off to the bathroom. When he came back, the old, normal menu was in front of him. This time when he touched it, well, you can guess what happened next. He got all excited, as did the others with him. I checked and verified. It was Kracken," Trish said as Amon leaned back, his belly making odd noises.

Kim spoke up, finally settling into the odd day. "He was high on the drug, then left. Could you tell if it was spiked?"

"That's how I knew something was off. Look, I ignore things at times. When Senator Powell walks through your doors, you take notice. I know people will be people. In the past, Kracken was not so frowned upon. Amon called me to the kitchen and told me he could feel hellion magic," Trish said as Amon nodded his head in confirmation.

"I take it that's not normal," I said inquisitively as Kim let out a whistle at the name.

Trish looked at me, pursing her lips. "You do understand that the hellion legions have been locked away for thousands of years, right?"

"Sure," I responded slowly, starting to think back to the stories my mother used to tell me. "The Old Gods used them against their masters. Then, when it was time for them to take their promised, rightfully acquired place on Earth—"

"Midgard," Amon corrected. Kim and I looked at each

other, starting to see larger implications.

"Midgard, the Old Gods tricked them, working with the lords of the Under and the Over, Heaven and Hell, whatever you call it, in a kind of peace treaty that would prove as always to favor the Old Gods. Anyway, so far, we've been dealing with these pirate-looking types. Why suddenly a hellion?" I asked, knowing the two already had that information in their back pockets. After all, supernatural bartenders had a flair for knowing things, especially when they were your landlady.

Amon spoke up, patting his belly. "Pirates, humph," he gurgled. "More like Soul Dealers. They broke a few hellions out of the Under many years ago. If the one around tonight had tusks, he was a general like me, and more than likely part of that gang. The others ... well, let's just say they are good at only a few things," Amon said as his gaze shifted to the kitchen.

"Great, so a senator, Vampire, and Mage walk into a bar," I jested. The joke took hold for once, garnering a chuckle out of the group.

Kim spoke up next. "The senator got the drug from the V, who I bet is connected to Cecil. That idiot. Even after everything that's happened the past few days, he's still running the stuff. The drug had the soul of a hellion somehow fused to it. That pile of goo in the middle of the fort was Senator Powell. Fucking great ..." Kim sighed.

"I would say that is a fair assessment," Trish said, looking over as Amon stood up. "We have company."

We said our goodbyes, heading back out into the bar area as the warded door clanked shut behind us. I realized it wasn't for the protection of others but for the protection and secrecy of Amon.

Looking around, it was clear the marshals and Council Mages had figured out the score of the night. More to the point, where the good senator had been that evening.

Kim turned, quickly grabbing my hand out of the sight

of others. "I had an amazing if less than stellar night, but I need to get some rest. I'll see what's going on here, then if you don't mind, can I crash on your couch?"

I stood frozen in place. *Did she just ask to have a sleepover?* "Uh, yeah, sure," I said, rubbing the back of my neck.

Trish looked over, smiling as I walked past the food service window as dishes started clanking, the smell of newly cooked food already wafting into the room.

CHAPTER 11

Die, Die, Die, My Darling . . .

"Good morning, sunshine," Kim's voice echoed down the hall. The smell of bacon and coffee wafting into my room brought me to immediate attention. Or was it the fact that Kim was cooking me breakfast? We had both been exhausted and had gone our separate ways last night, crashing for the evening.

The odd thing about the magical community was they liked to stay up later than most of the regular population. Sleeping in till around noon was acceptable, as was staying up till around 3:30 a.m. I was still on a normal schedule in most cases, but had also become accustomed to later nights.

"Morning," I said after quickly getting cleaned up before walking down the hall. Kim was standing there in one of my PD T-shirts and, well . . . I was staring. The laundry room was a couple of doors down, and she had helped herself to my clean shirt pile. There was something about a woman in your kitchen cooking breakfast in one of your rock band T-shirts that just got you in the feels.

"I got a text from Phil," Kim said, grinning. My obvious preoccupation with watching her prance around the room was clear. "He said you are all supposed to be at the Council chambers in an hour."

"What time is it?" I asked, taking the black cup of coffee from her. I paused as we both held the cup.

"Time for you to take a cold shower," she said jokingly. "Ten in the morning. You're supposed to be there at eleven."

"You're not coming?" I asked as she set a plate of bacon and eggs on the table for each of us.

"No. Did you listen to anything I said last night?" Kim chided, shaking her head. "Darkwater now has oversight of a portion of the marshals' team. I'm not sure it's a good time for me to just be showing up with you unless I'm asked to. I'd rather us appear to be separate. Ever since you peeled off from the NCTS and CSA, they have lost some visibility on what you are doing. Let's just keep it that way for now."

Kim was making perfect sense. While I didn't like the idea, not putting her in the middle of some unknown vendetta was good enough for me. Plus, after last night, I was pretty sure Darkwater knew we were out together, or at least fighting the same monster. For all I knew, he had been the one behind it. Over the past year, we'd spent time looking into his background, figuring out he had been the recipient of the water from the Fountain of Youth. While we couldn't prove it, we had a pretty good idea where he had gotten it from.

We parted ways as I messaged Tom and Ed. Before departing, we mapped out what to do about Bruce Teach and B&B LLC. The plan was simple: see how the shipments being transported by B&B were tied to Goolsby and Cecil. We would know by sundown.

Kim left, giving me a relatively close hug and peck on the cheek. Progress! It was a great thing. Before she took off, Kim received a text from the local news station looking for a comment. This one would not go unnoticed.

Before heading over to the Atheneum, I decided to give Belm a little ring. Time to go on the offensive.

◆ ◆ ◆

"Bruther," Phil hesitated. Petro had already given me a play-by-play of his rather sorted activities the day prior. James had been standing there listening to Petro, along for the ride. "You hear anything about Ned yet?"

"No, I was about to ask you the same thing," I said as we all stood around the gate behind the entrance. Tom and Ed had a closed-door meeting before I arrived, getting the information dump from last night's events. The two men stood outside the door looking at us, having a private conversation before walking over.

James was on duty, standing there taking it all in. He had become a trusted member of the team. While more of a satellite member, he was still in the gang. He also got stuck managing the front security entrance most of the time due to being a regular and fairly new to the marshals team. He was a young genius that had graduated early from college at seventeen. James had been recruited early to work for the Feds. Being a young black man not old enough to drink, with an IQ higher than anyone else but Jenny, he quickly made his name known. Not to mention he was game when fighting big scary monsters. Being a regular hadn't stopped him from working his way into the new world. When the Balance had finally occurred, he had been disappointed. He had known something everyone else hadn't, at least at the time.

"I'm not going to lie. I'm kind of glad I missed the whole thing," James said as he put his finger to his ear, getting called back to the front security entrance that had awkwardly been installed in front of the fountain, looking as out of place as a face tattoo on a nun.

"James, keep your ears and eyes open. Things might get a little dicey in Jacksonville," I said as he walked off, saluting lazily.

We turned our attention back to Ned. "Jamison stopped by last night before I finally got some rest. He doesn't think it's good. That lot has a way of telling, I think. But who knows? I only have half-Fae blood. I can't even tell when my socks are dirty," Phil said, attempting to lighten the mood.

"Right, gentlemen," Ed said as he and Tom walked over, patting me on the shoulder. "This isn't like the last few times we have been dealing with the Council. We need to let them know what we can. With Ned missing, it has escalated. The Supreme Council is involved, so a few of them will be in the meeting this morning."

"So we're just supposed to be one big happy family after everything that happened last year?" I asked.

Tom cleared his throat. "Darkwater and Goolsby will not be present at the meeting. The group assembled today is one we must work with." Tom had spoken and made it final. That was enough for me.

We walked over to the gate as Tom waved his hand, opening the portal. The cool, damp air of the Council chambers filled my lungs, a departure from Florida's humid fall environment.

After a short walk, I looked over to see Mouth standing at the door, talking with a woman. Upon further inspection and Phil's deviation from our strut into the chambers, it was clear she was one of Ying's people, the tall, stern-looking slim woman from FA's. Her name was Kristi. She and Phil had kept in touch off and on.

Mouth let out a rumbling throaty chuff. "Figured you two stiffs would be here."

"Nice to see you too, big guy," I retorted. The two of us had come to an odd type of professional truce. After fighting alongside each other on two occasions and me saving his boss, he had finally stopped threatening to pound my face into meatloaf. He was called Mouth because he would more than likely rather be punching you in the mouth than dealing with you. He was an ogre.

"Piss. Off . . ." Mouth drawled out, slightly grinning.

Phil shook Kristi's hand as the two made "call me later" signals with their fingers. We walked past the open doors into the main chambers, only to be shuffled off by Bull into a more private side chamber. I called the tall, bald man "Bull" basing his looks off the bailiff from an old sitcom called *Night Court*.

"Bruther, I think old Mouth there likes you. He at least respects you now," Phil commented, playing off his excitement on seeing Kristi.

"Yeah, the funny thing is I like him too. Calls it how it is, even when he's making fun of me," I said as we walked into the room.

Ana, Titus, Davros, Carvel, Ying, and Trish all sat at the U-shaped table's far end. "Trish?" I asked louder than intended as she looked up, smiling.

Bull corrected me. "That's Supreme Councilor Patricia to you." I looked over to see Ed and Tom grinning. Those asshats had known all along and had never bothered to tell me. I noticed the absence of the short, blonde Fae from my trial.

Petro, who had been riding on my shoulder, leaned over to whisper, "Guess we now know how your ass keeps getting pulled out of the fire, boss." He was right.

The team took their seats on the far end. Jenny had stayed behind and was working on samples of the drug with Macey, Lacey, and Casey. Try saying that ten times real fast. Frank, Angel, and another V I hadn't met before stood slightly off to Davros's right in the far corner. After the deaths of several Vampires, it was clear a line was being drawn in the sand.

Ana spoke first, as was often the case. "Good afternoon, everyone. I'll keep this short and to the point. As we all know, someone has been spiking Kracken. The unfortunate piece of this is that, as of last night and thanks to the team at the Atheneum, we have confirmed that necromancy is being used. This is, of course, to tap into the Everwhere and bring souls back to this Plane."

It was clear not everyone in the room knew this. Even Carvel shuffled in his seat. While he was still an angry old Mage, he would always do the right thing in the end, as Ed had stated. His pointed beak-like nose flared, taking in air.

Titus picked up where she had left off, his deep, gravelly voice fitting his large stature. "Per Max's confirmation on the docks with the packing slip and the picture of the symbol, it's clear the Thule Society is involved. We are looking into other assets that may be at play here."

I interrupted, much to the approval of Tom. "You mean Goolsby?" I asked, getting away with not calling him by his title, having a lower one myself.

Taking a deep breath, Titus continued, "Yes, we have strong evidence to suspect his involvement. I want to be clear: he may be an unwilling participant. Councilman Goolsby owns several businesses, and at times, is not privy to all that goes on."

Phil let out an audible snort, sharing my own sentiment in his own glorious way.

"That leads me to Ned," Titus said, gaining the laser focus of all the parties in the room. The man was well respected, and I could see why. He had even taken me under his wing as my sponsor that first year.

Tom spoke up. "What is the Supreme Council doing about this?"

Davros raised a finger as he often did, taking control of the room. "We are looking in all corners of this Plane and others. Our initial beliefs are that he is either hiding or no longer with us." That was the most Captain Obvious statement I had heard in months. I looked over to see Tom chewing on his lip, deep in thought. "We are putting all the assets we have toward finding him. Either way, we will know soon," Davros continued, following it up by the weirdest statement I would think one could hear out of an ancient Vampire's mouth. "I would suggest some prayers to whomever."

He was sending out a message of hope as best he could without showing doubt. I respected him. Plus, he also had some hellhounds I had rounded up for him. I liked animal people. Last year, we thought that one of the creatures had been killed in a blast from Terrance during our run-in saving Carvel. We actually found it sometime later in Florida, scaring people on the beach. It had survived, come back to life, and from what we could tell, swum across the Atlantic ocean searching for its partner.

I spoke up again. "Everyone cool with this pirate guy, Bruce, running around? I'm pretty sure he's the one at least shipping the stuff."

The room looked at me. As always, I'd jumped to conclusions. Fortunately, the room had learned I was often correct.

"We confirmed the company's ships have been moving Kracken. We need to discuss that with the team here today. We have coordinated with the Dunn, and are tracking another shipment heading to England. If there's a way to get on that ship undetected, we plan on doing so," Ying replied.

"I thought the drugs were coming here from overseas?" I asked, confused.

Carvel cleared his raspy throat. "The problem isn't the drug itself. It's what's being done to it. It seems that the Thule Society is shipping something overseas, but we can't find a trace of incoming shipments having any issues or being identified as hot."

"You all talk rather casually about this drug. Look, I get it. It used to not be a big deal. Things are changing though, and the way things used to be aren't going to work anymore," I said as Trish nodded in approval. My gut was starting to tell me that the retirement plan of others on the Council included the sale of Kracken. I'd also noticed the reluctance to mention the hellion. It was clear what it was.

"We are working through a plan with the Dunn, as noted. The details will be privy only to a small group," Carvel said quickly.

Tom looked around the room. "I'm working on finding where this stuff is being energized and blended. It's not a simple task. And I am betting there is a strong necromancer in the mix here."

Frank motioned to Bull as a few of us shifted our gazes at the light interruption. The two men murmured to each other as Angel walked out of the room.

Frank walked over, leaning down and talking with Davros. The group started to murmur.

"Everyone, there appears to be a situation in Jacksonville involving Councilman Goolsby. The Night Stalkers are being deployed," Davros said in a matter-of-fact tone.

Ana spoke up quickly. "Ed, send a group from your team to assist."

Phil and I looked at each other before standing up. The meeting hadn't taken long, and by the looks of it, only a handful of people would remain after we left. Tom and Ed knew what I did, plus the details from last night. It was clear by Ana's synopsis they already knew the score. I would get the details later.

Ed nodded as Phil, Petro, and I left the room. Mouth stood there as Kristi looked up. They both had their phones in hand, getting some type of alert. I looked at Mouth as he rolled his stony eyes. "Let me guess. You need me to—" Mouth was cut off by Carvel wailing out.

"I need you to go with Max to the docks. If Councilman Goolsby is in danger, please work to ensure his safety as he would ours."

Mouth grimaced as he shook his head. Carvel looked over at the three of us, giving us a slight nod. He hated that after saving his life, his nine hundred-year-old mother had taken a liking to me. She was a fantastic pie maker and still sent one once a month to the shop.

Kristi stood there expectantly. "Um, you coming, lass?" Phil asked as the stern woman smiled. "I'm driving," she replied, holding her palm out and opening a portal. She looked down at her phone, clearly receiving a text from Ying for her to go while the grown-ups made plans.

Gating like this was impressive. Gate Mages were fairly rare, and as of one year ago, their numbers had been reduced significantly. Kristi, for example, could gate to a location much like the Seekergate. Of course, my understanding was that there were a few more limitations.

We gated through to the far end of the Council chambers, saving a few minutes' walk. From there, we gated out to a field, followed by a patch of woods directly beside the docks. The sound of gunfire filled the air.

"I'm going to need a vacation after this week, Mouth. Any thoughts?" I asked as he just huffed, pulling out his signature twin MP5Ks, better known as 9mm funeral-home accelerators.

The quick gating had made me a little unfocused. We all took a moment to get caught up. And by "we," I meant Phil and I. Petro was hovering in the tree line already with Mouth and Kristi. We joined them after a minute.

"I think we beat the Night Stalkers here, boss," Petro said as we put in our communicators. Only Phil, Petro, and I had them. It was clear that Mouth didn't like being left out.

A rustle in the bushes behind us gained our immediate attention. Turning around, we were met by four fully suited black figures. Large white squares with a circle and crucifix in the middle adorned their armored chest plates. The Order Society had been hiding in the bushes where we just happened to land.

The Order Society was an organization that was best summed up as a new-age version of the Knights Templar, a.k.a. Crusaders. In reality, they were a modern-day group of reasonable zealots sworn to protect humankind from the evils of magic. In some ways, current events had justified their existence, and after the Balance, one part of the accords had acknowledged their existence. As one of the Council's regular members, Goolsby represented them, and had been vital in their inclusion. Rumor also had it he was still one of the senior leaders of the group.

These were the men and women that handled things if the magical world broke the rules against mankind. This included protecting certain aspects of society, such as artifacts and locations of significant importance.

"Hey, guys, super neat outfits. It looks like these bushes were already occupied. We can find some others?" I said as a silver-infused electrified net shot out from the far end of the group. A tall man had walked up, pointing the long tube holding the magic-grounding net. Normal silver was enough to shut most magic types down. Electrified silver would just make us drop on the ground drooling.

The wonderful thing about ogres was that they were uncommonly large. As the first net shot out, another foot soldier on the far end turned to point his at Mouth. The shot lost its coverage, bouncing off Mouth's back, who was holding back and had yet to shoot anything, much to my surprise.

I was fully under the first net, as was Kristi. Phil was down but had managed to punch a hole in the ground large enough to drop into. By the feeling underfoot, he was about to generate a whole new version of *Tremors*.

I looked over to see Mouth pulling up his weapons as the other two soldiers began moving. As soon as the action started, it ended. It was as if time had stopped, freezing everyone in place. It became clear why as ten Night Stalkers walked out from all angles. What caught my eye was the similarities in the armored uniforms, the Vampire special forces obviously pulling it off better. I also noticed neither party had pulled one of the five guns each of them carried. My favorite Night Stalker, Two, walked over, picking up the net with a katana she'd pulled from behind her back. I knew it was Angel, but I would never give it away, and she would never tell me. The slight limp, while improving, was still present.

"Alright, now that we have that out of the way," I chimed in as Two shook her head.

"I am Guardian Peter. We are not here to interfere in Council business." The slightly modulated voice came from the screened shield hiding his face.

"Understood," Two replied as she looked back at the warehouse on the far end of the dock. An explosion rocked the larger of the two buildings by the water as the sound of gunfire erupted.

The four Guardians lurched forward as the Night Stalkers and Mouth stood in their way.

"Phil, where you at?" I asked, directing my voice toward the ground.

"Bruther, say the word," Phil said. I could feel Two and the others all rolling their eyes.

"Now?" I said quizzically. Phil jumped out of the ground, two feet behind the group. He was covered in mud, and what you could see of his skin glowed. We all looked as he pulled out a soggy pack of cigarettes. The tattoos on the side of his neck started glowing.

Kristi walked over, pulling out her own pack and handing him one. "I think dinner and a drink are in or," she said, turning back to the tree line after winking at Phil.

"Guys, I think this is the part where we go." I approached the tree line, shaking my head.

Two held up her hand as she pointed toward the docks. The Night Stalkers all launched into the air, the brush around us shaking from the force.

"You guys have any neat tricks like that?" I asked as I looked over at Kristi. She had opened up a gate before the words finished getting out of my mouth, and we walked through, coming out on the back side of the larger warehouse.

A Vamp came flying down from the roof, its head turning to mist in the next second from a bullet I supposed originated from the tree line we had just left. *Note to self, limit yourself to only one smartass comment at the Guardians moving forward.*

Mouth kneeled as I pulled out Durundle, yelling, "Ignis!" Another jolt shook the building.

"Bruther, we need to go to ground. Petro, we clear?" Phil asked through the communicator. The other two had figured we were communicating with our field intelligence satellite, better known as Petro.

"Clear," Petro chirped as I saw him fly back up to the far end of the building. I raised my hand, pointing down the stairs as we all pushed against the wall with Phil leading the way down. Several spatters of gunfire erupted on the other side of the concrete wall. It was the familiar sound of the hushed barks from one of the Night Stalkers pistols. I walked up beside Phil as he shook his head.

"Can't see a damn thing, don't know who's who," he said, working to find a target with his pistol. Yes, we had finally gotten him to stop walking around with his shotgun.

I jumped around the corner as smoke rolled toward our position from the far end of the room. Two sword-wielding—you guessed it—pirates charged directly behind the smoke. My recently heightened senses allowed me to see through the obvious concealment spell.

As I rushed the fog pulling Durundle overhead, the two figures split off as another body appeared in front of me. On instinct, I slashed the sword downward, the blade hissing through the air as sparks of hellfire flew in all directions, cutting through my target like a katana through warm butter. I split the figure in half from top to bottom. The body stood in place for a second before falling to the ground.

"Shit," I said, not knowing who I had truly just cut in half. I rushed back around the corner as Mouth rattled off several rounds toward the far end of the dock. He was surgical with his submachine guns. Two gunmen were positioned on the other side of a power transformer, and the fact that the two goons hadn't hit us told me they were regulars, and more than likely, not going to be a problem moving forward.

"We need to get this under control now. I don't know who's who," I said loud enough for everyone to hear me.

As the words came out of my mouth, another louder, deep voice came from the other side of the wall. "It's the boss. He's dead!" the person exclaimed. Two and four other Night Stalkers came running down the stairwell we had just left, sleek guns in both hands.

I pointed at the opening at the far end of the wall Phil was still standing at. Two blurred around the corner as several thumps and sounds of weapons being dropped echoed. As if someone had flipped a switch, the gunfire stopped, and the sound of silence took hold of the recent violence.

Petro flew down as Mouth, Kristi, and Phil walked around the corner. I looked at the body I had given a split personality to, immediately feeling the blood drain from my face. I had cut Cecil in half, effectively killing a connected V. Even shittier than that, I had done Goolsby's dirty work once again, even if in a move of self-preservation. The entire event seemed orchestrated. Mouth walked around the corner holding two of Goolsby's men, both having been shot in the legs. He had played it safe. Me, on the other hand . . .

"Bloody hell," Phil said as the other cuffed Vs looked at me with hate in their eyes.

Kim and Frank came around the corner next. The calvary had arrived; at least the two people I knew would understand. I sat there for a few seconds, reflecting on the scene. In reality, I had killed a bad guy. Another drug dealer off the streets. Doing Goolsby's dirty work was what was truly bothering me.

The look on Frank's face said it all. Vs didn't like people killing their own kind, "Kristi, Mouth, your bosses want you back at the Council chambers. Max, what the hell happened here?" he asked, looking around and motioning to the Night Stalkers to fan out. They picked up the goons and walked out of the room. While unassuming, Frank was the head of the CSA for the Southern US, and from what I understood, he worked with the Night Stalkers. They obviously listened to him.

"Well, by my guess, Goolsby came down to the docks for a chat with Cecil here," I said, pointing at the two halves of his body, "and things didn't go as planned—" Petro cut me off mid explanation.

"Some Guardians were in the bushes," he barked out, gaining a wide-eyed glance from Frank.

"Max, I guess everyone showed up to the party today. Let's just get this cleaned up. I can see by the look on your face this is bothering you. That's why we are friends, brother," Frank said, walking over and letting loose a slight grin, whispering under his breath, "I hated this jackass anyway."

I still couldn't figure out why I was so concerned about Cecil. A thought started forming in the back of my mind, punching through the back of my eyes like a sledgehammer.

I let out a breath as Belm's voice came over the old internal thought-phone, better known as my head movie. *It's done,*

Belm's raspy voice echoed throughout my thoughts.

"Hey, guys," I said, getting everyone's attention. "Every single gunslinging bootlicker in the area and lord knows where was just here. Any chatter on the radio, Kim?"

"Nothing. Should we be expecting anything?" Kim replied.

A look of understanding washed over the group, except for Phil. He eyed me suspiciously, as did Petro. My mind wandered in an internal William Shatner voice. *Why was everyone there? What drew all the groups to the docks? Most importantly, did anyone notice that I set this whole event up, and while everyone was turning a blind eye, working a little plan?* Well, minus the cutting-Cecil-in-half thing.

I had no clue what Belm had truly done other than the one thing I needed him to. I guess more people than I thought had been watching the shipping yard at B&B's. The utter confusion of the event immediately signaled to me Belm's hand in it.

"Phil, I'm gating us back to the Atheneum. Frank, you want a lift?" I asked, turning to see Neil walk around the corner with a handful of plainclothes cops. "Great," I murmured.

Neil lit up a cigarette, walking up to the body as two marshals zipped up the bag with finality. "Every Tom, Dick, and Jane are out front. News, radio, I think I even saw a taco truck," he said, approaching Kim as she took a couple of steps over to me.

"Call me later," she said, reaching up to give me a light kiss on the cheek. I looked over at Neil smirking. Not just being a wiseass, but genuinely happy.

"Let's go, lover boy," Phil said, rolling his eyes. Frank motioned for us to go as I pulled out an Evergate stone, taking us back to the Atheneum.

CHAPTER 12

One Last Kiss Goodbye . . .

T he next morning lent itself to another meeting at the Council chambers. Twice in two days was more than enough. I followed up with Kim before leaving my room, and according to her, things looked to be okay after my little two-for-one special.

"Petro?" I barked, shuffling out into the hallway.

"Morning, boss," he replied, already up and dressed. Me, I was still in fuzzy slippers, my robe, and some boxers.

"Golden Grahams," I said, pulling out the box and grabbing a cap and bowl.

"Alright, what did you do?" Petro inquired, raising an eyebrow while stroking his mustache.

"Nothing—well, yet . . . Kim did kiss me yesterday. You think I'm in trouble again?" I asked, pouring the bowls full of cereal before adding the milk, just the way it had been engineered to be eaten. Phil was one of the few people to fail the *how do you eat your cereal* test that I hadn't given a hard time. While heavily intoxicated on Ambrosia, he had busted open a box and simply poured dry cereal down his throat.

"Nah, I think Goolsby's got some questions to answer. I saw that kiss; it was on the cheek, doesn't count. Anyway, I meant to ask before you and Tom started talking about all that gate stuff last night. Why were you all weird yesterday after everything went sideways?" Petro asked, taking several large bites.

He knew me too well. "The whole thing was a surprise to me," I said grinning, telling a half-truth. "Some of it, at least."

Petro squinted his eyes at me, grinning back. "You're up to something, boss. I know it. I'm in, don't care what it is."

We both shook our heads in silence. One thing I had learned about the magical world was, the less people knew about something, the better chances of it happening. Diviners were the main issue, but I had demon blood flowing through my veins, which meant I couldn't be divined. We had figured that was why Chloe'd had trouble seeing what I was going to do before my system had leveled out. Ed's problem reading my mind had been from a binding in the will Tom had done before he decided to show back up. I had been able to block him on a few occasions, it again being blamed on the demon blood. I was still figuring out the details, and had even worked on a chart with Jenny listing the negatives and positives.

Unlike yesterday, the Council chambers were packed this time around, the private meeting giving way to a full house. It was like my time in the hot seat last year. This time, however, Goolsby was in the chair. Carvel walked up with Tom and Titus.

"Max, glad you got some rest," Tom said, motioning me to follow the men. Phil had also just approached with Jenny.

We walked into the same side chamber from yesterday as Titus closed the door, ignoring the rest of the Council. I was sure people took notice of the little diversion.

"Everything is a go for tomorrow. You'll be meeting up with Inspector Holder this evening as the boat is set to dock in

Southampton," Titus informed the room.

"This information does not need to leave this room," Tom interjected, handing out a binding stone to the group, making sure everyone touched it. It would prevent divination and also keep us from physically being able to discuss it.

We walked out, and Phil decided to stay outside during the meeting talking with Kristi. I walked up the side stairs at the entrance, grabbing an empty seat next to an obvious witch. Witches stood out in a crowd, like my mother. They all dressed and looked like stylish hippies, if that makes any sense. Petro took off into the rafters where most of the other Pixies hung out. The smell of lavender wafted up from her as a breeze carried through the open doors. I looked at Goolsby as he sat in the middle of the room before I leaned forward to talk to the old lady.

"Hey, why don't they have that chair thingy hooked up to him?" I asked.

The lady jumped, calming after seeing my face. "Oh my, you're the Sand boy. I know your mother," she told me in a warm, welcoming tone.

"I'm Max. Nice to meet you," I greeted, holding out my hand.

"Teen, everyone calls me that. But look at you. I remember seeing you when you were in diapers," the old witch said, enjoying having someone to talk to other than, I was guessing, her cats.

"I'll tell Mom you said hello. Any idea?" I asked, again having the feeling he would somehow be exempt.

"Oh, he's human. According to the Balance Accords, they can't hook a regular up to the machine. Plus, I don't think it really works the same."

"Hmm," I hummed as Teen started talking about her recent haul of herbs from her garden. It wasn't that I was ignoring the witch, I was simply full up in the old head movie.

The doors closed as Teen turned around, patting me on the knee. I liked her. Now just wasn't the time.

Hell, I needed to call the folks.

The room was noisy, almost louder than during my little visit last year. "Order!" Bull yelled as the room went silent. I looked down at my watch, checking the time. I wasn't sure what time zone the Council chambers were in. It was 11:00 a.m. in Florida. One hour till game time.

That's right. I had a little plan.

The normal reverent hush came over the chamber. Goolsby stood up in front of the Supreme Councilors sitting high above the room. Davros was missing from the group. I knew deep down I had made an enemy somewhere, somehow, yesterday, but that was yet to be revealed.

Several Vs had been killed over the past few days, and it had not gone unnoticed. I was betting that was the reason Goolsby was here. I still had to chat ith Belm about what the hell he had done exactly.

"Marlow Goolsby, you are not under any accusations. You are here to answer questions concerning the events that happened yesterday at your shipping warehouse, and before that, at Riverplace Tower, where several Vampires were killed on both occasions. In addition, we are ensuring your safety and putting you under the protection of the CSA," Titus said in his deep voice as the room settled into their seats.

I looked at the sidelines to see who else was in the room. Directly across from Goolsby sat Councilman Dark-water. Flanking him were two individuals I had never seen before; one obviously looked to be a Mage, while the other looked indistinct. Directly across from that group sat Ed, Ana Vlad, and looking extremely out of place, Inspector Holder. Dick was becoming a regular on the scene, much against his wishes.

Ed spoke up first. "Mr. Goolsby, are you aware Ketonic-etho-entheriun, better known as Kracken, was found at both locations? First at your principal place of residence and business, Riverplace Tower, and then at the warehouses which you own at the docks."

Goolsby paused, sweeping his eyes around the room, hesitating momentarily as his eyes shifted past where I was sitting. I started getting anxious, hoping that Goolsby was finally going to be held accountable for something for once.

"Yes, I am sanctioned by the Council and civilian governments to transport the material for research purposes through Mags-Tech," Goolsby said matter-of-factly to the audience, his demeanor cool, calm, and calculating.

"Shit," I whispered under my breath. This guy had an out for any situation. Mags-Tech did have its hands in almost everything, and they had recently appointed a Mage as the operating CEO. Goolsby still sat on the board. However, he had given up his position when the Balance Accords were signed as part of his deal to have a civilian seat on the Council.

"Right, my understanding is that it is a very controlled substance. We also understand," Ed said, going into his full centuries-old-attorney mode, "the security and transportation of said material is part of your responsibility. Everyone in this room understands that so-called 'spiked' Kracken has been found in the bodies of several recently deceased victims. Including a senator."

"I do, and I would like to state for the record that my dealings in that operation are very limited. I am only on the board of Mags-Tech. The transportation and storage are often subcontracted for security reasons. I have supplied that information to the Senior Council for review."

He, of course, had distanced himself from the operation, and in doing so, shifted the focus off him as he always did.

"Thank you. We noted that B&B LLC shipping has been in charge of shipping the material over the past several months. Has their license to deal with Etherium-based materials been properly vetted and approved by the Council?" Ed asked. I didn't see what game Ed was playing. He obviously knew the answer; he was one of the strongest Mind Mages in the Southern US.

"Yes, Councilman Darkwater approved it in conjunction with the marshal's office several months ago," Goolsby responded as Darkwater, stoic as always, sat with his fingers crossed on the table in front of him.

"Point of order," the woman sitting beside Darkwater shouted.

"You have the floor," Titus replied, taking a sip of what looked like coffee.

Darkwater stood up. "Mr. Goolsby, are you aware that you are also being looked at concerning the recent deaths of several Vampires and regulars alike?"

"Might I remind the Council, that recent events have generated a significant strain on my business interest and operations? I would like to get to the bottom of these items as much as anyone. Bloodshed on my property is not acceptable, and will be dealt with," Goolsby countered, shooting a piercing glare at Darkwater.

I still couldn't tell if those two did business together. Goolsby hadn't looked happy last time I'd seen him around Darkwater, which in all fairness had been last year at the ball. I looked down at my watch to see time marching on. I had ten more minutes before it was go time.

The next eight minutes were spent going over the various details and issues concerning Cecil, when as always, the shoe dropped.

Darkwater looked at me, turning slightly. "Max Abaddon Sand was the person that killed Cecil at the docks, in cold blood, and without provocation. Do you know—"

Before he could ask Goolsby, I stood up. Time was ticking, and I figured I would use this to make a grand exit. "Hey,

Darkwater, fake news, buddy. That drug-dealing bag of ass was charging me. Better yet, I'm pretty sure he's the reason you are having all these drug problems," I bellowed at the top of my lungs as the room froze. Even Darkwater lost his composure for once, a look between shock and anger taking hold of his face.

The room erupted in a mix of guffaws and clapping, which echoed off the stone walls before Titus gaveled the room back to order. I had a minute left, and decided not to let Darkwater get the last word in. "Can anyone prove me wrong?" I walked down the stairs, shaking my head.

"Max, we have already cleared yesterday's scene. You were operating in the Council's interest and defended yourself as reported. The CCTV retrieved from the scene confirmed it," Ana said, taking over for Titus.

They had CCTV footage of the whole thing. That could be either a good thing or a bad thing for me. I needed to get my hands on that footage later and see if I could make out who else was in the smoke.

"I request Max's Council badge be held until a further investigation can be completed," Darkwater said, looking a little frazzled for once. Kim had mentioned before that he was not being his usual cool, calm, and collected self. He seemed almost desperate if you paid close enough attention.

"Denied. He was within his rights, as would you in the same situation," Ana replied coolly.

I finished walking out of the chambers, fist-bumping Bull as I left. Phil and Kristi were standing there smoking. "Time to go," I told Phil, grabbing my charm and whispering for Petro.

"Bruther, we could hear that mess from here. Holy hell. That guy probably called this meeting to try to get at you," he said, nodding his head to Kristi as Petro landed on my shoulder, throwing up some rock-and-roll devil horns.

"That was about as rock star as it gets, boss. You have to tell Abby and the gang about that one," Petro complimented.

We were already walking down the corridor before Phil stopped midstride. "Hold up. Where the hell are we going, and why are we leaving?"

"First, did I hear you giggling when I walked out?" I asked. Petro was stroking his mustache. The little guy had even started growing a beard; Casey had told him it had something to do with fertility.

Another round of jeers and yelling echoed down the hall. It must have been getting animated in the Council chamber. We were missing all the fun. Well, at least for now.

"Don't change the subject there, Jokey McJokerson," Phil chided as Petro pulled out his knife and picked at his fingernails jokingly.

"Alright, alright. Jesus Chri—"

"STOP!" Petro and Phil both yelled.

"Man, what is it with everyone and the J-man. Anyway, time to take a little field trip. We need to stop by the apartment and grab a few things, then we're off," I said, continuing to walk to what was known as the gate hall.

"Bruther, where are we going?"

"On a cruise, and drinks are on me," I replied as we reached the proper gate, coming out in the Atheneum only to walk through the Evergate back to the apartment. The Council chambers were highly warded, having been updated after the Balance, and traditional gating was now about the only way to get in and out. Also, I didn't really feel like testing out my luck.

CHAPTER 13

There's a Hole in the Bottom of the Sea . . .

Devin sat in the chair behind the office desk in the shop, the smell of freshly cracked pepper overtaking the other scents in the room. Today he was dressed in a black suit that had an etched pattern in it. Phil stopped and stared at the man, looking over at me.

The person who I pretty much figured was the devil—and my great-grandfather on mygrandmother Lilith's side—sat there with his fingers steepled.

His hair was as always cemented to his head and pulled back, revealing a lean, strong, and chiseled face. His smile was predatory and overly wide. Devin's nose was pointed and sharp like the rest of his features, and his skin was a shade too tan to be artificial, but also a bit red to make it look like the mild start of a sunburn on a person who lived their life by the sea.

"Maxxx . . ." Devin drawled out as Petro landed on the table. He knew who this was even though he still hadn't met him. He usually was preoccupied with one of Devin's companions.

"It's been a while. You sure it's a good thing to pop in like this?" I asked, referring to Phil.

"Oh, it's fine. It's about time I met your friends. Family and all, you know," Devin said, sitting up straight.

"Oy, you're that guy," Phil interjected, sitting in one of the chairs, looking skeptical.

Knowing there was always a purpose for his appearance and being on a schedule, I decided to speed things up. "It's great to see you, but we have places to be."

"Yes, about that. I understand Belm has been helping you out a good bit lately. I wanted to advise you to tread lightly. Things that are bigger than they may seem are in motion," Devin cautioned, pulling out a pitch-black cigarette, also tossing one to Phil.

Phil grabbed it admiringly. "I haven't had one of these in a long time. Are you the Devil?" he blurted as the two lit the burning-rubber-smelling smoke sticks.

Devin let out a throaty chuckle. "I've been called a lot of things," was all he replied.

"Do you know anything about the hellion that popped up?" I asked.

Devin took a long drag of the tar-smelling cigarette. *Note to self, put up a no-smoking sign.* "Yes, that. That got the attention of a few others. This particular hellion was a one-off. Otherwise, we would be having a much more serious conversation."

"You mean the legions?" Petro interjected. Being from the Plane, he was clearly more aware of certain aspects of the universe.

"Yes, little warrior. The legions, as you know, are all neatly tucked away, not to ever be released," Devin said as my memory kicked in.

"The Trojan horse of the Old Gods," I said, remembering the stories my mom used to read me at night.

Devin smiled. "Something like that. I can assure you that they are well secured. It would take an act of Go—" We all looked at Devin as he cut himself short.

"What do you know about this drug?" I asked.

"Oh, before I forget, you may want to remember that family is important. Be careful what you ask of others. Make sure you take time to appreciate that," Devin said, cryptic as always as he changed the subject. He wasn't going to answer my question.

Not wanting to get into a philosophical discussion with good old great-grandpa, I decided to save it for later. "Got it. I'll make sure to call more often."

With that, Devin stood up, throwing me a small bag with two coins in it. Opening it, I realized they were the two coins from my nightstand. One coin Davros had given me for rescuing a hellhound for him. The other I had received from an odd man called Penance as payment for doing him a favor. Oddly enough, that favor had been retrieving that very coin. I had an idea why, but had not yet taken any time to dig into it. I had forgotten about them. "Been in my underwear drawer?" I said, shaking my head, figuring these coins were more important than I'd thought.

Devin just grinned, shaking Phil's hand. "It was good to meet you, Phil." He stood there, looking at Phil as if he were reading the story of his life. There was something weird about the interaction. Something said without being spoken.

Devin popped out of existence as the smell of ozone filled the room, replacing the peppery aroma.

"What was that all about, boss?" Petro asked.

"I'm not sure. Phil?" I said, huffing out a lung-full of air.

"A weird one, that one. Yup, he's the Devil for sure. Just not sure which one," he replied as I looked over at him with a screwed-up face.

"Which one?"

"Doesn't matter. He wanted to meet me for some reason, though. Not sure. Hey, are those the coins from the summer?"

Phil said, changing the subject.

"Yup. Hey . . . " A thought clicked into place. "I know one of these coins opens a gate to Everwhere. Hell, that's where this Kracken stuff comes from, right?"

Phil's eyebrow's almost touched his forehead as Petro buzzed excitedly. "He's trying to tell you something, boss, without getting involved!"

"I think you're right. I forgot about these. We need to talk to Tom about them. I'm pretty sure the gate in the graveyard still works. This might even have something to do with the Postern." I said, trying to put my thoughts together.

"Bruther, where are we going?" Phil asked.

"Ah, yes, we need to grab a few things, and we'll be leaving in twenty minutes. Plan on us being gone maybe a day or two. Pack light. Here," I said, handing Phil and Petro a small cracker each. They just stood there, confused. I was playing my cards close to my chest to avoid any possible divination from stopping us. "Those are glamours; good ones. Mom made them for us. Once we eat them, we will be normal-looking folks blending in with the rest of whomever else is around."

Phil had a small stockpile of weapons at the shop, as well as a change of clothes. Petro zipped off to get his things together.

"My weapons are gone," Phil said, walking out of the back room.

"They're fine. Everyone ready?" I asked as I lead the team to the Postern.

The Seekergate shimmered to life as Phil and Petro just shook their heads. "I hate surprises," Phil said as we walked through.

◆ ◆ ◆

The smell of salt water filled my nostrils as I clapped my

hands, turning on the overhead light and revealing the shipping container we had gated into. Two footlockers sat at the far end, as well as two fold-up chairs and a table. I looked over, grinning.

"You sneaky son of a bitch. We aren't waiting for tomorrow," Phil said as he walked over to the footlocker with his name on it. The sound of the ship's horn signaled its departure from the dock.

"Nope. I figured that anything set up by the Council would have been compromised. When I met with Bruce, I saw a logbook on my way in. There was another vessel leaving today that didn't have a destination listed. The two guards were talking, so I figured they wouldn't mind me taking a quick look," I said as Petro zipped over to the box with his name on it.

Belm had packed the footlockers with weapons. Not just your everyday, run-of-the-mill weapons, but the heavy stuff. Grenade launchers, heavy caliber rifles, and of course, blue-tipped ammunition identifying them as special.

"What's the name of the ship?" Phil asked as I put my hand out, motioning for everyone's phones. We needed to keep a low profile until it wasn't needed anymore. Even if we didn't stick around long, I wanted to keep hidden as long as we could.

"The *Event Horizon*," I said as Petro and Phil stared at me. The name suddenly dawned on me. The *Event Horizon* was a ship in a movie that basically went to hell and came back with an extra passenger.

"Shit," Phil murmured, suddenly changing his attitude and holding up the six-shot M32 40 mm grenade launcher. "Mine," was all he said after that for a few seconds. He also grabbed a heavily modified AK-47, talking dirty to it under his breath. I reached down, pulling out an M4-style assault rifle and bandolier of grenades that shot out silver and iron when detonated.

"Look, I don't think we are going to need all this, but just in case . . ." I looked at my watch. "Let's hang loose for a few hours, and when we get into open waters, get out and stretch our legs. I have a feeling this boat is loaded down with goons."

"Hey, boss, I can't smell anything from in here," Petro said, pulling out a mini version of a sniper rifle.

"The container's warded; it goes both ways. Until we open it, we are blind for the most part. My thought is to wait until the sun goes down and then head out," I said.

"Why the strict timeline? And don't you think the Council will be pissed once they realize we are already gone?" Phil asked, taking out a flask and passing it over. I poured a small amount into the cap, twisting it off as was the routine.

"I couldn't gate in once out on the sea. Something about the salt water. Plus, the Council didn't say we couldn't, right?" I said as the three of us snickered.

"Bruther, I'm also guessing no one knows we are here?" He raised a good point.

"I left a note with Leshya before we left. She will get the word out at midnight. I figured if there is any trouble to be had, it will be had by then." I said, sitting down.

"You had something to do with that mess yesterday, didn't you," Petro asked in the form of a statement.

"Yup," I replied, leaving the rest to the imagination. I had asked Belm through our convenient mind link to make sure he created a distraction. He had sent me a photo via text now that he was hip to using his cell phone. The picture was a message in blood painted on the side of one of the boats at B&B's docks stating, *If you want your shipment, be at west dock 3.* It was accompanied by a specific time. I didn't bother asking where he got the blood; I knew better. Belm had a knack for theatrics. It was a hard message to miss, and in fact, had worked perfectly. Maybe a little too well.

"What was up with those Guardian chumps?" Petro asked, filling the reflective silence from the two forming mental images of what I may have done.

Phil interjected more animatedly than usual, "They are magic haters. Go around the world collecting magical artifacts to supposedly keep them out of others' hands, only to use them themselves. Countless Mages, Fae, Vs, and shifters have lost their lives at the end of a Guardian's sword."

"They all aren't like the ones we met though, according to the information Dr. Freeman pulled for me. Most of them are in civilian positions of power. Major players in the business world and the type. My understanding is that they are Crusaders, the same ones you read about in history. They operate in the background," I said, sounding smarter about the subject than I was.

"Sure, and I've been sober for the last twenty-four years. Don't fool yourselves. They want power just like everyone else does. The Balance Accords gave them some weird type of legitimacy, from what I hear. Kristi and I were talking about them," Phil said as Petro made kissy noises, getting a swat.

"I'm more worried about all these pirates and how Goolsby and the others are involved. Thing is, I don't think they are. I'm betting on it being our buddies at the Thule Society. Look at the children from last year," I said as the boat hit a wave, rocking the container.

"Those kids are scary powerful. I went to see them with Lacey and Macey, and they are already showing signs of Etherium after only a few years. Plus, they are growing faster than normal folks. Jenny said that they are aging four years to every one from a physical standpoint," Petro said. Jenny had the girls check on them monthly, and Petro had tagged along.

The Thule Society had made genetically engineered magical babies. While a mouthful, that was the simplest explanation I could come up with. The children had been the subject of much debate over the past year. Their existence was being kept a secret, and while the civilian governments knew it, even they wanted to keep it under wraps, which told me it was a bigger deal than I must have thought. They were currently kept in a secure location, and were allowed out one at a time and only under strict supervision.

"You think they are looking for us yet?" Phil asked, letting out a deep breath.

"Maybe. I made it look like we were taking the afternoon off. It sounded like everyone was focused on Goolsby for once. You guys notice that asshat Darkwater?" I asked.

"That wanker is on the take. He wants your head on a spike. But now that you mention it, he was acting a little odd. Not his cool, collected self," Phil said as Petro jumped up, hovering in the air.

"He was all sweaty; I could smell it on him. The other Pixies were making fun of him," Petro said, buzzing off to his box of goodies. A slight breeze flowed off his wings.

"It was like he was desperate, or—" I said slowly.

"Or not in control anymore. He may have lost whatever leverage he had," Phil cut me off, having a good point. I would talk to Ed about that when we got back, and see if they could look into it.

Eight hours and a flask down, my watch chirped, informing us the sun would soon go down. "Everyone ready?" I asked, pulling out the small cracker-like packet. The three of us ate the glamours, turning into nice little indistinct ship workers. These were top-notch. The one key element of these enchantments was that they would last at least a good hour and help our weapons blend in.

Phil stood there, holding what looked like a mop. I knew it was a grenade launcher. On the other hand, Petro was a work of art as he swooped down, looking like a small dark-colored gull with what looked like a twig hanging from his little clawed feet thingies.

"This is going to be fun," I said, steadying myself as the

boat again rocked. I pulled out the key, clicking it into the lock and slowly propping the door open. The hinges needed some WD-40 as they screamed to life, the saltwater pulling the moisture out of the air.

I grimaced as Petro shot out the door. The magic hit me immediately. Waves of thick, shifting Etherium passed through my body like radiation. Phil let out a slight snort as he shook off the sensation. "Nice dance moves," I said.

"There's something big on this ship, bruther," Phil said, his voice coming out with a little sass due to the glamour. These were good; they even tweaked your voice.

"Petro?" I asked, wanting to see if we were good to move. We had our communicators on.

"Clear, but . . . uhh . . . boss. Ned's on the ship," Petro said, confusion in his voice.

I picked up on his tone. "Doing what?"

"Well, there's about a dozen of those creepy-looking pirates, and they have Ned in a cage out in the open. Looks like a . . ." Petro trailed off.

"Petro," I barked quietly into the communicator.

Petro landed on my shoulder, making me jump. He started talking at warp speed. "They have Ned in the middle of a circle on the bow. Goons are crawling all over the place up there. I think we may be able to get over there if we can stay on top of the containers. At least get a clear line of sight of what's going on. It's not good."

When Petro said it wasn't good, he meant it. Ned's life was in danger.

I looked over at Phil as he nodded back. "Change of plans. We get to Ned. If we find out anything, that's a bonus," I said, doing the math in my head.

"Then we scuttle the ship," Phil followed up with no pushback from the team.

The container was luckily staggered with another group, giving us a larger than life staircase to climb. Petro took point, keeping us from being detected. As we climbed to the top row of containers, the smell of exhaust slammed into my face. The deck of the ship was forty feet below, give or take. Shadows from security patrols started to move as we got closer to the bow. Flashlights made the goons below look like fireflies dancing in the night.

I motioned ahead as Petro gave the all-clear to jump over to the next row of containers. Phil nodded to the far right as bright light glowed like a streetlight in the middle of an empty field. Reaching down, I checked on the rifle and, of course, Durundle.

The second layer of containers gave us cover as we moved forward. The roving flashlights below were picking up. While others often forgot how useful Pixies truly were, we never took having an eye in the sky for granted. Often ignored as lesser types by the Fae and Mage communities, the recent Balance Accords had leveled the playing field, giving them a seat on the Council. Lacey, Macey, and Petro had a lot to do with the Pixies' recent inclusion into politics.

We had successfully maneuvered to the bow of the ship undetected. Petro dropped back down as we could now see Ned tied up in a cage, sitting in the middle of a pentagram. The three of us kneeled down in the shadows of a container, barely out of sight.

Three men stood in front of Ned. One wore a long leather coat just like the Thule goons usually wore. He seemed larger than the rest and looked to be giving out instructions. To the side stood a row of the fashionable-looking pirates, with Pearl lingering behind them. On the other side of the pentagram stood a group of uniformed soldiers brandishing sleek sub-machine guns.

We fully retreated into the shadows as I leaned closer to

Phil. "What do you think?" I whispered, the sound of the wind and the boat's massive engines making it hard to hear.

Phil thought for a minute, a scowl on his face. "Mengele. That's the damn Angel of Death," he said in a low growl. This was the kind of situation in which I hated still being a newbie to the magical community. Picking up on my lack of recognition, Phil explained, taking a deep breath, "One of the Thule Society's head assholes."

I sat there reflecting for a minute on our options. *Was Lilith on this ship?* I thought for a minute before I heard shouting coming from below.

"It's time. Take your positions!" a deep, throaty voice bellowed, echoing off the containers. Petro buzzed to my shoulder, sensing our moods. Phil and I looked at each other, both coming to the same conclusion before whispering it at the same time.

"Diversion."

I pulled out one of the smaller explosive grenades from my bandolier, handing it to Petro. Without any words, Petro held out his claw-looking bird hand, sticking up one of the claws. "One minute," I whispered as Petro nodded, taking off.

"Hulk smash," I told Phil as a wicked grin crossed his face.

"I think we might just die today, bruther," he said, putting an unlit cigarette in his mouth. He looked odd under the glamour, like a janitor. Not that there was anything wrong with janitors, but seeing one pull out an enchanted hammer and large grenade launcher was just sending mixed signals.

Getting more comfortable with the plan that wasn't really a plan, rather just smashing everything and everyone down below to pieces, we started talking. Thirty seconds left . . .

"Mengele, is he dangerous?" I asked.

"The worst kind of scum. He's the one in charge here,

without a doubt. I still don't understand those pirates, but we just figured out who's peeing in the Cheerios back home," Phil said, checking the action on the M32 and clicking off the safety.

Chanting started, coming from the group below. "Shit, they're starting a ritual." I pulled up my rifle, putting it on full auto, and also grabbed a silver grenade, pulling the pin while holding the spoon. Phil held up his hand, counting down with his fingers. As he dropped the last one, a loud bang and flash of light reflected off the star-filled night sky.

I released the spoon on the grenade, dropping it directly below our location, clearing us an area to land. Shouts started, and after a slight pause, the chanting continued. Tactical lights began pouring over the landscape of the boat. We had to move while we were tucked away.

Phil looked over as I lifted my middle finger, a small flicker of hellfire tipping it off. He leaned in, lighting his cigarette off my finger while flipping me off in return as the grenade below us sprung to life. A silver-infused grenade wasn't full of high explosives. It did explode, but it focused on sending slivers of iron and mostly silver through the air, neutralizing magic and most of everything within a twenty-foot radius.

Shards of silver and iron whistled through the air as several grunts of surprised pain echoed off the containers. Chaos was one of my favorite things. A person with next to nothing could pretty much create a small riot if timed correctly. In this case, a mix of confusion and chaos ensued as Phil and I dropped down to the deck. Ned was roughly a hundred feet away, with mostly open space separating us.

Petro chirped over the communicator, "We just kicked the hornet's nest, boss!"

"Looks like it," I said, scanning the immediate area. Confused Thule goons and angry pirates came into sharp view. Several stunned people lay around the ground, having been in the immediate blast radius of the grenade.

JUSTIN LESLIE

It quickly dawned on me that we most likely looked like two deckhands holding mops. Mengele, as Phil had called him, yelled in a harsh German accent, "Stop them!" The larger than average man pointed in our direction, and a wave of heat passed over us, dissipating our disguises. Whatever he had thrown our way also seemed to smack into the surrounding goons.

I glanced quickly at Ned, seeing a look of recognition on his face. His eyes had a faint, growing orange glow coming from them. He didn't have much time.

Before I finished my thought, violence erupted—mainly in the form of Phil launching a real grenade directly at the pirates. It was clear the previous explosion had scattered the group, and Pearl must have immediately left, as I had yet to see him.

Bullets erupted from the left side of the deck as two men ran forward. Several of the pirates charged from the other direction. I pulled up the M4, releasing several three-round bursts of stinging death. The blue, glowing rounds led my aim into the group of pirates. Not to be outdone, the group split in two, with one spatter of bullets landing square in the chest of a forward-rushing pirate. His sword was up, and it was clear he was not used to being in a gunfight as he winked out of existence.

I didn't look behind as several rounds danced around me, coming from the other direction. Two large crashes and the rhythmic sound of a machine gun told me Phil was enjoying himself. Justified violence always put Phil in a good mood. It was different though, as his cadence was fast and direct; he was making his way to Ned without all the usual bravado.

A round from an old musket slammed past, as the smoke generated by the powder made it hard to see the figures moving in the shadows. I formed a larger than normal ball of hellfire in my hand, throwing it before the group could reorient or reload one of what I guessed was a blunderbuss. Mengele stood in front of the cage as he continued chanting.

I dropped down behind a crate, changing magazines, looking for movement. Another explosion rocked the deck as Phil launched another grenade. This was followed by a body flying overhead into the darkness, screaming as it fell into the dark abyss of the ocean.

"Petro," I said quickly into the communicator.

"Boss, incoming!" Petro screamed as lightning arched through the air. Pearl was back on the bow. Petro came flying through the air, homing in on me and slamming into the crate. He had been playing cat and mouse, keeping Pearl occupied. Pearl was indiscriminate with his arcs of electricity as he lit up the ship's deck. What I did notice was a protective bubble surrounding the cage and Mengele.

Phil must have missed the initial barrage as the sound of several rounds being fired drew my attention, giving me the chance to move. Pearl shifted as sparks erupted from the containers, the flack from Phil's grenade launcher bouncing off the metal and slamming into Pearl's back.

I let off another volley of rounds into the shadows where the pirates were, maneuvering before dropping the weapon to take a clear shot at Pearl. Hellfire poured from my inner self as I let loose several smaller spheres of dripping hellfire directly at the pale-white, all-around pain in my ass.

One ball of hellfire slammed directly into Pearl. He let out a throaty scream, "Gaaarhhh," as arcs of electricity exploded from his body. A look of realization crossing his face.

Time slows down often when you are in the heat of battle. Seconds turn into minutes as you take in the situation planning your next move. With my heightened senses, there was some truth to that. While I wasn't superhuman, I could move slightly faster than a normal being should be able to. I stared at Pearl as a grenade slammed into his torso. Everyone on the deck froze. Pearl's eyes had hate and confusion in them as he reached down, patting his chest.

Petro and I were still behind a large crate, as Phil jumped behind a container. The lucky silver-infused grenade Phil had shot into the mix finally exploded. Since it had low-level explosives, the effects were in Ultra HD.

Pearl's ribcage exploded outward with no flash, spraying red gore and slinging his lungs in several directions. He dropped to his knees as the chanting stopped. The explosion of pure energy and light that followed was blinding, the night amplifying its effects. Lightning spidered through the sky and deck, its bite flowing through my legs, freezing me in place. As soon as it happened, it stopped. The bright light imploded on Pearl as what was left of his body slumped over. It smacked on the deck with a wet thud.

As if things weren't bad enough already, lightning arched through the night sky as if in a nod to its old master, revealing an honest-to-God old-timey pirate ship directly beside our vessel.

"I don't think that was there a minute ago," I said into the communicator louder than needed. The gunfire and overall amount of grenades going off were catching up to my eardrums.

The boat rocked from the other side. Something had slammed into us, starting a violent vibration. The shock of the events began to wear off as shouts and gunfire started back up. This time our attackers were more cautious after seeing the onslaught of death we had brought with us. I would do anything in my power to not only save Ned, but my friends as well.

Mengele had turned back to the cage to start chanting again. Ned looked over at me and smiled. The Angel of Death stopped and looked over his shoulder, staring a hole through me. I stood up, pulling out Durundle. Petro pulled out his sword and darted into the darkness.

"*Ignis!*" I yelled, rushing from behind the crate. Two pirates waiting on me to move jumped out. I swung my sword down, effectively cutting them both in half, as I ran through their splitting bodies. Phil had started to engage the rest of the gun-wielding goons as I slammed into the protection circle with Durundle.

The blade bounced off, shaking my arms violently.

Unlike last time I had slammed the flaming sword into a protection circle, this one didn't budge. Mengele again turned as I stood there, staring the man in the face. He was the size of Mouth, but defined. The man was strong and large, avoiding the ogreish presence most things his size endured. He wore a black leather trench coat that had experienced decades of hard use, yet still looked cared for. A skull-and-bones insignia was pinned into the lapels. Scars pitted his face as hard eyes stared through me.

"You want some of me, ugly, come on out," I taunted, spittle flying from my mouth, its moisture hissing on the protective circle. I was so close it ignited my senses.

The boat rocked again as several grunts came from behind me. Petro was collecting eyes, giving the pirates a fashionable reason to wear two eye patches. Phil had also walked up on the other side of the protective circle around the cage. He was in full Mage mode, light gray smoke emanating from his body.

I took a breath as Mengele turned back to the cage as Ned convulsed. He looked over at me, as smoking orange flames started to seep from his eyes like smoke from a newly lit cigar. "Ned!" I screamed at the top of my lungs, gaining another sideglance from the hulking man. The reverberation of my voice causing a ripple in the circle.

A person who knew they were about to die and had come to terms with it often had a certain look on their face. One of peace and acceptance. Ned had that face as a pained grin smoothed across his mouth. He knew I was there, and was telling me it was already over.

I took a deep, centering breath. Stepping back, the crushing sounds of Phil slamming his hammer into the circle echoed in the night. Bodies were laid out in odd positions all over the place. We had effectively killed every goon on the deck. Sounds of gunfire still echoed as Petro flew around the ship keeping the others occupied.

Looking down, a chunk of Pearl's head lay at my feet. I kicked the fragment of skull, flinging it on the pile of bodies Phil had stacked up on the other side of the deck. The boat again shuddered and rocked.

"Hey, where's the boss?" I asked, again walking up to the circle.

"Far away, I can assure you," Mengele replied, turning his back on Ned as he convulsed again, his body starting to slowly glow.

"Lilith doesn't travel with you?" I asked, seeing if I could buy some time to figure out a plan. When I walked away, I had turned on my phone and activated the distress beacon tucked into my blazer. Not everything had to be magic to work.

Mengele bellowed from deep in his stomach, "That witch, she has what she wants. Plus, I'm pretty sure you know when family is around."

I stared, saving that information for later. A thought occurred to me as Ned spasmed again. Anger as hot as the sun started flowing through my body. Shouts began filling the air as the honest-to-God pirate ship docked onto the stern of the boat. The rest of the goons weren't coming after us; they were abandoning ship.

The ship shuddered again as rain started to fall. The thought that had crossed my mind was that a protective circle was just that: a circle, and we were on a boat. If we could cut through the deck and hull . . . well, that would be the end of that circle.

I put my hand to my ear, talking into the communicator. "Phil, let's sink this asshole."

Phil didn't respond in words, but with several rhythmic slams of his hammer on the deck.

I poured my will into Durundle as it exploded with raw, unharnessed energy, lighting up the front of the boat. It looked like someone had dropped several red flares on the deck. Ned let out a muffled scream as he tried to hold himself together. It was clear they were using him to bring someone over from the Everwhere.

I ran forward, slamming my sword down into the deck, pushing through it like a hot knife through butter. Walking forward, I started cutting alongside the circle as we caught Mengele's attention. He looked around as Phil and I kept hammering at the deck, making it a quarter of the way around before he stepped back, his body melting through the protective barrier.

"That did the trick," I said, pulling my blade out of the floor.

Mengele had come out on the other side close to Phil, who kept hammering. Finally realizing what had just happened, he stopped. I looked at Ned, also sizing Mengele up. He was going after Phil first. A bright light erupted from the man's hands as his right arm slammed forward, turning into a lightly glowing black double-bladed sword.

"Bloody hell," Phil let out breathlessly as I realized what Mengele was doing. He was giving me a choice. Help my friend, or help my past mentor.

The two men clashed as I started running around the circle, my feet slipping due to the water. The rain made the deck slippery, and I almost lost my footing. I caught myself focusing on the water around me, pushing it away from my body in a light wave.

Mengele backhanded Phil, as he flew into the containers.

It had been some time since I had witnessed Phil pushed around as this man had just done. I again focused as Mengele swung around, his sword humming through the air. I could hear it cutting through the rain. Ducking, I pulled up Durundle.

"You don't have to die tonight," Mengele said, his voice calm.

"I was about to say the same thing. Let Ned out of that cage now, and we can talk," I replied, not chancing a glance.

"He's already dead," he said, detached from the scene. Something slammed into the ship on the other side of the containers, sending several flying through the air. "Looks like you have other problems."

Lightning bolted through the air, lighting up a tentacle ten stories high. The large disembodied appendage with several containers in the curls of its limbs slammed back into the quickly angering ocean. Waves started crashing over the bow, filling my mouth with the taste of salt water. Mengele grinned, glancing over at the cage while a ray of orange light exploded from Ned as he let out a final scream, exploding into nothingness.

I lunged at Mengele, taking advantage of the distraction and swinging my sword down. I caught him slightly off-guard and sliced through his upper arm. The wound was superficial. I pulled back, realizing his massive blade was again swinging down.

My sword took the brunt of the blow, pushing me to the ground. I reached up. Pushing hellfire into my hands, I slammed the man in the chest only to see him absorb the flames into his body. Over the last thirty minutes, I had expended most of my power. After slinging that last ball of hellfire, I started to feel the pull in my chest telling me to keep an eye on my internal gas tank.

I had, however, caught him off-guard with the ball of

fire. The look on his face told me he didn't want that little trick of his being known. Either he was a demon, or he had demon blood.

I used his brief hesitation to get back on my feet, refocusing. If fire didn't work, I'd use water. Just saying, there was a good amount of water lying around.

Out of the dark, Phil came flying through the air, slamming his hammer directly into Mengele's back and launching him through the air several feet. I dove to the side as the man twisted unnaturally through the air, rolling to a stop on. Phil walked over as we both stood in front of the towering man. A wave crashed over the deck as Mengele started to laugh.

"Bruther, what's he laughing at?" Phil asked.

"I don't kno . . ." I trailed off as I looked over. As if in slow motion, a saber slammed down onto Phil's left hand, sending it flying through the air. Phil turned and faced off with the man I had left for dead in Everwhere several months ago. Blackbeard the Pirate stood there, rain running off his body, never taking his eyes off me.

Phil let out a bellow as he charged, blood flowing freely from his arm; he still had his hammer in his right hand. Blackbeard threw a ball of black smoke at Phil, laying him out on the spot. I stood there, glancing right and left. I was surrounded as Phil lay on the ground, more than likely bleeding out.

While I couldn't make much headway with Mengele, I knew from the last time we had met, I could absolutely lay the one-legged asshole out. I pulled hellfire into my hand, letting out several small flashes of light before jumping over Phil using my recently matured skills. While I wasn't superhuman, I could move a little faster, jump a little higher, and mostly use my senses to the best of their abilities.

It was clear as soon as I swung Durundle down, that the man that had erupted from Ned's now dead body was not fully in control of his faculties. He stumbled back, taken off by my charge. The cackling laugh of Mengele echoed behind me, getting further away.

"Remember me?" Blackbeard said, again pulling up his hand and pushing out a ball of black smoke. As soon as the cloud left his hands, it was like someone turned off the lights. All sound, light, and feeling disappeared. I swung my sword around blindly, landing a blow as the haze faltered.

I pushed my will out of my body, radiating hellfire as the haze lifted. Blackbeard had moved to my side and swung his saber again before I caught the blade with my sword. I looked down, seeing his peg leg. I kicked down hard, hearing the crack of the wood. Phil was ten feet away, still curled up and holding his bleeding stump.

"Yeah, I do. Remember me letting you live? Not again," I said, pushing a ball of hellfire into my hand. A tentacle five feet wide slammed into the deck behind me as I lost my balance, spinning around grabbing what I could. The tentacle had slammed through the deck, cutting the bow off from the rest of the ship.

Flames erupted from the gap as I pulled myself forward. Petro came over the radio. "I don't know what that thing is, but they are pissing it off. I think it's trying to sink the ship. Is all clear up there?"

"Get here," I huffed out as I looked up to see a gate shimmer to life in front of Blackbeard, who crawled through. It shut immediately behind him.

I got to my feet, running over to Phil. All I could think of was making sure he was okay. He was there because of me. I didn't care about the others. We would find them later. I looked around for Phil's hand as Petro came slamming down into my chest. Pixies couldn't fly well in the wind and rain. Last year we had worked on a few ways to help with that.

"What the hell, boss!" Petro exclaimed, making his way to my shoulder. The little warrior looked like he had flown through flames.

"His hand! His goddamn hand," was all I said as I lit up the shadows with hellfire, the last of my energy flowing from my body. Petro looked down, realizing Phil was hurt. He flew over to him, the rain pushing him in all directions.

The boat rocked as what sounded like a cannon being fired at the stern rang through the sky. Whoever was in the old galleon-style vessel was both sinking the ship, and fighting whatever the hell type of sea monster was now pulling its massive tentacle out of the hull behind us.

I lurched over, sliding into what was left of the silver cage Ned had been in, the metal burning my coat. Energy was still pulsating from the remains of the circle that Beardy—as he would now be called—had passed through.

Another roar of cannon fire filled the night air mixed with the crash of waves and thunder. The noise all came together in a crescendo of events.

Looking over, I saw Phil's hand sliding toward the gap in the deck. Gathering what little was left of my will, I pulled the water in front of it, channeling the appendage directly into my hands. That was a neat trick I had figured out after dropping the soap in the shower.

"It's time to go!" I yelled, breathlessly running over to Phil and Petro.

"Bruther, this better work," Phil gasped. I grabbed his good hand and pulled him up, placing his other hand in my pocket before pulling out an Evergate stone.

"Hey, buddy, I'm out of gas," I said as Petro got the message. I handed the small smooth stone to him as he smirked, the gate immediately shimmering to life in front of us.

The ship rocked violently as the deep howl of the sea monster below the ship shook my chest. It was time to leave.

CHAPTER 14

The Quiet Things That No One Ever Knows.

"What do you mean gone?" I asked as Jenny helped Phil sit in the wheelchair she had brought to the Postern.

"I just got a call from the team. They're flying over the area as we speak. There's a report of a debris field, but no signs of either of the ships," Jenny said in her motherly tone. She must have been relaxing if the pair of jeans and long sleeve T-shirt she had on were any indication. Lacey, Macey, and Casey hovered around Petro as they put some type of salve on his wings.

"Hey, man, you going to be good?" I asked. His left eye had swollen completely shut, and his severed hand lay in Phil's lap. Jenny quickly placed it in a bag of ice and put some type of hyper healing pad on the stump a few inches below his wrist.

Phil just looked up. Jenny, in an odd move, lit a cigarette, putting it in his mouth. "Hmmph," was all he got out.

"He'll be fine. I just need to get him into the medical bay," Jenny said. I hadn't realized they'd put a medical bay in. Most times we would just go to Jenny's lab. I guess things had continued to change at the Atheneum. I'd even heard they got another wing of the stacks digitized. I needed to spend a few days in the old haunt.

"Any clue when Tom and Ed will be back?" I asked.

"No, they gated to the closest Navy base and took a helicopter. Apparently, Tom has friends in high places. Oh, I almost forgot. Two things. Here," Jenny said, handing me an envelope.

"Early birthday card?" I asked, trying to lighten the mood.

"Letter from Kim. Plus, you're going to love this one. The secret superrich client that wants a high-end castor made just happens to be Councilman Darkwater's daughter." Jenny paused, holding back.

"Anddddd," I drawled out.

"She also happens to be the one and only widowed Carol Bellman. I only figured it out when I was finally sent a sample to verify what type of Etherium was likely in her system. We already knew this would not be an in-person transaction, and as always, I did a cross-reference in the system to see if anything popped up. You know, relatives, etc . . . The system lit up like a Christmas tree. Anyway, you may want to look into that," Jenny said as she rolled Phil out of the room.

I stood there, letting that information marinate in my brain like chicken in teriyaki sauce. "Darkwater's daughter," I whispered under my breath, letting the words roll around my mouth.

Petro flew over, landing on the table as the other Pixies followed Jenny out to help Phil. "That for real, boss?" he asked, smoothing out his mustache.

"If Jenny says so, I believe it. The issue is, I was pretty sure she wasn't a magical type when I met her. Though after everything we just witnessed, that doesn't mean much. I'm pretty sure there's now a way around that," I said sarcastically, picking up my phone and tapping out a message to Ed and Tom.

"This is going to get nasty boss. Ned was respected. I'm

sure they'll believe our story, but I'm not sure if how it ended up happening will go over too well," Petro said as I opened Kim's note, reading it out loud.

Max,

Don't reach out to me until I let you know it's clear. Things are like we discussed. My new proxy boss is about to make a play. Something's up with him. He's not in control like last year. Watch yourself, because they are watching you.

Kim

Petro and I both stood there, lost in thought. "You want me to check out Mrs. Bellman?" Petro asked.

"Sounds good. I have a sneaking suspension she's somehow going to be tied to Brucey boy," I replied, starting to figure out how lost I truly was with this whole situation. "Give me a shout if you find anything. I don't recommend getting too far away from home base."

"Sure thing, boss." He launched into the air only to hesitate, dropping back to the table, his eyes looking down. "Kim likes you. She trusts you, just as much as I do. Remember, you aren't bulletproof boss. That guy or whatever was bad news. Something smelled off about him. Like, like . . . something different. He reminded me of that Devil guy that you're related to, but more."

"I'll keep my eyes open. Hey, you were brave today. We did everything we could. Ned will be missed. I promise I'll personally send that son of a bitch back to wherever he came from. Both of them and his pirate goons," I said as Petro looked up, nodding his head in affirmation.

"Game time?" Petro asked.

"Game time," I replied as he left the Postern.

I reached down, pulling out the bag of coins from inside my old blazer recently turned long coat. In its new condition, it had indeed become a trench coat, as cliché as it sounded. A corduroy one to boot; it actually made sense why everyone in the books always wore one.

"Alright. Coins, show me your secrets," I said under my breath in my best *Lord of the Rings* impression, walking over to the far right gate. Tom had told me this gate went to the Everwhere, and was one of the gates he'd also happened to lose the key to.

Holding them in my hand, I started thinking about the graveyard and the crazy man with the alligator. I had lost a bet earlier in the year that had led me to an old graveyard in downtown Jacksonville. Part of it was retrieving one of the coins in my hand, that I just happened to be rewarded for acquiring.

That coin also opened a gate to Everwhere, a place where souls went to await whatever or wherever it was they were meant to do or go. Other people had called it purgatory. What I did know was that it was 100 percent real and somehow tied to recent events. I also knew that people around me were starting to get hurt, people I cared for.

I wasn't sure about the other coin. It was given to me by Davros for acquiring one of two hellhounds for him. We had believed one of the two hounds found at Carvel's house had been killed. Apparently, hellhounds were not that easily put down. After it jumped in front of a blast from Terrence, saving the day, it had decided to only play dead. Now Davros had both of them.

I walked over, running my hands along the dark, black obsidian gate. It didn't have a door like the others, just a black, empty void.

The cool thing about the Postern was that it was much like the entrance to the Fallen Angel. Devin had made the entrance tied to not only the Atheneum but my place as well. I quickly walked out of the Postern, moving into my bedroom. Grabbing the Postern journal, I turned, walking directly back.

Opening the journal, I turned it to the pages reflecting the black encrusted gate to the Everwhere. It was simply called the Mirrorgate. I initially thought it would take you to the Under—or Hell, as it is better known. After Tom returned, he quickly dispelled that notion, pointing at the blandest-looking gate in the room.

I repeated Tom's statement about the Mirrorgate. *"It's everywhere and nowhere. Out of all the gates in this room, this one is where it all started, and where it will all end."* The words lingered in my mind for several minutes. I hadn't thought about going back to the cemetery, but wondered what would happen if I did. That gravestone and this gate were connected, I was convinced of it.

A thought crossed my mind. When I was in Everwhere, it had been a close mirror to the real world I had just left. "What would happen if I went to Everwhere and just found the Postern and gated from there?" I murmured, rolling the coins in my hand. "Or don't be a dumbass and figure out this one," I scolded myself.

Tom had lost his access to the gate. While it did have a keyhole, I had learned there could be more than one way to use some of the gates. I pulled out the coin Davros gave me, sliding it over the sharp angles of the gate. The most striking part of it was its absolute deep blackness. It absorbed light, making the angles hard to make out.

My phone dinged with a text from Ed. They would be back in thirty minutes. I took a deep, calming breath, again focusing on the task at hand. A small rut caught the coin, making my hand stop. I lit a small flame on my finger and held it up. A slit the size of a coin reflected back. I snickered, wondering if I would get a bag of chips if I put the coin in the slot. But something was blocking the opening; it looked as if something had been broken off inside.

A ping again brought my attention away from the gate and to my phone. "Shit," I said. It was a message from Jamison. I had been hoping to deal with him later.

His text was simple and straightforward. *Is it true?* I responded simply with *yes*. There would be time to grieve later, and knowing Jamison, he was working to find out who was responsible. Even though I had a fairly good idea of who, I was struggling with the why and where. The man had dealt with secrets. While a powerful, full-blooded Fae, he'd preferred the subtle approach. I wondered how subtle Jamison was going to be. His father had been murdered to bring back some peg-legged asshole.

The voices of Ed and Tom filled the Postern as the two men arrived. Tom had an Evergate stone and had taken it with them. They acted like an old married couple, Tom pushing Ed in his modified wheelchair as they talked. I smiled, looking at the two of them as Tom walked around Ed and came to an abrupt halt in front of me, the look of aggravation evident on his face. The smell of ocean followed them before the Evergate winked out of existence.

"What the hell were you thinking!" Tom barked louder than I had ever heard him. Ed wheeled over.

I held my hands up in placation. "I was trying to help," I said, taking a step back. The look on Ed's face was something different. It was worry. I knew Tom had been closer to Ned than Ed, but I had yet to really get a good read on their past relationship.

"Tom, it would have happened anyway," Ed interjected, seeing the direction this was going.

While I rarely talked or reflected on my past in the military, the one thing I did keep was an uncanny ability to stay calm. Especially when being yelled at by others. I missed my time in the army; simpler times. Before I knew about magic —or for that matter, my background—I frequently found myself going with the flow. Not taking risks or calling the shots. Things had changed, I had changed, and more importantly, the world around me had changed. There were days when I even thought I would wake up and it would have all been a dream. I snapped back to the conversation after Ed's comment.

"Look, if I had gone tomorrow, the whole world would have known about it. Like Ed stated, I have a feeling what happened to Ned would have happened regardless. They didn't know we were there. Hell, if you want to get technical, news of our *planned*," I put emphasis on the word, "excursion more than likely sped up the event. Ever thought about that?"

Tom huffed lightly as his chest heaved. "You're reckless, and you're going to get yourself killed. I just heard Phil is missing a hand and Ed—"

Ed cut him off. "My condition has nothing to do with Max. If anything, he's probably one of the main reasons I'm still alive. If memory serves, this is in line with a certain someone present in this room," Ed said, directing his statement at Tom.

The comment deflated Tom. He let out another breath as the tension eased from his body. "Max, I'm going to say this one time and one time only. You're braver than most, I'll give you that, but this is bigger than you. It's bigger than me, and everyone else here. I know you're all about going out on your own, but we could have helped. I can't tell you how many times I wish you hadn't gotten caught up in all this. But in many ways, due to your lineage, you don't have a choice," Tom said, sighing again. He looked more tired the more he relaxed. I hadn't noticed his soaking wet clothes.

"Gentlemen, can we just let this be and focus? I understand your hesitation to follow well-laid plans due to diviners. So tell us what you can," Ed said, refocusing everyone. In many ways, there was still a lot that had been left unsaid between Gramps and me.

I started to tell them what I knew. When I got to the part about the titan-like creature on the ship, Tom interjected, and the mood shifted.

"It's been hundreds of years since I've heard of a titan on

Earth," Tom said, a puzzled look on his face. It was the expression one had when they placed their car keys somewhere specifically to be able to find them only to forget where that place was.

"I'll get with Doctor Freeman and see what he can find. It sounds like you weren't the only one out to shut the party down," Ed said, smirking at his hip use of language.

"Tom," I started, wanting to run my idea about the gates by him. "It's clear this whole thing has something to do with Everwhere. That much we all agree on. I was thinking about a way to travel in the Everwhere safely. Inspector Holder has already identified a location of significant activity on his side of the pond. Maybe we can use these coins," I said, dumping them out on the round table in the center of the Postern. Tom's eyes lit up.

"I never thought about approaching it this way. You may be onto something." Tom walked over, putting his hand on Ed's shoulder.

"How did you get around last time you were there?" I asked, never hearing many stories about his time in the Everwhere.

"A car," Tom replied, letting out a light chuckle at the memory of good times.

"A car?" I asked, remembering the vehicle that had come to my rescue. "It's the same one you left me in the will, isn't it?"

"That's what those keys were for? A vehicle you left in Everwhere?" Ed asked, shaking his head. The notion was ridiculous.

"Yup. It kind of has a mind of its own. You do still have the keys, right?"

"Sure, they're in a drawer over there," I said, pointing at the cabinet by the front entrance. It was locked, and after some modifications, able to hold several weapons and ammunition in case of emergencies—not to mention a few bottles of liquor.

I walked over, swiping my hand in front of the lock. As it clicked open, the smell of weapon oil hit me in the face. It was a good smell, one of comfort. I held up the keys, jingling them lightly as Tom walked over. I dropped them in his hands as he grinned.

"We need to talk to Dick. Max, check on Phil, and let's plan on meeting in the morning. Your place work?" Tom asked. It was clear a plan was forming in his head.

"Sounds good. I have Petro checking on something for me as well," I said, also filling them in on Jenny's wealthy customer.

"I think we may have just found some leverage," Ed said as he was now in planning mode.

Ed was right. This little detail may have just given us a sliver of hope. The plan to use the graveyard to get to Everwhere, then the Postern to gate solved one issue. We still didn't have a solid plan on how to flush anyone out.

"Anyone talked to Goolsby today?" I asked, thinking it may be time for him to pay me back for all the free dirty work I had done for him recently.

"No, maybe it's time you have a little chat with him." Tom grinned.

CHAPTER 15

The Long Dark Teatime for the Souls . . .

Aslynn was crying as I left the Atheneum. Jenny had taken the time to drop the bad news, knowing I didn't want to be around for the follow-up conversation. While Aslynn acted carefree, there was a different side to her that I knew lingered in the shadows. I had a feeling she and Jamison would be getting into the picture soon.

Petro had come up with some useful information on Carol Bellman. She often frequented St. Johns Town Center for shopping and lunch every other day. The young lady also had an expensive coffee habit that landed her at the same coffee shop every morning.

Before leaving the Atheneum, I'd checked with James in the crucible room for any updates on B&B LLC. As luck would have it, Brucey had left on a convenient business trip to an unknown location earlier in the day. The marshals and CSA had put an all-points bulletin out for him. *Do not engage, just report.*

Phil, on the other hand . . . pardon the pun, was doing better than I thought he would be. Due to some quick thinking, Jenny had knocked him out and was working on reattaching his hand, something that was way over my head. He looked rough, the lack of beard amplifying his looking out of place, but as Jenny put it, *"Due to the accumulated amount of alco-*

hol in his system, Phil should be able to pretty much live through anything."

Feeling good about leaving things as settled as they could be for the night, I decided a little break from the craziness was needed. That meant a trip to a normal place for some food and a drink. Looking on my phone, I picked the first place that came up: a small beach bar in Jacksonville that served burgers.

"This will do," I mumbled, pulling out the key to the Seekergate and walking through into the muggy October air on the beach.

The restaurant was moderately crowded. Several people lined the bar, leaving no room for newcomers. An attractive young hostess nodded at a corner table, looking out over the ocean. The air smelled of frying food, cigarette smoke, and cold beer. I liked the place immediately.

"What will you have?" a young girl in shorts about as brief as they could make them said.

"You have Vamp Amber?" I asked, quickly correcting myself. It was normal night, as Kim and I called it. "Never mind. Tell you what, how about a Miller Lite and a bacon cheeseburger, medium, with fries?"

"Thought you were one of those weirdos for a second," the girl chuckled, obviously taking a jab at magical types. The statement caught me off guard.

I hadn't really been out much since the Balance, and in many ways, hadn't paid much attention to what was going on in the real world. I knew some areas had gone to shit. Others, like Vatican City, had become strongholds of power overnight.

I sat there taking light pulls from my beer, letting the sounds of the ocean and partying twenty-somethings bring back old memories of days gone by. It also started bringing a certain clarity. Why had things gone to shit so quickly, and why around me. Sitting there overlooking the beach, I felt like

I could just walk away from everything. Maybe even further than I had when moving out of the Atheneum.

As the food arrived, the waitress again smiled with an innocent yet devilish grin. "Enjoy, and the second beer is on the house," she said, setting down a fresh glass of draft beer. I watched her saunter off to the kitchen. She looked back.

I nodded, immediately digging into the burger. The smell of beer, bacon, and cooked beef made my mouth water with every bite. It only took a few minutes to pound the burger down. Looking around, the crowd had thinned out significantly. "The party must have moved," I said under my breath into the glass, fogging the inside before taking another pull.

Either I was exhausted, or the last few days were starting to catch up with me. My legs felt sluggish as my arms began to slow down as if they were filled with concrete.

"Shit, check please," I said out loud as the waitress disappeared into the kitchen.

My body was not cooperating for some reason. The sounds of the kitchen doors swinging open filled the now hushed bar, and I noticed I couldn't turn my body.

I sensed her before I saw her. I leaned back and relaxed, hoping to reserve my strength as Lilith pulled out the chair across from me and sat down. She was tall and elegant, and like last time, was dressed in a black leather suit. Her hair was black and flowing over her chiseled features. Lilith's face was almost angelic. The look on it, same as last time, told another story.

"Max, I hope you enjoyed the burger. I had it made extra special just for you," she said, pulling back a long flowing scarf, exposing a biomechanical-looking arm.

As much as I wanted to react, my body was locked in place. "What the hell did you do to me? How did you know I was here?" I asked, figuring I'll buy some time to see if she wanted to talk, barter, or kill me.

"You know the problem with people like you, Tom, and

Ed? No? I'll answer that for you then," Lilith said, pulling out a cigarette and lighting it off her mechanical hand. This was the replacement for the one she'd lost last year.

I had gated Tom back through a portal with an enchanted gate rope as she held on to him. "You keep thinking that I am constantly shutting you out. Staying hidden in the shadows," She said, lightly chuckling.

Taking a deep breath, I focused on the message.

"When you try to find me in your mind's eye or whatever you want to call it, you see a roadblock. The thing is, I have a pretty good idea when someone is looking for me. If you had actually been paying attention, you would have realized that I'm much easier to find than you think," Lilith said.

She was being cryptic and making sense at the same time. It was clear she was powerful, and I didn't doubt she had more going on than hiding from the team. "How did you find me?" I asked, a slight strain in my voice.

"Well, just like when you looked for me, I did the same. Just a little better. Amazing what happens when you let your guard down or get distracted by *other things*," Lilith said, emphasizing the words.

The waitress walked back out with two glasses of tea. "Thank you, mistress," the young woman said, bowing slightly. Lilith raised a finger, as the woman turned and shuffled off.

Lilith reached over, putting her now clicking mechanical hand on mine as feeling started to seep back into my lower arm. "Drink. It will make you feel better. I'm not here to kill you; I'm just here to talk. That tea will start the process of loosening up your body," she said, taking a light sip from her cup.

I never in a million years thought I would ever want to punch my grandmother in the face. Odd how things work out.

"How?" I asked, seeing as she was in the mood to talk.

"Oh, I have eyes and ears everywhere. One day, when you

realize your full potential, you will understand. Plus, I'm aware you are particularly fond of diviners," she said, blowing smoke in my face. She was smoking one of those black, tar-smelling cigarettes. They were called Onyx and came from the Plane. I was betting they'd originated in the Under.

"The children, what the hell were you doing?" I asked, computing everything I had wanted to ask her over the year into a few pointed questions. I was trying to keep them in order. While the here and the now was important, not fully knowing the details from last year—not to mention the Fountain of Youth—had weighed heavily on me.

"Being a mother of sorts. That reminds me, I need to check in on the little ones. Let's save that for another day, Max," Lilith said, putting the conversation back in her court. She was smart and knew I was digging for as much information as I could.

I took a sip of the tea as a wave of relief flowed through my body. Not a release from my current situation, but a reprieve.

"Okay, to the point. Let's hear it," I said. A group of college-aged kids walked by, making faces as the odd-smelling smoke coming from Lilith's cigarette wafted into the street. It was clear she had somehow divined that I would be at this very location at this exact time.

"I'm here to ask you to stop following a dead end." She took another pull of her smoke before putting it out on the table. I had a feeling she meant "dead end" in another light. Nodding, I decided to use the old sales trick of keeping my mouth shut. "I have decided to no longer partake in the plans and antics of the Thule Society, that little organization you and your team are so fired up about. You do know they are small fish in a big sea, right? A means to an end. One that I have accomplished. I already have what I wanted out of the relationship." Lilith paused.

"You are the Thule Society," I stated as she let out a bark of laughter, which simmered into a deep, calming breath.

"That crew of flunkies. I was slaying souls thousands of years before those dissidents came around. I just gave them a little push in the right direction. The direction I needed at the time," she said, looking down at her mechanical arm.

"I don't get it. After everything I've heard and seen, you just decide to poison me then tell me you are quitting your day job, to do what?" I asked, my military intel instincts kicking in. I might not find out what was going on now, but I sure as hell was about to figure out what her true motivation was.

"Your mother ever read to you about demons or the Old Gods?"

"Sure, she used to always read me a story about the great divide, and how the Old Gods tricked the Lords of Heaven and Hell themselves into fighting each other. The Lords of the Underworld built an army that, if memory serves right, ended up being too large and obscene to control. Lost souls and all that stuff. In the end, the Old Gods turned Hell's own legions against itself and Heaven. By the time it was done, a part of the old world, Earth, became separated. The Lords of the Over and Under wanted the prize, Earth, for themselves. The legions decided they also wanted to keep Earth. The remaining Lords of the Planes or whatever you want to call them combined forces and overtook the hellion legions, locking them away never to be released again," I concluded reflectively, surprised I remembered most of the fairy tale.

I remember my mother always following up with a footnote. I heard her voice reverberating in my mind, *"It was a catch-22; kill the hellion legions, and the souls power the Old Gods beyond measure. Let them stay on Earth, and end up fighting them forever, stuck between the Lords of the Planes. Or lock them away for all time. After all, Terrum was the source of all power."*

"It's no fairy tale, Max. It's the truth. Even more, the Old

Gods want this piece of Terrum that they lost back. To do that, they need the help of the hellion legions. Is it starting to make sense? Anyway, as you know, our family is in the business of ensuring that does not happen. It gets complicated," Lilith said, taking another sip of her tea.

"The kids?" I asked again.

"Much like you, they are special; one in particular. One we all must protect, you know, family and all. To answer your question," Lilith said, her tone becoming hard. "With the Balance and everything else going on, there is a need for additional resources. While Father and the other Lords of the Planes are playing nice on the surface, under the water, the current is moving. Fast and unabated."

"So you're saying you are—well, were—creating an army of superdemons? Gods and graves," I said, already knowing the answer by the smirk forming on Lilith's face.

"Not as dumb as they say you are, young one. I'm no longer part of whatever it is Mengele and the bearded one are doing. They are truly playing with fire. My cards are on the table, except for a few. I'm also going to give you some much-needed information. That is, if you agree to not interfere in my work. Promise me this, and I'll give you more than you have now," Lilith said, wrapping up the conversation. She more than likely also knew my body was starting to fire back up.

"Tell me if you had anything to do with Chloe," I said, more focused on the past than the future.

Lilith sighed, blowing stale smoke in the air. "What have you learned over the last week?"

"You come to me with a request. By the looks of things, I don't have much of a choice, yet you are giving me one. I've learned that pirates can come back from the dead . . ." I trailed off. "What are you getting at?"

"Just because you appear to be dead, doesn't always mean you are," Lilith said, standing up.

"The Thule Society, along with the Soul Dealers—or as you call them so elegantly, pirates—are figuring out a way to let the hellion legions loose and control them. That's not on my list of things to do. They need all the soul stone they can get to build an army large enough to do just that. Soul stones are the base for Kracken, and the majority of it comes from England. More specifically, the Everwhere in England." She took a deep, clearing breath as the mechanisms in her new arm clicked.

"Promise me," I said, referring to her statement about not being part of the Thule Society anymore.

"I'll do my best. Before I forget, that man you call Black-beard, his name is Beleth; he is one of the Fallen Angels and someone you don't want to cross paths with," Lilith said as she walked off, leaving the bill on the table for me to pick up.

CHAPTER 16

No Rest for the Wicked . . .

"Τ his is troubling, especially if she has split off from the rest of the Thule Society," Tom said, taking a sip from his coffee. Trish had loaded it down with Fae honey.

After I was finally able to use my legs last night, I gated back to my apartment, passing out from a mix of Lilith's potion and pure exhaustion. Petro had popped out of his room before I left this morning, reminding me to stock up on Golden Grahams. He had also found a video feed of Bruce Teach and Mrs. Bellman having coffee.

After watching a clip of the video, the two looked more than comfortable together, furthering the twisting plot. Mages often had large egos, including a lack of appreciation or respect for technology, which frequently got them in trouble.

Stopping by FA's, I had picked up some of Trish's turbo coffee, messaging Tom that we needed to talk. The two of us had spent an hour so far going over everything Lilith said. Something was telling me he would know if there was more to it. And, of course, there was.

"She seemed to be content about something. It had to do with the children from last year. She mentioned one in particular," I said, taking a deep breath.

"Let me think about this. If we take everything she said at face value, that means we, in reality, weren't that far off the mark. I have a meeting with Dick and Dr. Freemen at noon. I would like you to be there," Tom told me in a concentrated tone, clicking his tongue on the roof of his mouth.

"I still need to catch up with Goolsby. I called Ed before I got here; he is working with a local detective named Neil to bring in Mrs. Bellman. He thought it would be best to keep the marshal's office out of it, especially with Darkwater having his hands in what they are doing," I informed him as my phone buzzed with a message from Phil.

It was a picture of him flipping me off with his newly reattached hand in typical Phil fashion. It was swollen, purple, and more than likely going to take several months to heal.

"Who was that?" Tom asked as I shook my head, tapping out a response.

I'll stop in later for a drink, get some rest. I need to get you caught up on last night.

"Phil. Looks like he's going to be okay."

I was thinking about what Phil could do in the background to help. People around me had started to get hurt at an abnormally high rate. The look on my face must have given my thoughts away because Tom spoke up. "Phil's hand is not your fault, and we are all upset about Ned, but it wasn't your fault either. They are going to hold a funeral for him next week. The Council is laying him to rest in the great hall. It's a prestigious honor," Tom said, walking out from behind the desk, sitting in the chair to my side, and handing me an old book.

"I don't think this can wait till next week. This needs to get worked out soon. I know you've been around and have witnessed things I can't even imagine, but . . . the look on that man or whatever's face was pure evil. Hell, both of them. Whatever it is they are up to, they are going to move faster now that they know we are at least in the game," I said, opening the book.

The book's title was simply *Fallen Angels*. The author's name was Patricia. It was a simple, well laid out book. The needed entry was under the letter *B*, and to the point.

Beleth: Commander and king of the lower eighty-five hellion legions. Prince of necromancy. Preferred to stay on Earth after the great divide. Double-crossed the generals of the lower eighty-five hellion legions to have them imprisoned.

There was a picture of a man with a massive beard holding a sword. "I'm pretty sure this is the guy," I said, turning the book toward Tom. It was obvious he already knew.

"Soul Dealers. The worst of the worst. I, to a point, see why Lilith is making a move on the chessboard," Tom said in a thoughtful tone. "I know she is not a fan of them. Plus, the Council theoretically eradicated them roughly two hundred years ago; it was a dark time for the Council. I was on that team, as was Ed. If this is Beleth as you say, bigger things are at work. Max, do you remember what the letter I left you in my will said?"

"What part?" I asked, seeing the dots starting to connect fully.

"I made a point to tell you that things were changing. They are, as you have realized. Ten years ago, I could have named most of the living Mages in the United States. Now a new Mage is coming into their power every day. There are demons, as you know, starting to show up, and we have had a recent outbreak of Vampires," Tom said reflectively.

"I already know the Balance was needed due to this. Are you saying something else is happening? Making all this trouble?" I asked slowly.

"Precisely. Some on the Council think the Old Gods are directly involved. Others just think things like we have been dealing with are power moves, the Thule Society being one of the most prominent behind them. The team took out most of their muscle last year. You even took out one of their main foot soldiers, Pearl. The deal with Kracken and Goolsby, I believe, can be resolved without violence. He's being dragged into this. The rest, I'm not so sure about." He took another sip of his coffee.

"It's pretty clear that Bruce, the Thule Society, and Beleth were working together to get Cecil and Goolsby to take each other out. I'm just not sure why," I huffed.

"Kim figured that piece out for us. She's a smart one. Goolsby and Cecil had the two things the Thule Society needed. The docks, the ability to control them, and a steady, reliable source of Kracken," Tom replied, the picture coming into focus with laser clarity. Why hadn't I been able to see this? It had been in front of my face the entire time. I, as always, had been too busy picking a fight to see things as they were. Oscar was right. I would listen to him more often from now on.

As I was about to speak, Tom interrupted.

"Haaa," Tom chuckled. "Much less convoluted than both of us thought."

"True. It makes sense. Glad we talked about this before me getting in front of Goolsby." I paused as the pieces fell into place, also letting out a light chuckle. "Hey, that reminds me, Mrs. Bellman and Bruce. Maybe it's just that simple. Carol Bellman, or Carol Darkwater as we now know her, is in love with Bruce. The two are together, and they plotted not only to take out her husband but also to use him as a vessel. Carol didn't have any magic in her blood, at least that we know of from our theory about her father being a fake. She cuts a deal with Bruce, and he somehow gets her to turn. She doesn't know any better and is obliviously blind, making the mistake of trying to get Jenny to make her a castor secretly. As an independent manufacturer, we don't have to register the owner."

Tom finished my thought, "I would even go as far as to say that Bruce is using Carol for her father's access to the Council. We've heard a few folks mention he's been acting odd lately.

Maybe with Lilith out of the picture, the mood has shifted. While ruthless, she always seemed to have patience. Lilith would never generate open discord on the Council. She knows we are watching Darkwater. Maybe that's part of it."

We both sat there for a minute, the entire puzzle starting to take form. "He's overextended himself. I bet he is working for the Thule Society and Lilith separately, yet together, if that makes any sense. Like he might not know, and the two sides are giving him conflicting information," I said again, looking down at my phone.

"Time for us to get going. We can lay the rest of this out later. Head to Goolsby's after we talk to the others just in case we're missing something. I'll fill them in when we get downstairs," Tom said as we both stood up, starting on our way.

Petro showed up as we walked into the dining room. It had been months, if not longer, since I had been in the room for a full-on meeting. Leshya had outdone herself with a spread of lunch salads and sandwiches. She even made one of her now famous cream cheese and cucumber sandwiches for me, the paper bag even having my name on it. I would thank her later.

Having Inspector Holder, better known as Dick Holder, in the room and not Kim felt weird. While I understood the reasoning, it still felt off.

Petro took his spot in front of my old seat, ripping into the small BLT in front of him. "Hey, boss," Petro said between noshing his food loudly.

"Petro, good job on finding out about Bruce and Carol Bellman. We think it's going to be a big piece of this. When this meeting is over, I'm heading over to see Goolsby, and I need my wingman," I said as Petro nodded his head in affirmation.

"Sure thing boss. I may need a nap after this sandwich though. That lady can cook," Petro mumbled as crumbs fell out of his mouth, the grease from the bacon gleaming off his hands.

"Agreed," was all I said, joining him by unwrapping my own sandwich. The sounds of the others following suit made for a chorus of crinkling, crackling paper.

At the far end, Jenny was tapping away violently on her keyboard as Phil walked in with his arm in a sling. "Well, well, well, looks like no one needs a hand getting lunch started," he said. The room went still. Phil had a particular way of not landing jokes when he was sober, which was . . . well, not often.

I stood up, grinning at him. The stone-cold look on his face didn't give anything away, making my grin falter for a second. *Was he mad at me for dragging him along?* I thought pensively.

Phil stepped forward as his now stubble-covered face split into a smile. "Come here, bruther," Phil bellowed, putting his good arm around my neck. The sounds of the others continuing their meals took back over.

"Nice to see you too, man. How are you holding up?" I asked as Jenny cut Phil's response off.

"Considering the sword used to cut his hand off was a soul sword, good. Plus, the ship you two were supposed to be on today just exploded in the middle of the ocean. They project no survivors. I believe the words were 'total disintegration,'" Jenny said bluntly.

"A what?" I asked, looking around the room for Dr. Freeman. Given a chance, he would let loose a torrent of knowledge.

"It's a sword that is more often used to keep whatever it cuts off alive," Dr. Freeman said in his slightly wavering voice, a mix of absolute knowledge and nerves.

Dr. Freeman was your typical old-school professor. He was, like always, wearing a button-down beige shirt with non-matching slacks, a pair of worn yet cared-for slip-on loafers on his feet. His hair was brown and clearly lacking on the top of his head. He had the classic comb-over and was not shy about it. The hair had, by the looks of his thick mustache, retreated from the top of his head and gone to his upper lip. He had finally invested in a newer pair of glasses, with thick wood grain rims. His frame wasn't full of strength, but you could tell by looking in his eyes that he was full of knowledge. Everyone loved the man, and when he spoke, people listened. At least for the first five minutes.

"You know all those beheadings back in the day? A good portion of them were done with a soul sword. There are only records of a handful of them. The Council has one, and if memory serves right, it's stored here in the stacks. Imagine taking your enemy's head as a show of force, then keeping them around as a pet or counterbalance. Kind of sick, but there are several cases of people taking heads just to keep them as confidants, promising to give them back a body and all that stuff," Dr. Freeman spit out.

"They have one on the Plane. The High Fae use it. I think Tatiana has it," Petro added, unfazed.

"Thing is, there are rumors of body parts still alive to this day that were cut off hundreds of years ago. People called them cursed when in reality, things like a hand," Dr. Freeman said, nodding to Phil, "just exist afterward. You know, not truly dead or alive. Rumor has it both parts could last an eternity."

Phil looked at his hand hanging out the end of a sling. "Great."

"It actually is. That is the reason your hand will be fine," Jenny said, going back to the ritual thrashing of her laptop keyboard.

"What about the boat?" I asked, looking over at Dick as he crammed what looked like a kipper sandwich in his mouth. The smell of salted raw fish oozed from him.

Dick stopped eating, slurping his fingers. "Bloody thing went up in flames, all fire and brimstone. No survivors—not even the crew. The chaps at the Dunn are trying to recon who was on the ship, if anyone."

"If anyone?" I asked, not doing the math in my head.

"Max," Ed spoke, rolling his wheelchair around the end of the table to get a clear view of everyone in the room. "We still wanted to keep an eye on the shipment. There are no records of the crew loading up or anyone from the Council or other agencies. After yesterday, it dropped off the radar. I . . ."

Jenny cleared her throat. "We believe it was a message, and also an opportunity to destroy evidence."

"We sure about that? Has anyone talked to Jamison or Aslynn?" I asked, having a gut feeling they'd had a hand in the obliteration of the shipping vessel. People, including myself, often forgot how powerful the Fae could be if provoked.

The room looked around, getting my point. The two were oddly absent and had a score to settle.

"Agreed. We need to look into their whereabouts. There is new information that I believe we need to discuss," Tom said. He took the next thirty minutes going over the details of my tea party with Lilith and our take on current events.

The team all came to the same conclusion we had. Unfortunately, the part about us going from the Everwhere to the Postern generated some confused looks.

"So, we need Dick here to tell us what's up with the docks in Southampton," I concluded, taking over for Tom as he got distracted by the Cuban hot-pressed sandwich Leshya set in front of him. He still got special treatment from her.

"The docks?" Dick asked as some type of juice dripped onto his shirt, his tie catching the majority of the onslaught. "We believe we found where their old ship was kept—the Isle of Wight. And even better than that, all the voodoo witchcraft activity seems to be centering around Stonehenge."

The group sighed. Petro snickered. "So we get to blow up another world-famous thing?" He was right. We had, in fact, already changed the landscape of several prominent structures.

"Gods and graves, can't we just get a house full of bad guys or something?" I complained, shaking my head.

"Even better, from what we understand, there's a tunnel underground that stretches close to Stonehenge. Never heard of such rubbish," Dick said as a stern look crossed his face. "Some of the Mages back home seemed to be reluctant to go anywhere near the place. Something about it being wrong."

Jenny stopped typing. "Ed and Tom may remember all the nonsense that surrounds that place. Max, for reference, it's like telling a bunch of kids about a haunted house in the woods, or some stupid rumor about a killer on the loose. It's more myth than reality."

"I would not completely ignore that. If memory serves right, there were reports of several Mages losing their powers after going there. Is that correct?" Tom said, looking back over at Dick.

"It's true. Not a rumor, but that's all. I talked with some of the other voodoo types, and they stated it was more than likely due to something those knuckleheads were doing," Dick said, knowing more than I thought he would.

"We get the point." Tom stood up. "Max and I will get a small team together and figure out our next move. Ed, as soon as Mrs. Bellman is in custody, please let me know."

"Right. I believe we should have her by this evening. I'll give you a call. Oh, and Max, there is some paperwork you need to fill out waiting for you back home. The whole Cecil deal has ruffled a few feathers on the V side of things," Ed said as the group started shuffling out of the room.

I noticed James was also missing. He was also part of the marshal's office agents assigned to the Atheneum. By appearances alone, it was clear that the marshal's office was outside the circle of trust. At least for now.

"Bruther," Phil said as Petro and I finished our lunches. "I want to talk to you about something later. It's private."

I looked at him, nodding my head. "Sure thing. I'll give you a call when we get back from Goolsby's. I know Jenny's not going to let you out of here yet."

Something in his face was contemplative, almost like he was a kid about to ask his dad for the keys to the new car.

CHAPTER 17

That's Not How It Works . . .

P etro and I drove the Black Beast to Riverplace Tower; I had even given Goolsby the courtesy of calling ahead, and for once, his secretary was more than accommodating. We were about to walk into a trap, or Goolsby needed something. I was much more in tune now when dealing with the man, and would not make the mistake of doing his dirty work again.

"You think he's going to listen?" Petro asked as I went over my plans.

"I do, and that's why we need to keep this to ourselves. At least for now," I said as we pulled the truck into the parking garage, the sound of the rumbling V8 echoing off the concrete announcing our arrival. They had finally started the repairs after Cecil and the Soul Dealers had come close to destroying the Blue House, Goolsby's restaurant and home base for operations.

The tall woman known only as the accountant was waiting for us in the lobby. No witty banter with the security guard today. After the Balance, the team that worked there more than likely knew most of the visitors that came to see Mr. Goolsby were not normal.

The elevator rocketed up the building at roughly three

hundred feet per minute, but the trip always took a while. I often wondered if the place was somehow a gate. I decided in the meantime to get to know our new friend. We had met on several occasions but never formally talked to each other.

"Name's Max, and you are?" I asked, seeing if the straightforward approach would work. The tall, business suit–wearing woman turned around. She had been facing the doors with her back to us.

Petro landed on my shoulder in anticipation of a response that never fully came.

"I'm here to take you to see Councilman Goolsby. If we need to discuss business, I will be made aware of this before we talk," the stern woman said, not giving anything away. An odd feeling of muffled power came from her; she could be a sensitive. It wouldn't surprise me if Goolsby hired Mages to work for him. What I did take note of was her calling him by his official Council title.

The elevator lurched to a stop as a bell chimed, and the doors slid open seamlessly. "Please follow me," the woman requested, walking out without acknowledging the workers in the lobby. The place was being fully renovated.

We walked into Goolsby's office. Blueprints were neatly stacked and laid out on his desk. I first assumed they were for the renovation. After taking a closer glance using my enhanced vision, I noticed they were for something larger and more complex.

"Max, Petro, thank you for stopping by," Goolsby greeted in an unusual welcome as he stood up. Seeing me taken off guard by this, he filled in the gaps. "I believe we both have something to gain from this meeting."

"Ah, of course. Look, I'm not going to beat around the bush here. I'm sure you know the basics of everything by now, and that you and Cecil were set up. What I can't figure out is how you didn't know?" I asked, remembering what Oscar had told me. *"You seem to always be asking the wrong people the right questions, and the right people the wrong questions."*

Something was telling me that looking backward would help. Goolsby sat back down, doing as he had every other time I had been in his office, which had been a grand total of . . . twice. Opening his top drawer and pulling out a bottle of scotch, Goolsby set three glasses on the table. Same as last time, he had a small cup for Petro.

"That is the same question I keep asking myself. I'm impressed you want to know. Max, we have a common enemy here. Something both of us want to ensure is no longer relevant," Goolsby said, his use of certain words deliberate. I could translate their meaning on my own. He started back after a slight pause. "My business has been compromised. My contract with the Council to work with Ketonic-etho-entheriun —Kracken—was just canceled. If I'm correct, which I am, my name is being connected to the magical drug trade run by the Thule Society."

It was clear that he had a firm grasp on the situation. "The others don't think there are any serious implications after yesterday," I said, seeing how much he already knew about my little cruise.

Petro had already downed his glass as I took my first light pull. While not my drink of choice, the scotch was amazing. It went down like velvet, only to leave a trailing bite in the back of my throat.

"I was updated about the situation, and understand. That doesn't mean the perception won't linger. You forget Max, many of these people and things have long memories. But to answer your question, I was preoccupied with other priorities. Cecil coming into Jacksonville was the least of my worries. While an issue that needed addressing, I can promise you it was minor," Goolsby said. As he waited for my response, he cocked his head sideways.

"I know you don't like the recent surge in magic. I also think you are working on Kracken for other reasons. Most importantly, I also believe you are using the Kracken for other purposes that the Council would not fully approve of," I said, waiting to see his response. Nothing. Goolsby just sat there stone-faced.

"Right," Goolsby said after a moment, something hitting home, "to a point. What if I told you a deal was made between the regular governments and the Council?

"I wouldn't be surprised," I replied, leaning back.

"The reason for the study of soul stone is simple: to level the playing field, and also through Mags-Tech, develop new weapons. Think about governments with the ability to turn people into Mages or the ability to take magic away. Not everything is as it seems. As frustrated as you might be not knowing this is going on, just look at all the prior conspiracy theories before the Balance. Not to mention the revenue stream such studies could produce for the Council. Some governments even believe this is necessary for our survival. They are, of course, wrong. But there is a silver lining. We are learning more about magic, as you would call it, than ever before." Goolsby paused. "I can see by the look on your face you are not surprised about the Council keeping secrets. Out of all the things going on, this isn't nearly as nefarious. What secrets are you keeping, Max?"

Goolsby made a point that I already knew but didn't want to accept. My time in the army had been enough to show me how governments often didn't want others to know what they're doing, and most importantly, why.

Petro spoke up, also handing his cup back to Goolsby for a refill. "There are too many roosters in the hen house. You know it, we know it, hell, everyone does. If you want things to stay as they are, you're going to need to bring something to the table. Plus, if I keep staying out late at night, Casey is going to kill me."

Goolsby and I both looked at Petro as he smoothed out his mustache.

"I'm listening," Goolsby said with a calm repose.

I sat there looking at Petro as he took a drink from his second shot. It would be extra Golden Grahams for him later. I might even introduce him to churros. He knew the stakes, and even worse, Casey must have laid the law down on him after we returned.

Taking another deep breath, I took a pull from my drink adding on to what Petro started. "We think we know where the Soul Dealers are coming from. Plus, we believe they are about to finish whatever it is they are doing."

"How does this pertain to me and bring something to the table?" Goolsby asked. You could tell he liked to negotiate; it was in his blood. I knew then and there he already had a plan.

"Tell me what you're planning to do," I stated flatly. Instead of playing cat and mouse, I would close the deal here and get to the point.

"Ah, you are focused for once. I guess hitting whatever it was over the head with a hammer didn't work this time. I'm sorry about Ned. I respected him," Goolsby said.

"We all are," I murmured under my breath in a show of respect. In reality, the gravity of his death hadn't settled in yet.

"My plan is a simple one. Find the source of the problem and remove it. I am willing to ensure my help, as well as that of my constituents, if available," Goolsby stated flatly, back in his business mode.

He was being genuine with me, if only momentarily because of Ned. "So, you're planning on finding the ship from my report, which you've obviously read, and sink it?" I clarified.

"No. We are." Goolsby leaned forward. "I'm sure you know who my constituents are. I just need to know when and where to place them on the chessboard. Plus, I think the ship is only one piece of the puzzle." He was talking about the Guardians, the now legitimized arm of the Order Society. Over time, they had garnered many designations: Crusaders, Knights Templar, just to name a few.

"Perfect. Now that's out of the way, here is what I'm thinking," I said, going over my plans for the mission.

"What you're thinking? Is this not an official Council operation?" Goolsby asked, getting the final bit of clarification he needed after I'd finished.

"I'm not too good at those, and no one's kicked me out of the Council yet. Plus, I've been chewed out before," I said, quoting one of my favorite Brad Pitt lines in his best voice.

"Your reputation for trust precedes you. I wish more people would take diviners as seriously as you do. You know how truly powerful they can be. The less people know, the better," Goolsby stated.

The plan was simple. Tom and I, including a small team, would gate to Everwhere. From there, we would make our way to the alternate version of the Postern, then gate to the Isle of Wight before heading toward Stonehenge.

Apparently, this version of Stonehenge was a true sight to behold and one of the main gates to the Everwhere, not to mention to the Above and Below. We had discussed simply gating to the location, but Tom had projected it would not work the same. He'd followed that by spouting out a bunch of rules that made little to no sense to me. I, of course, kept those pieces out of my conversation with Goolsby.

From there, it would be nothing more than getting Goolsby and the Guardians through. Take out Beleth, and hopefully, Mengele, eradicate whatever operation they had set up, and call it a day. Simple, right? What could possibly go wrong? Not taking into account Darkwater and whatever Mrs. Bellman had going on. I sat there watching Goolsby after laying out the plan. It also dawned on me that Lilith was still somehow in play.

Goolsby took a calming breath. "When?"

Petro and I looked at each other, not making that call yet. "Tomorrow," I said, deciding it would not benefit us to let this linger.

"Alright, is that all?" Goolsby asked, standing up.

I sat there, reflecting on the question. "I'll let you know when to use this," I said, handing him a stone from the Evergate. Goolsby picked it up, raising an eyebrow, surprised by the gesture. He reached into his pocket, passing me a black cylinder the size of an ink pen, the Mags-Tech logo on either end.

"Just push your thumb on the side with the logo. That will link us," Goolsby said, pulling out a matching communicator thingy. In retrospect, I hadn't thought that far ahead and had been assuming a simple call would do. I was still foggy on the rules of the Everwhere.

Petro and I left, taking a minute to talk before pulling out of the garage.

"You think he's going to help, boss?" Petro asked as I started the truck.

"Help, yes; do what we need him to? No," I said, having a feeling we may have just made a mistake.

"Well, at least we know he's not involved with the others. I think we need to figure out if that Neil guy has Mrs. Bellman yet. I think that's going to be a mess." Petro had a point.

"I'm not so sure about him not being involved. I think a backup plan is in order," I replied as we both grinned. Turning on the power ballad "Farrel Cats" by Planes Drifter, we pulled out of the garage as Petro sent out a text.

It only took twenty minutes to get to the holding building to which Neil, Kim's ex-husband, had taken Mrs. Bellman. She had apparently not been very cooperative. The building smelled like a musty old wet carpet which had been past its prime two decades ago.

"She call anyone yet?" I asked as Neil leaned against the wall, opening a bottle of pills and taking a handful of headache reducers. He proceeded to chew them up instead of washing them down with water.

"Nope. Well, I haven't handed her a phone yet. Since she is suspected of something on the OTN side of things, I'm not too sure what I can or can't do," Neil replied, blowing it off. He was either acting, or honestly didn't give a damn. I was leaning on him not caring.

Mrs. Bellman, better known as Carol Darkwater, sat there listening to us. Neil was either a complete idiot or playing the game. I wanted to see how far he would take it.

"Well, she is under suspicion for involvement in the murder of her husband, Mr. Bellman, through the use of magic," I said. She gasped.

"What? I want to talk to my lawyer," Carol said, huffing. She was not handcuffed to anything; however, it was clear she would not be let out of the room.

"Is it the same as Bruce Teach's?" I blurted out, garnering a snicker from Neil before he quickly corrected himself.

The color in her face turned several shades of white. Using Bruce's name had not only taken her off guard, but it had also shocked her that we knew about the two.

"I . . . what . . . no," she stuttered, deflecting.

"I don't think I have the jurisdiction to contact the Council," Neil said, snapping the lid back on his pill bottle before talking again. "Councilman Darkwater, from what I hear, is out traveling. I don't think we will be able to get a hold of daddy."

What was left of the color in Carol's face was now gone. Neil was playing the game. He surprised me with what he knew. Darkwater was indeed traveling, according to Ed.

"According to the Accords, you don't have any rights unless given to you by a member of the Council. Oh, looky here," I said, pulling out my Council shield. "You want to talk to us now, off the record, or do you want us to explain to every-one exactly what we know, which I can assure you has a lot to do with not only you, but your family as well. Oh, and the money you sent in for the castor will be returned by the end of the week," I said, glancing over at Neil, seeing a slight nod of approval.

"I'm not sure what you're talki—" Petro cut her off this time.

"Lady, I don't know you, but you know that as a Pixie, I can't break a promise, right?" Petro said quickly.

Carol nodded her head in understanding, realizing her fifteen minutes of fame were over.

"I promise you two things. First, these guys have you dead to rights. Secondly, you work with us, and we will leave you and your pops out of what's going on right now," Petro said. He had been taking a fair amount of liberties calling the shots lately. The funny thing about it was his ability to be spot on.

I raised an eyebrow at Petro as he winked. As if the gods had ordained it themselves, Carol Darkwater started singing like a bird. The one issue I saw was actually following through with Petro's promise. After a few seconds, I realized what he had said. She would be left out of the fallout for current events, but not the others. I could work with that.

"It's not what it seems. My father is not involved in this. He's just trying to help me," Carol explained, shuffling her hands in front of her nervously. She was no longer in charge.

"Trying to help with what?" I asked as Neil leaned against the wall talking to a female officer that had shown up. The two looked to be rather close. He must have called in some-one he could trust.

"I just want to be part of this new world. All my

friends . . ." Carol trailed off.

"Let me guess. All your rich friends want to buy their way into magic. I get that. Hell, I even understand it. We're not here to talk about drugs or what your friends are doing," I said, seeing her unease shift to panic.

"I don't know what you're talking about," Carol said, her voice wavering.

Petro, knowing that she was envious of true magic types, looked over as I nodded at him. "Lady, Max here is a sucker for a smile, but I'm not. I have a wife at home, and if I stay out past midnight again, she's going to leave me. We know Bruce is dealing in soul magic, and that he brought his dear old dad back from the grave. We also know that you two worked together to take out your husband, bringing one of those things over, which didn't work—just ask our buddy Phil's beard. Tell us the details, and you walk," Petro said, dusting lightly on the table in front of her.

I then realized he was mimicking the *CSI* show I had gotten him the box set of, playing the part. He was acting and was damn good at it. Petro was telling the truth about Casey, however.

Carol broke down crying, as Petro turned to me grinning. While I didn't condone pushing people's emotions, we needed leverage. Plus, she was a murderer, so there's that.

Hearing the sobbing, the woman that Neil had been talking to walked in. "Ma'am, are you okay?" she asked in a clear, smooth voice. While playing good cop, bad cop, she would be the nice one, but we weren't in a situation to be playing cat and mouse games—we needed answers. We also needed leverage to go back to Darkwater with.

It was clear that Carol was used to getting whatever she needed from the Council. I was even betting she had used her father's influence to get Goolsby's contract canceled. Realization started to set in, making the outcome clear as day. The contract was about to be outsourced to B&B LLC.

We had just peed in someone's flowerbed.

Carol looked up with a slight change in her mood. "I need some water, please?" she asked, the presence of another woman calming her.

"Can I have a word with you gentlemen in the hall?" the woman asked. She was dressed in a business suit and had intelligent eyes.

I nodded at Petro as we walked out into the hall. "I'm Max, and this is Petro. Are you a detective?" I asked, holding out my hand as Petro did a floating bow.

"My name is Tina, and no, I'm an attorney. I know Neil due to his frequent need for legal counsel—or representation, for that matter," she said, a slight blush crossing her cheeks. She liked him, so I liked her. Maybe she would keep the guy away from Kim. I thought about Kim and what she was up to. The lack of communication had been jarring.

Tina walked over to the cooler and poured a glass of water, walking it back into the room and closing the door behind her after she returned.

"Neil called. I'm afraid unless there is proof she is a Mage, she falls under the civilian legal code," Tina said, looking sternly at the three of us.

"Meaning?" I asked, drawing it out.

"Meaning, unless you have something to detain her for, she will need to be turned over to the proper authorities," Tina said sternly.

There was a thought forming in my mind that hadn't solidified yet. "We have plenty to hold her on," I said as the hairs on the back of my neck decided to straighten out like spikes on a porcupine.

I rubbed my neck.

"Like?" Tina asked, again making her point.

"Alright. Hey, Neil, is that room warded by any chance, or did you pat her down?" I asked as Neil turned in slow motion.

It was too late. Two green laser beams shot out from the room, cutting the wall and door in half in a zigzag pattern.

The group dived behind cover as the door fell in a smoking thump on the old stained carpet.

"You still got this?" I asked Tina as Petro flew to the far end of the hall. I pulled out my staff and leaned over to see Carol Darkwater's eyes glowing green, streaks of makeup running down her face. She had used the distraction to dose up on Kracken. While I was sure she was a sensitive, the drug kicked everything into overdrive.

Tina ducked further down as Neil pulled out his pistol. I shook my head, tapping my staff on the back of the flipped over lobby table.

Carol stalled, the power stunning her momentarily as Petro buzzed back over. "Hey, boss, there's water in the pipes behind that wall." He was implying that it might be a good idea for me not to set every building I was in on fire. I agreed.

"Distract her," I said as Carol looked up, the glow in her eyes starting to power back up. Petro zipped through the air toward her, giving me enough time to throw my hand out, willing the water in the pipes to rush out of the wall and burst in a semi-controlled fashion.

I shifted my hand, slamming the water directly into Carol at full force, knocking her out,and more importantly, giving me a clear shot with the stunning spell from my rod, one of the first items I'd ever blended.

I yelled, "Stupefacio!" as a ball of energy slammed into Carol when she started to look up, the mixture of the spell and water shutting her down immediately.

"What the hell?" I said, standing up and looking at her. The stunning spell and water shouldn't have completely grounded her. The magic had dissipated as soon as the water touched her body.

"It's ironized water, boss." Petro came to hover over my shoulder. Lights started flashing as the water continued to flow onto the floor. That stuff was illegal and was used to control Mages and Ethereals alike. What was it doing in this building? A building full of holding cells? Even more odd was the lack of other officers.

Neil picked up on my sudden interest in the building. He rushed forward, putting silver-infused handcuffs on Carol. Tina stood up, her hair wet and face in shock. She had never witnessed a Mage slinging magic around. Quarter Mage, at least. I had moved at unnatural speeds, the entire incident taking only a handful of seconds.

"At least I didn't burn the building down," I said as I picked up the phone and dialed Ed.

A team of Mages, including a handful of marshals, showed up to take Carol Darkwater into custody. After talking with Neil for a few more minutes, I assured him I would be looking into the building. Something felt off, and I didn't like the place.

Tina would not look directly at me; she was still stunned by what had happened. The regular population was still trying to sort these types of things out, many not fully believing as they hadn't witnessed it for themselves. After tonight, Tina would be a believer.

Stepping into the Postern, I turned to Petro. "Time to get plan B in motion. I'll get with Ed and Tom on Carol in a few minutes. She needs to be detained, and Darkwater called. That should take care of that piece." Petro stood on the table in the middle of the room, a meditative look on his face.

I shut my eyes, opening my internal phone line to Belm.

The demon—and come to find out relative—popped into existence as the smell of ozone filled the room.

"Figured you would call sooner," Belm rasped. While his voice had improved, it still sounded like dragging a bag of glass down a gravel road.

"Been busy, I take it?" I asked, seeing Belm's burnt arm.

"You could say that. Things are getting a little crazy back home. You should visit sometime; they would just love you. Oh, and Bo told me to say hello," Belm rasped. I hadn't heard from him in several months. The ambiguously fluid demon had wanted to take me for dinner the last few times we had seen each other. I was still trying to figure out if I was on the menu, or if he really wanted to try the local seafood.

"Great, so are you any good at gathering up a bunch of wandering souls in Everwhere?" I asked, putting plan B into motion.

CHAPTER 18

And Pass the Cemetery Gates . . .

T he next day, I received a message from Frank to meet him for coffee next door. After wrapping up with Belm last night, we had actually made it back home in time to avoid any significant issues with Casey. I was only threatened with having my underwear drawer cursed.

The familiar smell of FA's tantalized my senses, making me miss the place. Petro was staying with Casey for as long as possible to avoid any issue with the upcoming operation.

"Max," Trish said with a beaming smile.

"Trish, good to see you. Can I get a cup of the good stuff?" I asked, wishing for a cup of Fae honey coffee on the house. Trish handed over a cup, nodding at Frank, and to my astonishment, Davros sitting at a table.

"Thanks. Hey, I heard you're getting some help," I said grinning, referencing Sarah before walking over to the table. There was a small but busy crowd in FA's. Since the Balance, Trish had all but stopped regulars from coming in, only serving the magical communities.

"Max," Frank greeted, standing up and pulling out a chair. Davros looked up, a glass of synthetic blood sitting in front of him.

"Gentlemen, hope all is well," I replied as Davros sat there, still sipping on his drink.

"I heard you had a long night. Councilman Darkwater's daughter was Mr. Bellman's wife. Crazy," Frank said. He was wearing an immaculate form-fitting gray suit, and as always, smelled like freshly cut flowers. His thin yet strong figure demanded attention.

"You could say that."

Davros lifted a slender, thin-skinned finger. He was the scary as hell, old-type Vampire. "The Council is meeting this afternoon with Darkwater to get some questions answered. We will see what comes of it. As you are painfully aware, being a member of the Council affords one certain protections," Davros said in his silky yet strong aged voice. He must have figured out a way to cover the nauseating smell that he, as well as other old Vs, had.

I got along with Davros, and he even followed up his statement with a toothy grin that would make most people—and Mages, for that matter—uncomfortable. I knew that was him simply smiling. Vs were nothing more than cursed Fae—diseased, if you asked the Fae. Needless to say, the two groups didn't get along well.

"I doubt you wanted to meet with me over Darkwater getting scolded. What's up?" I asked, taking a sip of the hot coffee.

Frank took an unnecessary deep breath, considering he didn't need to breathe. "Max, we're here to tell you the Vampire Houses are not going to help you in whatever endeavor it is you and Tom are planning."

"Sounds like I can't keep anything a secret," I said flatly, the disappointment coming through in my voice.

"It's not that," Davros replied. "Too many of our kind have suffered from the final death. This problem is not one for us to solve."

There was a pause as the two let me take in the statement. I had been planning on asking Two, my favorite Night Stalker, to tag along.

"Yeah . . . I think this is about to become everyone's problem if it's not solved." I squinted my eyes as I let the comment drawl out.

"Max, Vampires and the Everwhere don't mix well," Frank said, looking over at Davros for support. It was clear the two men respected me enough to take the time to go over this.

Davros, taking the hint, spoke up. "We attract a certain type of entity in the Everwhere that is not what you would call . . . friendly."

"Vampires, as you know, are cursed Fae, not diseased. Our souls, in many ways, are stuck forever in the Everwhere. Over time, they twist and . . . well, let's just say things have not worked out well in the past," Frank explained.

While I hadn't fully heard this before, Phil had mentioned that other Ethereals considered the Everwhere off-limits. Well, most of them did, for the most part. Frank and Davros had come to inform me they couldn't support the mission. I still didn't understand how they knew about it in the first place. Maybe they had been guessing, then figured I was up to something, and before I finalized the plan, they were taking themselves off the chessboard. Or maybe not.

"Frank, can you do me a favor?" I asked. He nodded his head in agreement. "Can you get as many CSA agents over to B&B LLC and make sure they are no longer shipping or receiving anything?"

"You mean secure the facility?" Frank asked.

"Yup," I responded, finishing off my coffee.

"Yes," was all Frank said, standing up.

It would hurt not having a V with us, and even more troubling, Phil. The team was thinning out. I didn't want to get the full Council involved, and to be honest, they would probably ignore what I was saying. Tom could convince them with enough time, but it would be too late by then, and the whole thing would have leaked like gas after a late-night Taco Bell run.

"One last thing," Davros said, stepping directly in front of my face. "Good luck."

Frank followed up as Davros walked toward the bar to close out our tab. "Carvel wanted me to give you something. Here, it's a note. He said it might help Phil. I think in some odd way, he actually might just tolerate you."

The two men left as I walked over to Trish. "In over your head again, I see."

"Always. Hey, you have any more of those smoke charm thingies?" I asked.

"Thought you'd never ask," Trish said, winking. "I have something better. Here." She handed me a small metal cylinder.

"What's this?"

"Let's just say it carries the power of the sun. Crack it open and use a little hellfire. Just make sure you and whoever can leave the area you're in afterward. Oh, and don't let that off around regulars . . . or Mages or Ethereals. Just, use it if you get in a real pinch," Trish said as I delicately put it in my pocket.

Everyone knew I was up to something, and by this point, I didn't care. It was time to assemble my crew of flunkies, the dirty not quite dozen. It was game time.

"Bruther, I'm not supposed to be leaving the Atheneum till this hand's healed up," Phil said on the other end of the phone.

"Meeting me in the Postern doesn't count. Look, I know

you wanted to talk. I also have something you might be interested in," I told him as Petro zipped downstairs.

We did most of our work downstairs. It was set up like a reasonably normal office. While the space was eclectic, Petro and I did an excellent job of keeping the space's business side separated from our living area.

"Aye, I'll be there in ten minutes," Phil said as the sound of Jenny's voice echoed in the background.

"Boss, how's the V squad doing this morning?" Petro asked, stretching.

"Good. They just wanted to wish us good luck," I said, pulling out the note from Carvel Frank had given me. "Plus, some free chicken . . ."

"Free chicken?" Petro asked, not knowing the term.

"It's when someone gives you something you didn't ask for, but it's helpful," I explained, having already read the note. "Phil might not be getting that paid vacation just yet."

"We're doing this thing today, aren't we?" Petro asked in the form of an already known statement.

"Yup," I confirmed again, the word quickly becoming one of my favorites. "Grab what you need from here. I'm not sure when and if we will get a chance to stop back by."

After twenty minutes and what I guessed was a stern talking to by Casey, we gated to the Postern. Phil was standing by the center table, drinking a cup of coffee. He was supposed to be drying out.

"Bruther, look at you two," he said, noting Petro and I were wearing our field gear. Petro was in his body armor; I was wearing my enchanted trench coat, boots, and the rest of my gear. We had started keeping larger weapons in the Postern, plus other items we used before gating or if needed.

"What did you want to talk to me about? I figured it's okay if Petro's around," I said as Petro flew over to the weapons cabinet and picked up his small rifle.

"No problem. I understand you're gating to England. You know the missus was . . . well, we lost her there. I've never been to the Everwhere, and Tom was the only other person I knew who could go. After this summer and the graveyard, I started thinking bruther. You and Tom mentioned that lost souls or whatever are there," Phil said, taking extra time to make his point—or request.

"You want me to try and find her," I concluded, pulling the note from Carvel out of my pocket. "Her" being Phil's wife, who had been killed during an operation in Russia in 1908. It also happened to be the mission to recover the gate crystal and the bloodstone shard used to unsuccessfully summon a hellion legion. The bloodstone had been a critical part in tracking down the Thule Society's main base of operations last year.

"Uh . . . oy, ahh . . . pffft . . ." Phil stammered.

"Here," I said, handing Phil the note. "I get what you're asking. I think we need to talk to Tom about this one. Maybe when this is all over, we can dig into it. I give you my word."

Phil smiled, not having to voice it out loud. While it made some kind of sense, the thought of chasing a dead loved one through the Everwhere wasn't sitting well with me. I was sure it was a bad idea. That being said, Phil was my friend, and I would look into it.

Phil opened the note, reading it out loud. It was an old parchment with a handwritten note from Carvel at the top.

This seems like something you could use. C.I.

A soul sword has several effects on the body of the person at the end of the blade and that of the user. There are three such known blades in existence, one being on the Plane and the other two on Earth. When a person is cut by the blade, the energy used to enchant the body comes from the user. Over time, the enchantment takes hold and turns permanent. However, it has been shown that if the victim of the blade is in the Everwhere at the same time as the blade, the effects of the blade are negated most of the time.

"Is this true?" Phil asked as Tom walked in, having gotten my message from before we left the office.

"Let's ask the pro," I said as Phil handed the note over. Petro flew back over to the table with his rifle and remaining gear.

Tom read the note, letting out a thinking breath and rubbing his stubbled face. "This could be feasible. I'm not sure. The enchantment is what's making Phil's recovery take so long. Jenny is a superb Life Mage. In most cases, it would only take a day to get someone back on their feet, especially an Earth Mage like Phil."

Petro spoke up, "Only one way to find out. I'll get with Lacey and Macey and see if they can get some extra healing potion together." Before anyone could respond, Petro took off through a small hole by the weapons cabinet. I needed to ask him about that.

"Jenny's not going to be happy," Phil predicted, putting an unlit cigarette in his mouth and letting it roll around as he grinned.

"Is she ever whenever we do something like this?" I followed up. "Carvel sent this, in my opinion, knowing it should work. The guy deals in some pretty dark magic."

"Agreed, plus we will need the muscle. Max, I have a feeling you have a plan in mind," Tom said, patting Phil on the back.

I spent the next thirty minutes going over the plan with Phil and Tom, leaving out plan B and a few other details. Tom made it clear that getting to the Atheneum from the Old City Cemetery in Jacksonville would not be easy. From there, gating to the Isle of Wight would be easy. The one issue would be making sure Phil was good. If not, he would have to leave

"So the six of us—" Tom said as I cut him off.

"Six?" I interrupted.

"Oscar—don't leave home without him," Tom explained. "Plus, I would like to see if we can get Belm to tag along."

"I'm not sure he's going to be available right now," I warned, walking over to the weapons cabinet. "How about Ying? I have a few messages from her. I haven't checked them yet."

Tom pulled out his phone and dialed her number.

"Hello," Ying's Chinese accent came through the phone.

"Can you meet us in the Postern?" Tom requested, immediately hanging up the phone. Ying knocked on the door two seconds later. Considering she was the head of the Gate Mages guild, she had the uncanny ability to show up just about anywhere, including where she was not supposed to be due to wards. This included the Atheneum.

"Gentlemen," Ying greeted, Kristi following behind her.

"Ying, thanks for coming. Did you find anything?" Tom asked as I looked over. "Yes, Max, I can look into things too. Ying and her team have an uncanny ability to find out information."

"Yes, there is a shipment set to load up this afternoon. My connection in Southampton, as well as Inspector Holder, confirmed it. There is a lot of noise surrounding this shipment, almost like it is being used to cover for something else," Ying said. Kristi set a duffel bag on the table, pulling out several weapons and performing operation checks on them.

"If I were a betting man, I would say they are about to go underground completely. I would even bet that shipment will be easily tracked back to Goolsby—or Darkwater for that matter," Tom said.

"I also have this for you. A map of the underground tunnels going from the Isle of Wight to Stonehenge. It's an old map, but the tunnels have been there for a long time," Ying said, handing it to me. "Oh, and just so you are aware, once you get inside the tunnels, distance becomes relative."

"Let me guess, fifty miles might as well be twenty feet. I'm going to get a hold of Dick and see if his team can check out the docks," I said. The joke only registered with Phil, and he chuckled. "He's the one that gave us a pretty good idea of where to gate into as well."

"No marshals?" Ying asked, raising an eyebrow.

"Darkwater," is all Tom said as Ying nodded in understanding.

Petro was back after thirty minutes with a small potion vial. It was roughly 5:00 p.m., and between the change in time zones and however long it would take to get to the Atheneum in the Everwhere, we needed to go. We would drive to Jacksonville and from there use one of the coins to gate to the Everwhere.

Tom and Phil grabbed their gear as Kristi watched the preparations. Ying recommended for Kristi to come with us in case there was an issue with gating back. I was still feeling bad I hadn't filled Kim in on the plan. According to Tom, the fact that Davros had met me was a sign that we had the Supreme Council's blessing, even if off the record.

Dealing with Jenny and her insistence on Phil resting was our final roadblock. I let Ed get a read on our plans by letting my mental guards down. Within a few minutes, Ed was playing defense, and the two were going to monitor our movements as best they could. We were set.

The drive to Jacksonville was uneventful as the team reflected on the mission ahead. We truly didn't know what we would find. We all took time guessing only to figure out it didn't really matter, and we just needed to focus on our targets: Mengele, Beleth, and cutting off the supply of soul stone.

"I need to make a stop," I said, pulling into the 7-Eleven. Tom shook his head as Oscar shuffled on his lap, wanting behind his ears scratched. "I'll be right back. Mind pumping some gas?" I asked Tom as he jumped out of the truck, Oscar following behind.

The two keepers at the cemetery had an addiction for slushies, and in an abundance of caution, I would show up with two fresh, cotton candy flavored ones. As I opened the door, four men stepped out of the building, walking toward Tom.

"Hey, old man, nice cat," the greasy-looking man said as his friends chuckled. I shook my head, going in to get the slushies, knowing the probable outcome of the conversation. Most people would be nervous. Me? I was actually more worried about keeping the slushies frozen.

"Trouble?" the older man behind the counter asked in a gruff, lifelong smoker's voice.

I looked outside as Oscar started walking toward the men. "Nah, friends of yours?" I asked, figuring these men hung around the gas station often.

A loud crash came from outside. The aggressive man was on his back, and the other men were running toward him. Tom was still pumping gas.

Oscar dropped down from the canopy in half-human, half-battle cat form. I hadn't seen this one before, and it was just as scary as it sounded. A mix of hellcat and man. Long claws the size of hands protruded from his paws as he hissed and clicked his massive fangs. He pounced on top of the man, staring him in the face. Oscar's spiked tail promising more than a slight scratch.

Tom put the pump back up before walking over to the man, his partners running off around the back of the building. "He's a good cat. Hell on the furniture, though," Tom said. I looked back at the man behind the counter.

His expression was blank. He had witnessed this type of thing before. Picking up on it, I figured I would push the point that he needed to get those goons to relax. "Those guys come back in here, tell them they just tried to piss off a member of the Senior Council, and if it happens again, I'm coming back to talk with them."

I followed this up by creating a flaming pillar of hellfire in my hands after setting down the slushies. This time the man nodded, not responding. The point had been made. I figured the guardian from the cemetery probably came here with his pet alligator to get his fix of frozen beverages.

Dropping cash on the counter, I walked out, the door chiming behind me. Oscar was back in his cat form as we jumped back into the Black Beast.

"Bruther, one of those for me?" Phil asked, leaning forward.

"Remember the guardian and his pet alligator, Ralph?" I said, setting the drinks in the cup holder.

Oscar's ears pointed up as Tom turned toward me. "Old homeless-looking man with an alligator he calls Ralph when it's an animal and Al when . . . well, he's on two feet?" Tom inquired curiously. I quickly realized I hadn't fully explained my previous trip to the others, focusing on the events that had taken place in Everwhere and the coins.

"Yes," I answered as we pulled up to the front gates of the cemetery.

The sun was starting to set as the truck's automatic headlights came on. The sky was burning red as the sun started to fall into the St. Johns River. I turned the key on the Black Beast, the rumbling V8 coming to a rest creating a hushed eerie silence.

There, sitting on the curb in front of the cemetery gate, was the hobo and his pet alligator.

"Hermes," Tom said after seeing the figure, his lips twitching in impressed surprise.

"Hermes as in one of the sons of Zeus, Hermes?" I asked as Phil started laughing in the back seat.

"The one and only. This has more eyes on it than I thought. Hermes would only come here if he knew someone was passing through or traveling. He had a hand in the Postern at some point. I even met him once. It was not one of my best moments," Tom explained. The clicking of weapons and sounds of the doors opening filled the void Tom's statement had left. Had I actually met a Greek god? Had I just bought him a cotton candy slushy?

By the time we all poured out of the truck, Oscar was already in human form. I looked over to see Al taking on the same shape, again standing in a cheap green leisure suit.

Hermes cackled in his crackling voice. "Back again, and I see you brought company this time. Smart."

"Hello, Hermes," Tom greeted, walking around the truck. The man's eyes widened as he took a step back. "I'm not here on official business," Tom reassured him as I held up the slushies. A smile spread across Hermes's face upon seeing the still frozen sugar-filled drinks.

"At least one of you has manners. Thank you, my child," he said as Al quickly grabbed his, slurping it down before I could take my hand back. Oscar was now standing in front of the other shifter. They were having a conversation without it being shared. The two looked at ease with each other, a clear look of understanding between the two.

"Hermes, I apologize for our last encounter. Things were complicated at the time. We come in peace," Tom explained as Phil, Petro, and Kristi walked toward the cemetery gates.

The man let out a whooping cough, walking over to the others. "Max, are your friends afraid of ghosts?"

I didn't respond, giving them the opportunity. "Shitless!" Phil bellowed as Hermes focused on Petro.

"I'm just here for the free cruise," he replied as Hermes raised an eyebrow, smirking.

"And you, young lady?" the man asked, standing in front

of her.

"Can you kill them?" Kristi countered, shifting the weight of her weapon.

"You can, but you may not want to do that. You didn't answer my question." Hermes again pushed.

"Petro didn't. Well, yes, of course," Kristi said with a mix of nerves and confusion about the weirdness of the scene.

"Oh, he answered, and I can assure you he gave the wisest response." Hermes coughed again, taking a long slurp of his drink. "He's not here to disturb the souls of the dead during their final journey. Or, well, long-term accommodations."

I cut to the chase after letting Hermes get the theatrics out of the way. "Will the gate still work, and is it safe?"

"Work, yes; safe, never. I know why you are here, and I can say things have been rather busy on my side of things," Hermes said, reaching down into his tattered coat, pulling out a silver necklace.

"What's this?" I asked, taking the obviously enchanted item.

"A gift, if you can get the gatekeeper on the other side to relax long enough to give it to her." He grinned.

"Why didn't you give me this last time?" I asked.

"I didn't know if you would make it back, and I at least like a 50/50 chance of that happening before I give such a precious item. If you can give this to her, she will let you pass. Hopefully," Hermes said, stepping back as Al came to stand beside him.

"Hopefully?" Phil asked, spitting out the cigarette.

The final sliver of sun dropped into the river as we walked through the cemetery entrance, the cackling of Hermes echoing behind us. "Good luck, he, hah, hah, hahhh."

CHAPTER 19

Smokey and the Bandits . . .

"We couldn't do this during the day?" Phil asked as Petro landed on my shoulder.

"It's best we get our eyes acclimated to the dark. It's always dark in the Everwhere. Max, after you," Tom said as I stepped out in front of the group. My senses heightened, ready to spring into action.

Shadows danced off the tombstones and trees, making the space feel alive, the sounds of our steps on the unkempt grounds crunching underfoot. I needed a drink. Hell, I needed two. I was about to step into uncharted territory that few others had seen, Tom included. While I didn't know everything he had done in his centuries of life, I did understand he didn't like the Everwhere.

We arrived at Agnes's grave without any of the run-ins I'd had during the summer. The large statue stood out like a sore thumb even in the dark. It also had power pouring out of it, raising the hair on the back of my neck again.

Inspecting the statue, I pointed my flashlight at the angel's hand, reaching down to Agnes holding a child.

"This it, boss?" Petro asked, having been on his honeymoon during my last trip here.

"Yeah, this is it. Phil, how's your hand doing?" I asked, seeing him wince when shifting his new favorite toy, a highly modified AK-47—the same one he'd had on the *Event Horizon*.

"Could be better," Phil admitted out of character; he was hurting. If Carvel was correct, he would soon be back to full-on asshole.

I pulled out the gate rope, holding it out. "It's time. You all know the drill." The others grabbed the rope, Tom invocating the enchantment. The gate rope was a simple but highly outlawed enchanted item. According to Ed and Jenny, they were made via blood sacrifice. Once everyone was bound to it, if at any time the person in possession of the rope gated, the entire group would be pulled along for the ride.

I grabbed the coin out of my enchanted trench coat, holding it against Agnes's hand. With a twisting pull and pop of ozone, the team launched through the gate to Everwhere.

The change in temperature and general feel of the air was immediate. The team paused, regaining their faculties. I leaned over, taking several deep, heaving breaths.

"Everyone—" I was cut off as Phil yelled, setting the mood for the rest of the trip.

"Holy shit! Eat that, you bearded wanker," Phil bellowed, holding up his fully healed hand and flipping off the air with his unfortunately now working middle finger. The group froze, staring at him.

"Gods and graves, I guess flying under the radar is off the table," I said, shaking my head as the first flaming arrow thumped into the trees beside us.

"Down!" Tom yelled as another volley of flaming arrows slammed into the area around the grave marker.

The group spread out, still staying in a straight line, as I felt a pull on my trench coat. Petro, in a blur of motion, shot up into the sky.

"Hey," I barked, garnering more attention. I pulled out Durundle, yelling, *"Ignis!"* Flames erupted from the sword; for this rodeo, it had decided on flashy flames and billowing streaks of hellfire lighting up the surrounding area. Shadows danced red in the trees, looking as if someone had dropped a crate of red flares around us.

The soothing sound of Phil cocking his weapon came from behind me. Tom was a few feet in front of me behind a tree, just starring. He looked like he was mumbling.

"Petro, what do you see?" I said into the communicator in my ear. We had brought the enchanted earpieces that kept us on a secure channel.

The sounds of rustling leaves filled the night as whoever was slinging the arrows started to reposition in an attempt to flank us. Petro chirped over the communicator.

"Slow down, you jackrabbit," Petro said, talking to himself. He was chasing whoever it was.

"I'm guessing that is the keeper, don't fire. Petro is trying to give them the necklace," I said, making sure the others didn't destroy the graveyard, and possibly, our way home.

Making the situation even more chaotic, I looked over to see Tom whispering to the car keys he had taken from the Postern, that he had left me in his will. I was betting he was summoning his car. I sat there, thinking about how he could have gotten a car into the Everwhere.

A loud crash snapped me out of it as Petro came slamming down about as gracefully as I had ever seen him crash. He stood up, dusting himself off as silence suddenly filled the air, the only noise that of the approaching rumble of a car.

"Well, we are either about to die or . . ." Petro trailed off as a woman in glistening green armor stepped out from behind the tree in front of us. The bow in her hand was the same color as her armor. She was strong and agile. A helmet on her head with a small piece trailing down her nose left her eyes and pointed ears exposed, a tightly woven ponytail coming out of the back.

Tom walked out from behind the tree as Phil let out a whistle. Not a catcall but one of impressed awe.

I looked down, seeing Petro grinning. "Slowpoke," was all he said, smoothing out his mustache. Petro had pulled the necklace from my pocket and darted toward our attacker.

Durundle was still glowing, but the flame pulled itself in, letting off a lighter radiance after feeling the change in my mood.

"You're the one that closed the gate," the utterly intimidating woman said, her voice clear and precise, almost angelic. The necklace was now hanging around her neck.

"Yes, we brought you a gift for safe passage," I said, pulling the statement out of my third point of contact, better known as my ass.

"You have disturbed the balance, and you bring a Death Talker with you," she said, looking over at Tom.

"What's your name?" he asked, setting his feet. Headlights shone from behind the tree line.

"I know you," the woman stated bluntly. "My name is Lana."

"You're an Elf," Kristi said in awe.

Lana didn't respond. "Hey, so we have somewhere to go. We seek safe passage," I repeated, feeling as if I had to speak in some old-timey language from that movie about the short folks taking that ring to the volcano thingy.

Lana stood there as Tom spoke up. "We are here for Beleth."

The expression on Lana's face changed, hardening as she looked at Tom. "I will go with you," Lana said as the rest of the group walked up to the tree Tom was standing by.

"Go with us?" I asked as Phil popped a cigarette in his

mouth, not lighting it.

"I will go with you, and help you if I can," Lana said, bowing her head slightly toward Tom.

Two headlights lit up the area as the car finally made its way around the trees. Shadowed figures darted from the area, seeking cover from the light. Just like last year, whatever it was that occupied that space did not like the light.

"Our ride is here," Tom said as I stood firm.

"Why?" I asked, looking for a more direct approach.

"I am here to protect my part of the Everwhere. He has disturbed the balance. This is my charge. I was close to dispatching him when you came," Lana said, putting her hand up to the necklace.

"Well, lass, sounds like we have a middle-seat rider. Shotgun!" Phil barked as Lana looked at him, cocking her head sideways.

Kristi just kept staring at Lana, then a look of realization struck her face as she finally took in the rest of the area.

The Everwhere was much like a creepier mirror version of the regular world: a purple tint to the sky and a stale, earthy smell in the air, along with odd masses in the sky that looked like large chunks of Earth floating in the air. Shadows danced more freely as dark, black masses shuffled around the edges of your vision. While not a bad place, it wasn't good either. The Everwhere was, as described, the middle of the road. I had a feeling it leaned more toward the darker side of things.

The car willed to me a few years back was, in fact, a massive Cadillac from the 1970s. A DeVille, to be more precise. Chrome gleamed as the blood-red paint reflected the night sky. The engine, while strong, purred instead of rumbled, telling of a well-oiled and maintained engine.

"I think we'll have plenty of room," I said as Lana walked over to the door, waiting for someone to open it. I humored her, letting her take her seat next to the window. Kristi, being the slimmest of the group, reluctantly agreed to sit in the middle.

The blood-red leather interior was just as posh and showy as the outside. Tom grinned, grabbing the steering wheel. This was his baby, and the car seemed to know it. Phil was about to light up his cigarette as Tom slapped it out of his mouth without touching him.

"She doesn't like smoke," Tom said as the car revved, slightly agreeing.

"Is this car alive?" Kristi asked as Lana looked at her.

"Not sure," Tom replied, smiling from ear to ear.

"The road's dangerous. There are many lost souls on the roadway. I assume you are going to the room of gates?" Lana inquired, a light smell of honeysuckle coming from her hair.

"Why would you assume we're going to the room of gates?" I asked, pulling out my service pistol and slapping a clip of enchanted rounds into it. Lana was obviously talking about the Postern. There were notes in Tom's old journal calling it the room of gates.

Kristi had brought a small submachine gun that looked like a death machine. She was brave but fought her battles with her wits or the bandolier of gnarly looking charms she wore around her neck.

"I can smell it all over you, and the one driving used to travel through here," Lana said as Tom pulled out of the grave-yard onto the street.

The road was just as odd as the sky; while normal, it never looked clearly straight. Slight curves and waves made it look out of place. The buildings around seemed abandoned, full of glowing eyes and dark voids. Lana had her bow at the ready but no flaming arrows anywhere on her body.

Shadows continued to dance in the background as the car smoothly purred through the city streets heading to I-95. I peered out the window as a loud roar filled the air. Oscar, now in house cat form, stopped licking his paws, his ears perking forward.

"And that would be?" I asked, looking over at Lana.

"Trouble. Move this chariot," Lana said, whipping her head back around to focus on the tree line.

"What kind of trouble, lass?" Phil asked, squinting his eyes. His hand being healed had brought back the fire inside Phil. It was clear by his laser-like focus he was ready for a fight.

"A Chimera. It showed up over a year ago," Lana said. Phil looked back at me as I scowled.

I had often wondered what they had done with the massive creature I'd accidentally gated to the Council halls during the mess with the Transitions Office.

"Yeah, I'm with her, drive Gramps!" I barked, knowing what was now apparently looking for us.

"So, Lana. Do Chimeras have a good memory?" I asked as Petro flew to the back window, looking out into the dark void behind the car.

"The best. They are hunters and never forget the scent of their prey," she said, turning toward me after landing on the obvious reason I was asking.

"Max," Tom chimed in, clearing the air. "Didn't you and Phil really piss one off last year?"

"Yup," was all I said as the rest of the vehicle's occupants, including Lana, joined in a chorus of groans. The engine even seemed to rev slightly.

Tom floored the vehicle, swinging onto the interstate as what looked like apparitional vehicles swam in random spots. They must be from the regular Plane and bleeding over for some reason. I had figured out last year the reason I saw so many apparitions in the graveyard over the summer was all the lost souls tied to the location.

"Why can we see cars?" Phil asked as the car drove

through one as if it was nothing.

"You ever heard about Jesus taking the wheel? Something like that. There is either someone or something in that vehicle attached to Everwhere," Tom explained, knowing more about the place than he lead others to believe.

"Like a ghost in the back seat?" Kristi asked, shivering, a chill running through her body.

"Precisely," Tom said, looking in the rearview mirror.

"Hey, guys, is it normal for buildings to be flying in the air?" Petro asked just as a house landed in the middle of the interstate in front of the car.

Tom slammed on the brakes as the very real structure settled in the road, wood and sections of roof flying in several directions. *Note to self, things in or from the Everwhere are real here.*

Lana leaped from the vehicle, dispatching a volley of arrows at eye-blurring speed. Several landed, lighting up the familiar creature. The Chimera stood up on its back two feet, bellowing a guttural roar before landing back on the ground with a thud.

"Phil," Tom barked just as he was jumping out of the passenger seat.

"About to get busy," Phil said, aiming.

"Save it. Help me move that roof piece out of the road. We need to get moving, or we're stuck," Tom said as I nodded. Phil rolled his eyes, running over to meet Tom by the rubble. Petro had already taken to the sky. I was wondering if the colder air would affect his flying.

Kristi took position behind the car, taking aim.

The Chimera was built like a large gorilla without hair, carrying itself on legs that looked like they belonged to a large cat. Its front right leg was still burnt. Perched on top was an oval head that melted into its neck. It didn't have lips, just rows of pointed fangs disappearing inside its mouth, which happened to almost reach its broad, pinned-back ears. Even more intimidating—if that was possible—was its tail. It was slightly up its back and split into three long, spiked appendages, ready to end our little journey.

The flames from Lana's arrows faded away as I brought Durundle to life.

"Ignis!" I yelled. This time the blade was glowing, telling me that it was primed to throw some serious pillars of hellfire.

I looked over at Lana. "Ever been pulled over before?" I asked, making a joke out of the situation and wishing Phil had heard it.

She just looked at me as the creature, having sized us up, finally put its head down and charged.

Lana sent another volley of flaming arrows, the creature's momentum ensuring several of them missed. Kristi and I both let loose literal hell at the same time. Her enchanted rounds, which glowed neon blue and looked like a laser, peppered the creature, causing it to lose focus momentarily. Her ammunition seemed to pack a larger than usual punch.

I let a stream of hellfire out of the end of Durundle, which headed directly toward the Chimera's face. Or so I thought. The creature stopped on a dime, clearly remembering our last encounter, and scooped a portion of the road in its claw, slinging it directly at me before Durundle's beam landed on its side, causing it to fly backward several feet and slam into the median.

The slab of asphalt slammed into me, pushing me several feet back, pinning me to the ground. One or two years ago, before the demon part of my body started taking hold, the strike would have killed or, at the very least, maimed me. Now things were a little different; I had toughened up. While most other Mages and Ethereals didn't notice, I had to be careful with what I did in the open. I pressed my face against the slab, tasting blood in my mouth.

Kristi let out another round of precise submachine gunfire as something crashed behind me. Tom and Phil must have moved the roof. "Oscar!" I yelled, wondering where the hell he was in all this mess.

"Need some help?" Oscar's purring voice came from my side. I looked over. He was standing there in his half-human, half-cat form.

"Seriously?" I said as he snickered, heaving the chunk of road off me. "And?" I asked, pointing at the Chimera Lana was now in front of swinging her sword toward.

"I think we need to get going," Oscar replied, pointing behind the Chimera.

"What the hell is that?!" I asked louder than needed, getting Kristi and the others' attention as they walked toward the car.

Petro's voice came over the communicators, "Hey, guys, we have another problem."

"A bigger problem than that damn thing?" I asked as the car sprung to life, the motor purring once again.

"I'm out!" Kristi yelled as Phil pulled out his new favorite toy: a highly modified AK-47.

"Get in the car, princess," Phil bellowed, letting off several rounds into the upper part of the Chimera's face, causing it to shift the focus off Lana long enough for her to get a solid strike on its pushed-out chest. She was moving in a rapid angelic cadence, floating around the creature.

"I think he likes you," I said to Kristi, looking up to see Petro flying down at warp speed, needling his way through the open window into the car.

"We got to go, boss. Big dog, three heads, not happy," Petro barked as loud as he could into the communicators, forgetting he had it keyed.

"How do you know it's not happy?" I asked as the Chimera finally figured out we were not its biggest problem.

"Its three tails weren't wagging. That thing's pissed," Petro replied, jumping back into his spot.

"Lana!" I yelled. Lana turned around, not seeing or knowing about our new party guest. If this dog or whatever it was could occupy the Chimera long enough for us to get to the alternate version of the Atheneum, I was all game. "Time to go. Big dog!" I yelled.

The Elf flew back to the car, looking as if her feet never hit the ground. While she was slightly winded, she was otherwise untouched. Lana was a warrior.

I must have stood there a moment too long because Phil started singing his favorite song. "Max and Lana, sitting in a tree, K-I-S—"

"Enough, time to go," I urged as we jumped into the car, taking off at full speed. Whatever slammed into the Chimera made a loud, reverberating crash.

The engine purred as we lurched forward at blinding speeds. Everyone was silent for a few seconds before starting to talk at the same time, including Lana. Out of nowhere, the radio started blaring the Rolling Stones. The car was telling us to shut up. Petro flew over, landing on my knee.

"One at a time," I said, looking down at Petro. "What did you see?"

"Like I said, a big dog with three heads. It looked like someone had really pissed it off." Petro shivered slightly. The cold was getting to him. As if the car could read my mind, which by this point I was pretty sure it could, the heat came on.

"Cerberus," Lana muttered with a puzzled look on her face. Tom let out a deep breath.

"Is that bad? I kind of just assumed there would be some bigger than average monsters in Everwhere," I said, trying to rationalize the situation.

"Yes, very bad," Tom started, "Cerberus's job or purpose in whatever life it has is to prevent the souls of the departed from escaping. He effectively keeps the dead that have passed beyond the Everwhere from leaving the Over or Under, or whatever it is you choose to call it."

"I get it. Like the story. Souls were often used to power the Old Gods," I said, getting a look from Lana and Tom through the rearview mirror.

"He has never been in the Everwhere. At least not since I was posted here," Lana said, worry creeping into her flat smile.

"You keep saying that. 'Posted,'" Kristi interjected. She had finally calmed down enough to join the conversation. Phil was just chewing on an unlit cigarette as if he was daring Tom to slap it out of his mouth again.

"My master made a deal with Hades. On her behalf, I am bound to this part of Everwhere for one hundred winters," Lana said flatly. I already knew that time didn't mean much to Ethereals, and figured Elves were no exception to that rule.

"Hades," Phil interrupted. "Lord of the Underworld and all that jazz?"

"Yeah, all that jazz," Tom replied curtly.

"You don't believe Hades is real?" Lana asked, showing some actual emotion on her face by wrinkling her nose.

"Aghhh, I don't know, lass. I just . . . That's a lot to take in, even for me," Phil said.

"You believe in God and Jesus, right? Lucifer?" Tom asked as Phil nodded.

"Yeah, but I met that bloke," Phil finally said, not making it clear whom of the three mentioned he was referring to. I had yet to hear that story. After all, I had had frequent visits from the Devil myself.

"Look, even in our world, there are several layers to peel

back. People, well . . . Mages often forget that the Fae and others from the Planes see much more than we do and are much, much older. For example, unless you were a necromancer, which there are only a handful of, you would never see any proof of anything other than what the Council told you, or your own eyes saw," Tom said. I spoke up too, trying to calm my own nerves.

"It's like before I found out I was a Mage. I knew all about Vampires, ghouls, and hell, even Mages because of the movies. I just never thought they were real. Fuck me though, right?" I said smirking, the cuts on my face stinging as they stretched. Phil let out a laugh coming from deep in his chest. The rest of the car joined in as the car's old coil cigarette lighter popped out, glowing red.

Phil grinned, lighting up his cigarette as he petted the dashboard. "Good girl," Phil complimented as Tom again pushed the vehicle forward toward our destination.

CHAPTER 20

Plan A

O ther than the odd scene of hundreds of lost souls shuffling on the other side of the interstate heading toward Jacksonville, the rest of the trip went smooth. The most abnormal part of the journey was when we pulled up to the Atheneum. The looming facility shimmered under the purple sky. The lack of movement around it was the opposite of other areas in the Everwhere. It stood ominous and derelict. The souls of the dead didn't come here.

"Lana, anyone ever come here?" I looked for confirmation as the car came to a halt in the drive. Gravel crunching under the weight of the full vehicle.

"No," she replied, her pointed ears pinning back on the sides of her head. "This is a bad place in the Everwhere."

Tom sighed as he got out. "What Lana is referring to is the energy the Postern gives off here. It's sort of like bug repellent. It also means that anything in here is more than likely bad news. That being said, we warded the Atheneum in the Everwhere a long time ago, before we moved it here from Europe."

The facility was as old as most empires' histories, and as Jenny had explained, had been moved three times during its existence. Each time out of necessity.

"What does that mean?" I asked as Petro zipped into the

air.

"It means I'm not sure what may be inside. Oh, Kristi, you said you are out of ammunition?" Tom asked, inhaling deeply.

"Yes, I just kept pumping as many rounds as I could into that thing." Kristi shook her head, checking her vest to at least ensure she hadn't used all her blended items.

The trunk popped open without anyone doing so manually. Tom walked around, pulling a blanket off a pile of weapons. Some old, some newer, some . . . well, some were not from this Plane.

Lana's eyes widened as she leaned down, picking up a sash of blue-tinted throwing knives. "These are Elven," she said, throwing it over her shoulder. It was not a question if she could or could not take them . . .

Kristi leaned down, sorting through several weapons and picking up one of the pistols similar to the Night Stalkers. She also grabbed an odd-looking assault rifle identical to the ones the colonial marines used in the movie Aliens, the weapon even had a round count readout on the side.

Kristi, finding the holster, attached several more pouches and magazines to her vest. She was decked out in black gear, while I had opted for jeans, boots, a light tactical vest, and my enchanted trench coat.

"Bruther, expecting a party?" Phil said as his eyes glistened. He was already loaded to the teeth with weapons.

"Always have a plan B," Tom said.

"Hey, I'm the plan B guy here," I said, seeing the others shake their heads. Even Lana was picking up on the vibe. This time, I think they would have a change of heart. That is, of course, if it was needed, remembering what Belm and I'd discussed. Petro just snickered, knowing that very plan.

As the team finished resupplying, a loud crash echoed in the distance. The large wooden doors of the Atheneum loomed, dark and steadfast, as we walked up. Tom lifted his hand out, palm forward, and pressed it on the handle. Muttering under his breath, several gears and mechanisms started clanking in rapid succession.

After a few minutes, the door slowly creaked open. The sharp shrill of dried door hinges echoed in the still entrance hall. The fountain, which usually flowed with clear water and moved a globe on its axis, was now billowing a black substance that I figured was not something to be touched. In fact, it was so black it didn't glisten; instead, it absorbed the light as I beamed my flashlight toward it.

The one extra weapon I'd picked up was an M4-style assault rifle with all the fixings, gadgets, and do-floppers one could put on a gun. The underbarrel mounted flashlight was excessively bright, lighting up the entire space. I reached down and twisted the cap, making the beam of light more focused. Light, snowflake-looking particles hung in the air in all directions, making the far end of the entrance hall hard to focus on.

Slight noises ticked and creaked as we all stood there, still taking in the macabre version of the Atheneum.

"Let's get moving," Tom commanded, leading the team down the main entrance hall into the stacks.

Lana got in step behind me, not seeming to worry about the creepiness of the building. Come to think about it, she did pretty much work in the Everwhere. Chances were Lana had seen her fair share of creepy.

"What is your plan?" she asked as Petro landed on my shoulder, not liking the scenery.

"We're going to gate to England, then follow a trail to Stonehenge. From there, more than likely, pick a fight. Then see if we can shut things down," I explained, leaving out a few key details.

"That's bold for such a small team," Lana replied, her ears relaxing.

I suppose Elves showed their emotions through their ears. Much like a dog. Not that I was making comparisons. It was just one of those stupid observations I frequently made. *I wonder how she likes her cereal?* I thought.

"That's the point, lass. In and out. No big circus. We've learned that lesson with this lot. Plus, if things get out of hand, we will just pop out." Phil winked at her, not getting a reaction. He did, however, get a hard stare from Kristi.

"Think of this as more of a scouting mission. If we can, we will address Beleth if we find him. If not, we know where those goons are," I said. The stacks looked like a dark maze of books strewn everywhere in no particular order, much as they were back home. I wondered if they were the same.

"Ah, here," Tom said as we reached the door to the Postern, the dragon engraved in the door greeting us.

Tom once again unlocked the door and ward before he pushed the door open. "Stand back," he said as a violent rush of cold air surged out of the room as if it was pressurized.

We walked in to see an exact duplicate of the Postern back home, except all the doors were in the opposite order. The Evergate was on the right, the Seekergate on the opposite side. The Mirrorgate, being in the middle of the far wall, was still in its same location.

"Before you ask, yes, it's the opposite. It still works the same, from what I can tell. The Evergate can take you back to our Plane, but as more of a ghost," Tom explained, walking to the table sitting in the middle of the room. Petro zipped over to it, pulling out a small flask. He was acting winded and tired. The colder air was getting to him.

"I remember the lesson, and speaking of that—I'll be right back." I walked over to the Evergate. Pushing my will into it, I grabbed one of its stones, noticing several were missing compared to back home. I walked through into Marlow Goolsby's warehouse by the docks, the one we had basically destroyed the week prior. The sounds of confusion coming from behind me trailing off.

Looking down, my body was there, but not completely whole. I was a shadow of myself, a ghost.

Standing in the middle of the open space were Goolsby and two Guardians of the Order Society. The sight of my incorporeal body threw Goolsby off at first, the slight tensing of his jaw muscles giving it away. He hadn't expected to see me like this.

"Max, I see you know how to make an entrance," Goolsby said. While he was wearing tactical gear, it wasn't the same as the Guardians'.

I opened my mouth to find my voice sounding distant. I couldn't hear it in my head. "Is this the entire team you said would come?" I asked, thrown off. I had expected a full squad, if not more people.

It took a few seconds for what I said to register. "Oh, this is all we will need. At least for my part. The rest of the team is somewhere else at the moment. An apparent shipment of soul stone has been intercepted trying to leave the Southampton port. There are several parties all converging on that location as we speak. Your timing may just be good for once," Goolsby said, taking a jab at me as only he could.

Shaking my head, I held out the Evergate stone from the Everwhere Postern, willing a gate to appear. Goolsby and the two Guardians looked at each other. One was a woman and the other a man that towered at roughly seven feet tall. All three held rifles, with swords hanging off their backs, or in Goolsby's case, on his side.

While a little convoluted, the use of the Postern was fairly straightforward. To gate around the Everwhere, one would have to use a gate from the Everwhere Postern. If you tried to gate back to the regular world using anything other than a specific gate or place like the cemetery, you would basically be a ghost—not truly there, but there at the same time.

I assumed my body was back in the Postern in Everwhere, stiff as a board, lying in front of the gate. The feeling was hard to describe, but it was stable enough to function.

The Mirrorgate, according to Tom, was the only gate in the Postern that could fully take you to the Everwhere—that is, if you weren't already in the Everwhere, as I had figured out. The issue was, the key was broken off. This meant that unless you could use the Mirrorgate, the only way to accomplish what I had just done was to find another way through to Everwhere and then the Postern. Using the Evergate from the Everwhere Postern was one of those methods.

Last time I had gone through the cemetery, I had left my body behind. That was because I didn't actually have the coin in my possession to open the gate, according to Tom. It had let me in on its own, confused by my general makeup. I know the whole thing seemed backward, but it appeared to follow its own rules. Gating from the regular world to the Everwhere through the Evergate, as Goolsby and his team were about to do, would, in effect, leave them in one piece.

The three new additions to the team followed me as we walked back through the gate. Same as last time, I gasped, jumping up as Goolsby and the two others stepped over my body. Knowing what was happening, Tom reassured Phil he didn't have to save my life this time around. The math adding up in Phil's head generated a scowl.

"What the hell is this mess?" Phil complained as Tom shook his head.

"Plan A," I said, grinning, dusting myself off. I felt a small knot forming on the back of my head from falling earlier.

Lana's brow furrowed as Goolsby looked around, taking in the room.

"Was this your plan?" Tom said, walking over to Goolsby, not expecting me to respond. "Mr. Goolsby, I'm not sure what deal you made with Max, and I don't want to know. What I can tell you is, if you stray from our group, we are not coming to look for you."

The look on Tom's face was more than words could describe. Stern, forward, and unforgiving. He was saying this for a reason. Taking a second look at Goolsby, it was clear he had not been in the Everwhere before. The soul stone had been supplied to him through a third-party source. I stood there, reflecting on why I hadn't thought of this prior.

"Before we get going," I started, clearing the air. "How do you get the soul stone for your research? I don't think you have much experience here."

Goolsby stood there thoughtfully as the two Guardians pulled small backpacks off, heaving out additional gear and equipment. "Again, you seem to be asking the right questions," Goolsby said, looking at Lana longer than made me comfortable. I had a feeling she wanted to rip his throat out.

"Your Council—" Goolsby started.

"Our Council," I interrupted, snapping back. I wasn't being overly aggressive. I was just making sure all the cards were on the table.

"Our Council," Goolsby conceded, nodding in agreement, "has a team that supplies it from England. We pick it up, don't ask many questions, and that is all I know about that piece. I am not naive, and I know it comes from the Everwhere, as we talked about before. What I can tell you is this: Councilman Darkwater was the contract manager that I worked through on this project. You may want to have a conversation with him when you get back."

"When we get back," Petro said out of nowhere.

Kristi spoke up, being the voice of reason. "If we are done seeing who has the bigger shoe size, can we get this show on the road? I don't want to be here any longer than needed."

"Max, can I speak with you for a moment?" Tom said, walking over. "Outside."

I nodded over at Phil as he winked. He would keep an eye on things with Petro. In all fairness, I had a feeling Lana would take care of any issues at this point.

We walked outside, closing the door behind us. The iron dragon hanging on the entrance stared at us with empty eyes. Devin had given me a purple box that contained the gems to put in the sockets a couple of years ago.

"Why?" was all Tom said, not looking upset but intrigued.

"I would rather know what he's doing during all this. Plus, I'm starting to think a deal has been made that we are not fully aware of. I want to see what Goolsby does when he's forced to make a choice. I have a feeling he will have to sooner rather than later. Think about it, Darkwater and Goolsby have been working together on some type of project involving soul stone. I just don't know where Beleth and Mengele . . . and hell, for that matter, Lilith, come into play here," I said as Tom nodded.

"You need to stay focused. This is bigger than your personal vendettas," Tom warned. "I think it's as simple as we discussed before. Two groups with two separate agendas."

"Three groups," I said, reminding him that Lilith had pulled herself out of it.

"Don't count on it." He took another deep breath. Tom had been doing that a lot as of late. I needed to talk him into getting checked out by Jenny when we got back. "Don't look obvious when we go back in, but look at the Mirrorgate. The key is sitting in it in one piece."

I looked at Tom as he smiled. "I think I know what happened when I messed the key up. We can talk later, but I need to be the last person out. We must bring it with us; that gate is the key to everything in the Postern. That gate has more than one function."

I looked skeptically at Tom. "Alright," I replied, opening the door. Having the key to the Mirrorgate would allow us to not only come and go freely to the Postern in the Everwhere but travel as well on the Plane.

The team was ready to go as we walked back in. The two Guardians glared at Lana as she stared back.

"It's time," I said, holding out the rope. "Goolsby, I'm sure you know what this is. I need you all to grab a piece of it." I quickly glanced at the Mirrorgate, seeing the key sticking out of the keyhole. Goolsby had moved from one side of the room closer to the gate. I was betting he'd noticed the key and was going for it.

Goolsby's team walked over, grabbing the rope as I pushed my will into the enchanted item, binding them to our hopeful exit strategy from the Everwhere. After a quick pop of ozone, the binding was complete.

"I almost forgot. Did you bring that gate stone?" I asked. The look on his face clearly stated he hoped I had forgotten.

"Of course," Goolsby replied, looking around the room. "I'm just as invested in seeing this through as the rest of you." He was clearly feeling the lack of trust vibe in the room. Goolsby finished his sentence landing his gaze on Lana. He did not know where she came into play. Come to think of it, neither did I.

"Now that we have that out of the way, Max is going to be gating us to the location supplied by Inspector Holder. We should be on the beach close to the cliff walls," Tom instructed, walking over to the Seekergate, bringing it to life. It glowed a dull purple, moving like liquid.

I walked behind Goolsby, cutting him off from the key sitting in the Mirrorgate. Goolsby's eyes twitched slightly, telling me he was not happy that I'd forced him to move across the room away from the key.

"Ladies first," Phil said, putting his hand out for me to lead the way.

"Thanks, sunshine, you're always such a proper gentleman. I'll go last and make sure the gate closes," I said, keeping an eye on the key.

The rush of howling wind and the sound of crashing waves filled my senses as soon as I walked through to the other side. The tall white cliffs loomed several hundred feet overhead, and a dark purple tint engulfed everything, including the water. Large moving chunks of earth floated in the dark sky over the water.

The rest of the crew had also paused to take in the view.

"This is amazing," Kristi exclaimed as Petro flew over, hovering in front of me. I held out my hand for him to land.

"Stay out of the water, boss. Something smells funny about it. Kind of reminds me of the water in the fountain back at the Atheneum," Petro warned, dusting lightly.

"Got it. Now we just need to figure out where to go . . . " I trailed off, the rest of the team standing with their backs to the water.

There was a large opening in the cliff walls several hundred feet to our left, a waterway leading into the black abyss. The cave-like entrance was massive, large enough to hold the pirate ship we had encountered the night we lost Ned.

"*The Pearl* is there," I said, the fact clear as day in my mind.

"This is a bad place," Lana interjected, adding to the prospect of our impending doom lying inside the cave. Even worse, we might have some travel to do once inside, according to the plans.

"Now she tells us," Phil muttered as the others started to walk toward our destination. Odd clicking and shuffling sounds began to echo off the cliff walls the closer we got to the opening, the utter blackness of the space chilling.

CHAPTER 21

Plan B

The team walked through the large entrance as a veil lifted. A light pull in my chest told me we had just passed through a ward. Lights flickered and danced from various burning stones and breaks in the rocks, the light projecting at odd angles on the hulking galleon sitting in the water.

The ship was massive. Cannons protruded from its sides like spikes on a cactus, the sails still, lacking air movement. Snaps and pops of the wooden vessel echoed in the expansive cavern. It reminded me of One Eyed Willy's ship from the movie *The Goonies*, cave and all.

What didn't resemble the movie scene was the black obsidian stone that covered the interior walls. Someone had been here recently. By the looks of the ramp leading up to the ship, it appeared they had been in a hurry. Several intricately engraved crates were stacked up by the ramp. Tom shuffled over, rubbing his hands over the containers. The others spread around in a semicircle, mostly facing the dark walls to guard against the dancing shadows.

"It's a helluva lot hotter in here than the rest of this damn place," Phil said under his breath, attempting to be quiet for once in his life. He was nervous.

"Max, see these symbols?" Tom asked, motioning me over. The age and detail on the crates relayed the importance of the cargo inside.

"Some kind of binding spell mixed with something," I said, chewing my lip. A loud click from the far end beyond the reach of the light echoed, catching everyone's attention.

"It's a containment spell, knucklehead," Petro said, buzzing over. "They stink like death."

"That would be my assumption. They are full of soul stones. A good amount," Tom said, nodding over at Goolsby.

"Hey, Goolsby, didn't you say there was a big shipment of this stuff heading out of Southampton on the other side?" I asked as he walked up.

"Yes," Goolsby confirmed with a concerned look on his face. He pointed at the ship. "It's ready to get underway. It looks as if the crew left in a hurry."

Right on cue, loud banging and rumbling started coming from the far end as light radiated from another tunnel. The team, and more specifically Goolsby, didn't know that I had called in plan B when I realized Goolsby was not bringing his full team. He, as expected, had another agenda. A quick internal call on the old headphone to Belm had put plan B in motion.

The plan was simple. Belm was to gather up as many wandering souls as possible and attack the originators of the supposed shipment. Upon further inspection of the surrounding area, it was evident a fight had taken place, pushing the prior occupants of the ship deeper into the cave system. More pressing was the fact that it was still ongoing.

"Shit," I exclaimed out loud as Petro buzzed over.

"What's up, boss?" Petro asked, picking up on the situation.

"I probably should have given Belm a one-to-ten scale of how much ass he needed to kick," I said as Oscar came around the corner in full battle cat mode. He was impressive, and even Lana did a double take.

"Max," Tom said in a controlled tone. "What exactly was plan B?"

"Uh, yeah, so, Belm was supposed to gather a bunch of wandering souls and meet us here. Well, it looks like that kinda happened," I said, shrugging, checking the action on the M4 slung over my chest.

"Did you give him any further instructions?" Tom asked, pushing for more. He wasn't aggravated; he was calculating our next step. What I knew was that I had made the right call. Not only did we have more manpower or whatever one would call a small army of ghosts, but we had also stopped the shipment of soul stone from reaching topside.

Goolsby's men, as well as the marshals, would all be standing there waiting on a shipment that would never arrive. I was even betting there would be more interested parties.

"To stop the shipment if I were to call him," I said, realizing Belm was probably on cruise control at this point. He had summoned an army of souls, and they were fighting the Soul Dealers.

"Goolsby, I'm not going to ask you to come with us. You can just as well stay here and secure this location. We know about the shipment, so that is of no concern; we can track that down. Things are going to get a little sketchy from here," Tom said, pulling the long wooden staff off his back and pushing his will into the weapon. A black, smoky haze appeared around its surface. Whatever it was that staff did, I didn't want to be on the other end of it.

Phil, who as always was looking forward to justified violence, lit up a cigarette and smiled. "Game time," he said, checking the action on his toy.

Petro buzzed over to Oscar, taking a seat on his back. The two seemed to communicate without speaking. I would ask later about this. Oscar walked forward into the middle of the group, his massive size dwarfing everyone else. Lana grinned as Kristi just gawked. I had a feeling that while Kristi was an experienced Gate Mage, we had taken the term *overkill* to a whole new level.

I reflected on the group we had gathered. An overly brave Pixie with a kickass mustache, an Elf warrior, two Guardians, a very large scary-ass shifter, Phil (enough said), Goolsby, one of only a handful of living necromancers, and myself. To top it all off, I pulled out Durundle, bringing the flaming blade back to life once again. *"Ignis!"* It erupted from its slumber. For this rodeo, it decided to do the hellfire dripping showy lava thing. The ground hissed like an angry cat as several droplets hit the sandy stone.

I concentrated, reaching out to make a connection with Belm. Nothing. He was either preoccupied, or we would not be able to communicate in the Everwhere. What started to strike me as off was that I should have been nervous. I wasn't. Instead, a calm, steadying wave of warmth flowed through my body.

Goolsby and his small yet lethal-looking team pulled out matching pistols, similar to the ones the Night Stalkers carried. It was settled. Everyone would be going into the belly of the beast. Another, more distant explosion sounded from the cave as the motley crew started moving forward.

Tom lit several other dark stones hanging on the wall as we walked, lighting up the rest of the cave. Various pieces of transportation equipment sat lifelessly on the massive, sprawling floor. There had been a fight here.

A set of railroad tracks sat near the end of the cave with three separate rail systems leading into the far tunnel. This must have been the way the soul stone was being transported from Stonehenge. Two of the railcars were gone, presumably the method of escape for whomever Belm had found here. The absence of bodies piqued not only my but the others' interest as well.

"Where are the bodies?" Lana asked flatly.

"That's a good question, and one I don't have the answer to for once," Tom admitted.

Phil walked over to the remaining railcar and flipped a handful of switches. "It works," Phil told us, pulling himself into the front driver's seat.

The railcar looked very much like a van with its top sawn off, and railway wheels installed instead of tires. A large motor hung off the back of the vehicle. Phil pushed the start button, attempting to bring the vehicle to life. It hesitated for a moment, then buzzed to life. It sounded like a go-kart motor.

"You think they're going to hear us?" Petro asked as Oscar walked up beside the vehicle.

"No," I replied, standing on the side rail still holding a very angry sword. "Just listen." I held up a finger to my ear. "All hell's breaking loose. Whatever we're about to get into is some bad news."

Phil looked over at me, grinning. He placed his rifle on the dash pointing forward. "You knobs jumping on?" Phil asked as everyone started taking their places. Oscar let out a chuff, launching into the dark cave.

"Where are they—" Kristi started asking just as Phil slammed the railcar into motion. When Phil drove, which was next to never, he would find the maximum speed of whatever vehicle he was at the helm of and ensure that it got to its destination as quickly as possible.

The group collectively gasped as the railcar rocketed into the darkness. A dull light allowed only a few feet of visibility ahead of us. It wasn't clear whether we were going hundreds of miles per hour or just really fast. As Ying had stated, the distance wasn't a factor.

Piles of flaming bodies started appearing on the sides of the tracks, blurring due to the speed. Apparitional and physical masses lined the sides of the cave, and Phil was forced to slow down.

"Is that Oscar?!" I yelled over the sound of the rushing wind and whining motor.

"He's clearing a path!" Tom yelled back as Lana walked up to the front, standing on the rail beside me. The vehicle was moving at least twenty miles per hour when the Elf warrior launched herself into the darkness ahead at inhuman speeds, like a rocket.

"Anyone else?" I said as Phil lit up a cigarette. He was tapping his foot on the floorboard.

"Look," Tom pointed as Petro came flying back. The dust coming off his wings created a light glow behind him. Lana and Oscar were outlined in the light coming from the opening a few hundred feet ahead. By the looks of it, the tunnel was about to open back up. I couldn't really tell how fast we had been going. Much like the boat ride in *Willy Wonka*, we had probably traveled the distance to Stonehenge without really knowing it.

"We went a little farther. It's crazy up there. A bunch of ghosts, Soul Dealers, and hellions. Yup, there's a bunch of those up there," Petro confirmed sounding winded, spitting out the news like machine gun fire.

"Anyone else?" I asked as Phil turned off the railcar.

"That one guy that cut off Phil's hand and his butthead friend," Petro said, knowing how Phil would react.

"Well, time to make the biscuits," Phil said, standing up, a light silvery glow shimmering to life over his skin.

"Doughnuts. It's time to make the doughnuts," Kristi corrected, winking at him.

Tom looked down at his castor. "I don't think we have time to call for any more help. I can keep the souls that Belm brought from attacking us."

By the time we had all dismounted the railcar, loud howls of rage started echoing down the dark tunnel, followed by several large *booms*.

Tom held out his staff, pushing the dark smoke coiling around it over our team. Goolsby and the two Guardians twitched as the layer of smoke seeped into their clothes and uniforms.

"What's this?" Goolsby inquired with genuine interest.

"It will make you blend in with the others. I don't have time to explain, but understand that those souls out there are working on instinct alone. Attacking anything and everything nonapparitional," Tom said, the worry evident in his voice.

"What's the plan?" Kristi asked, taking note of the tone of Tom's voice.

"If it's not one of us or one of the hazy-looking figures fighting the monsters in there, then do your best not to die. That includes killing whatever monster or pirate-looking Soul Dealer you may run into. If you see Beleth or Mengele, let us all know on the communicator. They're not going to go down without a fight," I instructed, walking forward as the others started to follow.

I noticed a slight hesitation from Goolsby and his two companions. "You guys good?" I asked, not getting a response from the two Guardians.

"We'll follow your lead. If we believe our best interest is not to engage, then we will come back here," Goolsby said.

I finally lost my temper.

I swung around, grabbing Goolsby by the vest and lifting him off the ground with one arm. The demon part of my body taking over, pushing my strength into overdrive. The group froze as I felt the barrels of the Guardians' guns pointed at me.

"I've had about enough of your shit. We can either be on the same team or not. After all the crap I've inadvertently done for you, I would at least expect the all-powerful Goolsby the Great to maybe break a nail, or at least get your boots a little dirty," I said, spittle coming out of my mouth.

Goolsby waved off the two Guardians. "Set me down now."

"Or what?" Phil chimed in.

Taking a calming breath, Tom walked over. "Max, this isn't the time. Not to mention you are both members of the Council, and Goolsby is one of the few regular liaisons we have. This is exactly what Mengele and Beleth want us to do. He's spent the last several weeks trying to pull us all apart," Tom whispered to us.

I slowly lowered Goolsby, his face never wavering. Either he wasn't scared, or he was a master of not showing it.

"I can assure you we are on equal footing here," Goolsby said, implying as he had before that we both had the same goals. "If anything, we can at least agree to that."

Without saying anything, I nodded my head in agreement, walking back down the tunnel while squeezing the hilt of Durundle. My will flowing into the sword made it crackle in the dark.

CHAPTER 22

Blackbeard's Lament . . .

O scar flew through the tunnel opening, leaping over several rows of fighting men, creatures, and souls, crashing into what looked like a towering group of hellions. Lana, followed by myself and the others, charged as Petro took flight to higher ground. From there, he would report down, selectively choosing his targets.

Luckily for the team, there just happened to be several rows of rocks in front of the cave's entrance. We took cover, assessing our next move. The sounds of battle and the introduction of violence were immediate. The tunnel opened up into a cave triple the size of the one prior, so large it was hard to see the other side.

Flames erupted from what looked like rifles the Soul Dealers were wielding. Large masses of hellions stood like bulky death machines as souls flooded over them like ants on their prey. The smell of burning coal lingered as explosions rocked the other side of the cave. The battle was everywhere.

It reminded me of one of those battles you would see in movies based in medieval times. The type where the battlefield was fogged over while random foes attacked each other. I had never been able to figure out how they knew who they were supposed to be swinging a sword at. The scene in front of me matched that to a tee.

Squinting, I could just make out what looked like a replica of Stonehenge sitting in the middle of the vast, raging space. Two familiar figures stood in the center inside a large protection circle. Beleth and Mengele. My enhanced senses had sought out my targets like a hound dog.

"I think I found the bad guys," I said over the communicator. A few grunts of understanding responded. Gunfire from Kristi's rifle started ringing close by.

Tom and Phil crouched down, shuffling over to my location. Tom leaned over the rock, shooting several columns of the billowing black smoke at a group of Soul Dealers who had broken through the rear line. The four men crumpled lifelessly to the ground before what looked like souls exited their bodies. As if compelled, the now lost souls turned and started fighting their own men.

"Bloody hell," Phil said as he pulled up his rifle, sighting in on two more Soul Dealers. He landed several perfect shots directly through their skulls, the exploding heads splattering gore onto their surrounding companions, causing a shuffle of confusion.

A massive black, sprawling creature with a long spiked tail landed behind the rocks. Lana stood up, preparing to let loose an arrow on the horrific monster.

"Stop!" I bellowed as Belm crouched down, his eyes glowing red in rage.

Lana hesitated as Belm's eyes stopped glowing, returning to their normal pitch-black. His raspy voice came out of his transformed maw, the gore making me turn my head to avoid vomiting. "About time," Belm rasped before hacking out what looked like an arm.

"What the hell, mate?" Phil asked, shaking his head as Belm coughed out a laugh.

He continued to shrink, letting the violence-fueled rage

out of his body. Most demons were nightmare fuel when they let it all hang out, Belm especially so. He turned pitch-black in demon form, had an eight-foot-long spiked spear-like tail, and a face that would ensure a life of sleeping with the lights on. In reality, he wasn't exactly a demon. I had yet to figure it out, but knew he was some type of demigod. The son of the Devil, or as others called him, Lucifer . . . you get the point.

In human form, Belm looked like a greasy biker. He had a rumbling V8 for a voice and an odd shifting build.

"I've been busy," Belm said, finally resembling his partially human form. Lana stood there staring at him as if she was looking at a ghost, never mind the thousand or so actual ghosts in the room around us. Phil shook his head turning around, letting off another burst of rounds into the crowded battlefield. His shots were precise and landed their targets every time.

"What's up?" I asked as something slammed into the rocks, throwing debris over my head. Belm just stood there as small rocks bounced off his face.

"Well, Dad's not going to be too happy about this. I'm surprised he hasn't shown up yet. Anyway, they are pulling hellions through one at a time. We slowed them down for the first few waves, but I'll just say your timing is perfect," Belm rasped, blood and gore dripping from his face and now hand like claws.

"How long have they been doing this, and you think we can stop them?" I asked. Tom was staying oddly silent.

"I think they have been doing this for a few years at least, but not at this level. They figured out a way to stabilize the entrance," Belm said, ducking as a bolt of green plasma flew overhead, creating a dull green glow.

Tom spoke up, taking it all in. "Stonehenge is a type of prison entrance. It's also where soul stone comes from. We need to get inside that circle and shut this down before they really start moving."

"That sounds easy," I said, looking around. "Anyone seen Goolsby lately?"

Phil, Belm, and Tom all confirmed what I was thinking. "Petro, you see Goolsby and his asshat friends anywhere?" I asked, knowing the answer.

"No boss, but let me tell you, this place is crazy," Petro said, obviously staying above most of the action.

Tom took a deep breath, talking into the communicator. "Petro, any chance that if I give you something, you can drop it in the middle of the circle?"

"Sure thing. I might need a raise, though," Petro joked as he flew into the dirt, landing a little harder than usual.

"You alright, buddy?" I asked as Belm started shifting back into nightmare mode.

"Yeah, just a little banged up. I tried to get one of those big goons' eyeballs. It didn't work out so well," Petro replied, looking down at a trickle of blood on his leg.

"Extra Golden Grahams and rum when we get back," I said as he smoothed his mustache out in approval.

Tom shuffled over, taking a gold ring off his finger and handing it to Petro. "When you drop this, let us know over the communicator and get the hell out of there."

Belm walked over, getting in my face. "These souls will come at a price."

The message, while clear, was vague in its true meaning. "Gods and graves," I muttered as I turned around, dropped my rifle, and pointed Durundle at one of the tall hellions, firing a bolt of hellfire directly at its head, which in turn became engulfed in flames.

The hellion's screams of agony made me wince. Lana, though she still looked shaken from seeing Belm, had started shooting arrows again. Kristi and Phil had moved closer together, still firing into the battlefield with accurate bursts of fire, the coordinated attacks opening up gaps for the wandering souls to flood the Soul Dealers and hellions.

"What did you give him?" I asked as Tom ducked down, another volley of fire hitting the rocks.

"A vacuum of sorts. When it hits, everything in this room, not solid, is going to get smacked around. End of the day, it will dissolve that protective circle," Tom said, not laying out the exact details of where they were going. It reminded me of the Chimera. Gate it away and worry about it later. That is, until I was in the Everwhere trying to get something done.

The sound of Oscar roaring then shifting to a howl garnered Tom's attention. Without warning, he jumped over the rock wall, charging the crowd.

"Gods and graves." I let out a guttural shout, following behind Gramps.

The good thing about friends, true friends, was that they would truly go to hell and back with you. Even when it meant literally. Without hesitation, Phil and Kristi joined me, following Tom's path toward the sounds of Oscar struggling. I would handle Goolsby later; it was clear he had made his decision.

Tom parted the fighting souls, pushing them out of the way as black smoke formed a protective wall around our advancing group. Several arrows from Lana hissed overhead, surgically cutting through hellions and Soul Dealers alike, the scale and amount of pirate-dressed goons staggering. All these had once been people. People that had been tricked or taken advantage of, killed to bring back one of these monsters. I felt no pity as they dropped on the field of battle.

A hellion swung a large club down, breaking our advance. Phil took the brunt of the blow, flying several feet through the air, his rifle clattering to the ground. Kristi spun around, switching the MPK5 from semiauto to full-on eat shit and die. A spray of glowing blue rounds flew from the death machine. She swapped magazines, taking a handful of seconds to do so.

When the sounds of the gunfire started back, I whirled around to find a Soul Dealer pointing what looked like a trident in my general direction. A blue stream of solidified water shot from the end of his weapon as I pushed my will into Durundle, firing a wall of hellfire toward the now frowning pirate.

As the flame devoured the now retreating Soul Dealer's attack, I pulled back, opening my free hand palm up and willing the rest of the water to form a whip, slamming it into his legs. The goon dropped to the ground, crashing hard on his back.

Instead of making some stupid comment, I ended the man's life by pushing the water around his head, forming a bubble. The exertion of battle mixed with running and falling had the man heaving; he sucked in the bubble of water now surrounding his head. For good measure, I slung a small ball of hellfire directly at his skull.

The water boiled immediately. I would atone for this later. The fluidity of the kill had felt too at home for my comfort.

Phil, witnessing the scene from his back, rolled over, finally shaking off the blow as a hellion stood in front of us, several arrows lodged in inch thick leather armor sticking into the creature's chest. The hellion was almost upon Phil as Kristi grabbed a glass ball out of her sash, whispering into it before throwing it directly at the beast.

With a pop of ozone and disorienting flash, the hellion went from nine feet tall to roughly one foot. Phil quickly popped a cigarette in his mouth, lighting it with his finger as he stood up and took several steps back. The little hellion, looking strangely cute, charged as Phil raised his right hand into the air, mimicking a football kicker. The field goal was good. A trail of silver left behind told me he had put everything he had into the kick. The hellion let out a bark, flying several hundred feet through the air. The sound of bones cracking echoed.

"Jesus, what a shit show," Phil said, looking over at the dead pirate in front of me. Phil made a clicking noise while picking up his rifle. He grinned slightly, looking into the distance.

We advanced to a small group of large rocks that provided cover and a clear view of the center circle. Two hulking masses orchestrated what appeared to be a portal, pouring hellions into the cave.

"Petro, where are you?" I asked through the communicator as he buzzed overhead. The rest of the group converged on the small rock formation, forming a small semicircle.

"I'm going around the long way. I tried to fly up from the front, but that whole thing has some type of ward around it. The only chance I have is to hit it from the opposite side. They have everything focused on the front," Petro explained as Oscar let out another defiant roar.

Lana looked in the direction of Oscar's howls. "I'll be back," was all she said as she launched into the air several hundred feet.

"Dammit all to hell," Phil said as Kristi gave him a flat smile. He quickly corrected himself, grinning. Those two were getting close, the type of close where they had drinks late into the night, neither willing to ask the other in for a nightcap because they might just actually like each other.

The group stared as several loud crashes erupted from the area Lana had launched through the air toward. At the same time, Petro barked out frantically, "Bombs away!"

The confusion must have spread throughout the space because the cadence of fighting increased. A blast of air flew from the circle like an atomic bomb going off. Dust lifted off the ground, permeating the air as souls and bodies alike turned away from the bright eruption. Whatever Tom had given Petro was a top-shelf blended item.

I could hear Belm clearly in my head movie, as I liked to call it. "Hey," the raspy voice came through loud and clear. "I'm going to try to fill that hole with bodies."

"Yup, I'll get things handled out here," I said both out loud and internally as Oscar and Lana landed in the middle of the circle. Oscar was wounded and bleeding from his side. The mix of blood dripping from his fangs and body made him look like nightmare fuel. He was breathing hard, getting his second wind.

"Bruther, you okay?' Phil asked as Tom nodded at Lana. He walked over, petting Oscar on the neck. The rest of the group started to stir and concentrate once again on their prior targets. The violence resumed just as quickly as it had stopped.

"I'm fine. Where's Petr—?" I stammered as a small streaking missile headed straight for us. Petro was spiraling out of control, coming in hot.

Tom reached out with his hand, slowing Petro down and catching him in some type of force spell. Petro slowly landed at my feet. His right-wing was tattered and torn, the look on his face strained yet alert.

"Hey, buddy, you okay?" I asked as the others started looking around as the sounds of the fight escalated. Belm had landed inside the now destroyed protection circle and was attacking the hellions as they poured out.

"Tell Casey I love her, and my children that I went out bravely," Petro said, wincing.

"You're going to be fine, and you don't have any children," I said, letting a small ball of hellfire fly as a hellion walked from around a far rock. The others joined in the chorus, putting the massive creature swiftly to rest, a plume of dust coming from the now stopped freight train of pain.

I rolled my eyes. Scooping Petro up, I put him in my enchanted trench coat, inspecting his torn wing. I looked down at my pocket. "Stay put. You've done enough." Petro was knocked out before the final word escaped my lips.

"I've had about enough of this shit," I said. The others paused at my tone. Hellfire erupted from my hands while unbeknownst to me, Durundle became one with my arm, the hellfire forging a new bond with the weapon.

"Max, no!" Tom screamed, getting the attention of a few wandering souls. The group was thinning out. The others looked at me with odd expressions on their faces. I looked down, seeing the bizarre spectacle that was now my arm.

My vision was blurred as smoke started emanating from the rest of my exposed skin. I was on the verge of changing into something . . . something more, something different. I pulled back my will, focusing on the present. The tension quickly eased from my body as the sword still blazed like a beacon in the night.

Seeing my reaction, Phil let out a roar. "Gaghhh!" The two main people we had come to see turned around. Hate and fury shone from their faces. Mengele directed hellions from the fight back to the portal, attempting to stop the blood blender Belm had turned it into. It was clear neither one of them would go forward to pull him out. I couldn't see Belm, but as chunks of hellions flew from the portal, it was clear he was in a frenzy. I would have to buy him a few drinks later, if there was one.

Lana launched several arrows at Beleth, who dodged them with catlike reflexes. For a squat, fat man with a peg leg, he could move. Mengele looked indifferent, bringing his blazing sword to life. He pointed it toward the far right of the Everwhere version of Stonehenge.

A low rumble could be felt underfoot as at least a dozen hellions charged toward our location. In a moment of clarity, Tom barked out several orders.

"Phil, Lana, Oscar, and Kristi, take care of those hellions

while Max and I cut the head off the snake," Tom said in rapid succession. No questions asked, just a swift execution of his order.

The group shifted as Tom and I pushed forward, Mengele's eyes narrowing on our approach. He launched several purple laser-like flares at us, lighting up the area in a sparkling glow. Tom swiftly held up his staff, creating a wall of the black smoke he kept using, winking the spells out of existence as soon as they collided.

We slammed to a stop behind the farthest stone, looking at each other. The number of hellions kept growing. While Belm was laying waste to as many enemies as he could, several kept lumbering out of the hole, covered in gore.

"We have to stop that portal now before too many get through," Tom barked, pulling a small gel capsule out of his pocket and throwing it into the air.

"What was thaaaaaaaa . . ." I said as my speech modulated, slowing to a snail's pace, sounding like something from an '80s video game. Tom had thrown what Jenny called a time dilator. It slowed time momentarily, enough for the ones knowing it was being used to move.

Tom lurched forward, pulling me along. The surprise on Mengele's face turning to confusion. Mengele's lips started forming a scowl in slow motion, looking as if he had really bad gas. Beleth slowly started to turn; he had been facing the portal before the spell activated.

Mengele lifted a glowing white finger. Time started to catch up to the present as we came face to face with the two men now in front of us, ready to fight.

"I've got a bad feeling about this," I said jokingly in my best Han Solo voice, raising my arm now fused with Durundle into the guard over my head. Tom set his feet as Mengele grinned.

The sound of fighting echoed around us clearly, relaying

the message that Phil and the others were very pissed off and ensuring we got back not only in one piece, but in time for a drink.

"You think you can stop this?" Mengele asked, directing the question at Tom as the four of us slowly moved into position, seeing who would strike first.

"It's already over. There's no need to shed any more blood tonight," Tom said as Beleth laughed, turning it into a slow growl.

"Blood, what blood? All I see are souls suffering the final death and hellions. You want blood?" Beleth growled, danger dancing in his voice. He had a point. Besides a few cuts and scrapes, our team was otherwise unharmed. What had they truly done? I thought, then remembered Ned's exploding body.

"I'm going to shove that peg leg straight up your ass and then make you walk around using it as a crutch," I said, my chest heaving.

"Max, my dear friend. I left you a little present back home. I hope you enjoy the surprise," Beleth said as confusion washed over me.

"What surprise?" I said almost to the breaking point of extreme violence.

"Let's just say it will help you get ahead in life." Beleth chuckled as I lunged forward. I had taken the bait. I didn't care. I was going to end these two assholes here and now.

He shifted left as I brought Durundle—which was now part of me—down, slicing through air and stone. At the same time, Mengele blurred to life, rushing toward Tom. A large bloom of black smoke made the hulking figure miss his target.

Beleth pulled out a small knife, now having a weapon in each hand. The soul sword was dull and rusted from use. It was clear he never cleaned his blade.

"You had so much promise. Now you die," Beleth roared, this time taking my bait as I shifted left using my newly found speed, his attack missing by inches. I turned, bringing down my blade as he countered, catching the sword with his, the two of us standing face to face. The crackle of hellfire rang in the space between us, throwing Beleth off as he speared the knife into my stomach.

Lurching back, I saved the blade from fully penetrating my guts as he lunged forward again. Taken off guard by the agility of the man, I pulled up my free hand, ignoring his cutlass as I plunged my fist engulfed in hellfire directly into his face.

The sound and smell of burning flesh were immediate. Beleth let out a howl of pain as I swept my sword down, severing his legs from his body. The pure violence of the action again made me pause. This wasn't me. Was I capable of such actions?

I turned to my right to see the portal several feet away. The stampede of hellions was slowing down. I looked down at the defeated Beleth, still not registering the life-or-death battle Gramps was fighting beside me.

Calming my will, the blade in my hand winked out of existence; Durundle was no longer there. It was now a part of me, to control as I saw fit. The enchanted item had accepted me as an equal, making us one.

I grabbed the soul sword Beleth had dropped, putting it into the scabbard once reserved for Durundle. Holding the one part of his body that wasn't burning, I circled around like a discus thrower, throwing him into the portal.

I turned to see Tom on top of Mengele, the two in a fierce death lock, jockeying for position. I again mustered what was left of my will as Mengele started laughing. Tom landed several punches to his face before a glowing blade erupted from Tom's back.

"Nooooo!" I screamed, Gramps's body still struggling to finish its ordained task. I lurched forward, seeing red. Belm cut through the searing violence in the calmest, most normal voice I had ever heard. I knew it was him; I could feel it.

"Next time, make sure that you check your pockets," Belm said calmly, the sound of his actions saying otherwise.

I panicked, patting myself down, working to figure out what he was talking about. Then it struck me like a freight train. Belm had taken the vial Trish had given me. The one she had given explicit instructions to not use unless absolutely necessary.

I froze, realizing what Belm was about to do. I looked over at Tom to see a dark cloud circling the two men as Mengele struggled to get Tom off him. Tom grunted with the effort to keep Mengele down as I continued forward. The smoke from whatever spell Tom had unleashed pushed me back as I reached out like a bolt of lightning.

Belm again came through my thoughts. "Max, time to let go. We have to end this now." His voice remained cool and calm. Not raspy or anything like I had become accustomed to.

"It doesn't have to be this way!" I barked out loud and in my head at the same time.

Oscar roared in the background as a fresh round of hellions crashed into their group. Phil came over the communicator. "Bruther, it's getting sketchy over here. Grab the others, and let's boogie." His voice was strained yet determined.

I stood there, looking at the raging battle. "Max, this is something I have to do. I always wanted a brother," Belm said, catching me off guard, my rage melting into regret. I turned again, reaching out to the cloud of smoke around Tom and Mengele, again getting thrown back.

"Come out. We'll get reinforcements and come back," I again yelled out loud and in my mind.

"It's too late for that, Max. You've done your best. More than anyone ever expected," Belm trailed off as odd bangs started coming from the portal.

"No, Tom is still—"

Belm cut me off sharply this time.

"Tom has cast his fate. He knew this time would come and that this was a one-way trip." I screamed at the top of my lungs as Oscar joined me. He somehow knew what was happening to his friend, his mentor, his partner, and his master. "Goodbye, Max. We will see each other again. Tick, tock," was the last thing I heard Belm say as the air was sucked out of the cave, followed by a blinding white-hot light.

Reaching down, I grabbed the Evergate stone from the Everwhere Postern. Setting my jaw, I looked over at the cloud of smoke surrounding Tom and opened the gate. The rest of the team was pulled through the gate behind me, the rope burning in my pocket. I closed my eyes, willing Tom and Belm to get pulled through as well.

I finally opened my eyes, staring around the room, only to have my hopes crushed. Tom . . . Gramps was not here with us. The others were in various stages of being worn down. Goolsby stood in the room, as well as the two Guardians. I lunged at him as the two Guardians stepped in front of him. "Max, wait!" Goolsby yelled as I threw the two armor-clad Guardians as if they were made out of paper against the wall, neither getting up quickly enough. I grabbed Goolsby by the throat, white-hot heat surging through my body.

"You son of a bitch, we needed you, and you just left," I accused, spittle again flying from my mouth. Goolsby was mine, the look on his face one of stressed confusion. He hadn't realized that when I used the rope, it would bring him back as well.

A gentle hand touched my shoulder, the smell of cracked pepper filling my senses. "Max, there has been enough loss tonight," the calm yet firm voice of Devin echoed in the room.

"This piece of shit is the reason that Gramps and Belm . . ." I trailed off.

"The reason they are both gone. No, what happened tonight would have happened either way. Belm and Tom sacrificed themselves to save all of humanity. That pathetic thing you are holding up was called back to secure the soul stone shipment by your precious Supreme Council," Devin said, making it clear he did not approve or was part of the decision.

Oscar, now in human form, walked over, looking me in the eyes. "No one's ever truly gone," he said, blood seeping from wounds and scrapes all over his body.

The smell of lightly burning flesh started to radiate from Goolsby's neck. The two Guardians were back on their feet, moving toward us. Devin held up his hand, freezing them in place like popsicles.

"Change . . . it makes us who we are. What we may be, and what we will become. That is, unless you're unjustifiably ignorant; then, it's forced upon you by those that see you drowning in your own stupidity. No one in this room is your enemy. At least not today," Devin said, a hushed threat in his words directed at Goolsby and the two Guardians.

I let Goolsby down as he stared me directly in the eyes. "We will discuss this later. I'm sorry for your loss." Much to my surprise, Goolsby pulled out a small black box, setting it on the floor as a gate opened, and the three figures walked through. The small contraption sparked, then proceeded to crumble out of existence.

CHAPTER 23

Choices . . .

"More, please," Petro said as I set another small bowl of Golden Grahams in front of him.

"You can only milk a cow so long, man," I said, grinning as Casey buzzed over to the kitchen table with a change of bandages. The Pixie team had been working on healing Petro's wing over the past week. While he still wasn't able to fly, he had regained his appetite.

"I've got to get back up on my wings. Someone's got to keep an eye on you," Petro said, winking at Casey, smoothing out his mustache.

"I can't argue with that. Anything else you need before we head out?" I asked as Phil walked into the kitchen.

"I'm good boss. You might want to check your lab at some point. Casey said she smelled something funny down there. So what's going on today?" Petro asked as Phil walked over, handing me a drink from Gramps's bar.

"Probably a dead rat or something. I'll check out the lab when I get back. We have a meeting with the Supreme Council, followed by what I'm pretty sure is an ass-chewing. Then, if I were to guess, get a pat on the back behind the scenes. They aren't having the official wake for Gramps till Friday. I'm just going to get some answers," I said, sipping the glass full of Ambrosia.

"Bruther, you're going to need it. You get that text from Ed about Kim?" Phil belted out, finishing his drink before I finished my first pull. Sometimes I wondered why he just didn't walk around with the bottle.

Never mind, I thought as he pulled the bottle from behind his back.

"Yeah, I haven't heard from her yet. She told me specifically not to contact her until she let me know things were clear. Ed wants us to stop by the Atheneum after this today. You're not going to believe this shit," I said, holding out my now empty glass.

"What, your grounded?" Phil asked chuckling, quickly replaced by a light cough. Jenny had done her best to patch everyone up, and Phil was no exception. During the fight, he had figured out a way to break every single one of his ribs. Most normal humans—and Mages, for that matter—would be bedridden. Phil was already up and on his feet.

Lana had fared well, and per her parting statement, had to stay at her post. She had also confirmed that next time we were in Everwhere, there would be significantly fewer arrows to worry about. Oscar had taken off after we returned. He'd simply stated, "I'll be around," before leaving. Kristi was tough and had spent a good amount of her time hanging around Phil over the past week.

This recent development was a good thing. Ever since Phil had brought up looking for his wife in the Everwhere, I had been trying to figure out a way to distance him from that thought. Kristi seemed to be just what the doctor ordered.

After spending a few days being treated for cuts, bruises, and burns, I had focused on figuring out what may have happened to Gramps and Belm, Beleth's statement still front and center in my mind. He had left something behind. I didn't know what that was, but figured it would make itself known soon.

I still hadn't seen Frank. His absence was noticeably off. Ever since Cecil had ran into my sword (total accident, by the way), the Vs had been hands-off with everything I was working on.

My phone buzzed with a text from Ed. *Meet me in Tom's old office.* "Well, it looks like I have a stop to make before leaving. Do you want to gate over to the Atheneum with me? Ed wants a few minutes to talk before we go," I said as Phil looked down, seeing he hadn't received the same message.

"Nah, I'm good. I'll leave from here. Kristi wants to meet up for a few minutes before the briefing starts," Phil said, already knowing he was leaving early.

"Petro, hold down the fort. I'm heading to the Atheneum. I need to take that damn sword anyway," I said as he saluted.

The Atheneum was buzzing with activity. I went through the Postern in the stacks and was surprised to see several people getting a tour of the books and artifacts laid out. I garnered a look from the group as I walked out of the wooden door holding a cutlass in my hand.

I smiled, waved, and turned left, heading to Gramps's old place. The walk felt familiar yet distant at the same time. Over the past year, I had not taken this route but a handful of times. Memories of last week and what Devin had said floated through my mind.

"Max," Ed greeted, sitting behind the newer desk Gramps had shipped in after I took the old one.

"Ed, I see you're getting around a little better," I said, seeing he had made it up to the room on his own two feet.

"Yes, I spent last week trying a new type of Etho-Therapy in Japan. It has worked wonders. The good news is: no surgery. We are just concerned if it's going to take. Something about superdosing Etherium and all that. Anyway, how are you?" Ed asked in a good mood.

"As good as I can be, I guess, all things considered. Why did you want me to stop by?" I inquired, wanting to get to the point as always.

"Right," Ed said, taking a deep breath. "Do you notice anything different in here?"

"Besides it being empty and . . ." I trailed off, seeing the door to Gramps's old bedroom once again sealed off.

"So I'm not going crazy." Ed walked over, smacking the wall. Last time Gramps—as I would now call him again in his absence— had left and was not entirely dead, his room had sealed itself off.

"No shit," I said, a grin crossing my face. "That old son of a bitch. He's not gone."

"That would seem to be a fair assessment," Ed agreed as Leshya came out from my old room.

Ed and I both jumped.

"Good afternoon, gentlemen," Leshya said in a ghostly tone. She walked over, setting an old leather-bound briefcase full of papers on the desk, clicking it open. The smell of musty paper and burnt hickory escaped the sealed case.

"Leshya, where did you get this?" I asked, seeing what I thought was a grin on her face.

"This is our little secret," was all she said. Leshya turned and floated off back out of the room. The door closed behind her without her doing it.

"Looks like Tom left you a little something," Ed said, the excitement coming through in his tone.

"Looks like he left us something. She didn't say it was for me. Look, there's a letter." I pointed out. Ed picked it up, clearing his throat before reading it out loud.

Enclosed you will find the missing pages from my will. These pages were recovered recently.

Max,

If you are reading this, I need you to take these pages and finish what you have started. I believe you now understand the importance and power of the Postern. You have learned more in a few short years than I did in a hundred. Use these pages wisely.

Ed,

My old friend. Till Valhalla. Oh, and please make sure to keep Max out of trouble.

Tom

We looked at each other, the stack of papers sitting there with untold information on them beckoning me. I reached down, picking several of them up. There were sketches of the two coins, the key from the clock my mother had given me, and the Mirrorgate.

"You think this is over?" I asked.

"For now, yes," Ed confirmed, letting Toms message marinate

in his mind. "Tell you what. Why don't we head out."

"Sure, here. I need to leave this soul sword here. Everyone keeps saying it needs to be locked up in the enchanted items archives," I said, handing the crusty blade over to Ed.

"Right, when Tom was here, he gave me access to the archives. I haven't had a chance to go through them yet. Let's drop this off and head out," Ed said, looking at the sword as if it were talking to him.

I looked around the room as I turned the light switch off, closing the door behind us. There was a chance, a possibility, that Gramps might just be alive, or as I had recently learned, somewhere in between.

The two of us stayed silent as we walked through the stacks into the archives. I had never set foot inside the artifact archives; I'd only imagined what it would look like and what treasures it contained. As Ed placed the blade inside the room, I stayed outside of the fortified door, saving that adventure for another day.

The Council chamber was not as full as I'd expected. Familiar faces and a few that mixed into the crowd stood talking as the Supreme Council walked in: Ana, Titus, and Davros. Bull, whom I had yet to officially meet, brought the room to order as the massive chamber doors shut with a thud.

Looking around, I saw Darkwater, Carvel, and much to my surprise, Kim sitting next to Mouth. She wasn't even acknowledging my presence. My heart sank as Phil sat down beside me, the room finally coming to order. Ed, as he was now on the Senior Council, took his seat in the front row overlooking the floor.

"Councilman Darkwater, please step forward," Titus bellowed. Darkwater looked disheveled for once, the look of exhaustion and worry sitting on his face like a bad sunburn.

Darkwater stood up as I scanned the mood of the rest of the room. It was indifferent. I was sharply aware that others on the Council couldn't care less and didn't deal with the man on a daily basis. Or had him trying to kill them, for that mater.

"We will be discussing current events with you in a closed-door session. Can you confirm that Carol Bellman is your daughter?" Ana asked flatly. There was no emotion in her voice.

"Yes, she is," was all Darkwater said in response.

Bull stood up, walking over to Darkwater and escorting him into the side chamber we had met in a few weeks prior.

"Next order of business," Ana started back, waiting till Darkwater was out of the chamber. "Kim Kinder, please rise. You are hereby appointed Director of Regular Affairs, and with that, a member of this Council. Is there anyone present that censures this appointment?"

The room was silent as the gears started moving in my head. Phil smacked my leg, crooning, "You got a popular girlfriend. Ewww."

I sighed, smacking him back. The stern-looking woman in front of us turned around and gave us a death stare.

"I accept, since there are no objections," Kim said, looking around the room. Her stare landed firmly on me as my heart jumped through my throat.

"It's settled. Next order of business. Edward Rose, please stand," Ana indicated as Davros perked up, finally paying attention. They were using his full name, making this sound official. "It is our understanding that you planned and coordinated the venture that led to the death of Thomas Gabriel Sand, and the subsequent actions that followed," Ana said. Davros stood up and walked to the floor.

"I did, and take responsibility for the actions of those I directed," Ed said, not skipping a beat.

I started to stand up, but Phil, putting effort into it, pushed me down into my seat with authority. He growled under his breath. "They didn't put him under oath. They are giving him and you and hell, for that matter, me a stern warning. You sit there and take the tongue-lashing, lad."

"It's not his to take. It's mine to take," I said, confused.

"Is it? You don't think he knew everything we were doing and allowed it to happen? If you don't, then you underestimate the old bird," Phil replied with finality.

Davros spoke up, hushing the chamber. "Edward Rose, you

have a choice. You can either take a reduction on the Council or be assigned to the Artifact Retrieval Team."

I looked over to see Phil grinning from ear to ear. "This is bad, right?" I asked. Phil shook his head.

"It's all Ed has ever wanted to do. This means he will continue to work with Jenny, Dr. Freeman, and hell, us," Phil whispered.

I sat there, finally realizing this was all for show.

"I accept the assignment on the Artifact Retrieval Team, and with that, will retain my position on the Senior Council," Ed said quickly as if it had been planned.

"Mr. Rose, you are to report to the subchamber after this session is closed. You are to be accompanied by Maximilian Abaddon Sand and associates. That is all I have," Davros finished, sitting back down.

The next thirty minutes revolved around mundane items that needed to be addressed by the Council. Topics like education, a change in teaching the history of the Planes, and with that, how much information to offer up to the regular governments. My favorite topic was about the regulation of magical or blended items amongst regulars.

After the meeting was adjourned, we walked down to meet Ed. Mouth stood beside Carvel, talking with Kim.

"Great. I think if your ego gets any bigger, we will have to meet in a bigger room," Mouth growled, taking a good thirty seconds to spit out his insult. He smiled a toothy grin, holding out a hand the size of my head. I shook it as he nodded to Kim, turned, and walked off. Carvel talked with Ed as Kim blushed, looking down at her feet.

We both stood there, not saying anything. My heart again started to drop as a grin the size of the state of Texas spread across her face. "I think we're good now," Kim said, walking up and putting her arms around me in a tight hug. I looked down as she leaned forward, kissing me.

"Ahem, ahemmm," Ed grunted, clearing his throat.

Our lips slowly parted as I kept my eyes closed. That had actually happened. She'd kissed me. For once in my life, I had gotten the girl. Or at least I hoped so.

"You still owe me a drink," Kim flirted, her voice purring, uncaring of who was looking. Once we separated, we realized there was a small crowd around us.

Phil, as always, had something to say. "Get a room, mate."

Carvel walked over, holding out his hand. He whispered under his breath, "Good job." It was clear he didn't want others to hear his compliment. We were, after all, supposed to be getting punished. Truth be told, only a handful of Council members actually knew what had happened in the Everwhere.

We walked into the subchamber as Darkwater was leaving. The expression on his face had changed. He was no longer looking lost; now, he was wearing a determined smirk on his face.

"Hey, buddy," I stopped and said as he glared at me. "How's the fam?"

Darkwater didn't say anything as Ed slowly walked up beside me, grabbing my arm. "Not now." The rest of the group kept walking as I stared at Darkwater, my message clear.

Kim passed by, urging me, "Come on, big guy."

We walked into the room where the main players from the Supreme Council sat stoically. Frank was standing in the far corner, a large scar across his face. Angel stood beside him with a slight grin on hers. Dr. Freeman, Inspector Dick Holder, and James were already sitting at the table.

The room was large with dark stone walls, a large dark wood U-shaped table that went around the edges of the room, and several glass lights hanging from the ceiling, looking like they belonged above a fancy pool table.

"Please take a seat," Ana said, motioning for Bull to close the doors. "It looks like we have the whole gang together."

"Ana," Ed greeted before Phil could blurt out a smart-ass comment. I wished Petro was here.

"Let's cut the pleasantries, shall we," Davros said in a low growl loud enough to echo around the room. "Your team, with the help of a few others, has done a great service to not only this Council but to the civilian governments as well. While we might not share the depths of the service, the Supreme Council would like for you to know this."

"Excuse me," I interrupted, raising my hand, getting a snicker out of not only Phil but Kim. "I'm still trying to figure out exactly why you pulled us in here to kiss our asses. I mean, I'm not speaking for everyone."

"You actually are," Ed interjected. That got everyone's attention. "What deal did you just make with Councilman Darkwater?"

That was a fair point, and one I wanted to know. Ed must have been snooping around in the old head movie. Titus cleared his throat, speaking as Davros chuckled lightly. "His daughter has agreed to help us locate Bruce Teach in return for his continued presence on the Council."

"And . . . ?" I asked, raising my eyebrows, mouthing the words to keep Titus talking.

"We are clearing his daughter's record and not further investigating his office," Titus said under his breath. There it was. The hammer that they knew full well we would not be agreeable with.

"Are you all stupid, or just really ignoring the fact that asshat used water that the Thule Society gave him to get some type of magical power? Then he proceeded to blackmail his way onto the Council, only to get caught up in not only dealing, but becoming addicted to soul stone? The guy isn't even a real Mage," I said, the anger rising in my chest. The others sensing it stayed resolute. "I bet you guys are even letting Goolsby off."

Ed cleared his throat. "About that one. The Council deemed it important to secure the shipment of soul stone. That call didn't come from Goolsby. He, believe it or not, questioned it."

"I'm not going to ask who told him or how. That guy has it coming," I said, figuring there was a reason Goolsby wasn't present earlier.

Frank stepped forward. He was, after all, a senior commander in the CSA. "Max, there has been a lot going on in the background while you have been out running through everyone like a hellbound freight train. Frankly, I don't think anyone else could have done it. What we are saying is that we would rather keep our enemies close. As you know, there are other members on the Supreme Council.

They just choose not to attend these types of meetings, and that is a good thing." His voice was sharp and to the point.

"We are all on the same team here, Max. I can promise you if that were not the case, we would not be sitting here," Ana said in a more casual tone. "Over the past several weeks, you have basically broken every law, not only of the Council but I'm pretty sure of the regular governments."

She had a point. I looked over at Kim as she shrugged in agreement.

"Alright," I said, letting the tension out of my body. "What about Lilith, Tom, and Belm? Hell, has anyone seen Jamison?" I asked, not driving a point home but refocusing the conversation. I wanted answers. I'd keep the little assumed secret about Tom to myself.

"We will grieve our dead and bear witness to our living enemies," Davros said in a stone-cold voice, leaving no room for interpretation.

"Right, so what's next?" Ed asked, knowing there was more to the meeting.

"We need Max to continue studying and learning how to use the Postern. I may have accidentally spilled my coffee on the pages about the secondary version of the Postern in the Everwhere. Shame," Titus said, looking around the room to see if anyone would laugh at his joke. It landed flat. The guy was just too big and manly.

I took a deep breath, knowing that I had more than enough to try two of the other gates. "I've got one request."

"That seems reasonable," Davros replied lightly, letting the words trickle off his tongue.

"No more backdoor deals with Darkwater," I said as the others nodded approvingly.

"Agreed," was all Ana said. "For now, Ed, we are asking you to focus on securing the artifacts at the Atheneum. We plan on moving some things around. Jenny will need to be part of that conversation."

"Phil, we're going to need you to stay put for the time being," Titus continued, not sure how Phil would react.

Phil grinned, popping an unlit cigarette in his mouth. "I got to move first. I have new roommates, if they don't mind my drinking."

"And smoking," Angel added, walking over and taking the cigarette from Phil's lips.

"You good for the deposit and willing to sign some damage waivers?" I said as Phil proceeded to flip me off. We would have drinks for sure later.

"If we've had enough of this love fest, I suggest we all get back to work," Ana said. Ed nodded in agreement as he stood up, giving us all the cue to follow.

CHAPTER 24

The So What?

The Fallen Angel was packed. People lined the bar, and only Trish's promise of free drinks made them move. Kim, Phil, Jenny, Petro and the Pixie gang, Ed, and the rest of the crew all stood in a chaotic mass in the center of the bar.

"Get you something to drink?" the young lady behind the bar asked.

"That's the first time I've been asked . . . " I trailed off, seeing Sarah standing there with a tray full of Vamp Ambers.

Kim, taken aback by my pause, looked at me, pursing her lips. "Oh, you can have this one," Sarah said jokingly. "I'm already taken," she said as James leaned over and kissed her on the cheek.

The two grinned. For once, I didn't have anything to say, however, I had plenty to talk to Sarah about. She still owed me an explanation about her relationship with Tom.

"I see you've met the new help," Trish added as she leaned over the bar. "I heard the news. I'm sorry, Max."

"Yeah, I don't know if this is a celebration or a wake," I said as Trish saw the look of tired acceptance on my face.

"Both," she decided, heading over to the slit window on the wall and walking back with a plate of Fae honey tacos. "Amon says hello. You should go back and see him sometime."

I saluted the kitchen before I looked over at Kim. "So?"

"So what?" she replied, her red lipstick catching the light, drawing my attention.

"I want to know everything that happened with Darkwater."

She frowned. "Oh." I leaned forward, cupping her face in my hand.

"I'm just worried that this isn't over," I said, putting my hand down, the smile coming back to her face.

"It's not. It's never going to be. Let's relax tonight, and then tomorrow we can talk," Kim said, grinning again as Phil placed Petro on the table. He was drunk and telling the other Pixies of his heroic deeds.

"You sure you have enough room for me? His head gets any bigger . . ." Phil bellowed, taking a pull from his beer before letting out a long belch.

"When are you moving in?" I asked, actually surprised he was leaving the Atheneum.

"Tomorrow, bruther. I might get an early start on your couch," Phil said, picking up another beer and downing it in one long pull.

Jenny walked over, scratching my back as a mother would. Which reminded me, I needed to do some serious catch-up with my folks. "You should stop by Friday. Some of the children are stopping by. I heard they want to see uncle Max," Jenny said as she smiled at Kim. She was happy to see us together.

Last year, we had saved several special young children from the Thule Society and Lilith. They were like me—different, not normal—and a select few were determined to ensure they would not be used.

I sat there for a second as thoughts of Lilith floated through my mind. "Yeah, I'd like that," I agreed, looking at Petro. "I'll bring Mark Twain here."

"Perfect, it's settled," Jenny said walking over to Ed, putting her arm around him. I could tell Ed was struggling to stay on his feet. Ed leaning on the bar was the one thing keeping him standing. Also, the empty glasses of Magnus weren't helping.

I stood up, walked over to the jukebox Trish had installed, and picked one of Gramps's old favorites. David Bowie's "Life on Mars" started playing in the background.

After several hours of drinks and telling of glory days long since passed, I found myself staring at Gramps's old bar. It had somehow been transported to the apartment when I moved in. The rest of the party had gone their separate ways, and Phil, as mentioned, had passed out on the couch. Petro, on Casey's orders, had gone immediately to bed.

I walked over to my desk, flipping the switch underneath as the glass back popped open. My head swam from all the booze, mixing like a perfect storm in my head. Something was pulling me down to the lab. I hadn't spent much time there recently, and since Petro had mentioned something smelled bad, I decided to check it out.

Walking down the flight of stairs, I pushed the bulky iron door open. The smell of musty old books and fresh dirt greeted me like an old friend. I looked over at the fireplace, willing the wood to ignite, drowning the room in flickering yellow light. Shadows danced off the old bookshelves and odd collection of items, sending a shiver down my spine.

In the middle of the room sat a wooden box. I stared at it for what felt like several minutes. It was roughly the size of a basketball and had an odd aura surrounding it. Almost as if it wanted me to open it, but my body knew better. I took a deep breath, figuring it was too late and I was too full of drinks to mess with it. The mystery box would have to wait till morning.

As I went to turn, the sound of shuffling started emanating from the small crate. I whirled around as it shook slightly. "Shit, what's in the box?" I said under my breath in my best Brad Pitt impression. "Someone leave me a new pet?" I asked no one, slurring my words.

"Alright, dammit, hold on," I relented, talking to myself again. After removing a few screws, I took a deep breath as my hands shook lightly.

As I lifted the lid, Jamison's head stared up at me, gagged. His eyes moved wildly, showing living intelligence and desperation. A monster had cut his head off and put it in a crate alive. Someone had used a soul sword. No, not someone. Beleth; he had told me as much.

I took a deep breath, looking down at my trembling hands as I reached down, untying the gag . . .

EPILOGUE

"**A**re we going to play this game?" Lilith asked as the hooded figure walked out of the shadows. The sounds of the ocean crashing against the rock walls could be heard in the background.

"Are we?" Tom replied, taking a deep breath.

"I wasn't part of that mess. The Thule Society has made its choice, and now they can fight their own shitty war," Lilith said, walking over to a table and pouring a glass of wine in a gold chalice.

"I know who is pulling the strings and will ensure that fight stops. Where's the child?" Tom asked, referring to Lilith's reason to leave Mengele and the others to flounder.

"Oh, the child. I figured you didn't want another roll in the hay. Want to know how your great-grandchild is doing?" Lilith purred.

Tom stood there looking at Lilith as she drank her wine, the tightly wound bandage around his waist causing him to wince.

"How are the other children?" Lilith asked, finishing her glass.

"They're fine and off-limits. You will stay away from them," Tom warned with finality.

"Fair enough," Lilith agreed, pouring another glass of wine.

"You know what I have to do, and where I have to go. If you want my help, you will let me see the child," Tom said as he raised his head, staring directly into Lilith's eyes, the mechanical clicking of her new arm filling the silent void.

Tom reached into his pocket and pulled out the sash he had taken from her, throwing it on the table.

"You do want to play ball. When you awaken the sleeping giant, you will need me," Lillith purred as she formed a fist, banging it on the table three times.

A young woman walked in with her head down. "Yes, ma'am?" a defeated British accent inquired.

"Chloe, get the child and set another place for supper. We have company," Lilith said as recognition dawned on Tom's face. It was Chloe's lost soul. They were in the Everwhere.

"Hello, darling," Bo hissed as Devin walked into the dusty old shop. The Under was the place where demons lived, and Hell started. The air was tinted red due to the fire raging in the sky, and the large amount of dust permeating everything.

Bo's artifact shop was a place of wonder and nightmares. Screams could be heard in the background as spiked weapons and books lined the tattered walls. Bo was in his usual crushed red velvet suit straight out of the 1500s, a pair of round tinted spectacles covering his catlike eyes.

"I am guessing you heard about Belm," Devin said, lighting a black cigarette.

"My deepest condolences. He was such a good fellow," Bo said, the truth of his statement clear.

"I need you to keep an eye on someone for me on Earth," Devin said, blowing smoke in Bo's face as he fanned it away.

Bo grinned. "Oh my, I am going to have to get a new suit," Bo said, the light from the flames in the hanging lights gleaming off the hundreds of sharp razor-like teeth in his mouth.

BOOKOGRAPHY

The following books are available on both ebook (Amazon) and paperback (Amazon & Barnes & Noble). The audiobooks are an ongoing process and available through Audible and Apple.

Max Abaddon Books - A Urban Fantasy Series
 Max Abaddon and the Will -
 Audiobook by Luke Daniels
 Max Abaddon and the Purity Law -
 Audiobook by Luke Daniels -
 Winter 2021
 Max Abaddon and the Gate to Everwhere -
 Spring 2021

The Sinking Man Series - A Zombie Novella Series
Sheltered - Audiobook by Jarret Lemaster
Awakened - Audiobook - Winter 2021

ACKNOWLEDGMENTS

Special thanks go out to all my family, friends, and the authors that still inspire me to do more.

To everyone who has supported Max Abaddon through books one and two, cheers! Book three, can you believe it?

To my family, my wife, and two sons. This book is part of my legacy to you. When I am but a memory in time, you will always be able to pick this book up and remember what a nerd I really was and, well, still am . . . and will probably be some more.

www.ingramcontent.com/pod-product-compliance
Lightning Source LLC
Chambersburg PA
CBHW020909200626
46814CB00001BA/252